N. J. DAWOOD has also translated *The Koran* for the
Penguin Classics. Born in Baghdad, he came to England
as an Iraq State Scholar in 1945 and graduated from
London University. He is a director of Contemporary
Translations Ltd and managing director of The Arabic
Advertising and Publishing Company Ltd, London. He
has edited and abridged *The Muqaddimah of Ibn Khaldun*,
translated numerous technical works into Arabic, written and spoken radio and film commentaries, and con-
tributed to specialized English–Arabic dictionaries. He
has retold for children a comprehensive selection of
tales from *The Arabian Nights*, which will be published
shortly in an illustrated edition.

Tales from the
Thousand and One Nights

TRANSLATED
WITH AN INTRODUCTION BY
N. J. DAWOOD
ENGRAVINGS ON WOOD FROM
ORIGINAL DESIGNS BY
WILLIAM HARVEY

PENGUIN BOOKS

Penguin Books Ltd, Harmondsworth, Middlesex, England
Penguin Books Inc., 7110 Ambassador Road, Baltimore, Maryland 21207, U.S.A.
Penguin Books Australia Ltd, Ringwood, Victoria, Australia
Penguin Books Canada Ltd, 41 Steelcase
Road West, Markham, Ontario, Canada

—

This translation first published separately in Penguin Books as
The Thousand and One Nights (Penguin 1001) 1954
and as *Aladdin and Other Tales* 1957
The Thousand and One Nights reissued as a Penguin Classic in 1955
Reprinted 1961
This combined edition published with revisions and additions 1973
The illustrations are from *The Arabian Nights' Entertainments*,
translated by E. W. Lane, London, C. Knight, 1839–41
Reprinted 1974

—

Translation copyright © N. J. Dawood, 1973
Made and printed in Great Britain by
Richard Clay (The Chaucer Press), Ltd,
Bungay, Suffolk
Set in Monotype Garamond

CONTENTS

Contents

INTRODUCTION

THE folk-tales which have collectively survived in what is known as *The Thousand and One Nights* owe their origin to three distinct cultures: Indian, Persian, and Arab. They can be regarded as the expression of the lay and secular imagination of the East in revolt against the austere erudition and religious zeal of Oriental literature generally.

Written in a simple, almost colloquial style, and depicting a unique world of all-powerful sorcerers and ubiquitous jinn, of fabulous wealth and candid bawdry, these tales have little in common with the refined didacticism of Classical Arabic literature and have therefore never been regarded by the Arabs as a legitimate part of it. Yet it is a remarkable paradox that to the non-Arab world, and particularly to the West, the *Nights* is today the best known and most widely read book of Arabic authorship, while the more serious works of Classical Arabic literature, for the most part untranslatable verse, remain quite unfamiliar. In fact, in the course of the past two centuries the *Nights* has attained, mainly through the medium of translation, the status of a universal classic and has come to be recognized as such.

This is not surprising. The tales themselves are masterpieces of the art of story-telling. In inventiveness and sheer entertainment value they stand supreme among the short stories of all time. And in their minute accuracy of detail and the vast range and variety of their subject-matter they constitute the most comprehensive and intimate record of medieval Islam. For despite the fabulous and fantastic world they portray, with its emphasis on the marvellous and the supernatural, they are a faithful mirror of the life and manners of the age which engendered them. They are the spontaneous products of untutored minds, which would reach out in search

7

of the most imaginative and extravagant fancies and then relate them to the universal constants of this life.

The original nucleus of the *Nights* was derived from a lost Persian book of fairy-tales called *Hazar Afsanah* (A Thousand Legends), which was translated into Arabic about A.D. 850. The Arab encyclopaedist Al-Mas'oodi (d. A.D. 956) makes a casual reference to this book in his *Murooj al-Dhahab* (The Golden Meadows). He tells us that 'the people call it "A Thousand and One Nights"' and goes on to give a brief account of the Prologue which resembles that of our *Nights* in outline. Modern scholarship has traced this Prologue, which contains the framework story, back to Indian folk-lore. But there is no evidence that this 'Thousand and One Nights' of Mas'oodi contained the same stories that have come down to us in the manuscripts of the *Nights*, except the framework story. Several of the tales were undoubtedly taken, in some shape or form, from *Hazar Afsanah*; for they have unmistakable parallels in Indian and Persian folk-lore. The Arab *rawis*, or professional story-tellers, knew how to add local colouring to the foreign tale and how to adapt it to native surroundings. In the course of centuries other stories, mainly of Baghdad and Cairo origin, gathered round this nucleus, and, to make up the number of a thousand and one nights, more local folk-tales, generally of poor composition, were unscrupulously added by the various scribes and editors.

The final revision of this heterogeneous material was made in Egypt, probably in Cairo, by an unknown editor towards the end of the eighteenth century. Written in a language which constantly borders on the vulgar dialect, and in which the original marked differences of style and idiom are still apparent, this version has come to be regarded as the 'standard' text of the *Nights*. The present translation follows Macnaghten's Calcutta edition (1839–42) of this text, but the generally parallel first Bulaq edition (1835) has also been consulted wherever the Macnaghten text seemed faulty. Aladdin follows Zotenberg's text (Paris, 1888).

The Thousand and One Nights was first introduced to the Western world by Antoine Galland (1646–1715), a French orientalist and gifted story-teller who had travelled widely in the Middle East. His *Mille et une Nuits*, published in twelve volumes between 1704 and 1717, had a great popular success and was itself almost at once rendered into several European languages. Galland was by no means a faithful translator. He selected his materials and skilfully adapted them to contemporary European tastes, emphasizing the fantastic and the miraculous and carefully avoiding the candid references to sex. Nevertheless the Galland version possesses a vigorous narrative style and can still be read with enjoyment.

It was during 1706–8 that the first English rendering of the *Nights* made its appearance. Known as the 'Grub Street version', it was translated from Galland's French by an unknown hack-writer. This version, stilted and dull as it may well appear to the modern reader, established the popularity of the *Nights* with successive generations of Englishmen and was read with delight by the English Romantics in their childhood. For it was a very long time before an attempt to render a direct translation from the Arabic was made. In 1838 Henry Torrens published a literal translation of the first fifty Nights in which he tried to give the feel of the original. But today his version makes tedious reading. It was followed by E. W. Lane's translation (3 vols., 1839–41), a bowdlerized selection intended for the drawing-room. His notes are very valuable and show his deep knowledge of Egyptian life in the early nineteenth century. The first complete translation was made by John Payne (9 vols., 1882–4) and published in a limited edition of 500 copies. The rendering of this version is in sophisticated archaic English and its style is even more ponderous than that of any of its predecessors. In 1885–6 the last, and most celebrated, of the direct translations was published. This was Sir Richard Burton's (10 vols., with five supplemental vols.).

In translating *The Thousand and One Nights* Burton wrote, as he himself puts it, 'as the Arab would have written in English'. He 'carefully sought out the English equivalent of every Arabic word . . . and never hesitated to coin a word when wanted'. The result was a curious brand of English, a language which no Englishman has spoken or written at any time:

But she rejoined by saying, 'Allah upon you both that ye come down forthright, and if you come not, I will rouse upon you my husband, this Ifrit, and he shall do you to die by the illest of deaths'; and she continued making signals to them.

Thus I did for a long time, but at last I awoke from my heedlessness and, returning to my senses, I found my wealth had become unwealth and my condition ill-conditioned and all I once hent had left my hands.

'This, then, is the rede that is right: and while we both abide alive and well, I will not cease to send thee letters and monies. Arise ere the day wax bright and thou be in perplexed plight and perdition upon thy head alight!' Quoth he, 'O my lady, I beseech thee of thy favour to bid me farewell with thine embracement'; and quoth she, 'No harm in that.' So he embraced her and knew her carnally; after which he made the Ghusl-ablution; then, donning the dress of a white slave, he bade the syces saddle him a thorough-bred steed. Accordingly they saddled him a courser and he mounted and, farewelling his wife, rode forth the city at the last of the night, whilst all who saw him deemed him one of the Mamelukes of the Sultan going abroad on some business.

What Burton gained in accuracy he lost in style. His excessive weakness for the archaic, his habit of coining words and phrases, and the unnatural idiom he affected, detract from the literary quality of his translation without in any way enhancing its fidelity to the original. The notes are far more entertaining than the text.

In spite of Torrens, Lane, and Burton, however, the average English reader's acquaintance with the *Nights* begins and ends with the nursery adaptations. And it is this fact, as well as the absence of a readable version, which constitutes, in my opinion, the best justification for a fresh translation.

It has been my aim in this selection (originally published in two independent volumes – in 1954 and 1957 – by Penguin Books) to present the modern reader with an unexpurgated rendering of the finest and best-known tales in contemporary English. I have sought to reconcile faithfulness to the spirit of the original with fidelity to modern English usage. I have sometimes felt obliged to alter the order of phrases and sentences where English prose logic differs from Arabic. As the Macnaghten text, on which this translation is based, has never been properly edited, I have often found it necessary to make my own emendations. In the tale of 'The Hunchback', for instance, I have substituted Al-Muntasir Billah (who reigned in the year of the Flight 247, A.D. 861) for Al-Mustansir Billah (whose reign was more than three centuries and a half later) to avoid an obvious anachronism. I have generally tried to do without footnotes by bringing their substance up into the text itself whenever it reads obscurely. The only Arabic words used in this translation are those which have been assimilated into the English language, such as Caliph, Vizier, Cadi, etc. The spelling of all Arabic words has been simplified.

Here I must also mention that the verses have been left out. Apart from the fact that they tend to obstruct the natural flow of the narrative, they are devoid of literary merit. Internal evidence consistently shows that most of the verses were injected at random into the text by the various editors. I have also ignored the divisions of the tales into nights.

And now a few words on the tales themselves. 'Sindbad the Sailor' dates back to the time when Baghdad and Basrah had reached the zenith of their commercial prosperity. Originally the cycle seems to have been an independent work. It has many touches which remind one strongly of the *Odyssey*. Like Homer's epic, its background is the sea. The tale of the 'Third Voyage' has much in common with Book IX; the Black Giant is Polyphemus the Cyclops seen through Arab eyes. Yet it is almost certain that the author or authors of these tales did not know Homer. What they did know was the Odysseus legend, which, in the course of centuries, had reached the Arabs in the form of a romantic tale of sea adventures.

'The Hunchback' and 'The Porter' are excellent examples of the framework system of the *Nights*: the interlacing of several stories, narrated by different characters, into an organic whole; a system which owes its origin to Indian folk-tales and which was later on to be adopted by Boccaccio in the *Decameron* and by Chaucer in *The Canterbury Tales*. They present the reader with an admirable picture of social life in medieval Baghdad. 'The Hunchback' is full of social criticism, and above all it has, in the humorous figure of the barber, one of the most skilfully drawn characters in Oriental fiction.

'Aladdin' has been retold or otherwise presented to so many generations all over the world that it can perhaps be rightly described as the most renowned story invented by man.

'Judar' is of Cairo origin. Like 'Aladdin', it illustrates to a high degree the detachment with which the story-teller in the *Nights* treats the characters of his creation. The headstrong, idle, and worthless Aladdin makes good, but the kind and honest Judar is dispatched, with an utter disregard for 'poetic justice', unlamented to a foul death.

'The Fisherman and the Jinnee' combines Moslem superstition with Persian and Indian folk-lore. It is one of the oldest and simplest tales in the entire collection.

'Khalifah the Fisherman' is a humorous fantasy. It belongs to that group of Baghdad folk-tales which have Haroun Al-Rashid as their hero.

'Ma'aruf the Cobbler' is a sophisticated and elaborately thought-out social satire. It is one of the stories which were added to the *Nights* at a comparatively late period in Egypt.

'The Young Woman and her Five Lovers' and 'The Tale of Kafur the Black Eunuch' are short farcical skits, the first satirizing bureaucratic corruption, the second the extravagances of mourning in Islamic countries.

'The Historic Fart' and 'The Dream', which I have included in this edition, are typical of the amusing short folktales still current in the Middle East.

Finally, I would like to thank my wife for her research and for the invaluable help she has given me during the preparation of this translation. I should also like to record my gratitude to the late Dr E. V. Rieu, C.B.E., the founder editor of the Penguin Classics, for the keen personal interest he took in initiating this rendering for publication.

London, November, 1972   N.J.D.

IN THE NAME OF ALLAH
THE COMPASSIONATE
THE MERCIFUL

*P*RAISE be to Allah Lord of the Creation, and blessing and peace eternal upon the Prince of Apostles, our master Mohammed.

¶ The annals of former generations are lessons to the living: a man may look back upon the fortunes of his predecessors and be admonished; and contemplate the history of past ages and be purged of folly. Glory to Him who has made the heritage of antiquity a guide for our own time!

¶ From this heritage are derived the Tales of the Thousand and One Nights, together with all that is in them of fable and adventure.

THE PROLOGUE

*The Tale of King Shahriyar and his
Brother Shahzaman*

IT is related – but Allah alone is wise and all-knowing – that long ago there lived in the lands of India and China a Sassanid king who commanded great armies and had numerous courtiers, followers, and servants. He left two sons, both renowned for their horsemanship – especially the elder, who inherited the kingdom of his father and governed it with such justice that all his subjects loved him. He was called King Shahriyar. His younger brother was named Shahzaman and was king of Samarkand.

The two brothers continued to reign happily in their kingdoms, and after a period of twenty years King Shahriyar felt a great longing to see his younger brother. He ordered his Vizier to go to Samarkand and invite him to his court.

The Vizier set out promptly on his mission and journeyed many days and nights through deserts and wildernesses until he arrived at Shahzaman's city and was admitted to his presence. He gave him King Shahriyar's greetings and informed him of his master's wish to see him. King Shahzaman was overjoyed at the prospect of visiting his brother. He made ready to leave his kingdom, and sent out his tents, camels, mules, servants, and retainers. Then he appointed his Vizier as his deputy and set out for his brother's dominions.

It so happened, however, that at midnight he remembered a present which he had left at his palace. He returned for it unheralded, and entering his private chambers found his wife lying on a couch in the arms of a black slave. At this the world darkened before his eyes; and he thought: 'If this can happen when I am scarcely out of my city, how will this foul woman

act when I am far away?' He then drew his sword and killed them both as they lay on the couch. Returning at once to his retainers, he gave orders for departure, and journeyed until he reached his brother's capital.

Shahriyar rejoiced at the news of his approach and went out to meet him. He embraced his guest and welcomed him to his festive city. But while Shahriyar sat entertaining his brother, Shahzaman, haunted by the thought of his wife's perfidy, was pale and sick at heart. Shahriyar perceived his distress, but said nothing, thinking that he might be troubled over the affairs of his kingdom. After a few days, however, Shahriyar said to him: 'I see that you are pale and care-worn.' Shahzaman answered: 'I am afflicted with a painful sore.' But he kept from him the story of his wife's treachery. Then Shahriyar invited his brother to go hunting with him, hoping that the sport might dispel his gloom. Shahzaman declined, and Shahriyar went alone to the hunt.

While Shahzaman sat at one of the windows overlooking the King's garden, he saw a door open in the palace, through which came twenty slave-girls and twenty Negroes. In their midst was his brother's queen, a woman of surpassing beauty. They made their way to the fountain, where they all undressed and sat on the grass. The King's wife then called out: 'Come Mass'ood!' and there promptly came to her a black slave, who mounted her after smothering her with embraces and kisses. So also did the Negroes with the slave-girls, revelling together till the approach of night.

When Shahzaman beheld this spectacle, he thought: 'By Allah, my misfortune is lighter than this!' He was dejected no longer, and ate and drank after his long abstinence.

Shahriyar, when he returned from the hunt was surprised to see his brother restored to good spirits and full health. 'How is it, my brother,' asked Shahriyar, 'that when I last saw you, you were pale and melancholy, and now you look well and contented?'

'As for my melancholy,' replied Shahzaman, 'I shall now tell you the reason: but I cannot reveal the cause of my altered condition. Know then, that after I had received your invitation, I made preparations for the journey and left my city; but having forgotten the pearl which I was to present to you, I returned for it to the palace. There, on my couch, I found my wife lying in the embrace of a black slave. I killed them both and came to your kingdom, my mind oppressed with bitter thoughts.'

When he heard these words, Shahriyar urged him to tell the rest of his story. And so Shahzaman related to him all that he had seen in the King's garden that day.

Alarmed, but half in doubt, Shahriyar exclaimed: 'I will not believe that till I have seen it with my own eyes.'

'Then let it be given out,' suggested his brother, 'that you intend to go to the hunt again. Conceal yourself here with me, and you shall witness what I have seen.'

Upon this Shahriyar announced his intention to set forth

on another expedition. The troops went out of the city with the tents, and King Shahriyar followed them. And after he had stayed a while in the camp, he gave orders to his slaves that no one was to be admitted to the King's tent. He then disguised himself and returned unnoticed to the palace, where his brother was waiting for him. They both sat at one of the windows overlooking the garden; and when they had been there a short time, the Queen and her women appeared with the black slaves, and behaved as Shahzaman had described.

Half demented at the sight, Shahriyar said to his brother: 'Let us renounce our royal state and roam the world until we find out if any other king has ever met with such disgrace.'

Shahzaman agreed to his proposal, and they went out in secret and travelled for many days and nights until they came to a meadow by the seashore. They refreshed themselves at a spring of water and sat down to rest under a tree.

Suddenly the waves of the sea surged and foamed before them, and there arose from the deep a black pillar which almost touched the sky. Struck with terror at the sight, they climbed into the tree. When they reached the top they were able to see that it was a jinnee of gigantic stature, carrying a chest on his head. The jinnee waded to the shore and walked towards the tree which sheltered the two brothers. Then, having seated himself beneath it, he opened the chest, and took from it a box, which he also opened; and there rose from the box a beautiful young girl, radiant as the sun.

'Chaste and honourable lady, whom I carried away on your wedding-night,' said the jinnee, 'I would sleep a little.' Then, laying his head upon her knees, the jinnee fell fast asleep.

Suddenly the girl lifted her head and saw the two Kings high in the tree. She laid the jinnee's head on the ground, and made signs to them which seemed to say: 'Come down, and have no fear of the jinnee.'

The two Kings pleaded with her to let them hide in safety, but the girl replied: 'If you do not come down, I will wake the jinnee, and he shall put you to a cruel death.'

They climbed down in fear, and at once she said: 'Come, pierce me with your rapiers.'

Shahriyar and Shahzaman faltered. But the girl repeated angrily: 'If you do not do my bidding, I will wake the jinnee.'

Afraid of the consequences, they proceeded to mount her in turn.

When they had remained with her as long as she desired, she took from her pocket a large purse, from which she drew ninety-eight rings threaded on a string. 'The owners of these,' she laughed triumphantly, 'have all enjoyed me under the very horn of this foolish jinnee. Therefore, give me your rings also.'

The two men gave her their rings.

'This jinnee,' she added, 'carried me away on my bridal night and imprisoned me in a box which he placed inside a chest. He fastened the chest with seven locks and deposited it at the bottom of the roaring sea. But he little knew how cunning we women are.'

The two Kings marvelled at her story, and said to each other: 'If such a thing could happen to a mighty jinnee, then our own misfortune is light indeed.' And they returned at once to the city.

As soon as they entered the palace, King Shahriyar put his wife to death, together with her women and the black slaves. Thenceforth he made it his custom to take a virgin in marriage to his bed each night, and kill her the next morning. This he continued to do for three years, until a clamour rose among the people, some of whom fled the country with their daughters.

At last came the day when the Vizier roamed the city in search of a virgin for the King, and could find none. Dreading the King's anger, he returned to his house with a heavy heart.

Now the Vizier had two daughters. The elder was called Shahrazad, and the younger Dunyazad. Shahrazad possessed many accomplishments and was versed in the wisdom of the poets and the legends of ancient kings.

That day Shahrazad noticed her father's anxiety and asked him what it was that troubled him. When the Vizier told her of his predicament, she said: 'Give me in marriage to this King: either I shall die and be a ransom for the daughters of Moslems, or live and be the cause of their deliverance.'

He earnestly pleaded with her against such a hazard; but

Shahrazad was resolved, and would not yield to her father's entreaties.

'Beware,' said the Vizier, 'of the fate of the donkey in the fable:

The Fable of the Donkey, the Ox, and the Farmer

'THERE was once a wealthy farmer who owned many herds of cattle. He knew the languages of beasts and birds. In one of his stalls he kept an ox and a donkey. At the end of each day, the ox came to the place where the donkey was tied and found it well swept and watered; the manger filled with sifted straw and well-winnowed barley; and the donkey lying at his ease (for his master seldom rode him).

'It chanced that one day the farmer heard the ox say to the donkey: "How fortunate you are! I am worn out with toil, while you rest here in comfort. You eat well-sifted barley and lack nothing. It is only occasionally that your master rides you. As for me, my life is perpetual drudgery at the plough and the millstone."

'The donkey answered: "When you go out into the field and the yoke is placed upon your neck, pretend to be ill and drop down on your belly. Do not rise even if they beat you; or if you do rise, lie down again. When they take you back and place the fodder before you, do not eat it. Abstain for a day or two; and thus shall you find a rest from toil."

'Remember that the farmer was there and heard what passed between them.

'And so when the ploughman came to the ox with his fodder, he ate scarcely any of it. And when the ploughman came the following morning to take him out into the field, the ox appeared to be far from well. Then the farmer said to the ploughman: "Take the donkey and use him at the plough all day!"

'The man returned, took the donkey in place of the ox, and drove him at the plough all day.

'When the day's work was done and the donkey returned to the stall, the ox thanked him for his good counsel. But the donkey made no reply and bitterly repented his rashness.

'Next day the ploughman came and took the donkey again and made him labour till evening; so that when the donkey returned with his neck flayed by the yoke, and in a pitiful state of exhaustion, the ox again expressed his gratitude to him, and praised his sagacity.

' "If only I had kept my wisdom to myself!" thought the donkey. Then, turning to the ox, he said: "I have just heard my master say to his servant: 'If the ox does not recover soon, take him to the slaughterhouse and dispose of him.' My anxiety for your safety prompts me, my friend, to let you know of this before it is too late. And peace be with you!"

'When he heard the donkey's words, the ox thanked him and said: "Tomorrow I will go to work freely and willingly." He ate all his fodder and even licked the manger clean.

'Early next morning the farmer, accompanied by his wife, went to visit the ox in his stall. The ploughman came and led out the ox, who, at the sight of his master, broke wind and frisked about in all directions. And the farmer laughed so, he fell over on his back.'

When she heard her father's story, Shahrazad said: 'Nothing will shake my faith in the mission I am destined to fulfil.'

So the Vizier arrayed his daughter in bridal garments and decked her with jewels and made ready to announce Shahrazad's wedding to the King.

Before saying farewell to her sister, Shahrazad gave her these instructions: 'When I am received by the King, I shall

send for you. Then, when the King has finished his act with me, you must say: "Tell me, my sister, some tale of marvel to beguile the night." Then I will tell you a tale which, if Allah wills, shall be the means of our deliverance.'

The Vizier went with his daughter to the King. And when the King had taken the maiden Shahrazad to his chamber and had lain with her, she wept and said: 'I have a young sister to whom I wish to bid farewell.'

The King sent for Dunyazad. When she arrived, she threw her arms round her sister's neck, and seated herself by her side.

Then Dunyazad said to Shahrazad: 'Tell us, my sister, a tale of marvel, so that the night may pass pleasantly.'

'Gladly,' she answered, 'if the King permits.'

And the King, who was troubled with sleeplessness, eagerly listened to the tale of Shahrazad:

THE TALE OF THE
HUNCHBACK

ONCE upon a time, in the city of Basrah, there lived a prosperous tailor who was fond of sport and merriment. It was his custom to go out with his wife from time to time in quest of pleasure and amusement. It chanced that one evening, when they were returning home from a long jaunt, they met a sprightly little hunchback whose comic aspect banished grief and sorrow and drove away all care. Elated with drink, he was clashing a tambourine and singing gleefully. The tailor and his wife were so amused at the hunchback's drollery that they invited him to spend the evening with them as their guest. The hunchback accepted, and when they had returned to the house the tailor hurried out to the market-place, where he bought some fried fish, bread, and lemons, and honey for dessert.

The three sat down to a hilarious meal. Being fond of practical jokes, the tailor's wife crammed a large piece of fish into the hunchback's mouth and forced him to swallow it. But, as fate would have it, the fish concealed a big, sharp bone which stuck in his throat and choked him; so that when they examined him, they found, to their horror, that the hunchback was dead.

The tailor lifted up his hands and exclaimed: 'There is no strength or power save in Allah! Alas that this man should have met his fate at our hands, and in this fashion!'

'Your cries are of no avail,' said his wife. 'We must do something!'

'What *can* we do?' whimpered the tailor.

'Rise,' she said, 'and take the body in your arms; we will cover it with a shawl and carry it out of the house this very night. I will walk in front, crying: "My child is ill, my poor child is ill! Who will direct us to a doctor's house?"'

Encouraged by her plan, the tailor wrapped up the hunchback in a large silken shawl and carried him out into the street; his wife lamenting: 'My child! My child! Who will save him from the foul smallpox?'

So all who saw them whispered together: 'They are carrying a child stricken with the smallpox.'

Thus they proceeded through the streets, inquiring for the doctor's house as they went, until at last they were directed by the passers-by to the house of a Jewish doctor. They knocked, and the door was opened by a black slave-girl.

'Give your master this piece of silver,' said the tailor's wife, 'and beg him to come down and see my child; for he is very ill.'

When the girl went in to call the doctor, the tailor's wife slipped into the vestibule and said to her husband:

'Leave the hunchback here and let us run for our lives!'

The tailor propped up the body at the bottom of the staircase, and the pair made off as fast as their legs could carry them.

The Jew rejoiced on receiving the piece of silver. He rose in haste and, hurrying down the stairs in the dark, stumbled against the corpse and toppled it over. Terrified at the sight of the lifeless hunchback, and thinking that he himself had just killed him, the Jew called on Moses and Aaron and Ezra and Joshua son of Nun, and bethought himself of the Ten Commandments, and wrung his hands, crying: 'How shall I get rid of the body?' Then he took up the hunchback and carried him to his wife and told her what had happened.

'Why, then, do you stand there doing nothing?' exclaimed the terrified woman. 'If the corpse is still here by daybreak, we are lost! Come, we will carry the body up to the terrace and throw it into the house of our neighbour the Moslem.'

Now the Moslem was the steward of the royal kitchens, from which he seldom departed with his pockets empty. His house was always infested by cats and mice, which ate the butter, the cheese, and the corn; and on fine nights the dogs of the neighbourhood came down and feasted on the contents of his kitchen. So the Jew and his wife, carrying the hunchback, climbed down from their terrace into their neighbour's house, and propped him up against the wall of the kitchen.

It was not long before the steward, who had been out all day, returned to his house. He opened the door and lighted a candle – then started at the sight of a man leaning against the wall of his kitchen. 'So our thief is a man after all!' he thought; and taking up a mallet, he cried: 'By Allah, to think that it was you, and not the cats and the dogs, who stole all that meat and butter! I have killed almost all the cats and dogs in the district and never thought of you and your like, who come prowling down the terraces.'

So saying, he knocked down the hunchback with the mallet and dealt him another blow upon the chest as he lay on the ground. But the angry steward soon found that the hunchback was dead. He was seized with fear, and exclaimed:

'There is no strength or power save in Allah! A curse upon the meat and the butter, and upon this night which has witnessed your death at my hands, you wretch!' Then, perceiving his deformity, he added: 'Is it not enough that you are a hunchback: must you also be a kitchen thief? O Allah, protect me in your mercy!'

The steward took up the hunchback, and, carrying him on his shoulders, left the house. The night was already approaching its end. He walked with his burden through the deserted streets until he entered a lane leading to the market-place, and came to a shop that stood on a corner. There he leaned the hunchback up against the wall, and hurried away.

Soon after, a Christian, who was the King's broker, passed through the lane on his way to the public baths. Fuddled with drink, he reeled along muttering to himself, 'Doomsday has come! The Last Judgement has come!' and staggering from one side of the lane to the other. When he came close to the hunchback he stopped, and without noticing him, turned round to make water.

Now it so chanced that earlier in the evening the Christian had been robbed of his turban and was forced to buy another. Therefore, when he suddenly saw the figure of the hunchback against the wall, the drunken broker, imagining that he was about to snatch off his new turban, took him by the throat and knocked him down with a resounding blow. Then he raised a great outcry, screaming and cursing and calling out to the watchman of the market-place.

The watchman arrived to find a Christian beating a Moslem. 'Rise up and let go of him!' he shouted; and when he found that the hunchback was dead, he exclaimed: 'A pretty state of things when a Christian dares to kill a Believer!'

Confounded at the swift dispatch of his victim, the Christian began to call on Jesus and Mary: thus, as the proverb has it, intoxication departed and meditation came in its place. And the watchman took hold of the Christian broker, and manacled him, and dragged him away to the Governor's house.

In the morning the Governor gave orders for the hanging of the Christian. The town-crier proclaimed his crime in the streets, and a gallows was set up in the heart of the city. Then came the executioner. In the presence of the Governor, he placed the Christian beneath the gallows and threw the rope round his neck.

At this moment the King's steward pushed his way through the crowd, crying: 'Do not hang him! It was I who killed the hunchback!'

'Why did you kill him? asked the Governor.

'It all happened,' replied the steward, 'when I returned home last night and found him in my house, about to break into the kitchen. I struck him with a mallet and he fell down dead upon the instant. In despair, I carried him to a lane adjoining the market-place. Is it not enough to have killed a Moslem?' added the steward passionately. 'Must a Christian also die on my account? Therefore, hang no man but me!'

When he heard this the Governor set the Christian free and said to the executioner: 'Hang this man instead, on the grounds of his own confession.'

The executioner led the steward to the scaffold and had just placed the rope round his neck, when the Jewish doctor forced his way through the crowd, crying out: 'Do not hang him! I am the man who killed the hunchback!' And the Jew related to the Governor his own version of the hunchback's death. 'Is my sin not great enough that I have killed a man unwittingly?' he added. 'Must another be killed through my crime, and with my knowledge?'

On hearing this the Governor gave orders that the Jew be hanged in place of the steward. But when the rope was placed round his neck, the tailor came forward and cried out: 'Do not hang him! None killed the hunchback but myself!' And he related to the astonished assembly the circumstances of the hunchback's death.

The Governor marvelled at the story of the hunchback, and said: 'This episode ought to be recorded in books.' And he ordered the executioner to set the Jew at liberty and to hang the tailor.

'Would to heaven they would make up their minds,' muttered the executioner, who was becoming impatient at the delay. 'The day will end before we hang any of them.' And he resolutely placed the rope round the tailor's neck.

Now the hunchback, who was the cause of all this commotion, was the King's jester and favourite companion. When the King found that the hunchback had been absent from the royal palace all night and the next morning, he ordered some of his attendants to seek him. They soon returned to inform him of the hunchback's death and his self-confessed murderers.

'Go to the Governor,' said the King to his Chamberlain, 'and bring them all before me.'

The Chamberlain hurried at once to the city square, where the executioner was about to hang the tailor. 'Stop! Stop! Do not hang him!' shouted the Chamberlain, rushing through the crowd. And before the executioner could complete his work, the Chamberlain informed the Governor of the King's orders, and took him to the royal palace, together with the tailor, the Christian, the Jew, the steward, and the hunchback's body.

When they had all been admitted to the King's presence, the Governor kissed the ground before him, and related to him all that had happened. The King marvelled greatly, and gave orders that the story be inscribed on parchment in letters of gold. Then the King asked those who were present: 'Have you ever heard a story more marvellous than that of the hunchback?'

The tailor came forward, and said:

The Tailor's Tale

OF all the tales of marvel that I have heard, your majesty, none surpasses in wonder the incident which I witnessed yesterday. Early in the morning, before I met the hunchback, I was at a breakfast party given by a friend to some twenty tradesmen and craftsmen of the city, among them tailors and drapers and carpenters and others. As soon as the sun rose and the food was set before us, our host ushered into the room a handsome, but noticeably lame, young man, richly dressed in the Baghdad fashion. The young man greeted the company, and we all rose to receive him. But when he was about to be seated he caught sight of an old man in our midst who was a barber; whereupon he refused to sit down and made for the door again. We all hastened to prevent him, and the host, swearing that he should not leave the house, held him by the arm and earnestly pleaded with him to explain his abrupt departure.

'Sir,' he answered, 'do not try to detain me. If you must know, it is the presence of this sinister barber that compels me to leave at once.'

Our host was greatly astonished at these words, and we all wondered why the young man, a stranger in this city, should have taken such offence at the barber's presence. We begged him to tell us the reason.

'Gentlemen,' he answered, 'this barber was the cause of a grave disaster which befell me in Baghdad, my native city; thanks to him my leg was broken and I am now lame. I have sworn never to sit in the same room with him, nor live in any town where he lives. This is why I left Baghdad, yet here I find him again. Not another night will I spend in this city.'

'By Allah,' we said, 'let us hear your story.'

The barber hung his head, as the young man proceeded to tell of his adventure.

The Tale of the Lame Young Man and the Barber of Baghdad

You must know that my father was one of the chief merchants of Baghdad and I was his only son. When I attained manhood my father died, leaving me great wealth and a numerous retinue of slaves and servants. From that time I began to live sumptuously, wearing the richest clothes and eating the choicest dishes. But I always shunned the company of women, for Allah had made me strangely indifferent to their allurements.

It so chanced, however, that one day, as I was walking along a narrow lane in Baghdad, a crowd of women barred my way. To avoid them I slipped into a quiet alley, and sat down upon a bench. I had not been there long, when a window in the house opposite was flung open, and there appeared a young girl who was like the full moon in her beauty. She was watering the flowerpots on her window-sill, when she happened to glance around and caught sight of me; whereupon she shut the window and disappeared. My soul was enthralled with the vision of her beauty. Love suddenly burned like a flame in my heart. I sat lost in my new-born passion, till sunset, when the Cadi of Baghdad came riding by, with slaves before him and servants behind him. Imagine my feelings, gentlemen, when I saw him dismount and enter the very house where the young girl lived; for at that moment I realized that she was the Cadi's daughter.

I returned home downcast and melancholy, and threw myself upon my bed. My slave-girls came in and anxiously sat around me, afraid to inquire the cause of my dejection. Presently, however, there entered an old woman of the house who at once understood the truth of my condition. She sat

at my bedside and comforted me, saying: 'Tell me everything, my son, and let me be your messenger.'

When she had heard my story, she said: 'You must know that this girl lives with her father the Cadi in the strictest seclusion. I myself am a frequent visitor at their house, and will undertake to be the means of your union. Take heart, and do not despair.'

I was greatly consoled by her words, and the next day my people rejoiced to see me restored to good spirits. The old woman departed on her mission, but soon returned crestfallen. 'My son,' she said, 'do not inquire the outcome of my visit. Scarcely had I begun to speak of you, when the girl cried: "Hold your tongue, old woman, or you shall receive the treatment you deserve."'

Seeing that this news had dashed my spirits, the old woman added: 'But do not fear, I shall shortly approach her again.'

My anguish was renewed. After a few days, however, she came to me and said: 'Rejoice, I bring you good news! Yesterday I again visited the girl. When she saw me in tears, she asked me the cause of my grief. Weeping bitterly, I replied: "I have come from a youth who is languishing with love for you." Her heart was moved, and she asked: "Who is the youth of whom you speak?" "He is the flower of my life," I answered, "and as dear to me as my own son. Some days ago he saw you at your window, watering your flowers. He loved you from that moment. But when I told him of your harsh response he began to pine away, and took to his bed, where he now lies dying." "And all this on my account?" asked the girl, moved with pity. "Yes, by Allah," I replied. "Go back to him," she said, "give him my greetings and say my love is even greater than his. Ask him to come to me on Friday next, before the midday prayers. I shall let him in myself and bring him up to my chamber. But he must leave me before my father returns from the mosque." '

On hearing this, I was transported with joy and handsomely rewarded the old woman for her labours. My sickness left me, and my household rejoiced at my recovery.

When Friday came, I made ready for the great occasion, putting on my finest robes and sweetest perfumes, and then sat waiting for the hour of midday prayers. But the old woman hinted that a visit from the barber might do much to improve my appearance. I called my slave and said to him: 'Go to the market-place and bring me a barber. See that he is a man of sense who will attend to his business and will not split my head with idle chatter.' The slave went away and brought back with him a barber who was none other than the odious old man you see before you.

As soon as he entered, the barber remarked upon my pallor; and when I explained that I had but recently recovered from an illness, he congratulated me, saying: 'May Allah preserve you, sir, from all misfortune, all distress, all grief, and all sorrow!'

'Allah grant your prayer!' I replied.

'Now tell me, sir,' he said, 'do you wish to be shaved or to be bled? You doubtless know that the famous Ibn Abbas (may Allah rest his soul in peace!) has said: "He who has his hair cut on a Friday shall ward off seventy calamities." And to the same authority is also attributed the maxim: "To let blood on a Friday averts weakness of sight and a host of other diseases."'

'Enough of this talk, old man!' I cried. 'Come now, begin shaving my head at once.'

He rose, and produced from his pocket a large bundle. Imagine my astonishment when I saw him take from it, not a

razor or a pair of scissors as one might have expected, but an astrolabe consisting of seven plates of polished silver. He carried it to the middle of the courtyard, and, raising the instrument towards the sun, gazed intently at the reflection for a long time. Then he came back to me and said solemnly:

'Know, that of this day, Friday the tenth of Safar in the year two hundred and fifty-three after the Flight of the Prophet (upon whom be Allah's blessing and peace), and twelve hundred and thirty-one in the year of Alexander the Great, there have elapsed eight degrees and six minutes; and that, according to the strictest rules of computation, the planet Mars, in conjunction with Mercury, is this day in the ascendant: all this denoting an auspicious moment for hair-cutting. Furthermore, my instrument manifestly informs me that it is your intention to pay a visit to a certain person, and that of this nothing shall come but evil. There is also another sign in connection with a certain matter, of which I would rather not speak.'

'By Allah!' I cried, 'this is intolerable! You weary me with your tedious chatter, and what is more, your forebodings are far from encouraging. I sent for you to shave my head. Do so at once and cease your babbling!'

'If only you knew the gravity of the impending disaster,' he said, 'you would listen to my counsel and heed the portent of the stars!'

'Doubtless,' I cried, 'you are the only astrologer among the barbers of Baghdad: but, allow me to tell you, old man, you are also an impudent mischief-maker and a frivolous chatterbox.'

'What more would you have?' cried he, shrugging his shoulders. 'Allah has sent you one who is not only a barber of great repute, but also a master of the arts and sciences: one who is not only deeply versed in alchemy, astrology, mathematics, and architecture, but also (to mention only a few of my accomplishments) well schooled in the arts of logic, rhetoric, and elocution, the theory of grammar, and the commentaries on the Koran. Add to all this the maturity of judgement that can only be acquired through long experience of the world. Your late father, young man, loved me for my discretion; and it is the memory of his goodness and kind favours that prompts me to render you an honest service. Far from being a meddlesome gossip, as you seem to suggest, I am, in fact, renowned for my gravity and reserve; on account of which

34

qualities people call me the "Silent One". Instead of crossing
and thwarting me, young man, it would be much more befitting
to thank Allah for my sound advice and my concern for your
well-being. Would that I were a whole year in your service,
that you might learn to do me justice!'

Here I exclaimed: 'You will surely be my death this day!'
But when the old man was about to resume his soliloquy, I
felt as though my gall-bladder would burst, and I said to my
slave: 'In Allah's name, give this man a quarter of a dinar and
show him out; for I do not wish to have my head shaved after
all.'

'What kind of talk is this?' cried the barber. 'By Allah, I
will accept nothing before I have shaved you. You must know
that I would regard it as a pleasant duty and a great honour to
serve you even without payment. For although you do not
seem to appreciate my merits, I appreciate yours. I remember
one Friday when I was sent for by your late father (may Allah
have mercy upon him: he was a man of rare munificence). I
found him entertaining a company of visitors. He welcomed
me as he might have welcomed an old friend, and said: "I beg
you to let me a little blood." At once I took out my astrolabe,
computed the height of the sun, and soon ascertained that the
hour was clearly unpropitious for blood-letting. I did not
hesitate to tell him the truth. He accepted my judgement, and
readily agreed to wait for a favourable moment. Incidentally,
it might interest you to know that, while we waited, I com-
posed half a dozen verses in his praise and recited them before
the company. Your father was so pleased with them that he
ordered his slave to give me a hundred and three dinars and a
robe of honour. When the auspicious hour had come and the
operation was completed, I asked him in a whisper: "Why
did you pay me a hundred and *three* dinars?" "One dinar is for
your wisdom," he replied, "one for the blood-letting, and one
for the pleasure of your company; as for the remainder and the
robe of honour, pray accept them as a slight reward for your
excellent poem."'

'Then may Allah have no mercy on my father,' I burst out,
'if he ever had dealings with a barber like you!'

'There is no god but Allah, and Mohammed is His Prophet!'
exclaimed the barber, laughing and shaking his head. 'Glory
to Him who changes others and remains Himself unchanged! I
always took you for a sensible and intelligent young man: now
I see that your illness has slightly affected your head. You
would do well to remember that Allah in His sacred book
mentioned with especial praise those who curb their anger and
forgive their fellow-men. However, I will forgive you. As I
was saying, neither your father, nor your grandfather before
him, ever did anything without first seeking my advice. You
have doubtless heard the proverb: "He who takes good
counsel is crowned with success." Now you will find no one
better versed in the ways of the world than myself: and here I
stand, waiting to serve you. What I cannot understand, however, is that you seem to be a little tired of me, when I am not
in the least tired of you. But the high esteem in which I hold
your father's memory will always make me mindful of my
duty to his son.'

'By Allah,' I yelled, 'this has gone too far!' I was about to
order my slaves to throw him out of the house, when he
suddenly began to damp my hair, and before I knew what was
happening, my head was covered with lather.

'I shall take no offence, sir,' continued the wretched old
man, quite unruffled, 'if you are a little short-tempered. Apart
from the strain of your recent illness, you are, of course, very
young. It seems but yesterday that I used to carry you to
school on my shoulders.'

Unable to contain myself any longer, I said solemnly: 'My
friend, I must beg you to proceed with your work.' Then, I
rent my clothes and began to shriek like a maniac.

When he saw me do this, the barber calmly produced a
razor and began to strop it, passing it up and down the piece
of leather with deadly deliberation. At length, he held my head
with one hand and shaved off a few hairs. Then he raised his
hand and said: 'I do not suppose that you are aware of my
standing in society. These hands of mine have dressed the
heads of kings and princes, viziers and noblemen. Have you
not heard the poet's eulogy in my praise? . . .'

At this point I interrupted him, crying: 'You have stifled me with your nonsense!'

'It has just occurred to me that you might be in a hurry,' said the barber.

'I am indeed!' I shouted, 'I am indeed!'

'Well, well,' he went on, 'haste is a precept of the Devil, and leads only to ruin and repentance. The Prophet has said: "The best enterprises are those that are carried out with caution." I wish you would tell me the purpose of your hurry, as it is yet nearly three hours to midday prayers.' Here the barber paused, and then added: 'But the fallacies of mere conjecture are not to be relied upon by a man of my learning.'

So saying, he flung away the razor, took up the astrolabe, and went out into the courtyard. There he observed the sun for a long time, and at last came back, saying: 'It is now three hours to midday prayers, neither one minute more nor one minute less.'

'For Allah's sake,' I cried, 'hold your tongue: you have goaded me beyond endurance!'

Again he took up the razor and proceeded to strop it as he had done before. Scarcely had he removed a few hairs, when he said: 'I am somewhat anxious about you. It would be in your own interest to tell me the cause of your haste. For, as you know, your father and grandfather never did anything without consulting me.'

I realized that I should never be able to elude his persistent questioning. To cut the matter short, I said that I had been invited to a banquet at the house of a friend, and begged him to cease his impertinence.

At the mention of a banquet the barber exclaimed: 'This reminds me that I myself am expecting a few friends at my house today. But I have forgotten to provide anything for them to eat. Think of the disgrace!'

'Do not be troubled over this matter,' I replied. 'All the food and drink in my house is yours if you will only finish shaving my head.'

'Sir,' he cried, 'may Allah reward you for your generosity! Pray let me hear what you have for my guests.'

'Five different meat dishes,' I answered, 'ten stuffed chickens finely broiled, and a roasted lamb.'

'Be so good,' he said, 'as to let me look at them.'

I ordered the food to be brought before him, together with a cask of wine.

'How generous you are!' he exclaimed. 'But the incense and the perfume are wanting.'

I then ordered my slave to set before him a box containing aloe-wood, musk, and ambergris, the whole worth not less

than fifty dinars. Time was running short, so I said: 'All this is yours; only, for the sake of Mohammed, on whom be Allah's blessing and peace, finish shaving my head!'

'Pray allow me to see the contents,' he replied.

My slave opened the box, and the barber put aside his razor, and sat down on the floor examining the incense. He then rose and, taking up his razor again, held my head and shaved off a few hairs.

'My son,' he said, with great satisfaction, 'I do not know how to thank you. The party I am giving today will owe a great deal to your bounty. Although none of my guests might be considered worthy of such magnificence, they are all quite respectable. First, there is Zantoot, the bath-keeper; then

Salee'a, the corn merchant; Akrasha, the fruiterer; Hamid, the dustman; Silat, the grocer; Abu Makarish, the milkman; Kaseem, the watchman; and last, but by no means least, Sa'eed, the camel-driver. Each one of them is a delightful companion, and has a song and a dance of his own invention; and, like your humble servant, neither inquisitive nor given to idle talk. In truth, no description of my friends can do them justice. If, therefore, you would care to honour us with your company, you will have a more pleasant time, and we will all be the happier. One reason, in my opinion, why you would do well not to visit those friends of yours, is the possibility of meeting some busybody who will split your head with incessant chatter.'

Choking with rage, I burst into a fit of hysterical laughter, and said: 'I should be delighted to come some other time. Shave my head now, and let me go my way. Besides, your friends must be waiting for you.'

'But how I long to introduce you to these excellent fellows!' he continued. 'Once you meet them, you will give up all your friends for ever.'

'May Allah give you joy in them,' I said. 'I shall doubtless have the pleasure of meeting them one day.'

'Well, well,' said he, shrugging his shoulders, 'if you needs must go to your friends, I will now carry to my guests the presents with which you have favoured me. As I do not stand upon ceremony with them, I will return without delay to accompany you to your banquet.'

Here I lost all control of myself and cried: 'There is no strength or help save in Allah! Pray go to your friends and delight your heart with them, and let me go to mine; for they are waiting for me.'

But the barber cried: 'I will not let you go alone.'

'The truth is,' I said, 'that no one may be admitted to the house where I am going except myself.'

'Aha!' he exclaimed. 'It must be a woman, then, or else you would allow me to accompany you. Yet I am the right man for that kind of adventure, and could do much in an emergency; especially if, as I suspect, the woman proves to be a deceitful whore. Why, you would probably be murdered! Furthermore, you know how ruthless the Governor is about such irregular dealings, particularly on a Friday.'

'Vile old man,' I cried, 'how can you speak so to my face?'

'Did you imagine,' retorted the barber, 'that you could conceal such a design from me? My sole concern, young man, is to serve you.'

Afraid that my servants might hear the barber's remarks, I made no answer.

The hour of prayer had come and the imams had already begun their sermons when at long last the barber finished shaving my head.

'Take away this food to your house,' I said, 'and when you return we will go together to the banquet.'

But he would not believe my words. 'You want to get rid of me and go alone,' he replied. 'Think of the trap that may have been set for you! By Allah, you shall not leave the house until I come back to accompany you and watch over your safety.'

'Very well,' I said, 'but you must not be late.'

The barber took all the meat and drink I had given him and left me in peace. But the damnable dog hired a porter to carry the things to his house, and hid himself in one of the neighbouring alleys.

The muezzins had now intoned their blessings on the Prophet from the minarets of the city. I rose in haste and flung on my cloak and ran as fast as I could to the girl's house. Finding the door open, I hurried up the stairs to her apartment. But I had scarcely reached the first story when the Cadi arrived. Seized by a great fear, I rushed to one of the windows overlooking the alley, and was confounded to see the barber (Allah's curse be upon him!) sitting at the doorstep.

Now it so happened that immediately on his return from the mosque, the Cadi took it into his head to beat a maidservant. She raised an uproar, shrieking and screaming. A black slave interceded for her, but the furious Cadi fell upon him also, and the slave joined in the shrill tumult, yelling for help.

Imagining that it was I who was the victim, the incorrigible barber set up a great outcry in the street, tearing his clothes and scattering dust upon his head. 'Help! Help!' he cried. 'My master is being murdered by the Cadi!'

Then, running frantically to my house with a great crowd following him, he roused my people and my servants; and before I knew what was happening, they all came, men and women, to the Cadi's house, with torn clothes and loosed tresses, lamenting: 'Alas! Our master is dead!'

When he heard the loud clamour in the street, the Cadi ordered a slave to find out what had happened. The slave quickly returned and said: 'At the door there is a great multitude of men and women. They are all shaking their fists and crying: "Our master has been murdered!"'

The Cadi rose in anger and, opening the door, was amazed to find an infuriated mob shouting threats at him.

'What is the meaning of this?' he asked indignantly.

'Dog! Pig! Murderer!' shouted my servants. 'Where is our master?'

'What has your master done to me,' asked the Cadi, 'that I should kill him?'

'You have just been flogging him,' replied the barber. 'I myself heard his cries.'

'But what has your master done that I should flog him?' repeated the Cadi. 'Who brought him to my house?'

'Wicked old liar,' answered the barber, 'do not pretend to be so innocent; for I know the whole truth and every detail of the matter. Your daughter is in love with him and he with her. When you caught him in the house you ordered your slaves to flog him. By Allah,' added the barber vehemently, 'the Caliph himself shall judge this outrage! Give us back our master, or else I shall have to enter by force and rescue him myself.'

Embarrassed and perplexed, the Cadi said: 'If you are not lying, come and bring him out.'

When I saw the barber push his way through the door, I desperately looked about for a means of escape, but could find none. At length I saw in one of the rooms a great wooden chest which was empty. I jumped into it and pulled down the lid, holding my breath. Immediately after, the barber ran into the room. He looked right and left, and, instantly divining where I was, lifted the chest upon his shoulder and scrambled with it down the stairs. But as he rushed through the door, the barber tripped over the threshold, hurling me out of the chest into the crowded street. My leg was broken; but my single thought at that moment was to fly for my life. I took from my pockets handfuls of gold and threw them to the crowd. Whilst they were busy scrambling for the coins, I made off, hobbling through the back streets as fast as I could go.

The barber pursued me from one lane to another, crying: 'The blackguards would have killed my master! Praise be to Allah who aided me against them and saved my master from their hands!'

Then, calling out to me as he ran, the barber continued: 'Now you see the fruits of your rashness and impatience! Had not Allah sent me to your rescue, you would not have escaped alive today. I have risked my life in your service; but you would not even hear of taking me with you. However, I will not be angry, for you are very young, and exceedingly rash and foolish.'

Writhing with the pain in my leg and the anguish in my heart, I turned on my heel and solemnly said to the jabbering monster at my back: 'Is it not enough that you have brought me to this pass? Must you also hound me to my death in the midst of the market-place?' Then, entering a weaver's shop near by, I begged asylum of him and implored him to drive the barber away.

As I sat in the back room, I thought: 'If I return home, I will never be able to rid myself of this fiend. He will pursue me like a shadow, and I cannot endure the sight of him!'

I sent out for witnesses and wrote my will, dividing my property among my people. I appointed a guardian over them, and committed to him the charge of the young and the aged, and also the sale of my house and other estates. I then left Baghdad and came to live in your city, imagining that I had for ever freed myself from this monster. Yet no sooner had I stepped into this house than I found him sitting amongst you as an honoured guest. How, then, can my heart be at ease or my stay be pleasant, when I am under the same roof as the man who did all this to me and was the cause of my lameness?

The young man (continued the tailor) refused to sit down, and went away. When we had heard his story, we turned to the barber and asked: 'Is it true what this young man has said of you?'

'By Allah, gentlemen,' replied the barber, 'I must assure you that had it not been for my sagacity, resourcefulness, and personal courage this youth would have surely died. He should, indeed, be thankful that his folly cost him merely his leg, and not his life. This young man has accused me of being talkative and meddlesome – two vices from which, unlike my six brothers, I am entirely free. To prove to you the falseness of this charge, however, I shall now tell you the following story, and you shall judge for yourselves that I am a man not only of few words but also of great generosity and chivalry.'

The Barber's Tale

THE little adventure I am about to relate occurred to me some years ago during the reign of Al-Muntasir Billah (may Allah have mercy upon him: he was a truly munificent Caliph and a righteous man).

One day the Caliph was incensed against ten men, and he ordered his lieutenant to bring them before him. It so chanced that just as they were being embarked on a boat to cross the Tigris, I was taking the air along the river-bank. Drawing close to them, I thought to myself: 'This must be a pleasure party. They will probably spend the day in this boat eating and drinking. By Allah, I will be their guest and make merry with them.'

I jumped into the boat and sat in their midst. But as soon as we set foot on the opposite bank, the Governor's guards took hold of us and put chains round the necks of the men, and round my neck also. Yet I never breathed a syllable (which, I submit, is but a proof of my courage and discretion). Then they dragged us away to Al-Muntasir's court, and led us before the Prince of the Faithful.

When he saw us, the Caliph called the executioner and said to him: 'Strike off the heads of these ten wretches!'

The executioner made us kneel down in a row before the Caliph; then he unsheathed his sword and beheaded the unfortunate men.

Seeing me kneeling still at the end of the row, the Caliph cried, 'Why did you not kill the tenth man?'

The executioner counted aloud the ten heads and the ten bodies that lay on the ground; and the Caliph turned to me and said: 'Who are you, and how did you come to be among these criminals?'

Then, and only then, did I decide to break my silence.

'Prince of the Faithful,' I replied, 'I am called the "Silent One" and my wisdom is proverbial. I am a barber by trade and one of the seven sons of my father.' I then explained how

I was mistaken for one of the prisoners, and briefly outlined my life's history.

When he was satisfied that I was a man of rare qualities, the Caliph smiled, saying: 'Tell me, noble sheikh, are your six brothers like you, distinguished for their deep learning and the brevity of their speeches?'

'Gracious heavens!' I replied. 'Each of them is such a disreputable good-for-nothing, that you almost dispraise me by comparing me with them. Because of their recklessness, stupidity, and unusual cowardice, they have brought upon themselves all kinds of misfortunes and bodily deformities: the first is lame, the second loose-limbed and disfigured, the third blind, the fourth one-eyed, the fifth ear-cropped, and the sixth had both his lips cut off. Were it not for the fear that you might take me for an idle gossip I would gladly tell you their stories.'

Thereupon the Prince of the Faithful gave me leave to relate to him the story of my first brother.

The Tale of Bakbook
The Barber's First Brother

KNOW, Prince of the Faithful, that the eldest of my brothers, he who is lame, was in his youth a tailor and lived in Baghdad.

He used to ply his trade in a little shop which he rented from a wealthy man, who himself lived in the upper storey of the building. In the spacious basement below a miller worked at his mill and kept his ox.

One day, as he sat sewing, my brother chanced to raise his eyes and caught sight of a young woman looking out at the passers-by from an oriel window above his shop. She was the landlord's wife, and was as beautiful as the rising moon. Bakbook fell in love with her at first sight. He could sew no more and passed the whole day in gazing at her. Next morning he opened his shop at an early hour and sat sewing; but each time he sewed a stitch, his eyes wandered towards the window, and with every minute that passed, his longing for her grew more passionate.

On the third day, however, the woman, perceiving his love-sick gaze, cast at him a sidelong glance and smiled seductively. She then disappeared from the window, and shortly afterwards her slave-girl came to him with a parcel containing a length of red-flowered silk.

'My mistress sends you her greetings,' said the girl, 'and desires you to make her, with your own good hands, a shirt from this material.'

'I hear and obey,' replied my brother.

Bakbook set to work at once, so that the shirt was ready before the evening. Early next morning the slave-girl came to him again, and said: 'My mistress greets you and inquires if you slept well last night, for she herself, she says, could scarcely sleep a wink, thinking of you.'

Then the girl placed before him a piece of yellow satin, adding: 'From this my mistress wishes you to make her two pairs of drawers, and to have them ready by the evening.'

'I hear and obey,' replied my brother. 'Give her my most tender greetings, and say to her: "Your slave prostrates himself at your feet and waits your will and pleasure."'

He worked assiduously till the evening, when the woman looked out from her window, now smiling, now winking at him; so that Bakbook persuaded himself that he would soon enjoy her. Presently the slave-girl came to the shop and took the two pairs of drawers.

That night my brother lay on a sleepless bed, thinking of all the delights that were in store for him, and next morning the slave came again and said: 'My master wishes to speak to you and desires you to come into the house.'

Thinking that this was but a device to further the woman's intrigue with him, Bakbook gladly followed the slave-girl, and when he entered, he greeted his landlord, kissing the ground before him. The young woman's husband threw him a great roll of silk, and said: 'Make me a few shirts from this, good tailor.'

My brother went back to his shop and worked so diligently,

not allowing himself a moment for food or rest, that twenty shirts were ready by the evening. At supper-time he carried them to his landlord.

'How much do I owe you?' asked the landlord.

But as Bakbook was about to say: 'Twenty dirhams', the young woman made a sign to him that he should accept no payment. And the shallow-pated Bakbook, who did not for a moment suspect that the fair woman of his dreams was in league with her husband to make an ass of him, refused payment despite his woeful penury.

Early next morning the slave again came to him and said: 'My master wishes to speak with you.'

As soon as Bakbook entered, the landlord handed him a roll of stuff, saying: 'Make me five pairs of trousers.' He took the rascal's measurements and went back to his shop.

After three days of painful drudgery, my brother finished the trousers; and when he proudly carried them to their owner, the landlord complimented him on his needlework and loaded him with praises. But just as he put his hand into his pocket to take out his purse, the young woman again signed to Bakbook to accept no payment. So he feebly murmured a refusal and went back to his shop in exceedingly low spirits. For he was now not only afflicted with a love-sick heart and an empty stomach, but was also reduced to beggary.

However, to repay Bakbook for the services he had rendered them, the young woman and her husband decided to marry him to their slave-girl. My brother accepted without hesitation, and looked forward to becoming, in a sense, a member of the family. On the evening of the wedding they called him to their house and counselled him to spend the bridal night at the mill in the basement. Nothing, they assured my brother, was more conducive to connubial bliss than such a beginning.

After the marriage ceremony, the credulous Bakbook waited in the basement for his bride. But when she failed to come down he was obliged to sleep in that dreary place alone. At midnight he was awakened by the whip of the miller, who, at the instigation of the landlord, had tied my brother to the grinding-stone. He heard the miller's voice, saying: 'A plague on this lazy ox! The corn is waiting to be ground, and the customers are demanding their flour.'

Then the miller lashed Bakbook with his whip, crying, 'Rise up, and turn the mill!'

Yelling and screaming, my brother began to go round and round the millstone, and continued to do so for the rest of the night.

Early in the morning, the slave-girl to whom he had been married the night before came down to the basement. Seeing him still tied to the millstone, she unfastened him and said with affected concern: 'We have just heard of this unfortunate mistake. My mistress lacks words to express her grief.'

Bakbook was so overcome with exhaustion that he could make no answer.

Soon after, the clerk who had drawn up the marriage-contract appeared. He greeted my brother, saying: 'Allah give you a long and happy life, my friend!' Then, perceiving the haggard look on Bakbook's face, he added: 'If I am not mistaken, what a night of sport you must have passed, with billing and cooing and coupling from dark till day!'

'Allah confound all liars, you thousandfold scoundrel!' retorted my brother. 'Your contract and blessings have caused me to turn a mill all night.'

When the clerk heard the story of the unhappy bridegroom, he said: 'I think I know the reason. Your star is at variance with that of your bride. I can, for a small fee, draw you up a more auspicious contract.'

But my brother refused to listen to him and told him to go and play his tricks elsewhere.

He resumed his work with renewed determination, hoping to make a little money with which to buy something to eat. But while he was sitting at his needlework, the young woman appeared at the window. With tears running down her cheeks, she swore to him that she knew nothing of what had happened at the mill that night. At first Bakbook would not listen to her pleading; but before long her sweet words won his heart again, and all his troubles were forgotten.

For many days afterwards my brother sat sewing contentedly. One day the slave came to him and said: 'My mistress greets you and wishes to inform you that her husband is to spend the night at the house of a friend. She invites you to come to her at the fall of evening.'

Now you must know that the young woman and her husband had conspired to ruin my brother. The landlord had said to his wife: 'How shall we entice him into the house, so that I may seize him and drag him before the Governor?' And the wicked woman had answered: 'Let me play another of my little tricks on him, and he shall be paraded through the city as an example to others.'

In the evening my brother (who, alas, knew nothing of women and their cunning) was led by the slave to the landlord's house. The young woman welcomed him, saying: 'We are alone at last, thank heavens!'

'Waste no time,' urged my brother. 'First kiss me, and then . . .'

But before he could finish his sentence, the husband burst into the room. He gripped my brother, crying: 'By Allah, the Governor himself shall judge this outrage!'

Turning a deaf ear to Bakbook's pitiful entreaties, he dragged him away to the Governor, who whipped him, and mounted him upon a camel, and drove him through the streets of the city. Great crowds watched the spectacle, shouting: 'Thus shall adulterers be punished!'

During the procession Bakbook was thrown off the camel's back and broke his leg. Furthermore the Governor banished him from Baghdad. But I took pity on him and carried him back in secret to my house, where I have fed and clothed him ever since.

The Caliph was much amused by my story. He ordered a gift to be bestowed upon me, saying: 'You have spoken well, my silent sheikh.'

'Prince of the Faithful,' I replied, 'I will not accept this honour until I have told you the stories of my other brothers; although, indeed, I fear that you may think me a little talkative.'

And thereupon I began to relate the tale of my second brother.

The Tale of Al-Haddar
The Barber's Second Brother

M Y second brother, Prince of the Faithful, is called Al-Haddar, and was in his younger days as skinny and loose-limbed as a scarecrow.

One day, as he was slouching along the streets of Baghdad, an old woman stopped him, saying: 'I have an offer to make you, my good man, which you can accept or refuse as you think fit.'

'Tell me what it is,' said my brother.

'First,' continued the old woman, 'you must promise that you will talk but little and ask no questions.'

'Speak, then,' replied Al-Haddar.

'What would you say,' whispered the old woman, 'to a handsome house set about with beautiful gardens, where you may drink to your heart's content and embrace a pretty girl from night till day?'

'How is it, good mother,' said Al-Haddar, 'that you have chosen me from all others to enjoy this marvel? And what quality of mine has pleased you?'

'Did I not tell you,' replied the old woman, 'to ask no questions? Be silent, then, and follow me.'

My brother followed the old woman, his mouth watering at the delights which she had promised him, until they came to a magnificent palace, at the doors of which stood numerous slaves and attendants. As he entered, my brother was stopped by one of the servants, who demanded: 'What is your business here?' But his guide promptly intervened, saying: 'He is a workman whom we have hired for a certain task.'

The old woman led him up to the second storey, and then

ushered him into a great pavilion hung round with rich
ornaments. He had not waited long before a young woman of
shining beauty came in, surrounded by her slave-girls. Al-
Haddar rose and bowed to the ground before her, and she
welcomed him in a most amiable fashion. When they had all
sat down, the slaves placed delicate sweetmeats before their
mistress and her guest, and, as she ate, the young woman
jested with my brother and made a great show of affection for
him. Although she was laughing at him all the while, my
imbecile of a brother perceived nothing and fancied, in the excess of his passion, that the young woman was enamoured of
him and would soon grant him his desire.

When the wine had been laid before them, there entered the
pavilion ten beautiful girls singing to the accompaniment of
lutes. The young woman plied Al-Haddar with wine, and while
he drank she began to stroke his cheeks, more with violence
than with affection, and ended by slapping him hard on the
nape of his neck. My brother rose angrily, and would have
left the house had not the old woman reminded him, with a
wink, of his promise. Determined to control himself, he went
back in silence; but no sooner had he resumed his seat than
the young woman and her servants fell upon him, slapping and
cuffing him until he almost fainted. Upon this Al-Haddar made
up his mind that he was not to be trifled with any longer, and
resolutely made for the door. But the old woman hastened to
prevent him, whispering: 'Be patient a little, and you shall win
her.'

'How long, pray,' retorted Al-Haddar, 'have I to wait?
Never in all the days of my life have I been so vilely treated.'

'Once she is heated with wine,' replied the old woman, 'she
will be yours.'

Al-Haddar was prevailed upon to stay in the pavilion.
Presently, however, the young woman ordered her slaves to
perfume my brother and besprinkle his face with rose-water.
When they had done so, she called one of her slave-girls and
said: 'Take your master and do to him what is required. Then
bring him back.'

Not knowing what lay in store for him, my brother allowed

himself to be conducted into a neighbouring room. The old woman soon joined him and said: 'Be patient. Only little remains to be done and you shall enjoy her.'

'Tell me,' said Al-Haddar, his face brightening, 'what would she have the slave do with me?'

'Nothing but good,' replied the old woman. 'She will only dye your eyebrows and shave off your moustaches.'

'As for the dyeing of my eyebrows,' said Al-Haddar, 'that will come off with washing: it is the shaving of my moustaches that I cannot endure.'

'Beware of crossing her,' replied the old woman, 'for her heart is set on you.'

My brother patiently suffered the slave-girl to dye his eyebrows and remove his moustaches. But when the girl returned to her mistress to inform her that the task had been accomplished, the young woman said: 'There remains only one other thing to be done: his beard must be shaved off.' So the slave went back to him and told him of his hostess's orders.

'How can I,' said the blockhead, deeply perplexed, 'permit that which will disgrace me in the eyes of my fellow-men?'

But the old woman answered: 'She cannot love you otherwise: your face must first be as smooth as that of a beardless youth. Be a little more patient, and you shall attain your desire.'

My brother hopefully submitted to the slave-girl, who shaved off his beard and made up his face with red and white. When he was brought back to the young women, they were so amused by his grotesque appearance that they fell over on their backs and rolled laughing on the floor. The young woman complimented him on his looks and pressed him to dance before them. This he did, and while he hopped and capered about, they pelted him with citrons, lemons and oranges, and flung at his head every cushion that came to hand. When he was about to drop down unconscious, the old woman whispered in his ears: 'Now you have nearly attained your desire: there are no more blows, and one thing only remains to be done. It is her custom when overcome with wine to let no one approach her until she has put off all her clothes. When this is done, she will order you to do the same yourself and to run after her. You must obey her in every particular and run after her from one room to another until you catch her.'

Presently the young woman began to unrobe herself, and ordered the half-conscious Al-Haddar to put off his clothes. When they were both stark naked, she said to my brother: 'If you want anything, run after me until you catch me.'

With this she tripped out of the pavilion and rushed in and out of many rooms and galleries, Al-Haddar chasing her in a frenzy of desire. At length, she slipped into a darkened chamber, and as he was scampering after her, the floor suddenly gave way beneath him. In a twinkling he found himself down below, in the market of the leather-merchants.

When the merchants saw Al-Haddar drop in their midst – naked, shaven, with eyebrows dyed, his face painted, and his penis erect and rampant, they booed him, and clapped their hands at him, and thrashed his bare body with their hides, until he fell down senseless. Finally they threw him on a donkey's back and took him to the Governor, who asked: 'Who can this man be?'

'He fell down upon us,' they answered, 'through a hole in the Vizier's house.'

The Governor sentenced him to a hundred lashes and banished him from the city. As soon as this news reached me, I set out to search for him, and when I found him, brought him back in secret to Baghdad and made him a daily allowance of food and drink. But for my courage and generosity, I would not have taken such pains to succour such a fool.

I now beg you, Prince of the Faithful, to listen to the story of my third brother.

The Tale of Bakbak
The Barber's Third Brother

My third brother, he who is blind, Prince of the Faithful, is called Bakbak.

One day, as he was begging in the streets of Baghdad, Destiny directed his steps to a certain house. He knocked at

the door, hoping that he might be given a coin or something to eat. The master of the house called out from within: 'Who is there?' But my brother, who was well versed in the tricks of his profession, would not answer before the door was opened. Again he heard the master of the house call out at the top of his voice: 'Who is knocking?' and still he made no reply. Bakbak then heard the sound of approaching footsteps, and the door was opened.

'What do you want?' asked the master of the house.

'Some little thing for a poor, blind man, in the name of Allah,' replied my brother.

'Give me your hand,' said the man, 'and follow me.'

Bakbak stretched out his hand, and the man took him within and led him up from one flight of stairs to another until they reached the roof of the house: my brother thinking at every step that he was about to be given some food or money.

There the man stopped and asked Bakbak a second time:
'Now, what do you want?'

'Some little thing,' repeated my brother, 'in the name of
Allah.'

'Then may Allah have pity on you,' replied the man, 'and
open a door for you elsewhere.'

'Could you not have given me that answer when we were
below?' cried my brother indignantly.

'Vile wretch,' retorted the master of the house, 'why did
you not say you were a beggar when you first heard my voice?'

'What are you doing with me?' asked my brother helplessly.

'I have nothing to give you,' the man answered.

'Then guide me down the stairs,' said Bakbak.

But the master of the house coolly replied: 'The way lies
open before you.'

Unaided, my brother groped his way back to the stairs. But
when he was some twenty steps from the bottom, his foot
slipped, and he rolled down, nearly breaking his skull.

As he left the house, two of his blind fellow-beggars heard
his groans and went to ask him what had happened. He dolefully described to them the treatment he had received, adding:
'Now, my brothers, there is no way left for me but to go to

our house and take something from our common savings; or else I shall be hungry for the rest of this ill-omened day.'

Now all this time, the man from whose house my brother had just been so amiably dismissed was following Bakbak and his blind companions, and heard all that they said to each other. He continued to walk quietly behind them until they reached their dwelling. When the three had entered, he slipped into the house without a sound. Then said my brother to his friends: 'Shut the door quickly and search the house lest any strangers should have followed us.'

When he heard my brother's words the man, who was an accomplished thief, noiselessly caught a rope that was hanging from the ceiling, and, climbing it, held fast until the blind men had inspected every corner. They then sat down beside my brother and brought out their money and began counting it. It was more than twelve thousand dirhams. When they had finished, one of them took a coin and hurried out of the house to buy something to eat, while the other two put back the silver in its hiding-place beneath the tiles.

When their companion returned, they all sat down to eat. During the course of their meal, however, my brother gradually became aware of a fourth pair of jaws chewing by his side. 'There is a stranger in our midst!' shouted Bakbak, and as he stretched out his hand and groped around him, it struck against the thief.

The three men closed upon the stranger, punching and kicking him, and crying out: 'A thief! Help, good Moslems! A thief, help!'

But as soon as the neighbours and the passers-by came to their rescue, the thief shut his eyes, pretending to be blind like the three beggars. 'Take me to the Governor, good Moslems,' he cried out passionately, 'for, by Allah, I have important information to give him.'

At once the crowd seized the four and led them to the Governor's house.

'Who are these men?' asked the Governor, when they were brought before him.

'Noble Governor,' cried the thief, 'nothing but the whip

can make us confess the truth. Begin by flogging me, and then these others!'

'Throw this man down and thrash him soundly,' said the Governor.

The guards threw down the pretended blind man and fell upon him with their whips. When his buttocks had received the first few lashes, he yelled and opened one of his eyes; and after a few more he opened the other.

'Wicked imposter,' cried the Governor, 'so you are not blind after all!'

'Grant me your pardon,' replied the thief, 'and I will tell you the whole truth.'

The Governor nodded assent, and the man continued: 'For a long time we four have pretended to be blind beggars, entering the houses of honest Moslems and gaining admittance to their harems and corrupting their women. We amassed a large fortune, amounting to twelve thousand dirhams in silver. But when I demanded my share today, they rose against me and beat me. I beg protection of Allah and of you; and if, noble Governor, you doubt the truth of my confession, put them to the whip and they will open their eyes.'

'Scoundrels!' roared the Governor. 'Dare you deny Allah's most gracious gift and pretend to be blind?'

The first to suffer was my brother. In vain he swore, by Allah and by all that is holy, that none of them was blessed with sight. They continued to whip him until he fainted.

'Leave him till he comes to,' cried the Governor, 'and then whip him again!'

The others received a similar treatment; nor did they open their eyes in spite of the imposter's repeated exhortations. Then the Governor sent his guards to fetch the money from my brother's house. A quarter of it he gave the thief, and kept the remainder for himself. Furthermore, he banished Bakbak and his friends from the city.

When I heard of my brother's misfortunes I set out to search for him and brought him back in secret to my house, where he has lived ever since.

The Caliph laughed heartily at my story, and said to his attendants: 'Give him a reward and show him out of the palace.'

'By Allah,' I replied, 'I will accept nothing until you have heard the stories of my other brothers.'

The Tale of Al-Kuz
The Barber's Fourth Brother

MY fourth brother, one-eyed Al-Kuz, Prince of the Faithful was at one time a butcher and sheep-breeder in Baghdad. He catered for the rich and the high-born, so that he amassed great wealth and became in time an owner of many herds of cattle and large estates.

He continued to prosper until a certain day when, as he was attending to his customers, an old man with a long white beard entered the shop and asked Al-Kuz to weigh him some mutton. My brother did so, and when he examined the money which he had received from the stranger, he was so struck by the unusual brilliance of the coins that he kept them in a separate coffer. For five months the old man bought meat regularly from my brother, and each time he paid him Al-Kuz put the bright new coins aside.

One day, wishing to buy some sheep, my brother opened the coffer and found, to his astonishment and dismay, that it was filled only with little rounds of white paper. He set up a great clamour, beating himself about the face and calling out to the passers-by, until a huge crowd gathered round him. Whilst he was telling them his story, the old man himself came forward with the glittering coins ready in his hand as was his custom. My brother sprang upon him and, taking him by the throat, cried: 'Help, good people! Here is the scoundrel who has robbed me!'

But this did not seem to perturb the old man, who calmly whispered to my brother: 'Hold your tongue, or I will put you to public shame!'

'How will you do that, pray?' shouted Al-Kuz.

'By charging you here and now,' replied the old man, 'with selling human flesh for mutton!'

'You lie, accursed reprobate!' yelled my brother.

'None is more accursed,' rejoined the old man, 'than he who at this moment has a human corpse hung up in his shop instead of a sheep!'

'If you can prove this crime against me,' said Al-Kuz, 'my life and all my property are yours!'

Accepting the challenge, the old man turned to the bystanders and cried out: 'Good Moslems, for months this butcher has been slaughtering his fellow-men and selling us their flesh as mutton. If any one doubts this, let him enter the shop and see for himself!'

The crowd rushed in, and what should they see hanging from one of the hooks but the corpse of a man! Struck with horror, the infuriated mob gripped Al-Kuz, crying: 'Blasphemy! Sacrilege!' And those who were his oldest clients and dearest friends turned against him and beat him. In the hubbub, the sorcerer (for such was the wicked old man) struck my brother in the face, knocking out his left eye.

Then the crowd carried Al-Kuz and the supposed corpse to the chief of the city's magistrates. 'Your honour,' said the sorcerer, 'we bring before you a criminal who for months has been murdering human beings and selling their flesh as mutton. We call upon you to perform Allah's justice; and here are all the witnesses.'

My brother tried to defend himself, but the judge would not listen to him, and sentenced him to five hundred lashes. He confiscated all his goods and banished him from the city; and, indeed, had Al-Kuz been a poor man, he would have put him to a cruel death.

Penniless and broken, my brother left Baghdad and journeyed many days and nights until he arrived in the chief city of a foreign land. There he set up as a cobbler, making a precarious living in a little shop.

One day, as Al-Kuz was walking along the street, he heard the neighing of horses and the beating of hoofs. Upon inquiry he was informed that the King was going out hunting, and he stopped to watch the procession. Chancing to glance over his shoulder, the King caught sight of my brother's face, and with a start turned away his head, crying: 'Allah preserve us from the evil eye and from the portent of this day!' At once he turned his horse about and rode back to his palace, followed by the troops. As for my brother, he was set upon by the King's slaves and beaten, and then left for dead by the roadside.

Al-Kuz was so perplexed at this stroke of ill-fortune that he betook himself to one of the King's attendants and related to him what had happened. The courtier burst into a fit of laughter, and said: 'The King cannot bear the sight of a one-eyed man, especially if it is the left eye which is missing. Indeed, in this land death is the usual penalty for such a disfigurement.'

When Al-Kuz heard this he decided to fly the country, and set out at once for a far-off town where no one knew him. Many months afterwards, as he was taking a walk one day, he suddenly heard in the distance the neighing of horses and the beating of hoofs. He took to his heels in great panic, searching in vain for a hiding-place. At length he found himself on the threshold of a great door, and, pushing it open without a moment's thought, entered a long passage. Scarcely had he advanced one step, when two men sprang upon him, crying: 'Allah be praised that we have caught you at last! We have passed three sleepless nights in fear of your malice.'

'But, good people,' said my brother, 'what offence have I committed?'

'You are plotting to kill the master of this house and to ruin us all!' they replied. 'Was it not enough to reduce him to poverty, you and your friends? Where is the dagger with which you threatened us yesterday?'

So saying, they searched Al-Kuz and found his cobbler's knife in his belt.

'Good people,' whimpered my brother, 'have fear of Allah and let me tell you the whole of my story!'

But they refused to listen to him. They beat him and tore

his clothes to tatters. His body being thus uncovered, they saw the marks of whipping on his back. 'Black-souled reprobate,' they cried, 'these scars bear testimony to your other crimes!' Then they dragged him away to the Governor.

My brother tried to defend himself, but the Governor turned a deaf ear to his entreaties. 'Wretched criminal!' he cried indignantly. 'One need only look upon your back to see that you have practised every kind of crime!' And he ordered Al-Kuz to be given a hundred lashes.

Then the Governor's men hoisted Al-Kuz on the back of a camel, and drove him through the streets, crying: 'Thus shall house-breaking ruffians be punished!'

When I heard of my brother's misfortunes, I set out for his city, and searched for him until I found him. I then brought him back in secret to Baghdad, where he has lived under my care and protection ever since.

That is the story of Al-Kuz. But do not think, Prince of the Faithful, that it is in any way more extraordinary than the tale of my fifth brother.

The Tale of Al-Ashar
The Barber's Fifth Brother

My fifth brother, he who is cropped of both his ears, Prince of the Faithful, is called Al-Ashar. In his youth he was very poor, and used to beg alms by night and spend the proceeds by day. When our father died, we each inherited a hundred pieces of silver. For many weeks Al-Ashar did not know what to do with his share, and at length he decided to be a glass-merchant. He bought some glassware with his hundred dirhams, and, placing the articles in a large basket before him, sat at a corner in a busy thoroughfare.

On a certain Friday, as he squatted in his accustomed place, he sank into a reverie, and thought to himself:

'I have invested the whole of my capital in this glassware. It cost me a hundred dirhams and I shall no doubt sell it for two hundred. With the two hundred I shall buy more glass, which I shall sell for four hundred. I shall go on buying and selling till I make a large fortune. With this I shall buy all kinds of essences and jewellery, and make a vast profit. Then I shall be able to afford a splendid house, with slaves, and horses, and gilded saddles. I will eat the choicest dishes, drink the rarest wines, and be entertained in my own house by the sweetest singers of the city.

'When I have made a hundred thousand dirhams, I shall send for the subtlest marriage-brokers and instruct them to find me a wife amongst the daughters of kings and viziers. I shall perhaps ask for the hand of the Grand Vizier's daughter, for I hear she is a girl of incomparable beauty. I shall offer her a marriage-portion of a thousand pieces of gold; and should her father withhold his consent I will carry her away by force. I will buy ten young eunuchs to attend upon me, and dress myself in regal robes. My saddle shall be adorned with priceless jewels, and as I ride through the city to the Vizier's house, with slaves before me and servants behind me, men will bow reverently as I pass by them, greeting and blessing me.

'When I enter the Vizier's house, he will stand up to receive me. He will give me his own place and will himself sit down at my feet. Two of my eunuchs shall carry purses with a thousand dinars in each; one I shall lay before the Vizier as his daughter's marriage-portion; the other I shall present him as a gift, in proof of my worthiness and munificence. I shall be solemn and reserved, and for every ten words he addresses to me I shall answer with two. Then I shall return to my house. And when one of my future wife's relations returns my visit, I will give him gold and a robe of honour; but if he brings me a present I will return it to him, so that he will know how proud my spirit is.

'I will myself appoint the wedding-day, and then make preparations for the bridal festivities. On the wedding-night I will put on my most splendid robes and, surrounded by my guests, will recline upon a mattress of gold brocade. I will turn my head neither to the right nor to the left, but will look straight in front of me with an air of authority and contemptuous unconcern. When my bride is brought before me, decked with jewels and radiant like the full moon, I will not even look at her. Her women will plead with me, saying: "Our lord and master, here stands your wife, your slave, waiting for you to honour her with a gracious look." They will kiss the ground before me. I will cast one glance at her and resume my disdainful air. They will then conduct her to the bridal chamber, and I will rise and change into a finer robe. I shall order one of my slaves to bring me five hundred pieces of gold, which I shall scatter among my wife's attendants. Then I will go to my bride; and when I am left alone with her, I will neither speak to her nor even look at her. Presently the bride's mother will come in, kissing my head and hand, and saying: "My lord, look upon your slave-girl, who yearns for your favour; speak to her and heal her broken spirit." I will make no answer. She will throw herself down at my feet, kissing them again and again, and saying: "Your slave is a beautiful virgin and she has seen no man but you. On my knees I beg you to cease humbling her, or her heart will break!" Then the bride's mother will rise, and, filling a cup with wine, will give it to her daughter, who will offer it to me with all submission. But I, leaning idly upon my elbow among the gold-embroidered cushions, will take no notice of her. With a trembling voice she will say: "I beg you, my lord, to take this cup from the hand of your slave and servant." But I will maintain my dignified silence. She will raise the cup to my mouth, pressing me to drink from it. Then I will wave it away with my hand, and spurn her with my foot, thus –'

So saying, Al-Ashar kicked against the basket of glassware, knocking over the contents and crashing them in fragments to the ground.

My brother began to beat himself about the face, tearing his clothes and wailing, as the people went by to the midday prayers. Some stopped to say a kind word to him, and some passed by, taking no notice of his lamentation. Whilst he sat bitterly mourning the loss of all his worldly possessions, a woman rode by on her way to the mosque. She was very beautiful, and as she passed, surrounded by her servants, a sweet odour of the rarest musk hung about her. Moved with pity for my brother, she sent to inquire the cause of his distress. When she heard his story she called one of her servants and said: 'Give this unfortunate man the purse you are carrying.'

The servant took from his belt a heavy purse and gave it to Al-Ashar, who, on opening it, found that it contained five hundred pieces of gold. He almost died for joy, and fervently called down Allah's blessing on his benefactress.

Carrying the great purse, my brother returned to his house a rich man. He sat thinking of the happy turn of his fortune, and was on the point of conjuring up another vision, when he was roused by a knocking at the door. He went to open it, and found on the threshold an old woman whom he had never seen before.

'My son,' said the old woman, 'the hour of Friday prayers is almost past, and I have not yet made the necessary ablutions. I beg you to let me come into your house, so that I may prepare myself.'

Al-Ashar politely invited her to enter. He brought her a ewer and a basin, and retired to delight his eyes with his treasure.

A few minutes afterwards the old woman appeared in the room where my brother was sitting. She knelt and bowed twice in prayer and called down blessings on my brother. He thanked her, took two dinars from the purse, and offered them to her. But the old woman refused the gold with dignity, saying: 'Put this money back into your purse. If you have no need for it, return it to her who gave it to you.'

'Do you know her?' asked Al-Ashar in a transport of joy. 'I beg you to tell me how I can see her again.'

'My son,' she replied, 'I have served that lady for many years. I assure you that she has a great liking for you. But she is married to a rich, old man. Rise, my son, take with you all your money lest a thief should steal it, and follow me to the lady's house. When you are alone with her, let your words be loving and your deeds lusty. Thus shall her beauty and all her wealth be yours.'

Bursting with happiness, Al-Ashar rose, took all his gold,

and followed the old woman until she stopped at a great house and knocked. The door was opened by a Greek slave-girl, and the old woman went in, followed by my brother. Al-Ashar soon found himself in a spacious hall, hung with rich tapestry and spread with rare carpets. He sat down on a cushion, holding his turban on his knees, and before long a young woman, attired in splendid silks and blessed with more loveliness than the eyes of men had ever seen, appeared before him.

Al-Ashar rose to his feet as she entered, and when she saw him she welcomed him with a seductive smile. She took him by the hand and led him to a richly carpeted room, where they sat dallying together for an hour. Then the young woman rose from his side, saying: 'Stay here till I return.'

Whilst my brother was waiting, the door was flung wide open and there entered a tall black slave, holding an unsheathed sword in his hand.

'Vilest of men,' cried the Negro, 'who brought you to this house, and what are you doing here?'

My brother's tongue stuck in his throat and he did not know what to answer. The slave took hold of him and, stripping him of his clothes, beat him savagely with the flat of his sword until he fell down unconsious. Taking him for dead, the Negro called out in a terrible voice, and immediately a slave-girl ran in with a tray of salt. He filled my brother's wounds with salt, but Al-Ashar, who soon recovered his senses, neither moved nor uttered a sound lest he should kill him. Then the black slave gave another terrible cry, and the old woman appeared.

She gripped Al-Ashar by the feet and, dragging him into a dark cellar, threw him upon a heap of corpses.

For two days Al-Ashar remained among the dead, and would himself have surely perished had not Allah made the salt with which his wounds had been treated the means of preserving his life; for it prevented his flesh from festering and checked the flow of blood. At night-time, when his strength had returned a little, Al-Ashar crawled on all fours groping for the door. Having at length found it, he made his way, with Allah's help, out of the cellar to the vestibule, and concealed himself there. Next morning the old woman left the house in search of another victim; and before she had time to shut the door behind her, my brother slipped out without a sound, and made off as fast as his legs could carry him to his own house.

When his wounds had healed, Al-Ashar began to plan a punishment for the old woman and her accomplices. He kept a watchful eye on her movements and acquainted himself with her daily haunts. As soon as he was restored to his normal vigour, he disguised himself as a traveller from a foreign land. He tied to his waist a large bag filled with glass fragments, which seemed as though it were bursting with coins, hid a sword under his robe, and went out to seek the old woman.

When he saw her, Al-Ashar said with an uncouth foreign accent: 'Good mother, have you a pair of scales in which I can weigh nine hundred pieces of gold? I am a stranger here and do not know anyone in this city.'

The old woman answered: 'One of my sons is a money-changer, and has all kinds of scales. I will take you to him before he leaves his house, and he will gladly weigh your gold for you.'

My brother followed her until she stopped at the sinister house. The young woman herself opened the door for them, and her old servant whispered to her: 'I have brought you some fat meat today.' Then the young woman took my brother by the hand and led him to her room, where she did with him as she had done on the first occasion. Then she retired as before, and presently the black slave appeared with his naked sword.

'Rise up,' roared the Negro, 'and follow me!'

My brother rose, and as the slave turned his back, Al-Ashar drew his sword and sprang upon him, striking his head off with one blow. He then dragged him by the feet to the cellar and called out to the slave-girl, who promptly appeared with her tray of salt. Seeing Al-Ashar with a sword in his hand, she ran in terror out of the room. But he overtook her and killed her. He next called out to the old woman, and when she appeared, he cried: 'Black-souled hag, do you recognize me?'

'I do not, indeed,' replied the old woman.

'Know, then,' shouted my brother, 'I am the man to whose house you came to do your washings, and whom you betrayed so wickedly!'

The old woman implored him on her knees to pardon her, but with one stroke of his sword Al-Ashar cut her in two pieces. He then set out to look for her mistress. When he found her, the terrified young woman entreated him to spare her life. His heart was softened, and he pardoned her.

'How did you fall into the power of this black slave?' he asked.

'Three years ago,' she replied, 'before I was imprisoned in this house, I was a slave in the service of a merchant of this city. The old woman was a frequent visitor at our house. One day she invited me to accompany her to an entertainment. I accepted gladly, and, putting on my best clothes and taking with me a purse of one hundred dinars, went out with her. She led me to this house, where the Negro has kept me and made me the instrument of his crimes ever since.'

Al-Ashar ordered her to conduct him to the place where the stolen gold was hidden. He stood dumbfounded as she opened one coffer after another, all filled with glittering coins.

'You will never be able to carry all this gold alone,' she said. 'Go and bring some porters to take it out of the house.'

Al-Ashar went out at once and soon came back with ten strong men. But, on his return, he found the doors wide open and the girl and most of the money gone. He realized that the young woman had deceived him. Nevertheless, he contented himself with what she had left behind. He emptied the closets of their valuables and took everything to his house.

Al-Ashar slept in great happiness that night. But when he woke next morning, he was terrified to find twenty of the Governor's guards at his door. They seized him, saying: 'You are wanted by our master.'

The men dragged Al-Ashar before the Governor, who asked: 'Whence did you steal all this money and these goods?'

'Noble Governor,' replied Al-Ashar, 'grant me the pledge of mercy, and I will tell you the whole truth.'

The Governor threw him the white handkerchief of pardon, and my brother related to him the story of his adventures, and offered him a handsome share of the spoil. But the Governor seized everything for himself, and, fearing that the Caliph might hear of his action, decided to get rid of my brother by banishing him from the city.

Thus, Al-Ashar was forced to leave Baghdad. But he had not travelled far before he was set upon by a band of highwaymen, who, finding that they could rob him of nothing except his rags, beat him mercilessly and cut off both his ears.

When I heard of my brother's misfortunes, Prince of the Faithful, I set out to search for him and, having found him, brought him back in secret to my house, where I have provided for him ever since.

That is the story of Al-Ashar. I will now tell you the tale of my sixth and last brother, which, as you will readily agree, is even more extraordinary than the other tales.

The Tale of Shakashik
The Barber's Sixth Brother

My sixth brother, he who had both his lips cut off, Prince of the Faithful, is called Shakashik.

In his youth he was very poor. One day, as he was begging in the streets of Baghdad, he passed by a splendid mansion, at the gates of which stood an impressive array of attendants. Upon inquiry my brother was informed that the house belonged to a member of the wealthy and powerful Barmecide family. Shakashik approached the door-keepers and solicited alms.

'Go in,' they said, 'and our master will give you all that you desire.'

My brother entered the lofty vestibule and proceeded to a spacious, marble-paved hall, hung with tapestry and over-looking a beautiful garden. He stood bewildered for a moment, not knowing where to turn his steps, and then advanced to the far end of the hall. There, among the cushions, reclined a handsome old man with a long beard, whom my brother recognized at once as the master of the house.

'What can I do for you, my friend?' asked the old man, as he rose to welcome my brother.

When Shakashik replied that he was a hungry beggar, the old man expressed the deepest compassion and rent his fine robes, crying: 'Is it possible that there should be a man as hungry as yourself in a city where I am living? It is, indeed, a disgrace that I cannot endure!' Then he comforted my brother, adding: 'I insist that you stay with me and partake of my dinner.'

With this the master of the house clapped his hands and called out to one of the slaves: 'Bring in the basin and ewer.' Then he said to my brother: 'Come forward, my friend, and wash your hands.'

Shakashik rose to do so, but saw neither ewer nor basin. He was bewildered to see his host make gestures as though he were pouring water on his hands from an invisible vessel and then drying them with an invisible towel. When he finished, the host called out to his attendants: 'Bring in the table!'

Numerous servants hurried in and out of the hall, as though they were preparing for a meal. My brother could still see nothing. Yet his host invited him to sit at the imaginary table, saying: 'Honour me by eating of this meat.'

The old man moved his hands about as though he were touching invisible dishes, and also moved his jaws and lips as though he were chewing. Then said he to Shakashik: 'Eat your fill, my friend, for you must be famished.'

My brother began to move his jaws, to chew and swallow, as though he were eating, while the old man still coaxed him, saying: 'Eat, my friend, and note the excellence of this bread and its whiteness.'

'This man,' thought Shakashik, 'must be fond of practical jokes.' So he said: 'It is, sir, the whitest bread I have ever seen, and I have never tasted the like in all my life.'

'This bread,' said the host, 'was baked by a slave-girl whom

I bought for five hundred dinars.' Then he called out to one of his slaves: 'Bring in the meat-pudding, and let there be plenty of fat in it!'

Turning to my brother, the old man continued: 'By Allah, my friend, have you ever tasted anything better than this meat-pudding? Now, on my life, you must eat and not be abashed!'

Presently he cried out again: 'Serve up the stewed grouse!' And again he said to Shakashik: 'Eat your fill, my friend, for you must be very hungry.'

My brother moved his jaws, and chewed, and swallowed, while the old man called for one imaginary dish after another, and pressed his guest to eat. Then the host cried out: 'Serve up the chickens stuffed with pistachio nuts,' and turned to Shakashik, saying: 'Eat, for you have never tasted anything like these chickens!'

'Sir,' replied my brother, 'they are indeed incomparably delicious.'

Thereupon the host moved his fingers as though to pick up a morsel from an imaginary dish, and popped the invisible delicacy into my brother's mouth.

The old man continued to enlarge upon the excellences of the various dishes, while my brother became so ravenously hungry that he would have willingly died for a crust of barley-bread.

'Have you ever tasted anything more delicious,' went on the old man, 'than the spices in these dishes?'

'Never, indeed,' replied Shakashik.

'Eat heartily, then,' said his host, 'and do not be ashamed!'

'I thank you, sir,' answered Shakashik, 'but I have already eaten my fill.'

'Bring in the dessert!' cried the master of the house, and then said to my brother: 'Taste this excellent pastry; eat of these fritters: take this one before the syrup drips out of it!'

Shakashik helped himself to the imperceptible dainty, and, clicking his tongue with delight, remarked upon the abundance of musk in it.

'Yes,' agreed the old man, 'I always insist on a dinar-weight of musk in each fritter, and half that quantity of ambergris.'

My brother continued to move his jaws and lips and to roll his tongue between his cheeks, as though he were enjoying the sumptuous feast.

'Eat of these roasted almonds, and walnuts, and raisins,' said the old man.

'I can eat no more,' replied my brother.

'By Allah,' repeated the host, 'you must eat, and not remain hungry!'

'Sir,' protested Shakashik, 'how can one remain hungry after eating all these dishes?'

My suffering brother considered the manner in which his host was making game of him, and thought: 'By Allah, I will do something that will make him repent of his pranks!'

Presently, however, the old man clapped his hands again and cried: 'Bring in the wine!'

Numerous slaves ran in, moving their hands about as though they were setting wine and cups before their master and his guest. The old man pretended to pour wine into the cups, and to hand one to my brother. 'Take this,' he said, 'and tell me how you like it.'

'Sir,' said Shakashik, 'your generosity overwhelms me!' He lifted the invisible cup to his lips, and made as if to drain it at one gulp.

'Health and joy to you!' exclaimed the old man, as he pretended to pour himself some wine and drink it off. He handed another cup to his guest, and they both continued to act in this fashion until Shakashik, feigning himself drunk, began to roll his head from side to side. Then, taking his bounteous host unawares, he suddenly raised his arm so high that the white of his armpit could be seen, and dealt him a blow on the neck which made the hall echo with the sound. And this he followed by a second blow.

The old man rose in anger and cried: 'What are you doing, vile creature?'

'Sir,' replied my brother, 'you have received your humble slave into your house and loaded him with your generosity;

you have fed him with the choicest food and quenched his thirst with the most potent wines. Alas, he became drunk, and forgot his manners! But you are so noble, sir, that you will surely pardon his offence.'

When he heard these words, the old man burst out laughing, and said: 'For a long time I have jested with all types of men, but no one has ever had the patience or the wit to enter into my humours as you have done. Now, therefore, I pardon you, and ask you in truth to eat and drink with me, and to be my companion as long as I live.'

Then the old man ordered his attendants to serve all the dishes which they had consumed in fancy, and when he and my brother had eaten their fill they repaired to the drinking-chamber, where beautiful young women sang and made music. The old Barmecide gave Shakashik a robe of honour and made him his constant companion.

The two lived in amity for a period of twenty years, until the old man died and the Caliph seized all his property. My brother was forced to fly for his life. He left Baghdad and rode out into the desert, but before long a band of roving bedouin took him prisoner and carried him away to their encampment. Every day their chieftain put him to the torture, and threatened him, saying: 'Pay us your ransom or I will kill you!' Then my brother would weep and swear to him that he was no more than a penniless outcast.

Now the chieftain had a beautiful wife. Whenever her husband was away she would come to my brother and tempt him with the charms of her body. At first Shakashik would not yield to her advances, but the artful woman succeeded one day in seducing him. Whilst they were together the chieftain entered the tent and found his wife sitting upon my brother's knee.

'Vile wretch,' cried the furious Arab, 'you have corrupted my wife!'

He drew his knife (a blade that might have felled a camel with one stroke) and, seizing my brother, cut off his penis and his lips. Then he carried him upon a camel to a barren hill-side and left him there to perish.

However, Shakashik was rescued by some travellers, who recognized him and gave him food and drink. When news of his plight reached me, I journeyed to him and brought him back to Baghdad. I nursed him in my own house, and have provided for him ever since.

When he had heard the tale of my sixth brother (continued the barber to the guests), the Caliph Al-Muntasir Billah burst out laughing and said: 'I can well see, my silent friend, that you are a man of few words, who knows neither curiosity nor indiscretion. Yet I must ask you to leave this city at once and go to live elsewhere.'

Thus, for no conceivable reason, the Caliph banished me from Baghdad.

I journeyed through far countries and visited many foreign lands until I heard of Al-Muntasir's death and the succession of another Caliph. I then returned to Baghdad, and found that all my brothers had died also. It was soon after my return that I met this young man, whom I saved from certain death, and who has so unjustly accused me of being talkative and officious.

When the barber ended, your majesty (continued the tailor), we were all convinced that the lame young man had been the victim of an exceptionally garrulous and meddlesome barber. We therefore decided to punish him; so we seized him and locked him in an empty room. Then we sat in peace, eating and drinking and making merry until the hour of afternoon prayers.

When I returned home, my wife received me with angry looks. 'A fine husband you are,' she burst out, 'to enjoy yourself all day while your wife sits moping alone at home. If you do not take me out at once and give me a pleasant time, I shall divorce you!'

We went out together and passed the rest of the day in search of amusement. When we were returning home in the evening we met this hunchback, whose untimely death has caused all this company to assemble here.

The King of Basrah was much amused by the tailor's story, and said: 'The young man's adventure with the barber certainly surpasses in wonder the story of the hunchback.' And turning to the Chamberlain and the tailor, he added: 'Go, seek the barber and bring him before me. We will then bury the hunchback, for he has been dead since yesterday.'

The two men hurried to the house where the barber was still imprisoned. They set him free and brought him before the King, who found that he was an old man past his ninetieth year, with dark complexion, long white beard, and grey, bushy eyebrows; his nose was long, his ears shrivelled, and his manner lofty. After a good look at him, the King burst into a fit of laughter, and said: 'Silent One, we wish to hear some of your stories.'

'First, your majesty,' replied the barber, 'I would myself know the occasion of this gathering and the reason why the hunchback's body lies before you.'

The King said to the company: 'Tell the barber the story of the hunchback's death, and all that befell him at the hands of the tailor, the doctor, the steward, and the broker.'

When he had heard all, the barber exclaimed: 'By Allah, this is exceedingly strange! Lift the veil from the hunchback's body, and let me examine it.'

They did so; and the barber sat down, placing the hunchback's head upon his knees. After he had scrutinized the face for a while, he burst out laughing and exclaimed: 'Death is one of Allah's mysteries: but the death of this hunchback is a wonder that ought to be recorded for all time!'

The King and all the company were astonished at the barber's words.

'Explain your meaning,' said the King.

'Your majesty,' replied the old man, 'the hunchback is alive!'

So saying, the barber took from his belt a vial containing ointment, with which he rubbed the hunchback's neck. Then, producing a pair of iron forceps from his pocket, he put it down the hunchback's throat and pulled out the piece of fish and the bone. With a violent sneeze the hunchback sprang

to his feet. He passed his hands over his face, and said: 'There is no god but Allah, and Mohammed is His Prophet!'

The King and all the company marvelled greatly. 'By Allah,' exclaimed the King, 'I have never in all my life heard of an incident more strange than this!' Then, turning to the captains of his army, he added: 'Have any of you, good Moslems, ever seen a dead man come to life in this fashion? Had not Allah sent him this barber, our hunchback would have now been counted among the dead.'

And all those present said: 'By Allah, it is a rare marvel!'

The King ordered that the incident be recorded on parchment and that the scroll be kept in the royal library. He bestowed robes of honour upon the Jew, the Christian, the steward, the tailor, the hunchback, and the barber. He appointed the tailor to his court, and endowed him with a large annuity, and reconciled him with the hunchback, who again became the King's drinking companion. The barber also he appointed to his court, and conferred upon him many honours, and made him a favourite companion. And they all lived happily until they were visited by the Destroyer of all earthly pleasures, the Annihilator of men.

THE DONKEY

Iт is related that a pair of tricksters once saw a simpleton leading a donkey by its halter along a deserted road. 'I will steal that beast,' said one of them to his companion, 'and make an ass of its master. Follow me and you shall see.'

He went up behind the simpleton without a sound, and, deftly loosing the halter from the donkey, placed it round his own neck. He then jogged along as though nothing had happened.

When his friend had safely made off with the beast, the thief abruptly halted and would not yield to the repeated jerks of the rope. Looking over his shoulder, the simpleton was utterly confounded to see his donkey transformed into a human being.

'Who in heaven's name are you?' he cried.

'Sir,' replied the thief, 'I am your donkey; but my story is marvellously strange. It all happened one day when I returned home very drunk, as was my custom. My pious old mother received me with an indignant rebuke and pleaded with me against my evil ways. But I took up my staff and beat her. Whereupon she invoked Allah's vengeance and I was instantly transformed into the donkey which has faithfully served you all these years. Today the old woman must have taken pity on me and prayed to Allah to change me back into human shape.'

'There is no strength or help save in Allah!' cried the simpleton. 'I beg you to pardon the treatment you have received at my hands and all the hardships you have endured in my service.'

He set the robber free, and returned home in a pitiful state of bewilderment and dejection.

'What has happened to you, and where is your donkey?' asked his wife.

When he had related to her the strange story, the woman began to wring her hands, crying: 'The wrath of Allah will be upon us now for having used a human being so brutally.' And she fell down penitently on her knees, reciting verses from the Koran.

For several days afterwards the simpleton stayed idle at home. At length his wife counselled him to go and buy another donkey in order that he might resume his work. So he went off to the market-place, and, as he was inspecting the animals put up for sale, he was astounded to see his own donkey amongst them. Having identified the beast beyond all doubt, the simpleton whispered in its ear:

'The Devil take you for an incorrigible wretch! Have you been drinking and beating your mother again? By Allah, I will not buy you a second time!'

THE FISHERMAN AND
THE JINNEE

ONCE upon a time there was a poor fisherman who had a wife and three children to support.

He used to cast his net four times a day. It chanced that one day he went down to the sea at noon and, reaching the shore, set down his basket, rolled up his shirt-sleeves, and cast his net far out into the water. After he had waited for it to sink, he pulled on the cords with all his might; but the net was so heavy that he could not draw it in. So he tied the rope ends to a wooden stake on the beach and, putting off his clothes, dived into the water and set to work to bring it up. When he had carried it ashore, however, he found in it a dead donkey.

'By Allah, this is a strange catch!' cried the fisherman, disgusted at the sight. After he had freed the net and wrung it out, he waded into the water and cast it again, invoking Allah's help. But when he tried to draw it in he found it even heavier than before. Thinking that he had caught some enormous fish, he fastened the ropes to the stake and, diving in again, brought up the net. This time he found a large earthen vessel filled with mud and sand.

Angrily the fisherman threw away the vessel, cleaned his net, and cast it for the third time. He waited patiently, and when he felt the net grow heavy he hauled it in, only to find it filled with bones and broken glass. In despair, he lifted his eyes to heaven and cried: 'Allah knows that I cast my net only four times a day. I have already cast it for the third time and caught no fish at all. Surely He will not fail me again!'

With this the fisherman hurled his net far out into the sea, and waited for it to sink to the bottom. When at length he brought it to land he found in it a bottle made of yellow copper. The mouth was stopped with lead and bore the seal of our master Solomon son of David. The fisherman rejoiced, and said: 'I will sell this in the market of the coppersmiths. It must be worth ten pieces of gold.' He shook the bottle and, finding it heavy, thought to himself: 'I will first break the seal and find out what is inside.'

The fisherman removed the lead with his knife and again shook the bottle; but scarcely had he done so, when there burst from it a great column of smoke which spread along the shore and rose so high that it almost touched the heavens. Taking shape, the smoke resolved itself into a jinnee of such prodigious stature that his head reached the clouds, while his feet were planted on the sand. His head was a huge dome and his mouth as wide as a cavern, with teeth ragged like broken rocks. His legs towered like the masts of a ship, his nostrils were two inverted bowls, and his eyes, blazing like torches, made his aspect fierce and menacing.

The sight of this jinnee struck terror to the fisherman's heart; his limbs quivered, his teeth chattered together, and he stood rooted to the ground with parched tongue and staring eyes.

'There is no god but Allah and Solomon is His Prophet!' cried the jinnee. Then, addressing himself to the fisherman, he said: 'I pray you, mighty Prophet, do not kill me! I swear never again to defy your will or violate your laws!'

'Blasphemous giant,' cried the fisherman, 'do you presume to call Solomon the Prophet of Allah? Solomon has been dead these eighteen hundred years, and we are now approaching the end of Time. But what is your history, pray, and how came you to be imprisoned in this bottle?'

On hearing these words the jinnee replied sarcastically: 'Well, then; there is no god but Allah! Fisherman, I bring you good news.'

'What news?' asked the old man.

'News of your death, horrible and prompt!' replied the jinnee.

'Then may heaven's wrath be upon you, ungrateful wretch!' cried the fisherman. 'Why do you wish my death, and what

have I done to deserve it? Have I not brought you up from
the depths of the sea and released you from your imprisonment?'

But the jinnee answered: 'Choose the manner of your death
and the way that I shall kill you. Come, waste no time!'

'But what crime have I committed?' cried the fisherman.

'Listen to my story, and you shall know,' replied the jinnee.

'Be brief, then, I pray you,' said the fisherman, 'for you
have wrung my soul with terror.'

'Know,' began the giant, 'that I am one of the rebel jinn who, together with Sakhr the Jinnee, mutinied against Solomon son of David. Solomon sent against me his Vizier, Asaf ben Berakhya, who vanquished me despite my supernatural power and led me captive before his master. Invoking the name of Allah, Solomon adjured me to embrace his faith and pledge him absolute obedience. I refused, and he imprisoned me in this bottle, upon which he set a seal of lead bearing the Name of the Most High. Then he sent for several of his faithful jinn, who carried me away and cast me into the middle of the sea. In the ocean depths I vowed: "I will bestow eternal riches on him who sets me free!" But a hundred years passed away and no one freed me. In the second hundred years of my imprisonment I said: "For him who frees me I will open up the buried treasures of the earth!" And yet no one freed me. Whereupon I flew into a rage and swore: "I will kill the man who sets me free, allowing him only to choose the manner of his death!" Now it was you who set me free; therefore prepare to die and choose the way that I shall kill you.'

'O wretched luck, that it should have fallen to my lot to free you!' exclaimed the fisherman. 'Spare me, mighty jinnee, and Allah will spare you; kill me, and so shall Allah destroy you!'

'You have freed me,' repeated the jinnee. 'Therefore you must die.'

'Chief of the jinn,' cried the fisherman, 'will you thus requite good with evil?'

'Enough of this talk!' roared the jinnee. 'Kill you I must.'

At this point the fisherman thought to himself: 'Though I am but a man and he is a jinnee, my cunning may yet overreach his malice.' Then, turning to his adversary, he said: 'Before you kill me, I beg you in the Name of the Most High engraved on Solomon's seal to answer me one question truthfully.'

The jinnee trembled at the mention of the Name, and, when he had promised to answer truthfully, the fisherman asked: 'How could this bottle, which is scarcely large enough to hold your hand or foot, ever contain your entire body?'

'Do you dare doubt that?' roared the jinnee indignantly.

'I will never believe it,' replied the fisherman, 'until I see you enter this bottle with my own eyes!'

Upon this the jinnee trembled from head to foot and dissolved into a column of smoke, which gradually wound itself into the bottle and disappeared inside. At once the fisherman snatched up the leaden stopper and thrust it into the mouth of the bottle. Then he called out to the jinnee: 'Choose the manner of your death and the way that I shall kill you! By Allah, I will throw you back into the sea, and keep watch on this shore to warn all men of your treachery!'

When he heard the fisherman's words, the jinnee struggled desperately to escape from the bottle, but was prevented by the magic seal. He now altered his tone and, assuming a submissive air, assured the fisherman that he had been jesting with him and implored him to let him out. But the fisherman paid no heed to the jinnee's entreaties, and resolutely carried the bottle down to the sea.

'What are you doing with me?' whimpered the jinnee helplessly.

'I am going to throw you back into the sea!' replied the fisherman. 'You have lain in the depths eighteen hundred years, and there you shall remain till the Last Judgement! Did I not beg you to spare me so that Allah might spare you? But you took no pity on me, and He has now delivered you into my hands.'

'Let me out,' cried the jinnee in despair, 'and I will give you fabulous riches!'

'Perfidious jinnee,' retorted the fisherman, 'you justly deserve the fate of the King in the tale of "Yunan and the Doctor".'

'What tale is that?' asked the jinnee.

The Tale of King Yunan and
Duban the Doctor

IT is related (began the fisherman) that once upon a time there
reigned in the land of Persia a rich and mighty king called
Yunan. He commanded great armies and had a numerous
retinue of followers and courtiers. But he was afflicted with a
leprosy which baffled his physicians and defied all cures.

One day a venerable old doctor named Duban came to the
King's capital. He had studied books written in Greek,

Persian, Latin, Arabic, and Syriac, and was deeply versed in the wisdom of the ancients. He was master of many sciences, knew the properties of plants and herbs, and was above all skilled in astrology and medicine. When this physician heard of the leprosy with which Allah had plagued the King and of his doctors' vain endeavours to cure him, he put on his finest robes and betook himself to the royal palace. After he had kissed the ground before the King and called down blessings upon him, he told him who he was and said: 'Great King, I have heard about the illness with which you are afflicted and have come to heal you. Yet will I give you no potion to drink, nor any ointment to rub upon your body.'

The King was astonished at the doctor's words, and asked: 'How will you do that? By Allah, if you cure me I will heap riches upon you and your children's children after you. Anything you wish for shall be yours and you shall be my companion and my friend.'

Then the King gave him a robe of honour and other presents, and asked: 'Is it really true that you can heal me without draught or ointment? When is it to be? What day, what hour?'

'Tomorrow, if the King wishes,' the doctor replied.

He took leave of the King, and hastening to the centre of the town rented for himself a house, to which he carried his books, his drugs, and his other medicaments. Then he distilled balsams and elixirs, and these he poured into a hollow polo-stick.

Next morning he went to the royal palace, and, kissing the ground before the King, requested him to ride to the field and play a game of polo with his friends. The King rode out with his viziers and his chamberlains, and when he had entered the playing-field the doctor handed him the hollow club and said: 'Take this and grasp it firmly. Strike the ball with all your might until the palm of your hand and the rest of your body begin to perspire. The cure will penetrate your palm and course through the veins and arteries of your body. When it has done its work, return to the palace, wash yourself, and go to sleep. Thus shall you be cured; and peace be with you.'

The King took hold of the club and, gripping it firmly,

struck the ball and galloped after it with the other players. Harder and harder he struck the ball as he dashed up and down the field, until his palm and all his body perspired. When the doctor saw that the cure had begun its work, he ordered the King to return to the palace. The slaves hastened to make ready the royal bath and prepare the linens and the towels. The King bathed, put on his night-clothes, and went to sleep.

Next morning the physician went to the palace. When he was admitted to the King's presence he kissed the ground before him and wished him peace. The King hastily rose to receive him; he threw his arms round his neck and seated him by his side.

For when the King had left the bath the previous evening, he looked upon his body and rejoiced to find no trace of the leprosy: his skin had become as pure as virgin silver.

The King regaled the physician sumptuously all day. He bestowed on him robes of honour and other gifts and, when evening came, gave him two thousand pieces of gold and mounted him on his own favourite horse. So enraptured was the King by the consummate skill of his doctor that he kept repeating to himself: 'This wise physician has cured me without draught or ointment. By Allah, I will load him with honours and he shall henceforth be my companion and trusted friend.' And that night the King lay down to sleep in perfect bliss, knowing that he was clean in body and rid at last of his disease.

Next morning, as soon as the King sat down upon his throne, with the officers of his court standing before him and his lieutenants and viziers seated on his right and left, he called for the physician, who went up to him and kissed the ground before him. The King rose and seated the doctor by his side. He feasted him all day, gave him a thousand pieces of gold and more robes of honour, and conversed with him till nightfall.

Now among the King's viziers there was a man of repellent aspect, an envious, black-souled villain, full of spite and cunning. When this Vizier saw that the King had made the physician his friend and lavished on him high dignities and favours, he became jealous and began to plot the doctor's downfall. Does not the proverb say: 'All men envy, the strong openly, the weak in secret?'

So, on the following day, when the King entered the council-chamber and was about to call for the physician, the Vizier kissed the ground before him and said: 'My bounteous master, whose munificence extends to all men, my duty prompts me to forewarn you against an evil which threatens your life; nor would I be anything but a base-born wretch were I to conceal it from you.'

Perturbed at these ominous words, the King ordered him to explain his meaning.

'Your majesty,' resumed the Vizier, 'there is an old proverb which says: "He who does not weigh the consequences of his acts shall never prosper." Now I have seen the King bestow favours and shower honours upon his enemy, on an assassin who cunningly seeks to destroy him. I fear for the King's safety.'

'Who is this man whom you suppose to be my enemy?' asked the King, turning pale.

'If you are asleep, your majesty,' replied the Vizier, 'I beg you to awake. I speak of Duban, the doctor.'

'He is my friend,' replied the King angrily, 'dearer to me than all my courtiers; for he has cured me of my leprosy, an evil which my physicians had failed to remove. Surely there is no other physician like him in the whole world, from East to West. How can you say these monstrous things of him? From this day I will appoint him my personal physician, and give him every month a thousand pieces of gold. Were I to bestow on him the half of my kingdom, it would be but a small reward for his service. Your counsel, my Vizier, is the prompting of jealousy and envy. Would you have me kill my benefactor and repent of my rashness, as King Sindbad repented after he had killed his falcon?'

The Tale of King Sindbad
and the Falcon

ONCE upon a time (went on King Yunan) there was a Persian King who was a great lover of riding and hunting. He had a falcon which he himself had trained with loving care and which never left his side for a moment; for even at night-time he carried it perched upon his fist, and when he went hunting took it with him. Hanging from the bird's neck was a little bowl of gold from which it drank. One day the King ordered his men to make ready for a hunting expedition and, taking with him his falcon, rode out with his courtiers. At length they came to a valley where they laid the hunting nets. Presently a gazelle fell into the snare, and the King said: 'I will kill the man who lets her escape!'

They drew the nets closer and closer round the beast. On seeing the King the gazelle stood on her haunches and raised her forelegs to her head as if she wished to salute him. But as he bent forward to lay hold of her she leapt over his head and fled across the field. Looking round, the King saw his courtiers winking at one another.

'Why are they winking?' he asked his Vizier.

'Perhaps because you let the beast escape,' ventured the other, smiling.

'On my life,' cried the King, 'I will chase this gazelle and bring her back!'

At once he galloped off in pursuit of the fleeing animal, and when he had caught up with her, his falcon swooped upon the gazelle, blinding her with his beak, and the King struck her down with a blow of his sword. Then dismounting he flayed the animal and hung the carcass on his saddle-bow.

It was a hot day and the King, who by this time had become faint with thirst, went to search for water. Presently, however, he saw a huge tree, down the trunk of which water was trickling in great drops. He took the little bowl from the falcon's neck and, filling it with this water, placed it before the bird.

But the falcon knocked the bowl with its beak and toppled it over. The King once again filled the bowl and placed it before the falcon, but the bird knocked it over a second time. Upon this the King became very angry, and, filling the bowl a third time, set it down before his horse. But the falcon sprang forward and knocked it over with its wings.

'Allah curse you for a bird of ill omen!' cried the King. 'You have prevented yourself from drinking and the horse also.'

So saying, he struck the falcon with his sword and cut off both its wings. But the bird lifted its head as if to say: 'Look into the tree!' The King raised his eyes and saw in the tree an enormous serpent spitting its venom down the trunk.

The King was deeply grieved at what he had done, and, mounting his horse, hurried back to the palace. He threw his kill to the cook, and no sooner had he sat down, with the falcon still perched on his fist, than the bird gave a convulsive gasp and dropped down dead.

The King was stricken with sorrow and remorse for having so rashly killed the bird which had saved his life.

When the Vizier heard the tale of King Yunan, he said: 'I assure your majesty that my counsel is prompted by no other motive than my devotion to you and my concern for your safety. I beg leave to warn you that, if you put your trust in this physician, it is certain that he will destroy you. Has he not cured you by a device held in the hand? And might he not cause your death by another such device?'

'You have spoken wisely, my faithful Vizier,' replied the King. 'Indeed, it is quite probable that this physician has come to my court as a spy to destroy me. And since he cured my illness by a thing held in the hand, he might as cunningly poison me with the scent of a perfume. What should I do, my Vizier?'

'Send for him at once,' replied the other, 'and when he comes, strike off his head. Only thus shall you be secure from his perfidy.'

Thereupon the King sent for the doctor, who hastened to the palace with a joyful heart, not knowing what lay in store for him.

'Do you know why I have sent for you?' asked the King.

'Allah alone knows the unspoken thoughts of men,' replied the physician.

'I have brought you here to kill you,' said the King.

The physician was thunderstruck at these words, and cried: 'But why should you wish to kill me? What crime have I committed?'

'It has come to my knowledge,' replied the King, 'that you are a spy sent here to cause my death. But you shall be the first to die.'

Then he called out to the executioner, saying: 'Strike off the head of this traitor!'

'Spare me, and Allah will spare you!' cried the unfortunate doctor. 'Kill me, and so shall Allah kill you!'

But the King gave no heed to his entreaties. 'Never will I have peace again,' he cried, 'until I see you dead. For if you cured me by a thing held in the hand, you will doubtless kill me by the scent of a perfume, or by some other foul device.'

'Is it thus that you repay me?' asked the doctor. 'Will you thus requite good with evil?'

But the King said: 'You must die; nothing can now save you.'

When he saw that the King was determined to put him to death, the physician wept, and bitterly repented the service he had done him. Then the executioner came forward, blindfolded the doctor, and, drawing his sword, held it in readiness for the King's signal. But the doctor continued to wail, crying: 'Spare me, and Allah will spare you! Kill me, and so shall Allah kill you!'

Moved by the old man's lamentations, one of the courtiers interceded for him with the King, saying: 'Spare the life of this man, I pray you. He has committed no crime against you, but rather has he cured you of an illness which your physicians have failed to remedy.'

'If I spare this doctor,' replied the King, 'he will use his devilish art to kill me. Therefore he must die.'

Again the doctor cried: 'Spare me, and Allah will spare you! Kill me, and so shall Allah kill you!' But when at last he saw that the King was fixed in his resolve, he said: 'Your majesty, if you needs must kill me, I beg you to grant me a day's delay, so that I may go to my house and wind up my affairs. I wish to say farewell to my family and my neighbours, and instruct them to arrange for my burial. I must also give away my books of medicine, of which there is one, a work of unparalleled virtue, which I would offer to you as a parting gift, that you may preserve it among the treasures of your kingdom.'

'What may this book be?' asked the King.

'It holds secrets and devices without number, the least of them being this: that if, after you have struck off my head, you turn over three leaves of this book and read the first three lines upon the left-hand page, my severed head will speak and answer any questions you may ask it.'

The King was astonished to hear this, and at once ordered his guards to escort the physician to his house. That day the doctor put his affairs in order, and next morning returned to the King's palace. There had already assembled the viziers, the chamberlains, the nabobs, and all the chief officers of the realm, so that with their coloured robes the court seemed like a garden full of flowers.

The doctor bowed low before the King; in one hand he held an ancient book, and in the other a little bowl filled with a strange powder. Then he sat down and said: 'Bring me a platter!' A platter was instantly brought in, and the doctor sprinkled the powder on it, smoothing it over with his fingers. After that he handed the book to the King and said: 'Take this book and set it down before you. When my head has been cut off, place it upon the powder to staunch the bleeding. Then open the book.'

The King ordered the executioner to behead the physician. He did so. Then the King opened the book, and, finding the pages stuck together, put his finger to his mouth and turned over the first leaf. After much difficulty he turned over the second and the third, moistening his finger with his spittle at every page, and tried to read. But he could find no writing there.

'There is nothing written in this book,' cried the King.

'Go on turning,' replied the severed head.

The King had not turned six pages when poison (for the leaves of the book had been treated with venom) began to work in his body. He fell backward in an agony of pain, crying: 'Poisoned! Poisoned!' and in a few moments breathed his last.

'Now, treacherous jinnee,' continued the fisherman, 'had the King spared the physician, he in turn would have been spared by Allah. But he refused, and Allah brought about the King's destruction. And as for you, if you had been willing to spare me, Allah would have been merciful to you, and I would have spared your life. But you sought to kill me; therefore I will throw you back into the sea and leave you to perish in this bottle!'

'Let me out! Let me out, in the name of Allah!' cried the jinnee. 'Do not be angry with me, I pray you. If I have done you evil, repay me with good and, as the saying goes, punish me with kindness. Do not do as Umamah did to Atikah!'

'What is their story?' asked the fisherman.

'This bottle is no place to tell stories in!' cried the jinnee, writhing with impatience. 'Let me out, and I will tell you all that passed between them.'

'Never!' replied the fisherman. 'I will throw you into the sea, and you shall remain imprisoned in your bottle till the end of Time!'

'Let me out! Let me out!' cried the jinnee in despair. 'I swear that I will never harm you, and promise to render you a service that will enrich you!'

At length the fisherman accepted the jinnee's pledge, and after he had made him swear by the Most High Name, opened the bottle with trembling hands.

At once the smoke burst out and in a twinkling took the shape of a gigantic jinnee, who with a triumphant kick sent the bottle flying into the sea. When the fisherman saw the bottle disappear beneath the water, he was so overcome with terror that he wetted his drawers. 'This is a bad sign,' he thought, but quickly putting on a defiant air he cried: 'Mighty jinnee, Allah has said in His sacred book: "Be true to your promises, or We will call you to account." You have both promised and sworn that you would not deal treacherously with me. Therefore, if you break your pledge Allah will punish you; for He is a jealous God, and, though He may be slow in retribution, He does not forget. Remember that I said to you, as the physician said to the King: "Spare me, and Allah will spare you!"'

At this the jinnee fell into convulsions of laughter, and cried: 'Follow me!'

Still dreading the jinnee's intent, the fisherman walked on behind him until they left the city. They climbed a mountain and at length descended into a vast and barren valley in the middle of which there was a lake. At the shore of this lake the jinnee halted and bade the fisherman cast his net. The fisherman saw white fish and red fish, blue fish and yellow fish, sporting in the water. Marvelling at the sight, he cast his net into the lake, and, when he withdrew it, rejoiced to find in it four fish, each of a different colour.

'Take these fish to the King's palace,' said the jinnee, 'and he will give you gold. In the meantime, I must beg you to pardon the scant courtesy I have shown you; for I have dwelt so long at the bottom of the sea that I have forgotten my manners. Come and fish in this lake each day – but only once a day. And now, farewell!'

So saying, the jinnee stamped his feet against the earth, which instantly opened and swallowed him up.

The fisherman went back to his house, marvelling at all that had befallen him. He filled an earthen bowl with water and, placing the fish in it, carried it upon his head to the King's palace, as the jinnee had bidden him. When he had gained admission to the King's presence and offered him the fish, the King, who had never seen their like in size or colour, marvelled greatly and ordered his Vizier to take them to the black cook-maid. This slave-girl had been sent to the King as a present three days before by Caesar, and the King had as yet had no opportunity to test her culinary skill. So the Vizier took the four fish to the slave-girl and ordered her to fry them, saying: 'The King has reserved you, pretty negress, for a great occasion. Let us have proof today of your accomplishments.'

The King ordered the Vizier to give the fisherman four hundred pieces of gold. The fisherman received the coins in the lap of his skirt, and departed in a transport of joy. He bought bread, meat, and other necessities, and hurried home to his wife and children.

Meanwhile the slave-girl cleaned the fish, put them in the frying-pan, and left them over the fire. When they were well cooked on one side, she turned them over; but scarcely had she done so when the wall of the kitchen suddenly opened and through it entered a beautiful young girl. Her eyes were darkened with kohl, her cheeks were smooth and fresh, and her breasts round and shapely. She wore jewelled rings on her fingers and gold bracelets round her wrists, and her hair was wrapped in a blue-fringed kerchief of the rarest silk.

The girl came forward and, thrusting into the frying-pan a wand she carried in her hand, said: 'Fish, fish, are you still faithful?'

At the sight of this apparition the slave fainted away, and the young girl repeated her question a second and a third time. Then the four fishes lifted their heads from the pan and replied in unison: 'Yes, yes, we are faithful!'

Upon this the young girl overturned the pan and went out the way she had come, the wall of the kitchen closing behind her. When the slave-girl came to her senses, she found the fish burnt to cinders. She set up a great screaming, and hurried to tell the Vizier all that had happened. Amazed at her story, the Vizier sent at once for the fisherman and ordered him to bring four other fish of the same kind. So the fisherman went to the lake, and casting his net, caught four more fish. These he took to the Vizier, who carried them to the slave-girl, saying: 'Rise now and fry these in my presence.'

The slave cleaned the fish and put them in the frying-pan; but scarcely had she done so when the wall opened as before

and the girl reappeared, dressed in the same way and still holding the wand in her hand. She thrust the end of the wand into the pan and said: 'Fish, fish, are you still faithful?'

The four fishes raised their heads and replied: 'Yes, yes, we are faithful!' And the girl overturned the pan with her wand and vanished through the wall.

'The King must be informed of this!' cried the Vizier and, hurrying to his master, recounted to him all that he had seen.

'I must see this myself,' said the King in astonishment. He sent for the fisherman and ordered him to bring four more fish. The fisherman again hastened to the lake and promptly returned with the fish, for which he received four hundred pieces of gold. Then the King commanded his Vizier to cook the fish in his presence.

'I hear and obey,' replied the Vizier. He cleaned the fish and set the pan over the fire; but scarcely had he thrown them in when the wall opened and there appeared a great Negro, as ugly as a bull and taller than a warrior of the tribe of Aad. He held a green twig in his hand, and as soon as he set eyes on the pan, roared out: 'Fish, fish, are you still faithful?'

The four fishes lifted their heads and replied: 'Yes, yes, we are faithful!' Then the Negro overturned the pan with his twig and disappeared through the chasm in the wall, leaving the four fishes burnt to black cinders.

Confounded at the spectacle, the King cried: 'By Allah, I must find the answer to this riddle! No doubt these fishes have some strange history.'

He sent again for the fisherman, and asked him whence he had brought the fish.

'From a lake between four hills,' replied the fisherman, 'beyond the mountain which overlooks this city.'

'How many days' journey is it?' asked the King.

'It is barely half an hour's walk, your majesty,' he answered.

The King set out for the lake at the head of his troops, taking with him the bewildered fisherman, who led the way, muttering curses at the jinnee as he went. At length they came to the mountain and, climbing to the top, descended into a great desert which they had never seen before. They all marvelled at the mountains, the lake, and the fish of different colours which swam in it. The King asked the troops if any of them had ever seen a lake in that place, and when they all replied that they had not, he said: 'By Allah, I will never again enter my city or sit upon my throne until I have solved the mystery of this lake and these coloured fishes.'

He ordered his troops to pitch their tents for the night and, summoning his Vizier, who was a wise counsellor and a man of deep learning, said to him: 'Know that I have decided to go out alone this night and search for the answer to the mys-

tery of the lake and the fishes. I wish you to stand guard at
the door of my tent and tell anyone who may wish to see me
that I am ill and that no one is to be admitted to my presence.
Above all, you must keep my plan secret.'

At nightfall the King disguised himself, girt on his sword,
and slipped out from the camp unnoticed by his guards. All
that night and throughout the following day he journeyed on,
stopping only to rest awhile in the midday heat. Early next
morning he sighted a black building in the distance. He
rejoiced and thought: 'There perhaps I shall find someone
who can tell me the history of the lake and the fishes.'

Drawing nearer, he found that this was a towering palace
built of black stone sheeted with iron. He went up to the great
double door, one half of which was wide open, and knocked
gently, once, twice, and again, but heard no answer. The fourth
time he knocked hard, but still received no reply. Supposing
the palace to be deserted, he summoned up his courage and
entered, calling out at the top of his voice: 'People of this
house, have you any food for a weary traveller?' This he
repeated again and again and, getting no answer, walked
through the long vestibule to the centre of the building. The
hall was richly carpeted and hung with fine curtains and
splendid tapestries. In the middle of the inner court a beautiful
fountain resting on four lions of red gold spurted forth a
jewelled spray, and about the fountain fluttered doves and
pigeons under a golden net stretched above the courtyard.

The King marvelled greatly at the splendour of all that he
beheld, but grieved to find no one in the palace who could
explain the mystery. As he was loitering pensively about the
court, however, he suddenly heard a low, mournful voice
which seemed to issue from a heart laden with grief. The King
hastened in the direction from which the sound proceeded,
and presently came to a doorway concealed behind a curtain.
Lifting the curtain, he saw a handsome youth, dressed in a
gold-embroidered robe of Egyptian silk, lying on a bed in a
great marble hall. His brow was as white as a lily, and on his
cheek was a mole like a speck of black amber.

The King rejoiced to see the young man, and greeted him,

saying: 'Peace be with you!' But the youth, whose eyes were sore with weeping, remained motionless on the bed and returned the King's greeting in a faint voice, saying: 'Pardon me, sir, for not rising.'

'Pray tell me the story of the lake and the fishes,' said the King, 'and the reason of your tears and your solitary sojourn in this palace.'

At these words the youth wept even more bitterly and replied: 'How can I refrain from weeping, condemned as I am to this unnatural state?'

So saying, he stretched out his hand and lifted the skirt of his robe. The King was astonished to see that the lower half of his body was all of stone, while the upper half, from his waist to the hair upon his head, remained that of a living man.

'The story of the fishes,' said the youth, 'is indeed a strange story. If it were written with a needle on the corner of an eye, it would yet serve as a lesson to those who seek wisdom.'

Upon this the youth proceeded to recount:

The Tale of the Enchanted King

KNOW that my father was the King of an illustrious city which once flourished around this palace. His name was Mahmoud and he was lord of the Black Islands, which are now four mountains. He reigned for seventy years, and on his death I succeeded to the throne of his kingdom. I took in marriage my cousin, the daughter of my uncle, who loved me so passionately that she could not bear to part from me even for a moment. I lived happily with her for five years. It chanced one day, however, that my wife left the palace to visit the baths and was absent so long that I grew anxious for her safety. But I strove to dismiss these fears from my mind, and, entering my chamber, lay down to sleep upon my couch, bidding two of my slave-girls to fan me. One sat at my head and the other at my feet; and as I lay with my eyes closed, I heard one say to the other: 'How unfortunate is the

young King our master, Massoudah, and how pitiful it is
that he should have married our mistress, that shameless
woman, that black-souled whore!'

'Allah's curse upon all adulteresses!' replied the other.
'This harlot who revels away her nights in the beds of thieves
and cut-throats is a thousandfold too vile to be the wife of
our master.'

'And yet he must be blind not to see it,' said the first
slave.

'But how should he suspect her,' returned the other, 'when
every night she mixes in his cup a potent drug which so
benumbs his senses that he sleeps like the dead till morning?
How can he know what she does and where she goes? After
he has gone to sleep, she dresses and goes out of the palace.
She returns at daybreak, and wakes her husband by the fume
of aromatic incense.'

When I heard these words the world darkened before my
eyes and I was dazed with horror. At dusk my wife returned
to the palace, and we sat for an hour eating and drinking
together as was our custom every evening. At length I asked
for the final cup which I drank every night before retiring.
When she handed it to me, I lifted the cup to my lips, but
instead of drinking, poured it hastily into the folds of my garments. Then I lay down on my bed and pretended to fall asleep.

Presently I heard her say: 'Sleep, and may you never wake
again! O how I abhor you! My soul sickens at the sight of
you!' After this she dressed, perfumed herself, girt on my
sword, and left the palace. At once I rose and followed her.
She stealthily threaded her way through the streets of the
town, and, reaching the city gates, mumbled a magic charm.
Suddenly the heavy locks fell to the ground and the gates
swung wide open. Without a sound I followed her out of the
city until she came to a desolate waste-land strewn with
garbage heaps, and entered a ruined hovel surmounted by a
dome. I climbed up to the roof and crouched over a chink in
the ceiling. I saw her draw near to a pitch-black, thick-lipped
Negro. His skin was covered with sores and he lay in tattered
rags upon a mat of mouldering reeds.

Then I saw my wife, the daughter of my uncle, throw herself at his feet and kiss the ground before him. The Negro raised his head and growled: 'Execrable whore, why are you so late? All my black friends were in my house this evening, drinking, and enjoying their women. But I could not share in the merriment because you were not here.'

'Master, flower of my heart,' she answered, 'have you forgotten that I am married to that cousin of mine, whom I detest with all my soul? Had you permitted me, I would long ago have levelled this city to the ground and scattered its stones as far as the Mountain of Kaf, leaving only the cries of the owl and the raven to echo among its ruins!'

'Foulest of white whores,' replied the slave, 'do you dare trifle with me? I swear by the honour and chivalry of my tribe that, if you fail me once more, I will cast you off and never lay my body over yours again!'

When I heard these exchanges and witnessed with my own eyes what passed between them, the world blackened before me. Then I saw my wife, the daughter of my uncle, weep and humble herself before the black slave, saying: 'Light of my eyes, treasure of my heart, I care for none but you. Do not send me away, I beg you!'

When at length her lover was pacified, she rose, unrobed herself, and stood before him quite naked. Then she said: 'My lord, have you no refreshment for your slave?'

'In the pot,' he replied, 'you will find a stew of rats' bones, and there is some barley-water in the can which you may drink.'

As soon as she had finished her meal, she washed her hands and nestled close to the Negro on his bed of filth. Seeing all this I could control my rage no longer, and, jumping down from the roof, snatched the sword from my wife's belt and struck the Negro through the neck. A loud gasp convulsed his body. Thinking that the blow had killed him, I rushed out of the house and ran straight to the palace, where I tucked myself in bed and lay still. By and by my wife returned and lay down quietly beside me.

The next day I saw that my wife had cut off her tresses and

dressed herself in deep mourning. 'Son of my uncle,' she said, 'do not be angry with me for wearing these garments. I have just heard that my mother has died, that my father has lost his life in the holy war, that one of my brothers has been bitten to death by a serpent, and the other killed by the fall of a house. It is but right that I should weep and mourn.'

Showing no sign of anger, I replied: 'Do as you think fit. I shall not prevent you.'

She went in mourning for a whole year, and at the end of this time she had a dome built in the grounds of the palace. She called it the House of Grief, and to this monument she had the Negro carried: for he was still alive, though crippled and bereft of speech, and no longer able to gratify his mistress's lust. He still drank deep, and every day, early and late, my wife took to him wine and stews and broths, and fell to wailing under the dome. All this I suffered patiently.

One day, however, I entered upon her unawares and found her weeping and beating her face in a most violent fashion. Unable to contain my fury, I drew my sword and was about to strike her, when she sprang to her feet and, as it seemed, suddenly realizing that it was I who had wounded her lover, muttered some mysterious charm and cried: 'Now, Powers of Magic, let half his body be turned to stone!'

At that moment I became as you now see me, neither alive nor dead. Then she bewitched my entire kingdom, turning its four islands into mountains with a lake in their midst and transforming all my subjects – Moslems, Jews, Christians, and heathens – into fishes of four different colours. Nor was she satisfied with this, for every day she comes to torture me; she gives me a hundred lashes with a leather thong and puts a shirt of hair-cloth upon my wounds, all over the living part of my body.

When he had heard the young man's story, the King said to him: 'By Allah, your tale has added a heavy sorrow to my sorrows. But where is this enchantress now?'

'With the Negro in the monument, which you can see from the door of this hall,' replied the youth.

'By Allah,' cried the King, 'I will do you a service that shall be long remembered, a deed that shall be recorded for all time!'

At midnight the King rose, undressed, and, on the striking of the secret hour of sorcery, stole away towards the monument with his sword unsheathed in his hand. Inside he saw lighted lamps and candles, and braziers in which incense was burning. Without a sound he approached the Negro and struck him a mighty blow with his sword. The slave fell dead upon the instant, and the King, after stripping him of his clothes, carried the body upon his shoulders and threw it down a deep well in the grounds of the palace. Then he returned to the monument, put on the Negro's clothes, and sat down with his sword hidden in the folds of his garment.

Shortly afterwards the young enchantress entered her husband's chamber and, uncovering his body, gave him a hundred lashes. When he cried: 'Enough, for pity's sake!' she replied: 'Do you dare speak of pity? Did you show pity to my lover?' After she had wrapped him in a shirt of hair-cloth and put on him his other garments, she went off to the monument, taking with her a cup of wine and a bowl of hot soup. As soon as she entered, she said, weeping: 'Speak to me, my master! Let me hear your voice!'

Rolling his tongue in his mouth so that he should sound like a Negro, the King replied in a low voice: 'There is no power or majesty save in Allah!'

When she heard the voice of her supposed lover, who had for so long been silent, the young witch uttered a joyful scream and fainted away. But soon recovering herself, she cried: 'Praise to the Highest! My master is restored!'

'Wretch,' said the King in the same low voice, 'you are not worthy that I should speak to you!'

'Why, what have I done?' she asked.

'You have deprived me of all sleep,' he answered. 'Day after day you whip that husband of yours, so that his cries keep me awake all night. Had you had more thought for my comfort, I would have recovered long ago.'

'If it be your wish,' she replied, 'I will instantly restore him.'

'Do so,' said the King, 'and let us have some peace.'

'I hear and obey,' answered the witch, and, leaving the monument, hastened to the hall where the young man was lying. There she took a bowl filled with water and, bending over it, murmured some magic words. The water began to seethe and bubble as if in a heated cauldron; and sprinkling it upon her husband she said: 'Now, Powers of Magic, return him to his natural state!'

A quiver passed through the young man's body and, he sprang to his feet, shouting for joy, and crying: 'There is no god but Allah, and Mohammed is His Prophet!'

'Go!' shrieked his wife, 'and never return, or I will kill you!'

The young man hurried from her presence, and she came back to the monument, saying: 'Rise up, my master, that I may look upon you!'

In a feeble voice the King replied: 'You have remedied but one part of the evil. The root cause still remains.'

'What may that be, my master?' she asked.

'The people of this enchanted city and the Four Islands,' he replied. 'Night after night, when the hour strikes midnight, the fish raise their heads from the lake and call down curses upon us both. I shall not be cured until they are delivered. Free them, and return to help me from my bed, for by that act I shall be restored to health.'

Still taking him for her lover, she answered joyfully: 'I hear and obey!'

She rose and, going out of the palace, hastened towards the lake. At the shore she took a few drops of water in her palm and muttered an incantation. The spell was broken. The fish wriggled in the water and, raising their heads, changed back into human shape; the lake was transformed into a prosperous city, where people were buying and selling in the market-place; and the mountains became four islands.

Then the witch ran back to the palace and, hurrying to the King, said: 'Give me your hand, my master, and let me help you to your feet.'

'Come closer,' he murmured.

When she had drawn near, the King lifted his sword and thrust it into her breast, until the blade passed through to her back. Then he struck her down and chopped her body to pieces.

The King found the young man waiting for him at the palace gates. He congratulated him on his deliverance, and the youth kissed his hand and thanked him with all his heart. Then the King asked: 'Do you wish to stay in your own city or will you return with me to my kingdom?'

'Sir,' replied the youth, 'do you know how far your kingdom is from here?'

'Why, it is but two and a half days' journey,' answered the King.

The young man laughed and said: 'If you are dreaming, your majesty, then you must wake. Know that you are at least a year's journey from your capital. If you came here in two days and a half, that was because my kingdom was enchanted ... But I will never leave you again, even for a moment.'

The King rejoiced and cried: 'Praise be to Allah, who has brought us together! Henceforth you shall be my son, for I have not been blessed with an heir of my own.'

The King and the young man embraced one another and rejoiced exceedingly.

Returning to the palace, the young King told his courtiers of his intention to set out on a long journey. When all preparations were completed, the two Kings set forth from the Black Islands together with fifty slaves and fifty mules laden with priceless treasure. They journeyed for a whole year, and when at last they came in sight of the King's capital, the Vizier and the troops, who had abandoned all hope of his return, went out to meet their master and gave him a tumultuous welcome.

The King seated himself upon his throne in his own palace, and, summoning the Vizier and his other courtiers, recounted to them his adventure from beginning to end. Then he bestowed gifts on all who were present and said to the Vizier: 'Send for the fisherman who brought us the coloured fishes.'

When the fisherman, who had been the means of delivering

the enchanted city, was admitted to his presence, the King vested him with a robe of honour and questioned him about his manner of life and whether he had any children. The fisherman replied that he had one son and two daughters. The King took one of the daughters in marriage and the young Prince wedded the other, while the fisherman's son was appointed Keeper of the Royal Treasury. The Vizier became Sultan of the Black Islands, and departed thither with fifty slaves and robes of honour for all the courtiers of that kingdom.

The King and the young Prince lived happily ever afterwards. The fisherman became the richest man of his day, and his daughters were the wives of kings till the end of their lives.

THE YOUNG WOMAN AND
HER FIVE LOVERS

ONCE upon a time, in a certain city, there lived a rich and beautiful young woman whose husband was a great traveller. It so chanced that he once journeyed to a distant land and was absent so long that at last his wife succumbed to the temptations of the flesh and fell in love with a handsome youth who himself loved her tenderly.

One day the youth was engaged in a savage brawl and a complaint was lodged against him with the Governor of that city, who had him thrown into prison. The young woman was deeply grieved at the news of her lover's arrest. Without losing a moment she put on her finest robes and hurried to the Governor's house.

She greeted the Governor and handed him a petition which read: 'My noble master, the young man So-and-so, whom you have arrested and thrown into prison, is my brother and my sole support. He is the victim of a villainous plot, for those who testified against him were false witnesses. I hereby beseech you to consider the justice of my cause and to order his release.'

When he had read the petition the Governor lifted his eyes to the young woman and was so smitten with her seductive looks that he fell in love with her at sight. 'Wait in the harem of my house,' he said, 'whilst I write out an order for your brother's release. I will join you there presently.'

The young woman, who lacked neither cunning nor knowledge of the ways of men, at once perceived the Governor's intent and answered: 'You will be welcome, sir, at my own house, but custom forbids me to enter a stranger's dwelling.'

'And where is your house?' asked the old man, transported with joy.

'At such-and-such a place,' she replied. 'I will expect you there this evening.'

Taking leave of the enamoured Governor, the young woman went to the Cadi's house. 'Consider, sir, I pray you, the wrong that has been done me,' she began, 'and Allah will reward you.'

'Who has dared to wrong you?' asked the Cadi indignantly.

'Sir,' she answered, 'my brother, the sole pillar of my house, has on false witness been imprisoned by the Governor. I beg you to intercede on his behalf.'

But as soon as the Cadi set eyes on the young woman his heart began to throb with a violent longing for her, and he said: 'I shall instantly request the Governor to set your brother free. Meanwhile, wait for me in my harem. I will join you there presently.'

'My pious master,' she replied, 'it is more fitting that I should wait for you in my own house, where there are neither slaves nor maidservants to intrude upon our privacy.'

'And where is your house?' asked the Cadi eagerly.

'In such-and-such a place,' she answered. 'I will expect you there this evening.'

The young woman then hastened to the Vizier's house. She handed him her petition and implored him to release the youth from prison. Captivated by her beauty, the Vizier promised to do as she desired and pressed her to accompany him to his sleeping chamber. But the young woman put off his advances with winning grace, saying: 'I shall be delighted to receive you at my own house this evening.'

'And where is your house?' asked the Vizier.

'In such-and-such a place,' she replied.

Then she made her way to the royal palace and sought an audience with the King. She kissed the ground before him and begged him on her knees to order the youth's release. But as soon as his eyes fell upon the young woman, the King was seized with a passionate desire to lie with her.

'I will at once send for the Governor and order him to free your brother,' he said. 'Meanwhile, wait for me in my private chamber.'

'Your majesty,' she answered, 'a helpless woman cannot but obey the command of a mighty king. If this be indeed your majesty's wish, I shall regard it as a mark of high favour; but if the King will graciously consent to vouchsafe me a visit at my own house this evening, he will do me an even greater honour.'

'It shall be as you wish,' replied the King.

After directing him to her house, the young woman left the royal presence, and went to look for a carpenter's shop. When she had found one she said to the carpenter: 'Make me a large cupboard with four compartments, one above the other. To each compartment let there be a separate door fitted with a stout lock, and have it delivered at my house, at such-and-such a place, early this evening. What will be your charge?'

'Four dinars,' answered the carpenter. 'But if you will consent, sweet lady, to step into the backroom of my shop, I will ask no payment at all.'

'In that case,' said the young woman, 'you will be welcome at my own house this evening . . . But I have just remembered that I require five compartments in that cupboard and not four.'

'I hear and obey,' replied the carpenter, beaming with joy.

He set to work at once whilst the young woman waited in his shop. In a few hours a large cupboard with five compartments was completed, and his fair customer hired a porter and had it carried to her house.

She next took four strangely fashioned garments to a dyer, and after having them each dyed a different colour, returned home and made ready for the evening. She prepared meat and drink, arranged fruit and flowers, and burned incense in the braziers. At sunset she arrayed herself in splendid robes, putting on her richest jewels and sweetest perfumes, and sat waiting for her distinguished guests.

The first to arrive was the Cadi. She bowed low before him and, taking him by the hand, led him to a couch. No sooner had they seated themselves than the Cadi began to dally with her, and it was not long before he was roused to a frenzy of passion. But when he was about to throw himself upon her, the young woman said: 'First take off your clothes and turban. You will be more comfortable in this light robe and bonnet.'

Burning with desire, the Cadi promptly cast aside his clothes, and had scarcely put on the curious yellow robe and bonnet which his hostess handed him, when a knocking was heard at the door.

'Who may that be?' asked the Cadi, wincing with impatience.

'By Allah, that must be my husband!' she exclaimed in great agitation.

'What is to be done? Where shall I go?' cried the Cadi.

'Have no fear,' she replied. 'I will hide you in this cupboard.'

The young woman took the Cadi by the hand, and, after he had crouched low she pushed him into the lowest compartment of the cupboard, and locked the door upon him. Then she went to admit her next visitor.

This proved to be the Governor. The young woman kissed the ground before him and said: 'Pray regard this dwelling as your own. The night is still young; take off your robes and put on this nightshirt.'

Delighted at the suggestion, the Governor quickly stripped himself of his heavy robes and slipped on an ill-cut garment of red cloth, while his hostess swathed his head in an old rag of many colours.

'First,' said the young woman, as the Governor made ready to begin the amorous sport, 'you must write me an order for my brother's release.'

The Governor instantly wrote the order, and, setting his seal upon it, handed it to her. Then they dallied with each other, but as he was on the point of mounting her, there came a knocking at the door.

'That must be my husband!' exclaimed the young woman in terror.

'What is to be done?' cried the Governor, greatly perturbed.

'Climb up into that cupboard and stay there until I get rid of him,' said the young woman, as she bundled him into the second compartment and locked the door. Then she went to admit her third visitor.

This was the Vizier. She kissed the ground before him and gave him a courteous welcome. 'Sir,' she said, 'you do me great honour by stepping into this humble house.' Then she begged him to take off his clothes and turban, saying: 'Pray put on this light shirt and bonnet. They are better fitted for a night of revelry and merrymaking.'

When the Vizier had put off his ministerial vestments, his hostess helped him into a blue shirt and a long, red nightcap. But just as he was about to enjoy her, the King arrived. And the young woman made the worthy Vizier climb up into the third compartment of the cupboard, and locked the door upon him.

When the King entered the young woman kissed the ground before him, saying: 'Your slave lacks words to thank your majesty for this honour.'

Having invited him to sit down, she soon prevailed upon him to take off his costly robes and to put on a tattered old shirt scarcely worth ten dirhams. When the King was on the point of achieving his desire, however, a violent knocking at the door sent him scampering into the fourth compartment of the cupboard. Then she went to let the carpenter in.

'Pray, what kind of cupboard is this you have made me?' snapped the young woman at the carpenter as he stepped into the reception hall. 'Why, the top compartment is so small that it is quite useless.'

'It is a very large compartment,' protested the fat carpenter. 'It could hold me and three others of my size.'

'Try then,' she said. And when the carpenter had climbed up into the fifth compartment of the cupboard, the door was locked upon him.

The young woman took the Governor's order to the superintendent of the prison, and rejoiced to see her lover free at last. She told him all that had happened, adding: 'We must now leave this city and go to live in a distant land.' Then they hurried back to the house, packed up all their valuables, and set out for another kingdom.

Not daring to utter a sound, the five men stayed in the cupboard without food or drink for three days; and for three days they resolutely held their water. The carpenter, however, was the first to give in; and his piss fell on the King below him. Then the King pissed on the Vizier; and the Vizier pissed on the Governor; and the Governor pissed on the Cadi.

'Filth! Filth!' shouted the Cadi. 'Has not our punishment been cruel enough? Must we be made to suffer in this vile fashion also?'

The Governor and the Vizier were the next to speak, and the three recognized each other's voice.

'Allah's curse be upon this woman!' exclaimed the Vizier. 'She has locked all the senior officers of the kingdom in this cupboard. Thank Allah the King has been spared!'

'Hold your tongue!' muttered the King. 'I am here too. And if I am not mistaken, I must have been the first to fall into the snares of this impudent whore.'

'And to think that I made her this cupboard with my own hands!' groaned the carpenter from the top compartment.

It was not long, however, before the neighbours, seeing no one enter or leave the house, began to suspect foul play. They all crowded around the door debating what action they should take.

'Let us break down the door,' urged one, 'and find out if there is anyone at home.'

'We must investigate the matter,' said another, 'lest the Governor or the King himself should learn of it and have us thrown into prison for failing to do our duty.'

The neighbours forced open the door, and on entering the hall what should they find but a large wooden cupboard echoing with the groans of famished men!

'There must be a jinnee in this cupboard!' exclaimed one of the neighbours.

'Let us set fire to it!' cried another.

'Good people,' howled the Cadi from within, 'in Allah's name do not burn us alive!'

But they gave no heed to his cries and said to each other:

'The jinn have been known to assume human shape and speak with men's voices.'

Seeing that they were still in doubt, the Cadi intoned aloud some verses from the Koran and entreated them to draw closer. They came near, and in a few words he related to them all that had happened. The neighbours promptly called in a carpenter, who forced the locks, and delivered from the cupboard five men rigged out in fancy costume.

The luckless lovers burst out laughing when they saw each other and, after putting on their clothes, departed, each to his own house.

SINDBAD THE SAILOR AND
SINDBAD THE PORTER

ONCE upon a time, in the reign of the Caliph Haroun al-Rashid, there lived in the city of Baghdad a poor man who earned his living by carrying burdens upon his head. He was called Sindbad the Porter.

One day, as he was staggering under a heavy load in the sweltering heat of the summer sun, he passed by a merchant's house that stood in a pleasant, shaded spot on the roadside. The ground before it was well swept and watered; and Sindbad, seeing a broad wooden bench just outside the gates, put down his load and sat there to rest awhile and to wipe away the sweat which trickled down his forehead. A cool and fragrant breeze blew through the doorway, and from within came the melodious strains of the lute and voices singing. They mingled with the choirs of birds warbling hymns to Allah in various tongues and tunes: curlews and pigeons, merles and bulbuls and turtle-doves.

Moved with great joy, he went up to the door and, looking within, saw in the centre of the noble courtyard a beautiful garden, around which stood numerous slaves and eunuchs and such an array of attendants as can be found only in the courts of illustrious kings. And all about the place floated the aroma of the choicest meats and wines.

Still marvelling at the splendour of what he saw, Sindbad lifted up his burden and was about to go his way when there came from within a handsome and well-dressed little page, who took him by the hand, saying: 'Pray come in; my master wishes to speak with you.'

The porter politely declined; but the lad would take no refusal. So Sindbad left his burden in the vestibule with the door-keeper and followed the page into the house.

He was conducted into a magnificent and spacious hall, where an impressive company of nobles and mighty sheikhs were seated according to rank at tables spread with the daintiest meats and richest wines, and gaily decked with flowers and fruit. On one side of the hall sat beautiful slave-girls who sang and made music; and to the fore reclined the host, a venerable old man whose beard was touched with silver. Bewildered at the grandeur and majesty of all that he beheld, the porter thought to himself: 'By Allah, this must either be a corner of Paradise or the palace of some mighty king!'

Sindbad courteously greeted the distinguished assembly and, kissing the ground before them, wished them joy and prosperity. He then stood in silence with eyes cast down.

The master of the house welcomed him kindly and bade him draw near and be seated. He ordered his slaves to set before the porter a choice of delicate foods and pressed him to eat. After pronouncing the blessing Sindbad fell to, and when he had eaten his fill washed his hands and thanked the old sheikh for his hospitality.

'You are welcome to this house, my friend,' said the host, 'and may this day bring you joy. We would gladly know your name and calling.'

'My name is Sindbad,' he answered, 'by trade a porter.'

'How strange a chance!' smiled the old man. 'For my name, too, is Sindbad. They call me Sindbad the Sailor, and marvel at my strange history. Presently, my brother, you shall hear the tale of my fortunes and all the hardships that I suffered before I rose to my present state and became the lord of this mansion where we are now assembled. For only after long toil, fearful ordeals, and dire peril did I achieve this fame. Seven voyages I made in all, each a story of such marvel as confounds the reason and fills the soul with wonder. All that befell me had been pre-ordained; and that which the moving hand of Fate has written no mortal power can revoke.'

The First Voyage of Sindbad the Sailor

KNOW, my friends, that my father was the chief merchant of this city and one of its richest men. He died whilst I was still a child, leaving me great wealth and many estates and farmlands. As soon as I came of age and had control of my inheritance, I took to extravagant living. I clad myself in the costliest robes, ate and drank sumptuously, and consorted with reckless prodigals of my own age, thinking that this mode of life would endure for ever.

It was not long before I awoke from my heedless folly to find that I had frittered away my entire fortune. I was stricken with horror and dismay at the gravity of my plight, and bethought myself of a proverb of our master Solomon son of David (may peace be upon them both!) which my father often used to cite: ''The day of death is better than the day of birth, a live dog is better than a dead lion, and the grave is better than poverty.' I sold the remainder of my lands and my household chattels for the sum of three thousand dirhams, and, fortifying myself with hope and courage, resolved to travel abroad and trade in foreign lands.

I bought a large quantity of merchandise and made preparations for a long voyage. Then I set sail together with a company of merchants in a river-ship bound for Basrah. There we put to sea and, voyaging many days and nights from isle to isle and from shore to shore, buying and selling and bartering wherever the ship anchored, we came at length to a little island as fair as the Garden of Eden. Here the captain of our ship cast anchor and put out the landing-planks.

The passengers went ashore and set to work to light a fire. Some busied themselves with cooking and washing, some fell to eating and drinking and making merry, while others, like myself, set out to explore the island. Whilst we were thus engaged we suddenly heard the captain cry out to us from the ship: 'All aboard, quickly! Abandon everything and run for your lives! The mercy of Allah be upon you, for this is no

island but a gigantic whale floating on the bosom of the sea, on whose back the sands have settled and trees have grown since the world was young! When you lit the fire it felt the heat and stirred. Make haste, I say; or soon the whale will plunge into the sea and you will all be lost!'

Hearing the captain's cries, the passengers made for the ship in panic-stricken flight, leaving behind their cooking-pots and other belongings. Some reached the ship in safety, but others did not; for suddenly the island shook beneath our feet and, submerged by mountainous waves, sank with all that stood upon it to the bottom of the roaring ocean.

Together with my unfortunate companions I was engulfed by the merciless tide; but Providence came to my aid, casting in my way a great wooden trough which had been used by the ship's company for washing. Impelled by that instinct which makes all mortals cling to life, I held fast to the trough and, bestriding it firmly, paddled away with my feet as the waves tossed and buffeted me on every side. Meanwhile the captain hoisted sail and set off with the other passengers. I followed the ship with my eyes until it vanished from sight, and I resigned myself to certain death.

Darkness soon closed in upon the ocean. All that night and throughout the following day I drifted on, lashed by the wind and the waves, until the trough brought me to the steep shores of a densely wooded island, where trees hung over the sea.

I caught hold of one of the branches and with its aid managed to clamber ashore after fighting so long for my life. Finding myself again on dry land, I realized that I had lost the use of my legs, and my feet began to smart with the bites of fish.

Worn out by anguish and exertion, I sank into a death-like slumber; and it was not until the following morning when the sun rose that I came to my senses. But my feet were so sore and swollen that I could move about only by crawling on my knees. By good fortune, however, the island had an abundance of fruit-trees, which provided me with sustenance, and many springs of fresh water, so that after a few days my body was restored to strength and my spirit revived. I cut myself a staff from the branch of a tree, and with its aid set out to explore the island and to admire the many goodly things which Allah had planted on its soil.

One day, as I was roaming about the beach in an unfamiliar part of the island, I caught sight of a strange object in the distance which appeared to be some wild beast or sea-monster. As I drew nearer and looked more closely at it, I saw that it was a noble mare of an uncommonly high stature haltered to a tree. On seeing me the mare gave an ear-splitting neigh which made me take to my heels in terror. Presently a man emerged from the ground and pursued me, shouting: 'Who are you and whence have you come? What are you doing here?'

'Sir,' I replied, 'I am a luckless voyager, abandoned in the middle of the sea; but it was Allah's will that I should be rescued from the fury of the waves and cast upon this island.'

The stranger took me by the hand and bade me follow him. He led me to a subterranean cavern and, after asking me to be seated, he placed some food before me and invited me to eat. When I had eaten my fill he questioned me about the fortunes of my voyage, and I related to him all that had befallen me from first to last.

'But, pray tell me, sir,' I inquired, as my host marvelled at my adventure, 'what is the reason of your vigil here and for what purpose is this mare tethered on the beach?'

'Know,' he replied, 'that I am one of the many grooms of King Mahrajan. We have charge of all his horses and are stationed in different parts of this island. Each month, on the night of the full moon, we tether all the virgin mares on the beach and hide in shelters near by. Presently the sea-horses scent the mares and, after emerging from the water, leap upon the beasts and cover them. Then they try to drag them away into the sea. But this they fail to do, as the mares are securely roped. With angry cries the sea-horses attack the mares and kick them with their hind legs. At this point we rush from our hiding-places and drive the sea-horses back into the water. The mares then conceive and bear colts and fillies of inestimable worth. Tonight,' he added, 'when we have completed our task, I shall take you to our King and show you our city. Allah be praised for this happy encounter; for had you not chanced to meet us you would have surely come to grief in the solitude of these wild regions.'

I thanked him with all my heart and called down blessings upon him. Whilst we were thus engaged in conversation we heard a dreadful cry in the distance. The groom quickly snatched up his sword and buckler and rushed out, shouting aloud and banging his sword on his shield. Thereupon several other grooms came out from their hiding-places, brandishing their spears and yelling at the top of their voices. The sea-horse, who had just covered the mare, took fright at this tumult and plunged, like a buffalo, headlong into the sea, where he disappeared beneath the water.

As we sat on the ground to recover our breath, the other grooms, each leading a mare, approached us. My companion explained to them the circumstances of my presence, and, after exchanging greetings, we rode to the city of King Mahrajan.

As soon as the King was informed of my arrival he summoned me to his presence. He marvelled at my story, saying:

'By Allah, my son, your preservation has been truly miraculous. Praise be to the Highest for your deliverance!'

Thenceforth I rose rapidly in the King's favour and soon became a trusted courtier. He vested me with robes of honour and appointed me Comptroller of Shipping at the port of his kingdom. And during my sojourn in that realm I earned the gratitude of the poor and the humble for my readiness to intercede for them with the King.

There I witnessed many prodigies and met travellers from different foreign lands. One day I entered the King's chamber and found him entertaining a company of Indians. I exchanged greetings with them and questioned them about their country. In the course of conversation I was astonished to learn that there were no fewer than seventy-two different castes in India. The noblest of these castes is known as Shakiriyah, and its members are renowned for piety and fair dealing. Another caste are the Brahmins. They are skilled breeders of camels, horses, and cattle, and, though they abstain from wine, they are a merry and pleasure-loving people.

Not far from the King's dominions there is a little island where at night is heard a mysterious beating of drums and clash of tambourines. Travellers and men from neighbouring isles told me that its inhabitants were a shrewd and diligent race.

In those distant seas I once saw a fish two hundred cubits in length, and another with a head that resembled an owl's. This I saw with my own eyes, and many other things no less strange and wondrous.

Whenever I walked along the quay I talked with the sailors and travellers from far countries, inquiring whether any of them had heard tell of the city of Baghdad and how far off it lay; for I never lost hope that I should one day find my way back to my native land. But there was none who knew of that city; and as the days dragged by, my longing for home weighed heavy upon my heart.

One day, however, as I stood on the wharf, leaning upon my staff and gazing out to sea, a ship bearing a large company of merchants came sailing into the harbour. As soon as it was moored, the sails were furled and landing-planks put out. The crew began to unload the cargo, and I stood by entering up the merchandise in my register. When they had done, I asked the captain if all the goods had now been brought ashore.

'Sir,' he replied, 'in the ship's hold I still have a few bales which belonged to a merchant who was drowned at an early stage of our voyage. We shall put them up for sale and take the money to his kinsmen in Baghdad, the City of Peace.'

'What was the merchant's name?' I demanded.

'Sindbad,' he answered.

I looked more closely into his face, and, recognizing him at once, uttered a joyful cry.

'Why!' I exclaimed, 'I am Sindbad, the self-same owner of these goods, who was left to drown with many others when the great whale plunged into the sea. But through the grace of Allah I was cast by the waves onto the shores of this island, where I found favour with the King and became Comptroller at this port. I am the true owner of these goods, which are my only possessions in this world.'

'By Allah,' cried the captain, 'is there no longer any faith or honesty in man? I have but to mention a dead man's goods and you claim them for your own! Why, we saw Sindbad drown before our very eyes. Dare you lay claim to his property?'

'I pray you, captain,' I rejoined, 'listen to my story and you shall soon learn the whole truth.' I then recounted to him all the details of the voyage from the day we set sail from Basrah till we cast anchor off the treacherous island and reminded him of a certain matter that had passed between us.

The captain and the passengers now recognized me, and all congratulated me on my escape, saying: 'Allah has granted you a fresh span of life!'

At once my goods were brought ashore and I rejoiced to find the bales intact and sealed as I had left them. I selected some of the choicest and most precious articles as presents for King Mahrajan, and had them carried by the sailors to the royal palace, where I laid them at his feet. I informed the King of the unexpected arrival of my ship and the happy recovery of all my goods. He marvelled greatly at this chance, and, in return for my presents, bestowed upon me priceless treasures.

I sold my wares at a substantial profit and re-equipped myself with the finest produce of that island. When all was ready for the homeward voyage I presented myself at the King's court, and, thanking him for the many favours he had shown me, begged leave to return to my land and people.

Then we set sail, trusting in Allah and propitious Fortune; and after voyaging many days and nights we at length arrived safely in Basrah.

I spent but a few days in that town and then, loaded with treasure, set out for Baghdad, the City of Peace. I was over-joyed to be back in my native city, and hastening to my old street entered my own house, where by and by all my friends and kinsmen came to greet me.

I bought fine houses and rich farm-lands, concubines and eunuchs and black slaves, and became richer than I had ever been before. I kept open house for my old companions, and, soon forgetting the hardships of my voyage, resumed with new zest my former mode of living.

That is the story of the first of my adventures. Tomorrow, if Allah wills, I shall relate to you the tale of my second voyage.

The day was drawing to its close, and Sindbad the Sailor invited Sindbad the Porter to join the guests in the evening meal. When the feast was finished he gave him a hundred pieces of gold, saying: 'You have delighted us with your company this day.'

The porter thanked him for his generous gift and departed, pondering over the vicissitudes of fortune and marvelling at all that he had heard.

Next morning he went again to the house of his benefactor, who received him courteously and seated him by his side. Presently the other guests arrived, and when they had feasted and made merry, Sindbad the Sailor began:

The Second Voyage of Sindbad the Sailor

FOR some time after my return to Baghdad I continued to lead a gay and carefree life, but it was not long before I felt an irresistible longing to travel again about the world and to visit distant cities and islands in quest of profit and adventure. So I bought a great store of merchandise and, after making preparations for departure, sailed down the Tigris to Basrah. There I embarked, together with a band of merchants, in a fine new vessel, well-equipped and manned by a sturdy crew, which set sail the same day.

Aided by a favourable wind, we voyaged for many days and nights from port to port and from island to island, selling and bartering our goods, and haggling with merchants and officials wherever we cast anchor. At length Destiny carried our ship to the shores of an uninhabited island, rich in fruit and flowers, and jubilant with the singing of birds and the murmur of crystal streams.

Here passengers and crew went ashore, and we all set off to enjoy the delights of the island. I strolled through the green meadows, leaving my companions far behind, and sat down in a shady thicket to eat a simple meal by a spring of water. Lulled by the soft and fragrant breeze which blew around me, I lay upon the grass and presently fell asleep.

I cannot tell how long I slept, but when I awoke I saw none of my fellow-travellers, and soon realized that the ship had sailed away without anyone noticing my absence. I ran in frantic haste towards the sea, and on reaching the shore saw the vessel, a white speck upon the vast blue ocean, dissolving into the far horizon.

Broken with terror and despair, I threw myself upon the sand, wailing: 'Now your end has come, Sindbad! The jar that drops a second time is sure to break!' I cursed the day I bade farewell to the joys of a contented life and bitterly repented my folly in venturing again upon the hazards and hardships of the sea, after having so narrowly escaped death in my first voyage.

At length, resigning myself to my doom, I rose and, after wandering about aimlessly for some time, climbed into a tall tree. From its top I gazed long in all directions, but could see nothing save the sky, the trees, the birds, the sands, and the boundless ocean. As I scanned the interior of the island more closely, however, I gradually became aware of some white object looming in the distance. At once I climbed down the tree and made my way towards it. Drawing nearer, I found to my astonishment that it was a white dome of extraordinary dimensions. I walked all round it, but could find no door or

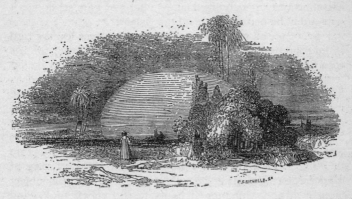

entrance of any kind; and so smooth and slippery was its surface that any attempt to climb it would have been fruitless. I walked round it again, and, making a mark in the sand near its base, found that its circumference measured more than fifty paces.

Whilst I was thus engaged the sun was suddenly hidden from my view as by a great cloud and the world grew dark around me. I lifted up my eyes towards the sky, and was confounded to see a gigantic bird with enormous wings which, as it flew through the air, screened the sun and hid it from the island.

The sight of this prodigy instantly called to my mind a

story I had heard in my youth from pilgrims and adventurers –
how in a far island dwelt a bird of monstrous size called the
roc, which fed its young on elephants; and at once I realized
that the white dome was no other than a roc's egg. In a
twinkling the bird alighted upon the egg, covering it completely with its wings and stretching out its legs behind it on
the ground. And in this posture it went to sleep. (Glory to
Him who never sleeps!)

Rising swiftly, I unwound my turban from my head,
then doubled it and twisted it into a rope with which I
securely bound myself by the waist to one of the great
talons of the monster. 'Perchance this bird,' I thought, 'will
carry me away to a civilized land; wherever I am set down, it
will surely be better than a solitary island.'

I lay awake all night, fearing to close my eyes lest the bird
should fly away with me while I slept. At daybreak the roc
rose from the egg, and, spreading its wings, took to the air
with a terrible cry. I clung fast to its talon as it winged its
flight through the void and soared higher and higher until
it almost touched the heavens. After some time it began to
drop, and sailing swiftly downwards came to earth on the
brow of a steep hill.

Trembling with fear, I hastened to untie my turban before
the roc became aware of my presence. Scarcely had I released
myself when the monster darted off towards a great black object
lying near and, clutching it in its fearful claws, took wing
again. As it rose in the air I was astonished to see that this
was a serpent of immeasurable length; and with its prey the
bird vanished from sight.

Looking around, I found myself on a precipitous hillside
overlooking an exceedingly deep and vast valley. On all
sides towered craggy mountains whose beetling summits
no man could ever scale. I was stricken with fear and repented
my rashness. 'Would I had remained in that island!' I thought
to myself. 'There at least I lacked neither fruit nor water,
while these barren steeps offer nothing to eat or drink. No
sooner do I escape from one peril than I find myself in another
more grievous. There is no strength or help save in Allah!'

When I had made my way down the hill I marvelled to see the ground thickly covered with the rarest diamonds, so that the entire valley blazed with a glorious light. Here and there among the glittering stones, however, coiled deadly snakes and vipers, dread keepers of the fabulous treasure. Thicker and longer than giant palm-trees, they could have swallowed whole elephants at one gulp. They were crawling back into their sunless dens, for by day they hid themselves from their enemies the rocs and the eagles and moved about only at night.

Overwhelmed with horror, and oblivious of hunger and fatigue, I roamed the valley all day searching with infinite caution for a shelter where I might pass the night. At dusk I came upon a narrow-mouthed cave, into which I crawled, blocking its entrance from within by a great stone. I thought to myself: 'Here I shall be safe tonight. When tomorrow comes, let Destiny do its worst.'

Scarcely had I advanced a few steps, when I saw at the far end of the cave an enormous serpent coiled in a great knot round its eggs. My hair stood on end and I was transfixed with terror. Seeing no way of escape, however, I put my trust in Allah and kept vigil all night. At day break I rolled back the stone and staggered out of the cave, reeling like a drunken man.

As I thus stumbled along I noticed a great joint of flesh come tumbling down into the valley from rock to rock. Upon closer inspection I found this to be a whole sheep, skinned and drawn. I was deeply perplexed at the mystery, for there was not a soul in sight; but at that very moment there flashed across my mind the memory of a story I had once heard from travellers who had visited the Diamond Mountains – how men obtained the diamonds from this treacherous and inaccessible valley by a strange device. Before sunrise they would throw whole carcasses of sheep from the top of the mountains, so that the gems on which they fell penetrated the soft flesh and became embedded in it. At midday rocs and mighty vultures would swoop down upon the mutton and carry it away in their talons to their nests in the mountain heights. With a great clamour the merchants would then rush at the birds and force them to drop the meat and fly away, after which it would only remain to look through the carcasses and pick out the diamonds.

As I recalled this story a plan of escape formed in my mind. I selected a great quantity of priceless stones and hid them all about me, filling my pockets with them and pressing them into the folds of my belt and garments. Then I unrolled my turban, stuffed it with more diamonds, twisted it into a rope as I had done before, and, lying down below the carcass, bound it firmly to my chest. I had not remained long in that position when I suddenly felt myself lifted from the ground by the talons of a huge vulture which had tightly closed upon the meat. The bird climbed higher and higher and finally alighted upon the top of a mountain. As soon as it began to tear at the flesh there arose from behind the neighbouring rocks a great tumult, at which the bird took fright and flew away. At once I freed myself and sprang to my feet, with face and clothes all bloody.

I saw a man come running to the spot and stop in alarm as he saw me. Without uttering a word he cautiously bent over the carcass to examine it, eyeing me suspiciously all the while; but finding no diamonds, he wrung his hands and lifted up his arms, crying: 'O heavy loss! Allah, in whom alone dwell all power and majesty, defend us from the wiles of the Evil One!'

Before I could explain my presence the man, shaking with fear, turned to me and asked: 'Who are you, and how came you here?'

'Do not be alarmed, sir,' I replied, 'I am no evil spirit, but an honest man, a merchant by profession. My story is an extraordinary one, and the adventure which has brought me to these mountains surpasses in wonder all the marvels that men have seen or heard of. But first pray accept some of these diamonds, which I myself gathered in the fearful valley below.'

I took some splendid jewels from my pocket and offered them to him, saying: 'These will bring you all the riches you can desire.'

The owner of the bait was overjoyed at the unexpected gift; he warmly thanked me and called down blessings upon me. Whilst we were thus talking, several other merchants came up from the mountain-side. They crowded round us, listening in amazement to my story, and congratulated me, saying: 'By Allah, your escape was a miracle; for no man has ever set foot in that valley and returned alive. Allah alone be praised for your salvation.'

The merchants then led me to their tent. They gave me food and drink and there I slept soundly for many hours. Early next day we set out from our tent and, after journeying over a vast range of mountains, came at length to the seashore. After a short voyage we arrived in a pleasant, densely wooded island, covered with trees so huge that beneath one of them a hundred men could shelter from the sun. It is from these trees that the aromatic substance known as camphor is extracted. The trunks are hollowed out, and the sap oozes drop by drop into vessels which are placed beneath, soon curdling into a crystal gum.

In that island I saw a gigantic beast called the karkadan, or rhinoceros, which grazes in the fields like a cow or buffalo. Taller than a camel, it has a single horn in the middle of its forehead, and upon this horn Nature has carved the likeness of a man. The karkadan attacks the elephant and, impaling it upon its horn, carries it aloft from place to place until its victim dies. Before long, however, the elephant's fat melts in the heat of the sun and, dripping down into the karkadan's eyes, puts out its sight, so that the beast blunders helplessly along and finally drops dead. Then the roc swoops down upon both animals and carries them off to its nest in the high mountains. I also saw many strange breeds of buffalo in that island.

I sold a part of my diamonds for a large sum and exchanged more for a vast quantity of merchandise. Then we set sail and, trading from port to port and from island to island, at length arrived safely in Basrah. After a few days' sojourn there I set out upstream to Baghdad, the City of Peace.

Loaded with precious goods and the finest of my diamonds,

I hastened to my old street and, entering my own house, rejoiced to see my friends and kinsfolk. I gave them gold and presents, and distributed alms among the poor of the city.

I soon forgot the perils and hardships of my travels and took again to sumptuous living. I ate well, dressed well, and kept open house for innumerable gallants and gay companions.

From far and near men came to hear me speak of my adventures and to learn the news of foreign lands from me. All were astounded at the dangers I had escaped and wished me joy of my return. Such was my second voyage.

Tomorrow, my friends, if Allah wills, I shall relate to you the extraordinary tale of my third voyage.

The famous mariner ended. The guests marvelled at his story.

When the evening feast was over, Sindbad the Sailor gave Sindbad the Porter a hundred pieces of gold, which he took with thanks and many blessings, and departed, lost in wonderment at all he had heard.

Next day the porter rose and, after reciting his morning prayers, went to the house of his illustrious friend, who received him kindly and seated him by his side. And when all the guests had assembled, Sindbad the Sailor began:

The Third Voyage of Sindbad the Sailor

KNOW, my friends, that for some time after my return I continued to lead a happy and tranquil life, but I soon grew weary of my idle existence in Baghdad and once again longed to roam the world in quest of profit and adventure. Unmindful of the dangers of ambition and worldly greed, I resolved to set out on another voyage. I provided myself with a great store of goods and, after taking them down the Tigris, set sail from Basrah, together with a band of honest merchants.

The voyage began prosperously. We called at many foreign

ports, trading profitably with our merchandise. One day, however, whilst we were sailing in mid ocean, we heard the captain of our ship, who was on deck scanning the horizon, suddenly burst out in a loud lament. He beat himself about the face, tore his beard, and rent his clothes.

'We are lost!' he cried, as we crowded round him. 'The treacherous wind has driven us off our course towards that island which you see before you. It is the Isle of the Zughb, where dwell a race of dwarfs more akin to apes than men, from whom no voyager has ever escaped alive!'

Scarcely had he uttered these words when a multitude of ape-like savages appeared on the beach and began to swim out towards the ship. In a few moments they were upon us, thick as a swarm of locusts. Barely four spans in height, they were the ugliest of living creatures, with little gleaming yellow eyes and bodies thickly covered with black fur. And so numerous were they that we did not dare to provoke them or attempt to drive them away, lest they should set upon us and kill us to a man by force of numbers.

They scrambled up the masts, gnawing the cables with their teeth and biting them to shreds. Then they seized the helm and steered the vessel to their island. When the ship had run ashore, the dwarfs carried us one by one to the beach, and, promptly pushing off again, climbed on board and sailed away.

Disconsolately we set out to search for food and water, and by good fortune came upon some fruit-trees and a running stream. Here we refreshed ourselves, and then wandered about the island until at length we saw far off among the trees a massive building, where we hoped to pass the night in safety. Drawing nearer, we found that it was a towering palace surrounded by a lofty wall, with a great ebony door which stood wide open. We entered the spacious courtyard, and to our surprise found it deserted. In one corner lay a great heap of bones, and on the far side we saw a broad bench, an open oven, pots and pans of enormous size, and many iron spits for roasting.

Exhausted and sick at heart, we lay down in the courtyard

and were soon overcome by sleep. At sunset we were awakened by a noise like thunder. The earth shook beneath our feet and we saw a colossal black giant approaching from the doorway. He was a fearsome sight – tall as a palm-tree, with red eyes burning in his head like coals of fire; his mouth was a dark well, with lips that drooped like a camel's loosely over his chest, whilst his ears, like a pair of large round discs, hung back over his shoulders: his fangs were as long as the tusks of a boar and his nails were like the claws of a lion.

The sight of this monster struck terror to our hearts. We cowered motionless on the ground as we watched him stride across the yard and sit down on the bench. For a few moments he eyed us one by one in silence; then he rose and, reaching out towards me, lifted me up by the neck and began feeling my body as a butcher would a lamb. Finding me little more than skin and bone, however, he flung me to the ground and, picking up each of my companions in turn, pinched and prodded them and set them down until at last he came to the captain.

Now the captain was a corpulent fellow, tall and broad-shouldered. The giant seemed to like him well. He gripped him as a butcher grips a fatted ram and broke his neck under his foot. Then he thrust an iron spit through his body from mouth to backside and, lighting a great fire in the oven, carefully turned his victim round and round before it. When the flesh was finely roasted, the ogre tore the body to pieces with his fingernails as though it were a pullet, and devoured it limb by limb, gnawing the bones and flinging them against the wall. The monster then stretched himself out on the bench and soon fell fast asleep. His snores were as loud as the grunts and gurgles that issue from the throat of a slaughtered beast.

Thus he slept all night, and when morning came he rose and went out of the palace, leaving us half-crazed with terror.

As soon as we were certain that the monster had gone, we began lamenting our evil fortune. 'Would that we had been drowned in the sea or killed by the apes!' we cried. 'That would surely have been better than the foul death which now awaits us! But that which Allah has ordained must surely come to pass.'

We left the palace to search for some hiding-place, but could find no shelter in any part of the island, and had no choice but to return to the palace in the evening. Night came, and with it the black giant, announcing his approach by a noise like thunder. No sooner had he entered than he snatched up one of the merchants and prepared his supper in the same way as the night before. Then, stretching himself out to sleep, he snored the night away.

Next morning, when the giant had gone, we discussed our desperate plight.

'By Allah,' cried one of the merchants, 'let us rather throw ourselves into the sea than remain alive to be roasted and eaten!'

'Listen, my friends,' said another. 'We must kill this monster. For only by destroying him can we end his wickedness and save good Moslems from his barbarous cruelty.'

This proposal was received with general approbation; so I rose in my turn and addressed the company. 'If we are all agreed to kill this monster,' I said, 'let us first build a raft on which we can escape from this island as soon as we have sent his soul to damnation. Perchance our raft will take us to some other island, where we can board a ship bound for our country. If we are drowned, we shall at least escape roasting and die a martyr's death.'

'By Allah,' cried the others, 'that is a wise plan.'

Setting to work at once, we hauled several logs from the great pile of wood stacked beside the oven and carried them out of the palace. Then we fastened them together into a raft, which we left ready on the seashore.

In the evening the earth shook beneath our feet as the black giant burst in upon us, barking and snarling like a mad dog. Once more he seized upon the stoutest of my companions and prepared his meal. When he had eaten his fill, he stretched himself upon the bench as was his custom and soon fell fast asleep.

Noiselessly we now rose, took two of the great iron spits

from the oven, and thrust them into the fire. As soon as they were red hot we carried them over to the snoring monster and plunged their sharpened ends deep into his eyes, exerting our united weight from above to push them home. The giant gave a deafening shriek which filled our hearts with terror and cast us back on the ground many yards away. Totally blinded, he leapt up from the bench groping for us with out-stretched hands, while we nimbly dodged his frantic clutches. In despair he felt his way to the ebony door and staggered out of the yard, groaning in agonies of pain.

Without losing a moment we made off towards the beach. As soon as we reached the water we launched our raft and jumped aboard; but scarcely had we rowed a few yards when we saw the blind savage running towards us, guided by a foul hag of his own kind. On reaching the shore they stood howling threats and curses at us for a while, and then caught up massive boulders and hurled them at our raft with stu-pendous force. Missile followed missile until all my com-panions, save two, were drowned; but we three who escaped soon contrived to paddle beyond the range of their fury.

Lashed by the waves, we drifted on in the open sea for a whole day and a whole night until we were cast upon the shore of another island. Half-dead with hunger and exhaustion, we threw ourselves upon the sand and fell asleep.

Next morning, when we awoke, we found ourselves en-circled by a serpent of prodigious size, which lay about us in a knotted coil. Before we could move a limb the beast sud-denly reared its head and, opening wide its deadly jaws, seized one of my companions and swallowed him to the shoulders, then it gulped him down entirely, and we heard his ribs crack in its belly. Presently, however, the serpent unwound its loathsome body and, heedless of my companion and myself, glided away, leaving us stricken with grief at the horrible fate of our comrade and amazed at our own narrow escape.

'By Allah,' we cried, 'we have fled from one form of death only to meet with another as hideous. How shall we now escape this serpent? There is no strength or help save in Allah!'

The warmth of the new-born day inspired us with fresh courage, and we struck inland to search for food and water. Before nightfall we climbed into a tall tree, and perched ourselves as best we could upon the topmost branches. But as soon as darkness fell we heard a fearful hissing and a noise of heavy movement on the ground; and in a twinkling the serpent had seized my friend and gulped him down, cracking all his bones in its belly. Then the vile creature slid down the tree and disappeared among the vegetation. That was the end of the last of my companions.

At daybreak I climbed down from my hiding-place. My first thought was to throw myself into the sea and thus end a life which had already endured more than its share of hardships and ordeals. But when I was on the point of putting my resolve into execution, my courage failed me; for life is very precious. I clung instinctively to the hope of a speedy rescue, and a plan to protect myself from the serpent began to form in my mind.

I collected some thick planks of wood and fastened them together into a coffin-shaped box, complete with lid. When evening came I shut myself in, shielded on all sides by the strong boards. By and by the snake approached and circled round me, writhing and squirming. All night long its dreadful hissing sounded in my ears, but with the approach of morning it turned away and vanished among the undergrowth.

When the sun rose I came out of my shelter and cautiously made my way across the island. As I reached the shore, what should I see but a ship sailing far off upon the vast expanse of water!

At once I tore off a great branch from a tree, and, yelling at the top of my voice, waved it frantically above my head. The crew must have instantly observed my signal, for, to my great joy, the ship suddenly turned off its course and headed for the island.

When I came aboard the captain gave me clothes to cover my nakedness and offered me food and drink. Little by little I regained my strength, and after a few days of rest became my old self again. I rendered thanks to Allah for rescuing me

from my ordeal, and soon my past sufferings were no more than half-forgotten dreams.

Aided by a prosperous wind, we voyaged many days and nights and at length came to the Isle of Salahitah. Here the captain cast anchor, and the merchants landed with their goods to trade with the people of the island. Whilst I was standing idly by, watching the busy scene, the captain of our ship came up to me, saying: 'Listen, my friend. You say you are a penniless stranger who has suffered much at sea. I will make you an offer which, I trust, will be greatly to your advantage. A few years ago I carried in my ship a merchant who, alas, was left behind upon a desert island. No news has since been heard of him, and no one knows whether he is alive or dead. Take his goods and trade with them, and a share of the profit shall be yours. The remainder of the money I will take back to the merchant's family in Baghdad.'

I thanked the captain with all my heart. He ordered the

crew to unload the merchandise and called the ship's clerk to enter up the bales in his register.

'Whose property are they?' inquired the clerk.

'The owner's name was Sindbad,' replied the captain. 'But henceforth they will be in charge of this passenger.'

A cry of astonishment escaped my lips and I at once recognized him as the captain of the ship in which I had sailed on my second voyage.

'Why!' I exclaimed. 'I am Sindbad, that very merchant who many years ago was left behind on the Island of the Roc. I fell asleep beside a spring and awoke to find that the ship had gone. The merchants who saw me on the Diamond Mountains and heard my adventure will bear witness that I am indeed Sindbad.'

On hearing mention of the Diamond Mountains, one of the merchants, who by this time had gathered round us, came forward and, peering closely into my face, suddenly turned to his friends, crying: 'By Allah, not one of you would believe the wonder which I once witnessed on the Diamond Mountains, when a man was carried up from the valley by a mighty vulture! This is he; Sindbad the Sailor, the very one who presented me with those rare diamonds!'

The captain questioned me about the contents of my bales, and I readily gave him a precise description. I also reminded him of a certain incident which had occurred in the course of our voyage. He now recognized me and, taking me in his arms, congratulated me, saying: 'Praise be to Him who has brought us together again and granted the restitution of all your goods!'

My merchandise was brought ashore, and I sold it forthwith at a substantial profit. Then we set sail and after a few days came to the land of Sind, where we also traded profitably.

In those Indian waters I witnessed many prodigies. I saw a sea-monster which resembled a cow and another with a head like a donkey's. I also saw a bird which hatches from a sea-shell and remains throughout its life floating on the water.

From Sind we set sail again and, after voyaging many days and nights, came at length with Allah's help to Basrah. I stayed there but a few days, and then voyaged upstream to Baghdad, where I was jubilantly welcomed by my friends and kinsmen. I bestowed alms upon the poor and gave generously to widows and orphans, for I had returned from this voyage richer than ever before.

Tomorrow, my friends, if Allah wills, I shall recount to you the tale of my fourth voyage, which you shall find even more extraordinary than the tales I have already related.

When the evening feast was ended, Sindbad the Sailor gave Sindbad the Porter a hundred pieces of gold, and the company took leave of their host and departed, marvelling at the wonders they had heard.

Next morning the porter returned, and when the other guests had assembled, Sindbad the Sailor began:

The Fourth Voyage of Sindbad the Sailor

THE gay and extravagant life which I led after my return did not cause me to forget the delights and benefits of travel in distant lands; and my thirst for seeing the world, despite the perils I had encountered, continued as violent as ever. My restless soul at length yielded to the call of the sea and, after making preparations for a long voyage, I set sail with merchandise from Basrah, together with some eminent merchants of that city.

Blessed with a favouring wind, we sped upon the foamy highways of the sea, trading from port to port and from island to island. One day, however, a howling gale suddenly sprang up in mid ocean, rolling against our ship massive waves as high as mountains. The captain at once ordered the crew to cast anchor, and we all fell on our knees in prayer and lamentation. A furious squall tore the sails to ribbons and snapped the mast in two; then a giant wave came hurtling down upon us from above, shattering our vessel and tossing us all into the raging sea.

With Allah's help, I clung fast to a floating beam, and bestriding it firmly, fought the downrush of the waves with those of my companions who had managed to reach it also. Now paddling with our hands and feet, now swept by wind and current, we were at length thrown, half-dead with cold and exhaustion, on the shore of an island.

We lay down upon the sand and fell asleep. Next morning we rose and, striking inland, came after a few hours in sight of a lofty building among the trees. As we drew nearer, a number of naked and wild-looking men emerged from the door, and without a word took hold of my companions and myself and led us into the building, where we saw their King seated upon a throne.

The King bade us sit down, and presently his servants set before us dishes of such meats as we had never seen before in all our lives. My famished companions ate ravenously; but my stomach revolted at the sight of this food and, in spite of my hunger, I could not eat a single mouthful. As things turned out, however, my abstinence saved my life. For as soon as they had swallowed a few morsels my comrades began to lose their intelligence and to act like gluttonous maniacs, so that after a few hours of incessant guzzling they were little better than savages.

Whilst my companions were thus feeding, the naked men brought in a vessel filled with a strange ointment, with which they anointed their victims' bodies. The change my companions suffered was astonishing; their eyes sank into their heads and their bellies grew horribly distended, so that the more they swelled the more insatiable their appetites became.

My horror at this spectacle knew no bounds, especially when I soon discovered that our captors were cannibals who fattened their victims in this way before slaughtering them. The King feasted every day on a roasted stranger; his men preferred their diet raw.

When my transformed companions had thus been robbed entirely of all their human faculties, they were committed to the charge of a herdsman, who led them out every day to pasture in the meadows. I myself was reduced to a shadow by hunger and fear and my skin shrivelled upon my bones. Therefore the savages lost all interest in me and no longer cared even to watch my movements.

One day I slipped out of my captors' dwelling and made off across the island. On reaching the distant grasslands I met the herdsman with his once-human charges. But instead of pursuing me or ordering me to return he appeared to take pity on my helpless condition, and pointing to his right made signs to me which seemed to say: 'Go this way: have no fear.'

I ran on and on across the rolling plains in the direction he indicated. When evening came I ate a scanty meal of roots and herbs and lay down to rest upon the grass; but fear of the cannibals had robbed me of all desire to sleep, and at midnight I rose again and trudged painfully on.

Thus I journeyed for seven days and nights, and on the morning of the eighth day came at last to the opposite side of the island, where I could faintly discern human figures in the distance. Drawing nearer, I rejoiced to find that they were a party of peasants gathering pepper in a field.

They crowded round me, and speaking in my own language inquired who I was and whence I had come. In reply I recounted the story of my misfortunes, and they were all amazed at my adventure. They congratulated me on my escape and, after offering me food and water, allowed me to rest till evening. When their day's work was done, they took me with them in a boat to their capital, which was in a neighbouring island.

There I was presented to their King, who received me kindly and listened in astonishment to my story. I found their city prosperous and densely populated, abounding in markets and well-stocked shops, and filled with the bustle of commercial activity. The people, both rich and poor, possessed the rarest thoroughbred horses; but I was bewildered to see them ride their steeds bare-backed.

In my next audience with the King I ventured to express my surprise at his subjects' ignorance of the use of saddles and stirrups. 'My noble master,' I remarked, 'why is it that no one in this island uses a saddle? It makes both for the comfort of the rider and his mastery over his horse.'

'What may that be?' he asked, somewhat puzzled. 'I have never seen a saddle in all my life.'

'Pray allow me to make one for you,' I replied, 'that you may try it and find how comfortable and useful it can be.'

The King was pleased at my offer. At once I sought out a skilful carpenter and instructed him to make a wooden frame for a saddle of my own design; then I taught a blacksmith to forge a bit and a pair of stirrups. I fitted out the frame with a padding of wool and leather and furnished it with a girth and tassels. When all was ready, I chose the finest of the royal horses, saddled and bridled it, and led it before the King.

The King was highly delighted with the splendour and usefulness of his horse's novel equipment, and in reward bestowed on me precious gifts and a large sum of money.

When his Vizier saw the saddle he begged me to make one for him. I did so; and it was not long before every courtier and noble in the kingdom became the owner of a handsome saddle.

My skill soon made me the richest man in the island. The King conferred upon me many honours and I became a trusted courtier. One day, as we sat conversing together in his palace, he said: 'You must know, Sindbad, that we have grown to love you like a brother. Indeed, our regard for you is such that we cannot bear the thought that you might some day leave our kingdom. Therefore we will ask you a favour, which we hope you will not refuse.'

'Allah forbid,' I replied, 'that I should refuse you anything, your majesty.'

'We wish you to marry a beautiful girl who has been brought up in our court,' he said. 'She is intelligent and wealthy, and will make you an excellent wife. I trust that you will settle down happily with her in this city for the rest of your days. Do not refuse me this, I pray you.'

I was deeply embarrassed and did not know what to answer.

'Why do you not speak, my son?' he asked.

'Your majesty,' I faltered, 'I am in duty bound to obey you.'

The King sent at once for a cadi and witnesses and I was married that day to a rich woman of noble lineage. The King gave us a magnificent palace and assigned to us a retinue of slaves and servants.

We lived happily and contentedly together, although in my heart-of-hearts I never ceased to cherish a longing to return home – together with my wife; for I loved her dearly. But, alas, no mortal can control his destiny or trifle with the decrees of Fate.

One day death took my neighbour's wife to eternal rest, and, as he was one of my closest friends, I visited him at his house to offer my condolence. Finding him overcome with grief, I tried to comfort him, saying: 'Have patience, my friend. Allah in His great bounty may soon give you another wife as loving and as worthy as the one He has taken from you. May He lighten your sorrow and prolong your years!'

But he never raised his eyes from the ground.

'Alas!' he sighed. 'How can you wish me a long life when I have but a few hours to live?'

'Take heart, my friend,' I said, 'why do you speak of death when, thank Allah, you are in perfect health, sound in mind and body?'

'In a few hours,' he replied, 'I shall be consigned to the earth with the body of my wife. It is an ancient custom in this country that when a wife dies her husband is buried with her, and if he should die first his wife is buried with him: both must leave this world together.'

'By Allah,' I cried in horror, 'this is a most barbarous custom! No civilized people could ever tolerate such monstrous cruelty!'

Whilst we were talking, my neighbour's friends and kinsfolk, together with a large crowd, came into the house and began to condole with him upon his wife's and his own impending death. Presently the funeral preparations were completed; the woman's body was laid in a coffin, and a long procession of mourners, headed by the husband, formed outside the house. And we all set out towards the burial ground.

The procession halted at the foot of a steep mound over-looking the sea, where a stone was rolled away from the mouth of a deep pit, and into this pit the corpse was thrown. Next the mourners laid hold of my friend and lowered him by a long rope, together with seven loaves of bread and a pitcher of water. Then the stone was rolled back and we all returned to the city.

I hastened with a heavy heart to the King's palace, and when I was admitted to his presence I fell on my knees before him, crying: 'My noble master, I have visited many far countries and lived amongst all manner of men, but in all my life I have never seen or heard of anything so barbarous as your custom of burying the living with the dead. Are strangers, too, subject to this law, your majesty?'

'Certainly they are,' he replied. 'They must be interred with their dead wives. It is a time-hallowed custom to which all must submit.'

At this reply I felt as though my gall-bladder would burst open. I ran in haste to my own house, dreading lest my wife should have died since I last saw her. Finding her in perfect health, I comforted myself as best I could with the thought that I might one day find means of returning to my own country, or even die before my wife.

But Allah ordained otherwise. Soon afterwards my wife was stricken with an illness and in a few days surrendered her soul to the Merciful.

The King and all his courtiers came to my house to comfort me. The body of my wife was perfumed and arrayed in fine robes and rich ornaments. And when all was ready for the burial I was led behind the bier, at the head of a long procession.

When we came to the mound, the stone was lifted from the mouth of the pit and the body of my wife thrown in; then the mourners gathered round to bid me farewell, paying no heed to my protests and entreaties. They bound me with a long rope and lowered me into the pit, together with the customary loaves and pitcher of water. Then they rolled back the stone and went their way.

When I touched the bottom of the pit I found myself in a vast cavern filled with skeletons and reeking with the foul stench of decaying corpses. I threw myself upon the earth, crying: 'You deserve this fate, Sindbad! Here you have come to pay the last penalty for your avarice, your insatiable greed! What need had you to marry in this island? Would that you had died on the bare mountains or perished in the merciless sea!'

Tormented by the vision of a protracted death, I lay in an agony of despair for many hours. At length, feeling the effects of thirst and hunger, I unfastened the loaves and the pitcher of water and ate and drank sparingly. Then I lay in a corner which I had carefully cleared of bones.

For several days I languished in that charnel cave, and at length the time came when my provisions were exhausted. As I lay down, commending myself to Allah and waiting for my approaching end, the covering of the pit was suddenly lifted and there appeared at its mouth a crowd of mourners, who presently lowered into the cavern a dead man accompanied by his screaming wife, together with seven loaves and a pitcher of water.

As soon as the stone was rolled back I rose and, snatching up a leg-bone from one of the skeletons, sprang upon the woman and dealt her a violent blow upon the head, so that she fell down lifeless upon the instant. Then I stole her provisions, which kept me alive for several days longer. When these in turn were finished, the stone was once again rolled away from the pit and a man lowered in with his dead wife. He, too, met the same end as the unfortunate woman before him.

In this way I lived on for many weeks, killing every new-comer and eating his food. One day, as I was sleeping in my accustomed place, I was awakened by a sound of movement near by. At once I sprang to my feet, and picking up my weapon followed the noise until I could faintly discern the form of some animal scurrying before me. As I pressed forward in pursuit of the strange intruder, stumbling in the dark over the bones and corpses, I suddenly made out at the far side of the cavern a tremulous speck of light which grew larger and brighter as I advanced towards it. When I had reached the end of the cave the fleeing animal leapt through the light and disappeared. To my inexpressible joy, I realized that I had come upon a tunnel which the wild beasts, attracted by the carrion in the cave, had burrowed from the other side of the mound. I scrambled into this tunnel, crawling on all fours, and soon found myself at the foot of a high cliff, beneath the open sky.

I fell upon my knees in prayer and thanked the Almighty for my salvation. The warm and wholesome air breathed new life into my veins, and I rejoiced to gaze upon the loveliness of earth and sky,

Fortified with hope and courage, I made my way back into the cave and brought out the store of food which I had laid aside during my sojourn there. I also gathered up all the jewels, pearls, and precious ornaments that I could find upon the corpses, and, tying them in the shrouds and garments of the dead, carried the bundles to the seashore.

I remained there several days, surveying the horizon from morning till night. One day, as I was sitting beneath a rock praying for a speedy rescue, I saw a sail far off upon the ocean.

I hoisted a winding-sheet on my staff and waved it frantically as I ran up and down the beach. The crew observed my signal, and a boat was promptly sent off to fetch me.

'How did you find your way to this wild region?' asked the captain in astonishment. 'I have never seen a living man on this desolate spot in all the days of my life.'

'Sir,' I replied, 'I was shipwrecked off this shore many days ago. These bales are the remnants of my goods which I managed to save.' And I kept the truth from him, lest there be some on board who were citizens of that island.

Then I took out a rare pearl from one of my packages and offered it to him. 'Pray accept this,' I said, 'as a token of my gratitude to you for saving my life.'

But the captain politely refused the gift. 'It is not our custom,' he said, 'to accept payment for a good deed. We have rescued many a shipwrecked voyager, fed him and clothed him and finally set him ashore with a little present of our own besides. Allah alone is the giver of rewards.'

I thanked him with all my heart and called down blessings upon him.

Then the ship resumed its voyage. And, as we sailed from island to island and from sea to sea, I rejoiced at the prospect of seeing my native land again. At times, however, a memory of my sojourn with the dead would come back to me and I would be beside myself with terror.

At length, by the grace of Allah, we arrived safely in Basrah. I stayed a few days in that town, and then proceeded up the river to Baghdad. Loaded with treasure, I hastened to my own house, where I was rapturously welcomed by my friends and kinsfolk. I sold for a fabulous sum the precious stones I had brought back from that barbarous city, and gave lavish alms to widows and orphans.

That is the story of my fourth voyage. Tomorrow, if Allah wills, I shall recount to you the adventures of my fifth voyage.

When the evening feast was over, Sindbad the Sailor gave Sindbad the Porter a hundred pieces of gold, and the company took leave of their host and departed, marvelling at all they had heard. Next morning the porter returned, and when the other guests had assembled, Sindbad the Sailor began:

The Fifth Voyage of Sindbad the Sailor

KNOW, my friends, that the gay and voluptuous life which I led after my return soon made me forget the suffering I had endured in the Land of the Cannibals and in the Cavern of the Dead. I remembered only the pleasures of adventure and the considerable gains which my travels had earned me, and once again longed to sail new seas and explore new lands. I equipped myself with commodities suitable for ready sale in foreign countries and, packing them in bales, took them to Basrah.

One day, as I was walking along the wharf, I saw a newly built ship with tall masts and fine new sails which at once caught my fancy. I bought her outright, and embarked in her my slaves and merchandise. Then I hired an experienced captain and a well-trained crew, and accepted as passengers several other merchants who offered to pay their fares beforehand.

Blessed with a favourable wind, we voyaged many days and nights, trading from sea to sea and from shore to shore, and at length came to a desert island where we caught sight of a solitary white dome, half-buried in the sand. This I recognized at once as a roc's egg; and the passengers begged leave to land, so that they might go near and gaze upon this prodigy.

As ill luck would have it, however, the light-hearted merchants found no better sport than to throw great stones at the egg. When the shell was broken, the passengers, who were determined to have a feast, dragged out the young bird and cut it up in pieces. Then they returned on board to tell me of their adventure.

I was filled with horror and cried: 'We are lost! The parent birds will now pursue our ship with implacable rage and destroy us all!'

Scarcely had I finished speaking when the sun was suddenly hidden from our view as by a great cloud and the world grew dark around us as the rocs came flying home. On finding their egg broken and their offspring destroyed, the birds uttered deafening cries; they took to the air again, and in a twinkling vanished from sight.

'All aboard, quickly!' I exclaimed. 'We must at once fly from this island!'

The captain weighed anchor and with all speed we sailed off towards the open sea. But before long the world grew dark again, and in the ominous twilight we could see the gigantic birds hovering high overhead, each carrying in its talons an enormous rock. When they were directly above us, one of them let fall its missile, which narrowly missed the ship and made such a chasm in the ocean that for a moment we could see the sandy bottom. The waves rose mountain-high, tossing us up and down. Presently the other bird dropped its rock, which hit the stern and sent the rudder flying into twenty pieces. Those of us who were not crushed to death were hurled into the sea and swallowed up by the giant waves.

Through the grace of Allah I managed to cling to a floating piece of wreckage. Sitting astride this, I paddled with my feet, and, aided by wind and current, at length reached the shore of an island.

I threw myself upon the sand and lay down awhile to recover my breath. Then I rose and wandered about the island, which was as beautiful as one of the gardens of Eden. The air was filled with the singing of birds, and wherever I turned my eyes I saw trees loaded with luscious fruit and crystal brooks meandering among banks of flowers. I refreshed myself with the fruit and water, and when evening came lay down upon the grass.

Early next morning I rose and set off to explore this solitary garden. After a long stroll among the trees I came to a rivulet where, to my astonishment, I saw, seated upon the bank, a decrepit old man cloaked in a mantle of leaves.

Taking him for a shipwrecked mariner like myself, I went up to him and wished him peace; but he replied only by a

mournful nod. I asked him what luckless accident had cast
him in that place, but instead of answering he entreated me
with signs to take him upon my shoulders and carry him
across the brook. I readily bent down and, lifting him upon
my back, waded through the stream. When I reached the
opposite bank I stooped again for him to get off; but instead
of alighting the old wretch powerfully threw his legs, which

147

I now saw were covered with a rough black skin like a buffalo's, round my neck and crossed them tightly over my chest. Seized with fear, I desperately tried to shake him off, but the monster pressed his thighs tighter and tighter round my throat until I could no longer breathe. The world darkened before my eyes and with a choking cry I fell senseless to the ground.

When I came to myself I found the old monster still crouching upon my shoulders, although he had now sufficiently relaxed his hold to allow me to breathe. As soon as he saw that I had recovered my senses he pushed one foot against my belly and, violently kicking my side with the other, forced me to rise and walk under some trees. He leisurely plucked the fruits and ate them, and every time I stopped against his will or failed to do his bidding he kicked me hard, so that I had no choice but to obey him. All day long he remained seated upon my shoulders, and I was no better than a captive slave; at night he made me lie down with him, never for one moment loosening his hold round my neck. Next morning he roused me with a kick and ordered me to carry him among the trees.

Thus he stayed rooted upon my back, discharging his natural filth upon me, and driving me relentlessly on from glade to glade. I cursed the charitable impulse which prompted me to help him, and longed for death to deliver me from my evil plight.

After many weeks of abject servitude I chanced one day to come upon a field where gourds were growing in abundance. Under one of the trees I found a large gourd which was sun-dried and empty. I picked it up and, after cleaning it thoroughly, squeezed into it the juice of several bunches of grapes; then, carefully stopping the hole which I had cut into its shell, left it in the sun to ferment.

When I returned with the old man a few days afterwards, I found the gourd filled with the purest wine. The drink gave me fresh vigour, and I presently began to feel so light and gay that I went tripping merrily among the trees, scarcely aware of my loathsome burden.

Perceiving the effect of the wine, my captor asked me to let him taste it. I did not dare to refuse. He took the gourd from my hand, and raising it to his lips gulped down the liquor to the dregs. When he was overcome with the wine, he began to sway from side to side and his legs gradually relaxed their clasp round my neck. With one violent jerk of my shoulders I hurled him to the ground, where he lay motionless. Then I

quickly picked up a great stone from among the trees and, falling upon the old fiend with all my strength, crushed his skull to pieces and mingled his flesh with his blood. That was the end of my tormentor: may Allah have no mercy upon him!

Overjoyed at my new freedom, I roamed the island for many weeks, eating of its fruit and drinking from its springs. One day, however, as I sat on the shore musing on the vicissitudes of my life and recalling memories of my native land, I saw to my great joy, a sail heading towards the island. On reaching the beach the vessel anchored, and the passengers went ashore to fill their pitchers with water.

I ran in haste to meet them. They were greatly astonished to see me and gathered round, inquiring who I was and whence I had come. I recounted to them all that had befallen me since my arrival, and they replied: 'It is a marvel that you have escaped from that fiend; for you must know that the monster who had crouched upon your shoulders was none other than the Old Man of the Sea. You are the first ever to escape alive from his clutches. Praise be to Allah for your deliverance!'

They took me to their ship, where the captain received me kindly and listened with astonishment to my adventure. Then we set sail, and after voyaging many days and nights cast anchor in the harbour of a city perched on a high cliff, which is known among travellers as the City of Apes on account of the hosts of monkeys that infest it by night.

I went ashore with one of the merchants from the ship and wandered about the town in search of some employment. We soon fell in with a crowd of men proceeding to the gates of the city with sacks of pebbles on their shoulders. At the sight of these men my friend the merchant gave me a large cotton bag, saying: 'Fill this with pebbles and follow these people into the forest. Do exactly as they do, and thus you will earn your livelihood.'

Following his instructions, I filled the sack with pebbles and joined the crowd. The merchant recommended me to them, saying: 'Here is a shipwrecked stranger; teach him to earn his bread and Allah will reward you.'

When we had marched a great distance from the city we came to a vast valley, covered with coconut-trees so straight and tall that no man could ever climb them. Drawing nearer, I saw among the trees innumerable monkeys, which fled at our approach and swiftly climbed up to the fruit-laden branches.

Here my companions set down their bags and began to pelt the apes with pebbles; and I did the same. The furious beasts retaliated by pelting us with coconuts, and these we gathered up and put into our sacks. When they were full we returned to the city and sold the nuts in the market-place.

Thenceforth I went out every day to the forest with the coconut hunters and traded profitably with the fruit. When I had saved enough money for my homeward voyage I took leave of my friend the merchant and embarked in a vessel bound for Basrah, taking with me a large cargo of coconuts and other produce of that city.

In the course of our voyage we stopped at many heathen islands, where I sold some of my coconuts at a substantial profit and exchanged others for cinnamon, pepper, and Chinese and Comarin aloes. On reaching the Sea of Pearls I engaged the services of several divers; and in a short time brought up a large quantity of priceless pearls.

After that we again set sail and, voyaging many days and nights, at length safely arrived in Basrah. I spent but a few days in that town, and then, loaded with treasure, set out for Baghdad. I rejoiced to be back in my native city, and hastening to my old street, entered my own house, where all my friends and kinsmen forgathered to greet me. I gave them gold and countless presents, and distributed a large sum in charity among the widows and orphans.

That is the story of my fifth voyage. Tomorrow, my friends, if Allah wills, I shall recount to you the tale of my sixth voyage.

When the evening feast was ended, Sindbad the Sailor gave Sindbad the Porter a hundred pieces of gold, and the company departed, marvelling at all they had heard.

Next morning the porter returned and, when the other guests had arrived, Sindbad the Sailor began:

The Sixth Voyage of Sindbad the Sailor

I was one day reclining at my ease in the comfort and felicity of a serene life, when a band of merchants who had just returned from abroad called at my house to give me news of foreign lands. The sight of these travellers recalled to my mind how great was the joy of returning from a far journey to be united with friends and kinsmen after a prolonged absence; and soon afterwards I made preparations for another voyage and set sail with a rich cargo from Basrah.

We voyaged leisurely many days and nights, buying and selling wherever the ship anchored and exploring the unfamiliar places at which we called. One day, however, as we were sailing in mid-ocean, we suddenly heard the captain of our ship burst out in a loud lament. He beat himself about the face, tore at his beard, and hurled his turban on the deck. We gathered round him, inquiring the cause of his violent grief.

'Alas, we are lost!' he cried. 'The ship has been driven off its course into an unknown ocean, where nothing can save us from final wreck but Allah's mercy. Let us pray to Him!'

Then, quickly rising, the captain climbed the mast to trim the sails, while the passengers fell on their knees weeping and bidding each other farewell. Scarcely had he reached the top when a violent gale arose, sweeping us swiftly along and dashing the ship against a craggy shore at the foot of a high mountain. At once the vessel split to pieces and we were all flung into the raging sea. Some were drowned outright, while others, like myself, managed to escape by clinging to the jutting rocks.

We found scattered all along the shore the remains of other wrecks, and the sands were strewn with countless bales from which rare merchandise and costly ornaments had broken loose. I wandered among these treasures for many hours, and then, winding my way through the rocks, suddenly came upon a river which flowed from a gorge in the mountain. I followed its course with my eyes and was surprised to find that instead of running into the sea, the river plunged into a vast rocky cavern and disappeared. The banks were covered with glittering jewels, and the bed was studded with myriads of rubies, emeralds, and other precious stones; so that the entire river blazed with a dazzling light. The rarest Chinese and Comarin aloes grew on the adjacent steeps, and liquid amber trickled down the rocks onto the beach below. Great whales would come out of the sea and drink of this amber; but, their bellies being gradually heated, they would at length disgorge it upon the surface of the water. There it would crystallize and, after changing its colour and other properties, would finally be washed ashore, its rich perfume scenting the entire region.

Those of us who had escaped drowning lay in a sorrowful plight upon the shore, counting the days as they dragged by and waiting for the approach of death. One by one my companions died as they came to the end of their provisions, and we who were left washed the dead and wrapped them in winding sheets made from the fabrics scattered on the shore, and buried them. Then my friends were stricken with a sickness of the belly, caused by the humid air, to which they all succumbed; and I had the melancholy task of burying with my own hands the last of my companions.

Realizing that death was at hand, I threw myself upon the earth, wailing: 'Would that I had died before my friends! There would at least have remained good comrades who would have washed my body and given it a decent burial! There is no strength or help save in Allah!'

At length I rose and dug a deep grave by the sea, thinking to myself: 'When I sense the approach of death I will lie here and die in my grave. In time the wind will bury me with sand.' And as I thus prepared to meet my end, I cursed myself for venturing yet again upon the perils of the sea after having suffered so many misfortunes in my past voyages. 'Why,' I cried in my despair, 'O why were you not content to remain safe and happy in Baghdad? Had you not enough riches to last you twice a lifetime?'

Lost in these reflections, I wandered to the banks of the river, and as I watched it disappear into the cavern I struck upon a plan. 'By Allah,' I thought, 'this river must have both a beginning and an end. If it enters the mountain on this side it must surely emerge into daylight again; and if I can but follow its course in some vessel, the current may at last bring me to some inhabited land. If I am destined to survive this peril, Allah will guide me to safety; if I perish, it will not be worse than the dismal fate which awaits me here.'

Emboldened by these thoughts, I collected some large branches of Chinese and Comarin aloes and, laying these on some planks from the wrecked vessels, bound them with strong cables into a raft. This I loaded with sacks of rubies, pearls, and other stones, as well as several bales of the choicest ambergris; then, commending myself to Allah, I launched the raft upon the water and jumped aboard.

The current carried me swiftly along, and I soon found myself enveloped in the brooding darkness of the cavern. My raft began to bump violently against the ragged sides, while the passage grew smaller and narrower until I was compelled to lie flat upon my belly for fear of striking my head. Very soon I wished I could return to the open shore, but the current became faster and faster as the river swept headlong down its precipitous bed, and I resigned myself to certain death. At length, overcome by terror and exertion, I sank into a death-like sleep.

I cannot tell how long I slept, but when I awoke I found myself lying on my raft close to the river bank, beneath the open sky. The river was flowing gently through a stretch of pleasant meadowland, and on the bank stood many Indians and Abyssinians.

As soon as these men saw that I was awake, they gathered about me, asking questions in a language I did not understand. Presently one of their number came forward and greeted me. in Arabic.

'Who may you be?' he asked, 'and whence have you come? We were working in our fields when we saw you drifting down the river. We fastened your raft to this bank and, not wishing to disturb your slumbers, left you here in safety. But tell us, what accident has cast you upon this river, which takes its perilous course from beneath that mountain?'

I begged him first to give me some food, and promised to answer all their questions after I had eaten. They instantly brought me a variety of meats, and when I had regained my strength a little, I recounted to them all that had befallen me since my shipwreck. They marvelled at my miraculous escape, and said: 'We must take you to our King, so that you may yourself tell him of your adventure.'

Thereupon they led me to their city, carrying my raft with all its contents upon their shoulders. The King received me courteously and, after listening in profound astonishment to my story, congratulated me heartily on my escape. Then, opening my treasures in his presence, I laid out at his feet a priceless choice of emeralds, pearls, and rubies. In return he conferred upon me the highest honours of the kingdom, and invited me to stay as his guest at the palace.

Thus I rose rapidly in the King's favour, and soon became a trusted courtier. One day he questioned me about my country and its far-famed Caliph. I praised the wisdom, piety, and benevolence of Haroun Al-Rashid, and spoke at length of his glorious deeds. The King was profoundly impressed by my account. 'This monarch,' he said, 'must indeed be illustrious. We desire to send him a present worthy of his greatness, and appoint you the bearer of it.'

'I hear and obey,' I replied. 'I will gladly deliver your gift to the Prince of the Faithful, and will inform him that in your majesty he has a worthy ally and a trusted friend.'

The King gave orders that a magnificent present be prepared and commissioned a new vessel for the voyage. When all was ready for departure I presented myself at the royal palace and, thanking the King for the many favours he had shown me, took leave of him and of the officers of his court.

Then I set sail, and voyaging many days and nights at length safely arrived in Basrah. I hastened to Baghdad with the royal gift, and when I had been admitted to the Caliph's presence I kissed the ground before him and told him of my mission. Al-Rashid marvelled greatly at my adventure and gave orders that the story be inscribed on parchment in letters of gold, so that it might be preserved among the treasures of the kingdom.

Leaving his court, I hastened to my old street and, entering my own house, rejoiced to meet my friends and kinsfolk. I gave them gold and costly presents, and distributed lavish alms among the poor of the city.

Such is the story of my sixth voyage. Tomorrow, my friends, I shall recount to you the tale of my seventh and last voyage.

When the evening feast was ended, Sindbad the Sailor gave Sindbad the Porter a hundred pieces of gold, and the guests departed, marvelling at all they had heard.

Next morning the porter returned and, when the other guests had assembled, Sindbad the Sailor began:

The Last Voyage of Sindbad the Sailor

FOR many years after my return I lived joyfully in Baghdad, feasting and carousing with my boon companions and revelling away the riches which my farflung travels had earned me. But though I was now past the prime of life, my untamed spirit rebelled against my declining years, and I once again longed to see the world and travel in the lands of men. I made preparations for a long voyage and, boarding a good ship in company with some eminent merchants, set sail from Basrah with a fair wind and a rich cargo.

We voyaged peacefully for many weeks, but one day, whilst we were sailing in the China Sea, a violent tempest struck our ship, drenching us with torrents of rain. We hastily covered our bales with canvas to protect them from the wet and fervently prayed to Allah to save us from the fury of the sea, while the captain, rolling up his sleeves and tucking the skirts of his robes into his belt, climbed the mast and from the top scanned the horizon in all directions. Presently he climbed down again, all in a tremble with terror and, staring at us with an expression of blank despair, beat his face and plucked the hairs of his beard.

'Pray to Allah,' he cried, 'that He may save us from the peril into which we have fallen! Weep and say your farewells, for the treacherous wind has got the better of us and driven our ship into the world's farthermost ocean!'

Thereupon the captain opened one of his cabin chests and

took from it a small cotton bag filled with an ashlike powder. He sprinkled some water over the powder and, after waiting a little, inhaled it into his nostrils; then, opening a little book, he intoned aloud some strange incantations and at length turned to us, crying: 'Know that we are now approaching the Realm of Kings, the very land where our master Solomon son of David (may peace be upon him) lies buried. Serpents of prodigious size swarm about that coast, and the sea is filled with giant whales which can swallow vessels whole. Farewell, my friends; and may Allah have mercy upon us all!'

Scarcely had the captain uttered these words when suddenly the ship was tossed high up in the air and then flung down into the sea, while an ear-splitting cry, more terrible than thunder, boomed through the swelling ocean. Terror seized our hearts as we saw a gigantic whale, as massive as a mountain, rushing swiftly towards us, followed by another no less huge, and a third greater than the two put together. This last monster bounded from the surging billows and, opening wide its enormous mouth, seized in its jaws the ship with all that was in it. I hastily ran to the edge of the tilting deck and, casting off my clothes, leapt into the sea just before the whale swallowed up the ship and disappeared beneath the foam with its two companions.

With Allah's help I clung to a piece of timber which had fallen from the lost vessel and, contending with the mighty waves for two days and nights, was at length cast on an island covered with fruit trees and watered by many streams. After refreshing myself I wandered aimlessly about, and soon came to a fast-flowing river which rolled its waters towards the interior of the island. As I stood upon the bank I hit upon the idea of building a raft and allowing myself to be carried down by the current, as I had done in my last voyage. 'If I succeed in saving myself this time,' I said, 'all will be well with me and I solemnly vow never in all my life to let the mere thought of voyaging cross my mind again. If I fail, I shall at last find rest from all the toils and tribulations which my incorrigible folly has earned me.'

I cut down several branches from an exotic tree which I

had never seen before and bound them together into a raft with the stems of some creeping plants. I loaded the raft with a large quantity of fruit and, commending myself to Allah, pushed off down the river.

For three days and nights I was hurried swiftly along by the current, until, overcome by dizziness, I sank into a dead faint. When I recovered consciousness I found myself heading towards a fearful precipice, down which the waters of the river were tumbling in a mighty cataract. I clung with all my strength to the branches of the raft and, resigning myself to my fate, prayed silently for a merciful end. When I had reached the very edge of the precipice, however, I suddenly felt the raft halted upon the water and found myself caught in a net which a crowd of men had thrown from the bank. My raft was quickly hauled to land, and I was released from the net half dead with terror and exhaustion.

As I lay upon the mud, I gradually became aware of a venerable old man who was bending over me. He wrapped me in warm garments and greeted me kindly; and when my strength had returned a little he helped me to rise and led me slowly to the baths of the city, where I was washed with perfumed water. Then the old man took me to his own house. He regaled me sumptuously with excellent meats and wines and, when the feast was ended, his slaves washed my hands and wiped them with napkins of the rarest silk. After this my host conducted me to a noble chamber and left me alone, after assigning several of his slaves to my service.

The kind old man entertained me in this fashion for three days. When I had completely recovered, he visited me in my chamber and sat conversing with me for an hour. Just before leaving my room, however, he turned to me and said: 'If you wish to sell your merchandise, my friend, I will gladly come down with you to the market-place.'

I was greatly puzzled at these words and did not know what to answer, as I had been cast utterly naked in that city.

'Do not be troubled over your goods, my son,' went on the old man. 'If we receive a good offer, we will sell them outright; if not, I will keep them for you in my own storehouse until they fetch a better price.'

Concealing my perplexity, I replied: 'I am willing to do whatever you advise.' With this I rose and went out with him to the market-place.

There I saw an excited crowd admiring an object on the ground with exclamations of enthusiastic praise. Pushing my way among the gesticulating merchants, I was astonished to find the centre of attention to be no other than the raft aboard which I had sailed down the river. And presently the old man ordered a broker to begin the auction.

'Who will make the first bid for this rare sandalwood?' began the broker.

'A hundred dinars!' cried one of the merchants.

'A thousand!' shouted another.

'Eleven hundred!' exclaimed my host.

'Agreed!' I cried.

Upon this the old man ordered his slaves to carry the wood to his store and walked back with me to his house, where he paid me eleven hundred pieces of gold locked in an iron coffer.

One day, as we sat conversing together, the old man said: 'My son, pray grant me a favour.'

'With all my heart,' I replied.

'I am a very old man, and have not been blessed with a son,' went on my benefactor. 'Yet I have a young and beautiful daughter, who on my death will be sole mistress of my fortune. If you will have her for your wife, you will inherit my wealth and become chief of the merchants of this city.'

I readily consented to the sheikh's proposal. A sumptuous feast was held, a cadi and witnesses were called in, and I was married to the old man's daughter amidst great rejoicings. When the wedding guests had departed I was conducted to the bridal chamber, where I was allowed to see my wife for the first time. I found her incomparably beautiful, and rejoiced to see her decked with the rarest pearls and jewels.

My wife and I grew to love each other dearly, and we lived together in happiness and contentment. Not long afterwards my wife's father died, and I inherited all his possessions. His slaves became my slaves and his goods my goods, and the merchants of the city appointed me their chief in his place.

One day, however, I discovered that every year the people of that land experienced a wondrous change in their bodies. All the men grew wings upon their shoulders and for a whole day flew high up in the air, leaving their wives and children behind. Amazed at this prodigy, I importuned one of my friends to allow me to cling to him when he next took his flight, and at length prevailed on him to let me try this novel adventure. When the long-awaited day arrived, I took tight hold of my friend's waist and was at once carried up swiftly in the air. We climbed higher and higher into the void until I could hear the angels in their choirs singing hymns to Allah under the vault of heaven. Moved with awe, I cried: 'Glory and praise eternal be to Allah, King of the Universe!'

Scarcely had I uttered these words when my winged carrier dropped headlong through the air and finally alighted on the top of a high mountain. There he threw me off his back and took to the air again, calling down curses on my head. Abandoned upon this desolate mountain, I lifted my hands in despair and cried: 'There is no strength or help save in Allah! Every time I escape from one ordeal I find myself in another as grievious. Surely I deserve all that befalls me!'

Whilst I was thus reflecting upon my plight, I saw two youths coming up towards me. Their faces shone with an unearthly beauty, and each held a staff of red gold in his hand. I at once rose to my feet, and, walking towards them, wished them peace. They returned my greeting courteously, and I inquired: 'Who are you, pray, and what object has brought you to this barren mountain?'

'We are worshippers of the True God,' they replied. With this, one of the youths pointed to a certain path upon the mountain and, handing me his staff, walked away with his companion.

Bewildered at these words, I set off in the direction he had indicated, leaning upon my gold staff as I walked. I had not gone far when I saw coming towards me the flyer who had so unceremoniously set me down upon the mountain. Determined to learn the reason of his displeasure, I went up to him and said gently: 'Is this how friends behave to friends?'

The winged man, who was now no longer angry, replied: 'Know that my fall was caused by your unfortunate mention of your god. The word has this effect upon us all, and this is why we never utter it.'

I assured my friend that I had meant no harm and promised to commit no such transgression in future. Then I begged him to carry me back to the city. He took me upon his shoulders and in a few moments set me down before my own house.

My wife was overjoyed at my return, and when I told her of my adventure, she said: 'We must no longer stay among these people. Know that they are the brothers of Satan and have no knowledge of the True God.'

'How then did your father dwell amongst them?' I asked.

'My father was of an alien race,' she replied. 'He shared none of their creeds, and he did not lead their life. As he is now dead, let us sell our possessions and leave this blasphemous city.'

Thereupon I resolved to return home. We sold our houses and other property, and hiring a vessel set sail with a rich cargo.

Aided by a favouring wind, we voyaged many days and nights and at length came to Basrah and thence to Baghdad, the City of Peace. I conveyed to my stores the valuables I had brought with me, and, taking my wife to my own house in my old street, rejoiced to meet my kinsfolk and my old companions. They told me that this voyage had kept me abroad for nearly twenty-seven years, and marvelled exceedingly at all that had befallen me.

I rendered deep thanks to Allah for bringing me safely back to my friends and kinsfolk, and solemnly vowed never to travel again by sea or land. Such, dear guests, was the last and longest of my voyages.

When the evening feast was ended, Sindbad the Sailor gave Sindbad the Porter a hundred pieces of gold, which he took with thanks and blessings and departed, marvelling at all he had heard.

The porter remained a constant visitor at the house of his illustrious friend, and the two lived in amity and peace until there came to them the Spoiler of worldly mansions, the Dark Steward of the graveyard, the Shadow which dissolves the bonds of friendship and ends alike all joys and all sorrows.

THE HISTORIC FART

It is related that in the town of Kaukaban, in Yemen, there was once a bedouin of the Fadhli tribe called Abu Hasan, who, having given up the life of the desert and settled down as a townsman, became, after much diligence and enterprise, a merchant of considerable wealth.

His wife had died while they were both young, and his friends were always pressing him to marry again. Weary of a widower's life, he at length gave in to their persuasions and engaged the services of an experienced marriage-broker, who found him a bride as beautiful as the moon when it shines on the sea. He celebrated the wedding with a sumptuous feast, to which he invited his near and distant kinsfolk, the ulema and fakirs of the town, and friends and acquaintances from all over the countryside. His whole house was thrown open to the wedding guests. There was rice of every hue and flavour, sherbets, lambs stuffed with walnuts, almonds, and pistachios, and a young camel roasted whole. Everyone ate, drank, and and made merry; and the bride was displayed, according to custom, in seven different robes – and again in yet another robe as befitted such a grand occasion – to the great joy of the women, who marvelled at her exceptional beauty.

At last came the moment when Abu Hasan was summoned to the bridal chamber. Slowly and solemnly he rose from his divan; but, horror of horrors, being bloated with meat and drink, he let go a long and resounding fart. The embarrassed guests, whose attentions had been fixed upon the bridegroom, turned to one another speaking with raised voices and pretending to have heard nothing at all. Abu Hasan was so mortified with shame that he wished the ground would open up and swallow him. He mumbled a feeble excuse, and, instead of going to the bridal chamber, went straight to the courtyard, saddled his horse, and rode off into the night, weeping bitterly.

After a long journey he reached Lahej, where he boarded a ship ready to sail for India, and in due course arrived in Calicut on the Malabar Coast. Here he met many Arabs, especially from Hadramaut, and was recommended by them to the King, who, though an unbeliever, took him into his service and in time promoted him to the captainship of his bodyguard.

He lived there in peace and contentment for ten years, and at the end of that time he was seized with a longing for his native land as strong as that of a lover pining for his loved one, so that he almost died of his self-imposed exile.

One day, unable to resist this yearning any longer, he absconded from the King's palace, boarded a ship, and eventually landed at Makalla in Hadramaut. Here he disguised himself in the rags of a dervish and, keeping his name and identity secret, travelled to Kaukaban on foot, enduring hunger, thirst and exhaustion, and braving a thousand dangers from lions, snakes, and ghouls. By and by he reached the hill which overlooked his native town. He gazed upon his old house with tears in his eyes, saying to himself: 'Pray God, no one will ever recognize me. I will first wander about the town and listen to the people's gossip. Allah grant that after all these years no one will remember what I did.'

He went round the outskirts of the town, and, as he sat down to rest at the door of a hut, he heard the voice of a young girl within, saying: 'Please, mother, what day was I born on? One of my friends wants to tell my fortune.'

'My daughter,' replied the woman solemnly, 'you were born on the very night of Abu Hasan's fart.'

When he heard these words, he got up and fled. 'Abu Hasan,' he said to himself, 'the day of your fart has become a date which will surely be remembered till the end of time.'

He travelled on until he was back in India, where he remained in exile until his death. May Allah have mercy upon him.

ALADDIN
AND THE ENCHANTED LAMP

ONCE upon a time there lived in a certain city of China an impoverished tailor who had a son called Aladdin. From his earliest years this Aladdin was a headstrong and incorrigible good-for-nothing. When he was ten, his father wished to teach him a decent trade; but as he lacked the means to pay for his training he took him into his own shop to teach him the trade of a tailor. Being accustomed to pass his time playing with the urchins of the quarter, however, Aladdin never stayed in a single day. Whenever his father went out of the shop or was attending to a customer, he would run off to the parks and gardens with little ruffians of his own age. He thus persisted in his idle and unruly ways until his father, grieving over the perverseness of his son, fell into an illness and died.

Seeing that her husband was dead and her son good for nothing, Aladdin's mother sold the shop with all its contents and took to cotton-spinning in order to support herself and her child. No longer restrained by the fear of a father, the young vagabond grew more wayward and perverse; he spent all his days away from home and returned only for his meals. And in this way he carried on until he was fifteen years of age.

One day as he was playing in the street with his companions, a dervish who was passing by stopped there and eyed Aladdin attentively. This dervish, who had come from the far interior of Morocco, was a sorcerer; he was deeply versed in astrology, and could, by the power of his magic, uproot a high mountain and hurl it against another. Having examined the boy closely, he muttered to himself: 'This is the youth I need; the very youth in quest of whom I left my native land.'

He drew aside one of the other boys and inquired of him

Aladdin's name, who his father was, and the circumstances of his life. When he had learnt everything concerning him, he went up to Aladdin and, leading him away from his companions, said: 'My child, are you not the son of So-and-so the tailor?'

'Yes, sir,' Aladdin replied, 'but my father has been dead a long time.'

At these words the Moor threw his arms about Aladdin's neck and kissed him again and again with tears running down his cheeks.

'Why do you weep, sir?' asked the boy in bewilderment. 'Did you know my father?'

'How can you ask me such a question, my child?' replied the Moor in a sad and broken voice. 'How can I refrain from weeping when I suddenly hear of my own brother's death? I have been travelling abroad these many years, and now, alas, that I have returned in the hope of seeing him, you tell me he is dead! But when I first caught sight of you, your blood cried out you were my brother's son. I recognized you at once, although, when I left this land, your father was not married yet. But, alas, no man can escape his fate or trifle with the decrees of Allah. My son,' he added, taking Aladdin again into his arms, 'you are my only comfort now; you stand in your father's place. He that leaves an heir does not die.'

With that the Moor took ten pieces of gold from his purse and gave them to Aladdin, asking where his mother lived. When the youth had directed him to his mother's house, the magician said: 'Give these ten dinars to my brother's wife, together with my kindest greetings. Tell her that your uncle has come home, and that, if Allah wills, I shall visit her to-morrow. Say that I desire to greet her, to see the house where my brother lived, and to look upon his grave.'

Aladdin rejoiced at the ten dinars. He kissed the Moor's hand and ran home to his mother, arriving long before supper-time.

'Mother,' he cried, 'I bring you good news. My uncle is back from his travels and sends you his greetings.'

'Are you making fun of me, my child?' the woman

answered. 'Who may this uncle be? And since when have you had a living uncle?'

'How can you say I have no living uncles or relations?' Aladdin protested. 'That man is my father's brother. He embraced and kissed me, and wept bitterly when he heard of my father's death. He himself bade me tell you of his arrival.'

'Indeed, child,' replied his mother, 'you did have an uncle once. But he is dead, and I never heard of any other.'

Next morning the Moorish sorcerer left his lodgings and began wandering about the town in search of Aladdin, for he could not bear to lose sight of him. Before long he found him playing in the streets with his companions. He hurried up to him, embraced and kissed him, and gave him two dinars.

'Run along to your mother,' he said, 'and give her these two dinars. Bid her prepare something for supper, and say your uncle is coming to eat with you this evening. And now, my boy, show me the way to your house again.'

'Gladly, sir,' replied Aladdin, and when he had pointed out the road to him, took the two dinars to his mother.

'My uncle is coming to have dinner with us,' he told her.

Aladdin's mother hastened to the market-place and bought all the food she needed. Then she borrowed pots and dishes from her neighbours and began to cook the meal. When evening came she said to Aladdin: 'Dinner is ready, my son. Perhaps your uncle does not know the way to our house. Go out and see if you can find him in the street.'

Just as Aladdin was about to go, there came a knocking on the door. He ran to open it, and found the Moorish sorcerer standing on the threshold with a porter laden with fruit and drink. Aladdin led him into the house, and when the porter was dismissed the Moor greeted the old woman and begged her, with tears in his eyes, to show him where her husband used to sit. Aladdin's mother showed him the place, and he fell on his knees and kissed the ground.

'Alas, my brother, light of my eyes!' he cried. 'Oh, my irreparable loss, my great sorrow!'

He thus continued to weep and mourn until the woman was

convinced that he really was her husband's brother. At length,
seeing him distracted with grief, she lifted him gently from
the ground, crying: 'Forbear, I pray you, or you will kill
yourself!'

She spoke comforting words to him and made him sit down.
And when all three were seated the Moor began:

'My good sister, do not be surprised at not having seen or
known me when my late brother was alive. It is now forty
years since I left this land and began my wanderings in the
far-flung regions of the earth. I travelled in India, Sind, and
Arabia; then I went to Egypt, and sojourned for a while in
the city of Cairo, the wonder of the world. Finally I journeyed
into the deep interior of Morocco, and there I dwelt for thirty
years. One day, however, as I was sitting all alone, I sank into
a reverie and began to think of my native land and my brother.
I was seized with a great longing to see him, and wept to find
myself so far away from home. At length my yearning for him
so overpowered me that I resolved to journey back to the
country of my birth. "Unhappy man," I said to myself, "how
long will you stay an exile from your native city, the home of
your only brother? Rise and seek him before death overtakes
you; for who is secure from the assaults of fate or knows what
the vicissitudes of time may bring? It would indeed be a heavy
grief if you should die before you have seen your brother
again; he is perhaps in poverty and want, while, thanks to
Allah, you are a man of wealth. Go, visit your brother, and
help him in his need."

'Thereupon I rose and made preparations for the journey.
After reciting Friday's prayers and the opening verses of the
Koran, I mounted my horse and set forth. It would be fruitless
to tell you of all the hardships and perils I encountered on the
way until the Almighty brought me to this city. Then the day
before yesterday, whilst I was wandering about the streets, I
saw Aladdin playing with his companions. My heart leapt for
joy and I forgot all my troubles when I recognized my
nephew. But when he informed me of my poor brother's
death I nearly swooned for grief; he has perhaps told you how
I received the sorrowful news. Still I consoled myself in having

Aladdin as my brother's son. For does not the proverb truly say: "He that leaves an heir does not die?" '

Perceiving that his words had brought tears into the old woman's eyes by the memories they had evoked, the Moorish sorcerer changed his theme, and, to complete the trick, turned to Aladdin.

'Aladdin, my son, what trade have you learnt?' he said. 'What business do you follow to support yourself and your mother?'

Aladdin hung his head, and his mother replied: 'Oh, do not ask about Aladdin's trade! By Allah, he knows nothing at all, nor have I ever seen a more worthless child. All day long he idles away his time with the young vagabonds of the street. Alas, it was he that sent his poor father to his grave, and I myself shall follow him soon. Day and night I toil at the spinning-wheel to earn a couple of loaves for us. Brother of my husband, I swear by your life he never comes home except for meals. That is all I see of him. I have a good mind to turn him out of doors and leave him to fend for himself; for I am getting old and have not the strength to wear myself out as I used to do.'

'That is not well, nephew,' said the Moor, turning to Aladdin. 'Are you not ashamed to pursue this reckless and unprofitable path? Such conduct is not worthy of a young man like yourself, blessed with intelligence and born of decent folk. It does you little credit to let your old mother work to keep you, when you are old enough to support yourself. Allah be thanked, there are many good craftsmen in our city. Choose whatever trade you wish to learn and I will put you to it, so that when you are a man you will be well-equipped to earn a living. Perhaps you did not like your father's trade; choose another that you prefer, and I will do all I can to help you.'

Aladdin made no answer, and the Moor, realizing that he still preferred his idle life, continued: 'Take no offence, dear nephew. If you have no mind to learn a trade, there is no harm in that. I will open a shop for you and furnish it with silks and costly stuffs, so that you shall soon become a well-known merchant in the town.'

On hearing this, Aladdin rejoiced at the prospect of being a merchant dressed in fine clothes. He smiled at the Moor and nodded his head in acceptance.

'Now, my nephew,' went on the Moor, 'since you are willing to accept my offer and become a merchant with a shop of your own, be a man and prove yourself worthy of your new station. Tomorrow, if Allah wills, I will take you to the market-place and buy you a fine merchant's suit. After that I will look for a suitable shop for you.'

Deeply impressed by the munificence of her new-found relation, Aladdin's mother thanked the Moor with all her heart and exhorted her son to cast off his idle ways and show obedience to his uncle. Then she got up and served the meal; and, as the three ate and drank, the Moor chatted with Aladdin about trade and business affairs. When the night was far advanced the Moor took his leave and went off to his lodgings, promising to return next morning.

That night Aladdin could scarcely sleep for joy. In the morning there was a knocking on the door, and, when the old woman went to open it, she found the Moor outside, asking for her son. Aladdin ran out to meet him; he greeted his uncle and kissed his hand. The dervish took him by the hand, and went off with him to the market-place. There he entered a shop stocked with all manner of clothes and asked for an expensive suit. The merchant showed him numerous costly outfits and the Moor bade Aladdin choose the one he fancied most. Overjoyed at the liberality of his uncle, Aladdin picked out a magnificent suit, and the Moor paid the merchant on the spot. From there he took Aladdin to the city baths; and, after they had washed and refreshed themselves, Aladdin put on his new clothes and rejoiced to see himself so finely dressed. Beaming with delight, he kissed his uncle's hand and thanked him for his generosity.

Then the Moor led Aladdin to the merchant's bazaar, and let him see the traders buying and selling in their stores.

'My son,' he said, 'as you are soon to be a merchant like these men, it is but proper that you should frequent this market and get acquainted with the people.'

He showed him the sights of the city, the great buildings and the mosques, and at midday took him to an inn where they were served a meal on plates of silver. They ate and drank until they were satisfied; and then the Moor took Aladdin to see the Sultan's palace and the surrounding parks. After that he took him to the foreign merchants' khan where he himself was staying, and invited some of the merchants there to dinner. They accepted his invitation, and when they came he introduced Aladdin to them as his brother's son.

At nightfall he escorted Aladdin back to his mother's house. Seeing her son attired like a merchant, the poor woman was transported with joy and called down a thousand blessings on the Moor.

'Brother of my husband,' she said, 'I do not know how to thank you for your kindness.'

'Dear sister-in-law,' the Moor replied, 'I have done nothing to deserve your thanks. Aladdin is my son; I am in duty bound to be a father to him. Have no more fears for his future.'

'I pray to Allah, in the name of all the prophets,' exclaimed the old woman, 'to bless you, brother, and prolong your life for my sake, so that you may keep this orphan boy under the wing of your protection. May he, for his part, be ever obedient to you and render himself worthy of your favours.'

'Aladdin is no longer a child,' replied the Moor, 'but a man of sense. It is my dearest wish that he should follow in his father's footsteps and be a comfort to you in your old age. I am deeply sorry, however, that, tomorrow being Friday, the market will be closed and I shall not be able to open a shop for him as I promised. But, Allah willing, we shall do so on the day after. Tomorrow I shall come and take Aladdin to visit the parks and gardens beyond the city, that he may get to know the merchants and notables who frequent them.'

And the Moor took his leave and went back to his lodgings.

That night Aladdin lay in an ecstasy of bliss, thinking of his good fortune and the delights that were in store for him. Next morning he rose early and, as soon as he heard the knocking on the door, ran out blithely to receive his uncle. The dervish took him into his arms and kissed him, saying: 'Today, dear nephew, I will show you some fine things the like of which you have never seen in all your life.'

Hand in hand they walked along until they came out of the city gates and reached the fine parks and tall palaces that lay beyond. Aladdin, who had never seen these before, exclaimed for joy as they came in sight of each fresh building. When they had walked a long way from the city and were tired out, they entered a beautiful garden and sat down to rest beside a fountain of crystal water, set about with brazen lions as bright as gold. Here the Moor undid his belt and pulled out of it a kerchief filled with fruits and sweetmeats.

'Eat, my nephew, for you must be hungry,' he said.

The two ate together, and after they had rested and refreshed themselves the Moor bade Aladdin rise and walk with him a little farther. Aladdin got up, and they walked on through the gardens until they reached the open country and came to a high mountain.

'Where are we going, uncle?' asked Aladdin, who had never walked so far in all his days. 'We have passed all the gardens now, and can see nothing before us except that mountain. Let us go back to the city, for I am worn out with walking.'

'Be a man, my boy,' replied the Moor. 'I wish to show you another garden, which surpasses in beauty all you have yet seen; no king has the like of it in the whole world.'

And to divert Aladdin, the Moor proceeded to tell him all manner of strange stories, until they came to the goal which the magician had set himself. To see that spot he had come all the way from Morocco to China.

'This is the place we have been seeking,' said the Moor. 'Sit down and rest a little. Here, if Allah wills, I am going to show you strange and wondrous things such as the eyes of man have never seen before.'

He allowed the boy to rest a while, and then said to him: 'Rise up now, Aladdin, and gather up some dry sticks and fragments of wood, that we may light a fire. Then you shall see the marvel for which I brought you here.'

Wondering what his uncle was about to do, Aladdin forgot

his weariness and went among the bushes to search for dry twigs. He gathered up a great heap, and carried them to the old man. Presently the magician set fire to the wood and, when it was all ablaze, opened a small box he had about him and threw a pinch of incense from it into the flame, muttering mysterious charms. At once the sky was overcast with darkness and the earth shook and opened before him, revealing a marble slab topped with a copper ring. The boy was terrified at all this and wanted to run away; but the Moor, who could never achieve the object of his quest without Aladdin's help, at once caught hold of him and, raising his fist, dealt him a mighty blow on the head, so that his teeth were almost knocked out. Aladdin fell back fainting; nor did he recover his senses until the Moor brought him round by his magic.

'What have I done to deserve this, uncle?' Aladdin sobbed.

'I struck you to make a man of you, my child,' replied the Moor in a gentle tone. 'I am your uncle, your father's brother, and you must obey me. If you do my bidding, you shall be richer than all the monarchs of the world. Now listen carefully to my instructions. You have just seen how I opened the earth by my spells and incantations. Below that marble slab there is a treasure which none may open but yourself; only you can lift that stone and go down the stairs which lie beneath. Do as I bid you, and we will divide the hidden riches between us.'

Amazed at the magician's words, Aladdin forgot his tears and the smarting blow he had received.

'Tell me what to do, uncle,' he cried, 'and I will obey you.'

The Moor went up to him and kissed him. 'Nephew,' he said, 'you are dearer to me than a son. I have no other relative in all the world; you are my only heir. For your sake I bore the hardships of my long journey; to see you a fine, rich man is my utmost wish. Come, take hold of that ring and lift it.'

'But, uncle,' Aladdin replied, 'I am not strong enough to lift it all alone. Come and help me.'

'No, nephew,' said the Moor. 'If I help you we shall gain nothing and all our labours will be lost. Try by yourself, and you shall find that you can lift it with great ease. I told you, no one can move it but you. Just take hold of the ring and, while raising it, pronounce your name and your father's and mother's.'

Aladdin summoned up all his strength and did as the magician told him. The slab moved easily under his hand; he set it aside and saw below him a vaulted cave with a stairway of a dozen steps leading to the entrance.

'Now be careful, Aladdin,' cried the Moor. 'Do exactly as I tell you and omit nothing. Go down into the cave, and at the bottom you will find a great hall divided into four apartments. In each apartment you will see four gold coffers and other valuables of gold and silver. Do not halt for a single moment and take care not to touch the coffers or the walls, so much as with the skirt of your gown; for if you do you will at once be changed into a black stone. When you reach the fourth apartment you will find another door, which opens on a handsome garden shaded with fruit-trees. Pronounce the names you spoke over the slab and enter. After walking some fifty yards you will come to a staircase of about thirty steps, leading up to a terrace. On the terrace you will find a suspended lamp. Take down the lamp, pour out the oil in it, and hide it away in the breast of your robe. Do not fear for your clothes, for its oil is no ordinary oil. On your way back you may pause among the trees and pluck off whatever fruit you like.'

When he had finished speaking, the Moor drew a ring from his finger and put it on one of Aladdin's.

'My boy,' he said, 'this ring will deliver you from all evils and all perils, so long as you observe what I have told you. Be bold and resolute, and have no fears. You are a man now, no longer a child. In a few moments you shall be the richest man alive.'

Aladdin jumped down into the cave and found the four apartments with the four gold coffers in each. Bearing in mind the Moor's instructions, he made his way through them with infinite caution, and came out into the garden. From there he climbed up the stairway to the terrace, took the lamp down, poured out the oil, and put it into the breast of his robe. Then he returned to the garden and stopped for the first time to look upon the trees and the birds among their branches, warbling

hymns to the Creator. The trees were laden with fruits of
every shape and hue: white, red, green, yellow, and other
colours. Aladdin was too young to realize that these were
pearls and diamonds, emeralds and rubies, and jewels such as
no king ever possessed. He took them for coloured glass of
little value, and yet was so delighted with their lustre, which
outshone the sun in his midday brightness, that he gathered a
great quantity of them and stuffed them into his pockets and
into the folds of his belt and gown. When he had loaded himself with as much as he could carry, he hurried back through
the four apartments without touching the gold coffers and
quickly climbed the stairway at the cavern's mouth. But the
last step, being higher than the rest, he could not climb because
of his heavy load.

'Uncle,' he shouted, 'lend me your hand and help me to get
out.'

'Give me the lamp first,' the Moor replied. 'It is weighing
you down.'

'I cannot now,' said Aladdin. 'Just give me your hand, and
you shall have the lamp as soon as I am up.'

The sorcerer, whose sole concern was to gain possession
of the lamp, impatiently repeated his demand; Aladdin, on the
other hand, had so encumbered himself with his burden that
he could not get at it, and was therefore unable to give it to him.
Provoked at Aladdin's delay, and thinking that he wished to
keep the spoil for himself, the Moor flew into a terrible rage;
he ran to the blazing fire, cast more incense upon it, and howled
a magic charm. At once the marble slab moved into its place
and the earth closed over the cave, leaving Aladdin below
ground, unable to come out.

Now, as I have said before, the Moor was really a stranger
and no uncle of Aladdin's. He was an evil sorcerer from the far
interior of Morocco, an African deeply versed in the renowned
black arts of his native land. From his earliest days he had
applied himself to necromancy and witchcraft, so that, after
forty years' study of magic and divination, he learnt one day
that among the remotest cities of China there was a city called
Al-kolo-ats, and that in that city there was a vast treasure the

like of which no king ever amassed. He had also learnt that that treasure contained an enchanted lamp which could make its possessor richer and more powerful than any monarch in the world, and that it could be opened only by a youth of poor parentage called Aladdin, a native of that city. Convinced of the truth of his discovery, he set out forthwith for China, and, after a long and arduous journey, sought out Aladdin and reached the place where the treasure was hidden. But all his labours went in vain, and he resolved to entomb Aladdin underground, so that neither he nor the lamp should come up out of the earth. His great hopes having thus been cheated, the Moor abandoned his quest and journeyed back to Africa with a heavy heart. So much for him.

As for Aladdin, when the earth closed over him he began to shout frantically for help, begging his uncle to stretch out his hand to him and help him to come up out of the cave. When there was no answer to his cries he realized that he had been grossly deceived, and that the Moor was no uncle of his. Giving up all hope of escape, he went down weeping to the bottom of the stairs and felt his way through the dark towards the garden; but the door, which had been opened by enchantment was now shut by the same means. He returned to the cave's entrance and threw himself despondently on the steps. There he sat for three days, without having any food or drink, and finally abandoned all hope of living. He wept and sobbed, praying to Allah to deliver him from his predicament and wringing his hands in despair. Whilst he was wringing his hands together, he chanced to rub the ring which the Moor had given him as a protection. At once a great black ifrit, as tall as one of Solomon's jinn, appeared before him.

'I am here, master, I am here!' the jinnee cried. 'Your slave is at your service. Ask what you will, for I am the slave of him who wears my master's ring.'

The sight of this apparition struck terror to Aladdin's heart. But when he recalled the magician's words, his hope revived and he summoned up all his courage.

'Slave of the ring,' he cried, 'I order you to carry me up to the surface of the earth.'

Scarcely had he uttered these words when the earth was rent asunder and he found himself above ground on the very spot where the marble slab had been. It was some time before his eyes could bear the light after having been so long in total darkness; but when at length he looked about him he was amazed to see no sign of cave or entrance, and would not have recognized the place but for the black cinders left by the magician's fire. In the distance he saw the city shimmering amidst its gardens and hastened joyfully towards it, giving deep thanks to Allah for his deliverance. He reached home worn out with hunger and fatigue, and dropped down fainting before his mother, who, for her part, had been grieving bitterly ever since he left her. The old woman did all she could to restore her son to his senses; she sprinkled water over his face and gave him aromatic herbs to smell. As soon as he came to he begged for something to eat.

'Mother, I am very hungry,' he said. 'Bring me some food, for I have had nothing to eat or drink these three days.'

His mother brought him all the food that she could find, and when he had eaten and recovered his strength a little, he said: 'Know, mother, that the man who said he was my uncle is a Moorish magician, a wicked impostor, a very fiend. He made me those promises only to destroy me. To think how we were deceived by his fine words! Listen, mother, to what he did . . .'

And with that Aladdin proceeded to tell his mother of his adventure with the Moor from beginning to end.

When she had heard his story, Aladdin's mother shook her head. 'I might have known from the very start that the old wretch was no uncle of yours but an unbeliever and a hypocrite,' she said. 'Praise be to Him who has delivered you from his treachery and deceit.'

She went on soothing him in this way until Aladdin, who had not slept a wink for three days, was overcome by sleep. He did not wake till nearly noon the following day, and as soon as he opened his eyes he asked his mother for something to eat.

'Alas, my boy,' she sighed. 'I have not a crust of bread to give you; you ate yesterday all the food I had. But be patient a little. I have some cotton here which I have spun; I shall presently go to the market-place and sell it, and buy you something to eat with the money.'

'Leave your cotton for the time, mother,' Aladdin answered, 'and give me the lamp I brought. I will go and sell it, for it is sure to fetch a better price than your spinning.'

Aladdin's mother brought him the lamp and, noticing that it was dirty, said: 'If we wash and polish it, it will sell for a better price.'

She mixed a little sand in water and began to clean the lamp. But no sooner had she rubbed the surface than a fearsome jinnee of monstrous stature appeared before her, saying: 'What is your wish, mistress? I am your slave and the slave of him who holds the lamp: I and the other slaves of the lamp.'

The old woman, who was not used to seeing such apparitions, was so overcome with terror that she could make no answer; her tongue became knotted in her mouth and she fell fainting to the ground. Now Aladdin had seen the jinnee of the ring in the cave; and when he heard this jinnee speaking to his mother he ran quickly to her aid and snatched the lamp out of her hands.

'Slave of the lamp,' he said, 'I am hungry. Bring me some good things to eat.'

The jinnee vanished and reappeared in a twinkling, carrying upon his head a priceless tray of virgin silver which held twelve dishes of the choicest meats, together with a pair of silver goblets, two flasks of clear old wine, and bread whiter than snow. All these he set down before Aladdin and disappeared again. Seeing that his mother still lay unconscious on the floor, Aladdin sprinkled rose-water over her face and gave her fragrant scents to smell. When she returned to her senses he said: 'Rise, mother. Let us sit down and eat this food which Allah in His great bounty has provided for us.'

Aladdin's mother was much amazed to see the massive silver tray. 'Who may this generous benefactor be who has discovered our poverty and hunger?' she cried. 'We are surely much indebted to him for his kindness. It seems that the Sultan himself has heard of our wretched plight and sent us this tray.'

'Mother,' replied Aladdin, 'this is no time for such questions. Rise, and let us eat. We are famished.'

They sat at the tray and fell to with great relish. Aladdin's mother had never in all her life tasted such delicate food, which was worthy of a king's table. Nor did they know whether the tray was valuable or not, for they had never seen such things before. They ate until they were satisfied; yet enough was left over for supper and the next day. Then they got up, washed their hands, and sat chatting together.

'Now, my child,' said Aladdin's mother, 'tell me what you did with the jinnee. Allah be praised, we have now eaten our fill of his good things. You have no longer the excuse of telling me that you are hungry.'

Aladdin recounted to his mother all that had passed between him and the jinnee from the time she fainted.

'It is quite true,' said the astonished woman. 'The jinn do appear to men; but I never saw any before this. He must be the same jinnee who rescued you in the cavern.'

'No, mother,' Aladdin answered. 'That was another jinnee. The jinnee that appeared to you was the jinnee of the lamp.'

'How is that, my child?' she asked.

'This jinnee was of a different shape,' replied Aladdin. 'The other was the slave of the ring; the one you saw belonged to the lamp which you were holding.'

When she heard this the woman was greatly alarmed. 'My child,' she cried, 'I beg you by the milk which you sucked from me to throw away the lamp and the ring. I am terrified of them, and could not bear to see those jinn again. Besides, it is unlawful for us to have any dealings with them. The Prophet himself, upon whom be Allah's blessing and peace, warned us against them.'

'I would gladly obey you in anything, mother,' Aladdin replied, 'but I cannot afford to lose the lamp or the ring. You have yourself seen how profitable the lamp proved to be when we were hungry. And remember: when I went down into the cave that impostor of a Moor did not ask me for gold or silver, although the four apartments of the treasure were full of them.

He told me to fetch him the lamp and nothing else; for he must have known its great value. If he had not, he would never have endured such hardships or come all the way from his native land in search of it; nor would he have locked me up in the cavern when I refused to hand it to him. That is why we must keep this lamp and take good care of it, for in having it we shall never again be poor or hungry. Also, we must never show it to anyone. As for the ring – I could not bear to lose that either. But for its jinnee I would have surely perished under the earth, inside the treasure. How then can I take it off my finger? Who knows what troubles and misfortunes the future holds for me? This ring will surely save my life. Still, I will hide the lamp away, if you like, so that you need never set eyes on it again.'

'Very well, my boy,' agreed his mother. 'Do as you please. For my part, I will have nothing to do with them, nor do I wish ever to see that fearsome sight again.'

For two days they went on eating the food which the jinnee had brought them, and when it was finished Aladdin took one of the dishes from the magic tray and went with it to the market-place. There he was approached by a Jewish silversmith who was craftier than the Devil. Aladdin, who did not know that it was all of solid silver, offered him the plate; and when the silversmith saw it, he drew his customer aside so that none should see him. He examined the dish with care and found that it was of the purest silver, but did not know whether Aladdin was aware of its true worth, or if he was a gullible fool.

'How much do you want for it, sir?' asked the silversmith.

'*You* should know how much it is worth,' Aladdin answered.

Hearing the boy's competent reply, the silversmith was at a loss how much to pay him. He was at first tempted to give him very little, but feared that Aladdin might know its value. Then he was inclined to give him a substantial sum, but thought it might well be that Aladdin had no knowledge of its worth. At length he took out a gold dinar from his pocket and offered it to him. When Aladdin saw the piece of gold, he took it and ran off in the highest feather, so that the silversmith, realizing that the boy had no idea of its value, bitterly regretted that he had not given him less.

Aladdin hurried away to the baker's and got change by buying some bread; then he ran home and gave the bread and the money to his mother.

'Mother,' he said, 'go and buy for us what we need.'

His mother went down to the market-place and bought all that they required; and the two ate until they were satisfied. Whenever the money ran out, Aladdin would go to the market-place and sell another dish to the silversmith; and thus the cunning old man bought all the plates for very little. Even then he would have wished to give him less; but, having rashly paid him one dinar on the first occasion, he feared that the boy would go and sell elsewhere. When the twelve dishes were all gone Aladdin decided to sell the silver tray. As this was large and heavy, he fetched the old merchant to the house and showed it to him. The silversmith, seeing its tremendous size gave him ten dinars; and with this money Aladdin and his mother were able to provide for themselves several days longer.

When the ten dinars were finished Aladdin took out the lamp and rubbed it. The self-same jinnee appeared before him, saying: 'Master, ask what you will. I am your slave, and the slave of him who holds the lamp.'

'I order you,' said Aladdin, 'to bring me a tray of food like the one you brought before. I am hungry.'

The jinnee vanished, and in the twinkling of an eye returned with a tray exactly like the first one, holding twelve splendid dishes full of delicate meats, two flasks of sparkling wine, and a fine clean loaf. Having been warned beforehand, Aladdin's mother had left the house so that she should not see the jinnee a second time; but when she returned and saw the tray with the silver dishes, and smelt the rich aroma, she marvelled greatly and rejoiced.

'Look, mother!' Aladdin cried. 'You told me to throw the lamp away. See how valuable it is.'

'May Allah richly reward him!' replied the old woman. 'Still, I do not wish ever to see that jinnee again.'

She sat down with her son, and the two ate and drank until they were satisfied. What was left over they stored for the following day. When this was finished, Aladdin took one of the dishes and, hiding it under his robe, went off to search for the old merchant in order to sell it to him. It chanced, however, that whilst he was walking through the market-place he passed by the shop of an honest goldsmith, well known for his piety and fair dealing. The old sheikh stopped Aladdin and greeted him.

'What brings you here, my son?' he asked. 'I have often seen you pass this way and do business with a Jew. I have watched you giving him some articles, and perhaps you have something with you now which you intend to sell him. What an easy prey he must have found you! If you have something to sell, my son, show it to me and, by Allah, I will pay you the right price for it, not a copper less.'

Aladdin showed him the plate, and the goldsmith took it and weighed it in his scales.

'Have you been selling him plates like this one?' inquired the old man.

'Yes,' Aladdin replied.

'How much have you been getting for them?' asked the goldsmith.

'A dinar for each,' Aladdin answered.

'What a blackguard,' exclaimed the goldsmith, 'to rob Allah's servants in this fashion! You must know, my son, that this rogue has cheated you and made a proper fool of you. This dish is made of the purest silver and is worth no less than seventy dinars. If you are willing to accept this price, take it.'

The goldsmith counted out seventy dinars, and Aladdin took the gold and thanked the old man for his kindness. In due course he sold him the other dishes, at the same honest price. In this way Aladdin and his mother grew wealthier and wealthier, yet they continued to live modestly, avoiding extravagance and ostentatious waste.

Aladdin now renounced his idle ways and old companions and passed all his time in the markets of the city, conversing with personages of distinction and merchants great and small.

He also visited the bazaars of the goldsmiths and jewellers, where he would sit and watch the jewels being bought and sold. Before long he came to realize that the varied fruits which he had brought back from the treasure were no coloured glass or crystal but gems beyond the wealth of kings. He examined all the jewels in the market, but found none to be compared with the smallest of his own. Thus he went on frequenting the jewellers' shops, so that he might become acquainted with the people and learn from them the affairs of trade. He asked them questions about buying and selling, taking and giving, and in time came to know what was cheap and what was costly.

It so chanced one morning that whilst he was on his way to the jewellers' market he heard a herald crying in the streets: 'By command of our Royal Master, King of the time, Sovereign of the age and the moment! Let all the people close their shops and retire at once behind the doors of their houses: for the Princess Badr-al-Budur, the Sultan's daughter, desires this day to visit the baths. If anyone disregards this order he shall be punished by instant death and his blood shall be upon his own head.'

When he heard this proclamation Aladdin was seized with a great desire to see the Sultan's daughter, for her loveliness was the talk of all the people. He began casting around for some way to look upon her, and at length decided that it was best to stand behind the door of the baths and see her face as she entered. Without losing a moment, he ran straight off to the baths and hid himself behind the great door, where none could see him. Presently the Princess left the palace, and, after riding through the streets and seeing the sights of the city, halted at the baths. She lifted her veil as she went in; and her face shone like the radiant sun, or a brilliant pearl.

'Truly,' murmured Aladdin to himself, 'she is a wondrous tribute to her Maker! Praise be to Him who created her and decked her with such loveliness and beauty!'

As he gazed upon her Aladdin felt confused and bewildered; his eyes were dazzled and love took full possession of his heart. Many a time he had heard tell of Badr-al-Budur's beauty, but he had thought that all women looked like his mother. He returned home, all in a daze. His mother began questioning him anxiously, but he made no answer; she brought him his dinner, but he refused to eat.

'What has come over you, my child?' she asked. 'Are you ill? Have you any pain? Tell me, my son, I pray you.'

'Let me alone, mother,' he replied.

His mother went on pressing him to eat, and at last he ate a little. Then he threw himself upon his bed, where he lay musing listlessly all night and throughout the following day. Greatly troubled over his odd behaviour, the old woman questioned him again, saying: 'If you are in pain, my child, tell me and I will call the doctor. There is an Arab doctor in our city now; he was sent for by the Sultan. Stories of his great skill are on every tongue. Shall I go and fetch him for you?'

'I am not ill,' Aladdin replied. 'I am quite well. Only I thought that all women looked like you, mother. But yesterday I saw the Princess Badr-al-Budur when she was going to the baths. I saw her as she really is, for when she entered she lifted off her veil. As I looked on her face and saw her exquisite features, my heart and all my limbs quivered with love for her, mother. I shall know no rest until I have won her in marriage from her father the Sultan.'

When she heard him say this, his mother thought he had gone mad.

'The name of Allah shield you, my child!' she exclaimed. 'You must be out of your mind. Come, return to your senses and do not behave like a madman.'

'I am not mad, mother,' Aladdin replied. 'Whatever you say, I shall never change my mind. I cannot rest until I win the fair Badr-al-Budur, the treasure of my heart. I am resolved to demand her of her father.'

'Do not say such things, I beg you!' cried the old woman. 'If the neighbours hear you they will say you are possessed. Think no more of these extravagant fancies. Why, who would undertake to demand such a thing of the Sultan? Even if you do embark on such a hazard, through whom do you intend to present your suit?'

'Who else should present my suit for me when I have you, mother?' he answered. 'Whom can I trust more than you? I want you to go yourself and deliver my petition.'

'Allah preserve me from such a thing!' she exclaimed. 'Do you think I am mad too? Consider who you are, my child. Your father was the poorest tailor in this city and I, your mother, come from scarcely nobler folk. How then can you presume to demand the Sultan's daughter? Her father will marry her only to some illustrious prince, no less powerful and noble than himself.'

'I have thought about all this, mother,' replied Aladdin, who had been listening to her patiently. 'But nothing will deter me in the least from my resolve. If you love me as your son, mother, I beg you to do this kindness for me. Do not let me perish; for I shall surely die if I fail to win my heart's beloved. Remember, mother, I am your son.'

'Yes, my son,' the old woman sobbed. 'I am your mother, and you are my only child. My dearest wish is to see you married, and to rejoice in your happiness. If you want to marry, I will seek for you a wife who is your equal. But even then I shall not know what to answer when they ask me if you have any trade or property. And if I cannot give any answer to humble people like ourselves, how can I presume to ask the King of China for his only daughter? Think of it, my child. And who is it that wants to wed her? A tailor's son! Why, I know for sure that if I speak of such a thing we shall be utterly ruined; it may even put us in danger of our lives. Besides, how can I ever bring myself to make so impudent and reckless a demand? How am I to gain access to the Sultan? If they ask me questions, what answers can I give them? They will probably think I am a maniac. And supposing that I do gain admittance to the Sultan, what gift can I present him with? Yes, my son, I know that our Sultan is very kind and never sends away any of his subjects empty-handed or without justice done; I know that he extends his munificence to all men. But he bestows his favours only upon those who deserve them or have acquitted themselves nobly in his service. Now tell me, child; what have you done for the Sultan or his kingdom to be worthy of such a favour? Again, as I said before, no one ever goes to petition the Sultan without a rich present to lay at his feet. What gift have you to offer him that is worthy of his royal station?'

'What you say is quite true, mother,' Aladdin replied. 'You ask me what present I have to offer the Sultan. Know then that I can offer him a gift the like of which no monarch has ever possessed. Those coloured fruits which I brought with me from the treasure, supposing them to be glass or crystal, are jewels of incalculable worth; not all the kings in the world have the least one of them. I have been going round with jewellers of late, and I know now that they are priceless gems. If you wish to judge them for yourself, bring me a large china dish and I will show you. I am convinced that with a present such as this your errand will be quite easy. Make no mistake about the value of these jewels. I have often seen the jewellers sell at enormous prices stones that are worth but little compared with ours.'

Half in doubt, the old woman rose and brought him a large china dish. She set it before Aladdin, who took out the jewels from their hiding-place and ranged them skilfully on the plate. As she looked upon them, his mother's eyes were dazzled by their rich lustre.

'Do you see, mother?' said Aladdin to the dumbfounded woman. 'Can there be a more magnificent present for the Sultan? I have no doubt that you will be well received and highly honoured by him. Rise now, take the dish, and go to the Sultan's palace.'

'Yes, my son,' she answered. 'I admit that your present is both precious and unique. But who in heaven's name could make so bold as to stand before the Sultan and demand of him his daughter? When he asks me: "What do you want?" my courage will surely fail me and I shall be speechless with confusion. And supposing that, by Allah's will, I did have enough courage to deliver your proposal, they would certainly think me insane and dismiss me from his presence with contumely and insults; and what is more, both you and I might well incur the penalty of death. Still, for your sake I must take heart and go. But, my child, if the Sultan was pleased to accept your present and ask me, as people always do on such occasions, about your standing and your income, what am I to tell him? Indeed, this may well be the first question he will ask me.'

'The Sultan will never ask you that after seeing these splendid jewels,' Aladdin replied. 'Do not burden your mind with groundless fears, but go boldly about your errand and offer him these gems; for, remember, I have a lamp that brings me whatever I want. If the Sultan asks you such a question, the lamp will provide me with the answer.'

They went on chatting together for the rest of that night. In the morning Aladdin's mother rose and made ready for her interview with a cheerful heart, especially when she understood the properties of the lamp and all that it could do. After Aladdin had charged her to tell no one about the secret, she wrapped the dish of gems in a handsome shawl and made her way betimes to the Sultan's palace, in order that she might gain access to the audience-hall before it was crowded. When she arrived the hall was not yet full; so she watched the Vizier and some of the nobles as they passed into the Sultan's court. Presently the hall was filled with viziers and courtiers, nabobs and princes and great ones of the palace; then the King himself entered, while the others stood up in respectful silence. The Sultan sat upon his throne, and at his bidding all those present took their seats, according to their rank.

The petitioners were now summoned before the King, and every cause was judged upon its merits; but the greater part of them had to be dismissed for lack of time. Among these last was Aladdin's mother; for though she had arrived before the others, no one spoke to her or offered to take her before the Sultan. When the audience had finished and the Sultan had retired, she made her way back to her own house. As soon as Aladdin saw his mother returning with the dish, he knew that something untoward must have occurred; but he did not wish to question her until she had come in and told him what had happened.

'Allah be thanked, my son,' she said at last. 'I plucked up enough courage to enter the audience-hall today, even if, like many others, I could not speak to the Sultan. But have no fears. If Allah wills, I shall speak to him tomorrow.'

Although vexed at the delay, Aladdin rejoiced at his mother's words and consoled himself with hope and patience. Next morning his mother took the dish and went again to the Sultan's palace, but found the audience-chamber closed. Upon inquiry she was informed that the King held an audience only thrice a week, so that she was obliged that day to return home. Thenceforth she went to the palace every day; when she found the hall open she would stand helplessly by until the audience was finished and then make her way home; on other days she would find it closed. This she continued to do for a whole week, and at the end of the final session the King, who had noticed her presence at every audience, said to his vizier as they left the court: 'For six or seven days I have seen that old woman come to the palace with something under her cloak. What does she want?'

'Women have petty minds, your majesty,' answered the Vizier. 'Perhaps this woman has been coming to complain of her husband or one of her people.'

The King, however, would not be put off by this reply. He ordered the Vizier to bring her before him if she came once more.

'I hear and obey, your majesty,' answered the Vizier, lifting his hand to his brow.

Next morning the King saw Aladdin's mother standing wearily in the audience-hall, as on the previous days.

'That is the woman about whom I spoke to you yesterday,' he said to his vizier. 'Bring her to me now, so that I can look into her cause and grant her her request.'

The Vizier rose at once and led Aladdin's mother before the Sultan. She fell on her knees and, kissing the ground before him, wished him long life and everlasting glory.

'Woman,' said the King, 'I have seen you come to the audience a number of times and stand there asking nothing. Make known to me your request, that I may grant it.'

Aladdin's mother again called down blessings upon the Sultan and, once more kissing the ground, said: 'Before making my request, great King, I beg you to promise me immunity, in case my plea sounds strange to your majesty's ears.'

Being of a generous and indulgent nature, the Sultan promised her immunity and ordered the audience-chamber to be cleared so that she might speak up freely. When all but the Grand Vizier had been dismissed, he turned to Aladdin's mother and said: 'Speak, woman, for you are now under Allah's protection.'

'Great King,' she said, 'I also beg your forgiveness.'

'Allah forgive you,' he replied.

'I have a son called Aladdin, your majesty,' the old woman began. 'One day he heard the crier bidding the people keep to their houses because Princess Badr-al-Budur was going to the baths. When my son heard this he longed to see her; he hid himself behind the door of the baths and saw her as she went in. He loved her from that instant, and has not known a moment's peace ever since. He has asked me to entreat your majesty to marry her to him; and try as I might, I could not free his mind of this obsession. "Mother," he has said to me, "if I do not win my heart's beloved, I shall surely perish." I beg you, great King, to be indulgent and to forgive me and my son for the audacity of this request.'

When she had finished speaking, the Sultan laughed benevolently and said: 'Now tell me what you are carrying in that bundle.'

Noticing that the Sultan was not angry, Aladdin's mother undid the shawl and presented him with the plate of jewels. At once the entire hall was lit up as if by chandeliers and coloured torches; and as he gazed at the jewels the dumbfounded King marvelled at their brilliance, their size, and their beauty.

'Never in all my life have I seen the like of these jewels!' he exclaimed. 'I do not think there is a single stone in my treasuries to be compared with them. What do you say, Vizier? Have you ever seen the like of these marvels?'

'Never, your majesty,' agreed the Vizier. 'I doubt if the smallest of them is to be found in all your treasures.'

'Then do you not think,' said the Sultan, 'that this young man who sent them to me is worthier of my daughter's hand than any other?'

The Vizier was greatly troubled to hear this, and did not know what to answer; for the King had promised Badr-al-Budur to his own son.

'Great King,' he ventured after a short silence, 'perhaps you will be so indulgent as to let me remind your majesty that you have promised the Princess to my son. I therefore beg your highness to allow him a delay of three months in which to find, if Allah wills, a dowry greater than this.'

The Sultan knew full well that neither the Vizier nor the richest monarch in the world could find him a dowry equal to the present which he had just received; but, as he did not wish to offend his minister, he granted him the delay he had requested.

'Go to your son,' he said to the old woman, 'and tell him that my daughter shall be his. Only the marriage cannot take place before three months, as there are preparations to be made.'

Aladdin's mother thanked the King and called down blessings upon him. Then she hurried back to her house in a transport of joy. When Aladdin saw her return without the dish, and observed the happy smile on her face, he took it as a good omen.

'Allah willing, mother,' he cried, 'you have brought me good news. I pray that the jewels have won the Sultan's heart. He has received you graciously and listened to your request.'

His mother told him how the Sultan had received the jewels and marvelled at their size and beauty.

'He promised that the Princess should be yours,' she added. 'But the Vizier whispered to him in private, and after that he said the marriage could not take place before three months. My son, I fear that the Vizier may use his cunning to change the Sultan's mind.'

Despite the long delay, Aladdin was overjoyed at the Sultan's promise and warmly thanked his mother for her labours.

'By Allah, mother,' he said, 'it seems as though I have been dead and you have given me fresh life. Allah be praised for that. Surely now I am the richest and happiest of men!'

For two months Aladdin patiently counted the days that separated him from the great occasion. Then one evening his mother went out to buy some oil and, as she walked down the street, noticed that the shops were closed and all the city decked and lighted. The windows were hung with flowers and candles, and the squares thronged with troops and mounted dignitaries carrying torches in their hands. Puzzled by all this, the old woman entered an oil-shop that was open and, after buying what she needed, inquired the cause of the commotion.

'Why, good woman!' replied the oil-vendor. 'You must surely be a stranger in our city, not to know that this is the bridal night of Princess Badr-al-Budur and the Grand Vizier's son. He will soon be coming out of the baths; those officers and soldiers will escort him to the palace, where the Sultan's daughter is waiting for him.'

Aladdin's mother was profoundly dismayed on hearing these words. She returned home with a heavy heart, not knowing how to break the alarming news to her son.

'My child,' said she, as soon as she entered the house, 'I have some bad news to tell you. But I fear that it will deeply grieve you.'

'What news, mother?' asked Aladdin impatiently.

'Alas, the King has broken his promise to you,' she answered. 'This very night the Vizier's son is to wed Princess Badr-al-Budur. Oh, how I dreaded that the Vizier would change the Sultan's mind! I told you he whispered something to him after he had accepted your proposal.'

'And how do you know,' asked Aladdin, 'that the Vizier's son is to marry Badr-al-Budur tonight?'

His mother described to him all that she had seen in the city: the lights and decorations, the soldiers and dignitaries waiting to escort the Vizier's son on his bridal night. On hearing this Aladdin was seized with a feverish rage; but soon, remembering the lamp, he regained possession of himself.

'Upon your life, mother,' he said, 'I do not think the Vizier's son will enjoy his bride tonight. Let us say no more about this. Rise, and cook the dinner. After that I will go into my room and see what can be done. All will be well, I tell you.'

After dinner Aladdin shut himself in his own room and locked the door. He then brought out the lamp and rubbed it. At once the jinnee appeared, saying: 'Ask what you will. I am your slave, and the slave of him who holds the lamp: I and the other slaves of the lamp.'

'Listen carefully,' said Aladdin. 'I asked the Sultan for his daughter and he promised that I could wed her after three months. But he has not kept his promise, and is marrying her instead to the Vizier's son. Tonight the wedding takes place. Now I command you, if you are indeed a trustworthy slave of the lamp, to carry the bride and bridegroom in their bed to this house as soon as you see them lie down together. I myself will look after the rest.'

'I hear and obey,' replied the jinnee. 'Is there anything else you require me to do?'

'Nothing at present,' Aladdin answered.

The jinnee vanished, and Aladdin went back to his mother and sat talking with her. When he thought the time had come for the jinnee to return, he shut himself in his room again. In a few moments the slave of the lamp appeared with the newly wed couple lying in their bed. Aladdin rejoiced exceedingly.

'Take up this wretch,' he cried to the jinnee, 'and put him to sleep in the privy.'

At once the jinnee carried away the Vizier's son; he laid him down in the privy and, petrifying his body with a single breath, left him there in a pitiful state. Then he returned to Aladdin.

'Master, what else do you require?' he asked. 'Speak, and it shall be done.'

'Come in the morning,' Aladdin answered. 'Then you may carry them back to the palace.'

'I hear and obey,' replied the jinnee; and so saying he vanished.

Aladdin could scarcely believe that all this had truly come to pass. When he found himself alone with Badr-al-Budur, he did not for a single moment allow his longing to get the better of him, although he loved her with a consuming passion.

'Fairest of women,' he said, 'do not think that I brought you here to abuse your honour; Allah forbid. I did this only to let no one else enjoy you, for your father the Sultan gave me his word that you should be my bride. Do not be alarmed; no harm shall touch you here.'

When the Princess suddenly found herself in that dark and dismal dwelling, and heard Aladdin's words, she was so overcome with terror that she could make no answer. Presently Aladdin got up, undressed, and laid himself beside her on the bed, placing an unsheathed sword between them. But because of her fright the Princess slept not a wink all night. Nor did the Vizier's son, who lay petrified in the closet, fare any better.

Next morning the jinnee returned without Aladdin rubbing the lamp.

'Master,' he said, 'command, and I will gladly do your bidding.'

'Go,' cried Aladdin. 'Carry the bride and bridegroom back to the Sultan's palace.'

In a twinkling the jinnee did as Aladdin told him. He laid the Vizier's son beside Badr-al-Budur and carried them both to the royal palace, so swiftly that the terrified couple could not see who had thus transported them. Scarcely had the jinnee set them down and disappeared, when the Sultan came in to visit his daughter. This greatly distressed the Vizier's son, for he was just beginning to warm himself after his dreary night in the closet. However, he jumped to his feet and put on his clothes.

The Sultan kissed his daughter between the eyes and bade her good morning. Then he asked her if she was pleased with her husband. But the girl looked dolefully at him and said nothing. He questioned her again and again, and still she made no answer. At length he angrily left her room and, betaking himself to the Queen, gave her an account of his daughter's strange behaviour.

'Your majesty,' said the Queen, wishing to allay his anger,

'most brides are a little coy and bashful after their wedding night. Do not be harsh with her. In a short time she will return to her former ways and talk to people freely; it is sheer modesty that prevents her now. But I will presently go and speak to her myself.'

So saying, the Queen put on her clothes and went to visit her daughter. She came up to Badr-al-Budur and, kissing her between the eyes, wished her good morning. But the Princess uttered not a word in reply.

'Something very odd must have befallen her to upset her so,' thought the Queen to herself. 'What grief is this, my daughter?' she asked. 'Tell me what has happened. Here I am, wishing you good morning, and you do not even return my greeting.'

'Do not be angry with me, mother,' said the Princess, raising her head, 'but forgive the scant courtesy with which I have received you. I pray you to let me explain my present state. Look what a miserable night I passed! Scarcely had we lain down together, when someone came – we could not see who he was – and carried us away, bed and all, to a mean, dark, and squalid place.'

Badr-al-Budur recounted to her mother all that had passed during the night: how her husband had been taken away from her and replaced by another youth who slept by her side with a sword between them.

'Then, this morning,' she continued, 'he who took us away returned and brought us back to this very chamber. As soon as he had set us down and gone, my father entered; but such was my terror at that moment that I had neither heart nor tongue to speak to him. If, for this reason, I have incurred his displeasure, I pray you to explain to him what has happened, so that he should not blame but pardon me for my offence.'

'Dear child!' exclaimed the Queen. 'Take care not to tell this story to anyone else. They will say the Sultan's daughter has gone mad. You were wise not to tell your father of all this. Say nothing about it to him, I warn you.'

'But, mother, I am not mad,' replied Badr-al-Budur. 'I have

told you nothing but the truth. If you do not believe me, ask my husband.'

'Rise up, child,' said the Queen, 'and think no more of these wild delusions. Put on your clothes, and go and watch the festivities that are being held all over the city in your honour. Listen to the drums and the singing; and look at these decorations, all celebrating your happy marriage.'

The Queen at once called her women, who dressed the Princess and made her toilet. Then, returning to the Sultan, she told him that Badr-al-Budur had had dreams and nightmares, and begged him not to be angry with her. She next sent in secret for the Vizier's son and questioned him.

'Your majesty, I know nothing of what you say,' he answered, fearing lest he should lose his bride.

The Queen was now convinced that Badr-al-Budur was suffering from some nightmare or hallucination. The festivities went on all day, with dancers and singers performing in the palace, to the accompaniment of all manner of music. The Queen, the Vizier, and the Vizier's son did all they could to stir the revelry, to cheer the bride and dissipate her gloom. But for all their efforts she remained silent and morose, brooding over the happenings of the previous night. True, having slept in the privy, the Vizier's son had suffered even more than she. But he denied it all and chose to forget his wrong, fearing that he might forfeit his bride and the honour that had been done him, especially as everyone envied him his luck in marrying a girl so noble and so fair as Badr-al-Budur.

Aladdin went out that day and watched the rejoicings in the city and the palace with laughter in his heart; particularly when he heard the people speak of the distinction which the Vizier's son had gained, and how fortunate he was to have become the Sultan's son-in-law.

'Poor fools!' he thought to himself. 'If only you knew what happened to him last night!'

In the evening Aladdin went into his room and rubbed the lamp. When the jinnee came he ordered him to bring the Sultan's daughter and her bridegroom as on the previous night, before the Vizier's son could touch her. The slave of the lamp vanished, and returned at once with the bed and the couple. Then he carried the young man to the closet, where he left him petrified with fear. Aladdin rose, placed the sword between himself and the Princess, and slept by her side. In the morning the jinnee brought back the husband and returned the bed to the palace. Aladdin was greatly pleased with the progress of his plan.

When the Sultan woke up, his first thought was to go and visit his daughter, to see if she would act as on the day before. Immediately rising, he put on his clothes and betook himself to Badr-al-Budur's apartment. On hearing the door open the Vizier's son leapt up from the bed and hurriedly dressed himself, his ribs almost splitting with the cold; for the slave of the lamp had just brought them back to the palace. The Sultan came up to his daughter, lifted the curtains, and kissing her between the eyes wished her good morning. He asked her how she was, but instead of answering she frowned and looked sullenly at him; for she was now in a desperate state of bewilderment and dejection. Her silence greatly provoked the Sultan, who at once knew that she was hiding something from him.

'What has come over you, my girl?' he cried, drawing his sword. 'Tell me the truth, or I will cut off your head this instant. Is this the respect you owe me? I speak to you, and you do not answer me with a single word.'

Badr-al-Budur was terrified to see her father brandishing his sword at her.

'Do not be angry with me, I beg you,' she replied, raising her head. 'When you have heard what I have suffered these last two nights, you will excuse and pity me; for I have always known you as a most loving father.'

Thereupon she recounted to the Sultan all that had happened.

'And now, father,' she added, 'if you wish to confirm what I have said, ask my husband. He will tell you everything. I do not know what they did to him when they took him away, or where they put him.'

The Sultan was profoundly moved by his daughter's words,

and his eyes filled with tears. He sheathed his sword, and, kissing her tenderly, said: 'My child, why did you not tell me of all this, so that I could have protected you from those terrors last night? But have no fear; rise up, and dismiss these morbid thoughts. Tonight I will post guards about your room, and you shall be secure from all dangers.'

The Sultan returned to his apartment, and at once sent for the Vizier.

'What do you think of this business?' he cried, as soon as the Vizier presented himself before him. 'Perhaps your son has told you what happened to him and my daughter?'

'Your majesty, I have not seen my son these two days,' the Vizier answered.

The King told him Badr-al-Budur's story.

'Now go to your son,' he added, 'and find out the whole truth from him. My daughter may be so frightened that she does not really know what has happened; though, for my part, I am inclined to believe her.'

The Vizier summoned his son and asked him if what the Sultan had said was true or not.

'Allah forbid that Princess Badr al Budur should tell a lie,' answered the young man. 'All that she says is true. These last two nights have been a nightmare to us both, instead of being full of delight and joy. What happened to me was even worse. Instead of sleeping with my bride, all night I was locked up in the privy, a dark, frightful, stinking place. My ribs were almost split with cold.'

And he related the story to him in all its details.

'I now beg you, dear father,' he concluded, 'to speak to the Sultan and request him to release me from this marriage. I know it is a great honour to be the Sultan's son-in-law, especially as I am so deeply in love with the Princess. But I cannot endure again what I suffered these last two nights.'

The Vizier was greatly troubled by these words. His fondest wish had been to marry his son to the Sultan's daughter and thus make him an illustrious man. He brooded long over the ordeal, and did not know what he should do; for it grieved him much to terminate the marriage, which he had striven with such zeal to bring about.

'Be patient a little, my son,' he said at last. 'Let us see what happens tonight. We will post armed men about your chamber. Do not so rashly cast away this great honour; no one else but you has achieved it.'

The Vizier left his son and, returning to the Sultan, informed him that the Princess's story was true.

'Then here and now,' rejoined the Sultan, 'I declare the marriage null and void.' And he at once gave orders that the rejoicings should cease and the marriage be dissolved.

The people of the city were amazed at the sudden change, especially when they saw the Vizier and his son coming out of the palace with a forlorn and angry look. They began to ask what had happened and why the marriage had been broken off. But nobody knew the secret except Aladdin, who was full of glee at the odd proceedings.

Now the King forgot the promise he had given to Aladdin's mother. When the three months elapsed, Aladdin sent his mother to demand the fulfilment of the Sultan's pledge. So the old woman went off to the palace, and as soon as she entered the audience-hall the King recognized her.

'Here comes the woman who presented me with the jewels,' said the Sultan, turning to his vizier. 'I gave her my word that after three months I would marry my daughter to her son. Go and bring her before me.'

The Vizier brought Aladdin's mother before the Sultan, and after she had kissed the ground and wished him everlasting glory he asked her what she wanted.

'Your majesty,' she said, 'the three months are up after which you promised to wed your daughter Princess Badr-al-Budur to my son Aladdin.'

The Sultan was at a loss what to answer, for it was all too plain that the woman was very poor, one of the humblest of his subjects. Yet the present she had brought him was indeed beyond price.

'What do you suggest now?' he asked the Vizier in a whisper. 'It is perfectly true that I made her such a promise.

But it is obvious they are lowly folk, with nothing to recommend them socially.'

The Vizier, who still bitterly resented his humiliation, was overwhelmed with envy and thought to himself: 'How can such a wretch marry the Princess, and my son forfeit the honour?'

'Your majesty,' he replied, 'that is no difficult thing. We must surely rebuff this stranger; for it scarcely befits your highness to give away your daughter to such an ignorant upstart.'

'But how can we get rid of him?' rejoined the Sultan. 'I gave him my word, and a king's word must needs be kept.'

'I suggest,' said the Vizier, 'that you demand of him forty dishes of pure gold filled with jewels like the ones he has already sent you; the dishes to be carried in by forty slave-girls, attended by forty slaves.'

'By Allah, you have spoken well, my vizier,' replied the Sultan. 'That is something he can never do; in this way we shall once for all be rid of him.'

The Sultan then turned to Aladdin's mother and said: 'Go to your son and tell him that I stand by my promise. The marriage will take place when he has sent a fitting dowry for my daughter. I shall require of him forty dishes of pure gold filled with the same kind of jewels you brought me, together with forty slave-girls to carry them and forty slaves. If your son can provide this dowry, my daughter shall be his.'

Aladdin's mother silently retired, and set out for home crestfallen.

'Where will my poor boy get all those dishes and jewels from?' she thought to herself, shaking her head. 'Even if he returns to the treasure and strips the magic trees of their jewels – not that I really believe he can do this, but suppose he does – where in heaven's name are the forty girls and forty slaves to come from?' Deep in these reflections, the old woman trudged along until she reached her house, where Aladdin was waiting for her.

'My child,' she said, as soon as she entered, 'did I not tell you to give up all thought of Badr-al-Budur? Did I not warn you that such a thing was impossible for people like ourselves?'

'Tell me what happened,' Aladdin exclaimed.

'The Sultan received me very kindly,' she replied, 'and I believe he was well disposed towards you. But your enemy is that damnable Vizier. When I had spoken to the Sultan and reminded him of his promise, he conferred with his vizier, and the scoundrel whispered to him in secret. After that the King gave me his answer.'

And she told Aladdin of the dowry the Sultan had demanded.

'My child,' she added, 'the King expects your answer now. But I do not think there is any answer we can give him.'

'So that is what you think, mother?' Aladdin replied, laughing. 'You think it is quite impossible. Rise up, now, and get for us something to eat; then, Allah willing, you shall see the answer for yourself. Like you, the Sultan thought that his demand was beyond my power. In fact, he has demanded but a trifle. Go, I say, and get dinner ready. The rest you can leave to me.'

His mother got up, and went off to the market-place to buy the food she needed. Meanwhile Aladdin entered his room, took the lamp, and rubbed it. At once the jinnee appeared, saying: 'Master, ask what you will!'

'The Sultan is willing to give me his daughter,' Aladdin said. 'But I must send him forty dishes of pure gold, each ten pounds in weight, filled to the brim with jewels like those in the garden of the treasure-house. The dishes must be carried by forty girls, with forty slaves to attend them. Go and bring me these without delay.'

'I hear and obey,' replied the jinnee.

The slave of the lamp vanished, and after a while returned with forty girls, each attended by a handsome slave; on their heads the girls bore dishes of pure gold full of priceless gems. The jinnee led them before his master, and asked him if there was any other service he could render.

'Nothing at present,' Aladdin answered. 'If I require anything else I shall call you.'

The jinnee disappeared again. Presently Aladdin's mother

returned from the market-place, and was much amazed to see the house crowded with so many slaves.

'Can all this be the work of the lamp?' she exclaimed. 'May Allah preserve it for my boy!'

Before she had time to take off her veil, Aladdin said: 'Mother, there is not one moment to be lost. Before the Sultan enters his palace and goes into his harem, take him the dowry he has asked for. Go to him now, so that he may know that I can give him all he demanded, and more besides. Then he will realize that he has been fooled by the Vizier, and that I am not to be put off by such excuses.'

With that Aladdin rose and, opening the door of the house, led out the girls and the slaves in pairs headed by his mother, so that they filled the entire quarter. When the passers-by beheld this wondrous spectacle they stopped and marvelled at the beauty of the girls, who were arrayed in robes woven of gold and studded with jewels the smallest of which was worth a fortune. They also gazed at the dishes, and saw that they surpassed the sun in their flaming brightness; each dish was covered with a kerchief embroidered in gold and sewn with precious gems.

Aladdin's mother led forth the great procession, and as they passed from street to street the people crowded round, agog with wonder and exclamation. At length the procession came to the palace and wound its way into the courtyard. The commanders and the chamberlains marvelled greatly at the sight, for never in all their lives had they seen the like: especially the girls, whose beauty would have ravished the heart of a hermit; yet the commanders and the chamberlains were all high-born and worthy men. They were even more astonished at the magnificent robes the girls were wearing, and the dishes upon their heads, which glowed with such fiery radiance that they could scarcely open their eyes to look at them.

The courtiers went and informed the Sultan, who at once ordered them to be brought in. Aladdin's mother led them into his presence, and they all gravely saluted the King and called down blessings upon him. Then they set down their plates and, after lifting the covers, stood upright with their arms crossed over their breasts. The Sultan was filled with wonderment at the rare elegance of the girls, whose beauty beggared description. He was dumbfounded when he saw the golden dishes brim-full with dazzling gems, and was even more bewildered as to how all this could have happened in such a short time. Presently he ordered the slave-girls to carry their dishes to Badr-al-Budur's apartment, and when they had done so Aladdin's mother came forward and said: 'Your majesty, this meagre present is by no means equal to Badr-al-Budur's nobility. She deserves much more than those jewels.'

'What do you say now?' said the Sultan in a whisper, turning to the Vizier. 'What shall be said of a man who can produce so much riches in such a short time? Does he not deserve to be the Sultan's son-in-law and take the Sultan's daughter for his bride?'

Now the Vizier had been even more amazed than the Sultan at this prodigious wealth; but envy rankled in his heart, especially when he knew that the King was pleased with Aladdin's dowry.

'Your majesty,' he cunningly replied. 'Not all the treasures of the world are worthy of Badr-al-Budur's fingernail. Surely you overrate this dowry in comparison with your daughter.'

Realizing that the Vizier's words were prompted by his envy, the Sultan turned to Aladdin's mother and said: 'Woman, go to your son and tell him that I accept his dowry. I stand by my promise; my daughter shall be his bride. Tell him to come to the palace, that I may meet him. He shall be received with the utmost honour and consideration. The wedding shall begin this very night; only, as I told you, let him come here without delay.'

Enraptured at her son's prospects, the old woman ran home more swiftly than the wind to give the good news to Aladdin. As soon as she was gone the King dismissed his court, and, repairing to the Princess's chamber, ordered the slave-girls to be brought in with the dishes, so that Badr-al-Budur could look at them. The Princess marvelled at the size of the jewels and the beauty of the slave-girls, and was delighted to know that all this had been sent to her by her new husband. Her father, too, rejoiced to see her so happy, and no longer cast down with gloom and dejection.

'Are you pleased with this present, my daughter?' he asked. 'I am sure that this young man will prove a better husband than the Vizier's son. Allah willing, you will be happy with him.'

So much for the Sultan. As for Aladdin, when he saw his mother enter the house beaming with joy, he knew that her mission had been successful.

'Glory to Allah!' he exclaimed. 'My hopes are now fulfilled.'

'Rejoice, my boy,' cried the old woman. 'You have attained your wish. The Sultan has accepted your present, and the Princess is to be your bride. This very night the wedding will take place. The King has proclaimed you before the whole world as his son-in-law, and desires that you should call on him without delay. Allah be thanked, my task is done.'

Aladdin kissed his mother's hand and thanked her with all his heart. Then he retired to his chamber, took up the lamp, and rubbed it. At once the jinnee appeared, saying: 'I am here. Ask what you will!'

'Slave of the lamp,' said Aladdin, 'I order you to take me to a bath more magnificent than any in the world, also to bring me a splendid regal suit such as no king has ever worn.'

'I hear and obey,' replied the jinnee.

So saying, he took Aladdin upon his shoulder and in a twinkling brought him to a bath such as neither king nor emperor ever saw. It was made of agate and alabaster, and adorned with wondrous paintings that dazzled the eye. No mortal troubled the peace of that white vault. The slave of the lamp led him into an inner hall, thickly studded with jewels and precious stones, and there he was received and washed by a jinnee in human shape. After his bath Aladdin was led back into the outer vault, where, instead of his former clothes, he found a magnificent regal suit. Cool drinks were brought to him and coffee flavoured with amber; and when he had refreshed himself there came into the hall a train of slaves who perfumed him and dressed him in his sumptuous robes.

Aladdin, as you know, was the son of a poor tailor; yet anyone who saw him now would have taken him for some illustrious prince. Glory be to Him who changes others and remains Himself unchanged!

As soon as Aladdin was dressed, the jinnee appeared again and carried him back to his own house.

'Master,' said the jinnee, 'is there anything else that you require?'

'Yes,' Aladdin replied. 'I want you to bring me a retinue of four dozen slaves, two dozen to ride before me and two dozen to ride behind me, complete with livery, horses, and weapons. Both slaves and horses must be arrayed in the finest and the best. After that bring me a thoroughbred steed worthy of an emperor's stable, with trappings all of gold studded with rich jewels. You must also bring me forty-eight thousand dinars, a thousand with each slave. Do not delay; all these must be ready before I go to the Sultan. Lastly, be careful to select twelve girls of incomparable beauty, dressed in the most exquisite clothes, to accompany my mother to the royal palace; and let each girl bring with her a robe that would do credit to a queen.'

'I hear and obey,' replied the jinnee.

He vanished, and in the twinkling of an eye returned with everything that Aladdin had asked for. In his hand he held the bridle of a horse unrivalled among all the Arabian steeds for beauty, with trappings of the finest cloth-of-gold. Aladdin at once called his mother and gave her charge of the twelve girls; he also gave her a robe to put on when she went with her attendants to the royal palace. Then he sent one of the slaves to see whether the Sultan had come out of his harem. The slave departed, and in a flash returned, saying: 'Master, the King awaits you.'

Aladdin mounted his horse, while his attendants (glory be to Allah who created them and endowed them with such comeliness and beauty!) mounted before and behind him. As they rode they scattered handfuls of gold among the crowd before their master Aladdin, who would have put to shame the greatest of princes: so handsome and radiant he looked. Glory be to the bountiful Giver, the Everlasting! All this was due to the power of the magic lamp; for whoever possessed it acquired beauty, wealth, and all knowledge. The people marvelled at Aladdin's generosity and surpassing munificence; they were amazed at his good looks, his politeness and dignified bearing. They praised the Merciful for such a noble creature, and called down blessings upon him, although they knew him to be the son of a humble tailor. No one envied him: they all swore that he deserved it.

Meanwhile the Sultan had assembled the great ones of his kingdom to inform them of the impending marriage. He bade them wait for Aladdin's arrival and go forth in a body to receive him. He also summoned the amirs and viziers, the chamberlains, nabobs, and commanders of the army; and they all stood waiting for Aladdin at the gates of the palace. Presently Aladdin arrived and would have dismounted at the entrance; but one of the amirs, whom the Sultan had stationed there for the purpose, hastened to prevent him.

'Sir,' he said, 'it is his majesty's wish that you should enter riding and dismount at the door of the audience-chamber.'

The courtiers walked before him, and when he had reached the audience-hall some came forward to hold his horse's stirrup, others to support him on either side, while yet others took him by the hand and helped him to dismount. The amirs and dignitaries ushered him into the hall, and as soon as he approached the throne and was about to prostrate himself on the carpet the Sultan stepped down and took him in his arms; he kissed him and made him sit down on his right. Aladdin exchanged greetings with him, and wished him long life and everlasting glory.

'Your majesty,' he said, 'you have been graciously pleased to bestow on me your daughter, although, being the humblest of your subjects, I am unworthy of so great an honour. I pray to Allah that He may preserve and keep you. Great King, I lack the words to thank you for this signal favour. I beg your

majesty to grant me a plot of land where I can build a palace
worthy of Princess Badr-al-Budur.'

The King was greatly astonished when he saw Aladdin
dressed in such regal splendour. He looked intently at him,
marvelling at his comeliness and beauty, and then at the stalwart and handsome slaves who stood around him. He was even
more amazed when Aladdin's mother made her entrance,
resplendent like a queen in her costly robes and surrounded
by the twelve graceful girls, who were attending her with the
utmost dignity and deference. He also marvelled at Aladdin's
eloquence and cultured speech; and so did all the others
present in the audience-hall except the Vizier, who almost
perished with envy. Having listened to Aladdin's words and
observed his magnificence and modest bearing, the Sultan
took him in his arms again and kissed him.

'It is a great pity, my son,' he said, 'that Destiny has not
brought us together before today.'

He ordered the musicians to start playing; then he took
Aladdin by the hand and led him into the palace hall, where
the wedding feast had been prepared. The Sultan sat down
and made Aladdin sit on his right. The viziers, dignitaries, and
notables also took their seats, each according to his rank.
Music filled the air, and all the palace echoed with the sounds
of great rejoicing. The Sultan spoke to Aladdin and jested with
him, while Aladdin replied with gallantry and wit, as though
he had been bred in a royal palace and all his life consorted
with kings. And the longer the Sultan talked to him the more
impressed he grew with his accomplishments.

When they had eaten and drunk, and the tables were
removed, the King ordered the cadis and witnesses to be
brought in. They came, and duly wrote the marriage contract
for Aladdin and the Princess. As soon as the ceremony was
over Aladdin rose and begged leave to go; but the Sultan
prevented him.

'Where are you going, my son?' he cried. 'All the wedding
guests are here and the feast is not yet finished. The contract
has just been written.'

'Your majesty,' Aladdin replied, 'I wish to build Badr-al-

Budur a palace befitting her degree. I cannot make her my wife until I have done that. Allah willing, the palace shall be finished, by your slave's unremitting zeal, in the shortest possible time. Eager as I am to fulfil my joy in the Princess, my duty prompts me to do this first, in proof of the great love I bear her.'

'Take whatever land you please, my son,' the Sultan said. 'It is for you to choose. But to my mind it would be best to build it here, on the great square in front of my palace.'

'I could wish for nothing better,' replied Aladdin, 'than to be so near your majesty.'

With that he took leave of the Sultan and, mounting his horse, returned to his own house amidst the acclamations of the people. As soon as he reached home he entered his room and rubbed the lamp.

'Master, ask what you will,' said the jinnee, as he appeared before him.

'I have an important task to set you,' Aladdin replied. 'I wish you to build me, with the least possible delay, a palace in front of the Sultan's: a marvel of a building, the like of which no king has ever seen. Let it be furnished royally and fitted with every comfort.'

'I hear and obey,' the jinnee answered.

He disappeared, and, just before daybreak, returned to Aladdin, saying: 'Master, the task is accomplished. Rise and look upon your palace.'

Aladdin got up, and in the twinkling of an eye the slave of the lamp carried him away to the palace. When Aladdin saw it he was overwhelmed with wonder; it was all built of jasper and marble, lazuli and mosaics. The jinnee conducted him into a treasury heaped with all manner of gold and silver, and precious stones beyond count or value. He then led him into the dining-hall, where he saw plates and ewers, cups and spoons and basins, all of gold and silver. He next took him to the kitchen, and there he saw the cooks with their pots and utensils, also of gold and silver. From there he led him into another room, which he found stacked with coffers containing rich and wondrous garments, Chinese and Indian silks embroidered with gold, and thick brocades. After that he ushered him into several other chambers full of treasures beyond description, and finally brought him into the stables, where he saw thoroughbred horses whose like no monarch ever possessed. In an adjoining store-room lay costly saddles and bridles, cunningly wrought with pearls and rich jewels. All this had been accomplished in one night.

Aladdin was bewildered and amazed at these marvels, which were beyond the dreams of kings. The palace was thronged with slaves and serving-girls, who would have bewitched a hermit by their beauty. But the most wondrous thing of all was the dome of the building, which was pierced with four-and-twenty windows encrusted with emeralds, rubies, and other precious stones. At his own request, one of the windows had not been properly finished, for he wished to challenge the Sultan to complete it. Overjoyed at the splendour of all that he beheld, Aladdin turned to the slave of the lamp and said: 'There is but one thing wanting, which I forgot to mention.'

'Ask,' replied the jinnee, 'and it shall be done.'

'I require a carpet of rich brocade, woven with gold,' said Aladdin. 'It must be stretched from this palace to the Sultan's, so that Princess Badr-al-Budur may walk upon it without treading the ground.'

The jinnee vanished, and in a trice returned, saying: 'Master, your request is granted.'

He took Aladdin and showed it to him: a wonder of a carpet, stretching from his palace to the Sultan's. Then the jinnee carried him back to his own house.

When the Sultan woke that morning, he opened the window of his bedroom and looked out. In front of his palace he saw a building. He rubbed his eyes, opened them wide, and looked again. The building was still there, a towering edifice of astonishing beauty, with a carpet stretched from its threshold to the doorstep of his own palace. The doorkeepers and everyone else who saw it were no less astounded. At that moment the Vizier entered the King's apartment, and he too was utterly amazed to see the new palace and the carpet.

'By Allah,' they cried together, 'no king on earth could ever build the like of that palace!'

'Now are you convinced that Aladdin deserves to be my daughter's husband?' said the Sultan, turning to the Vizier. 'You have seen that splendid building, whose extraordinary richness transcends the most prodigious fancy.'

'Your majesty,' answered the Vizier, stung with envy, 'nothing short of magic could have produced that edifice. Not the richest man alive can build such a palace in one night.'

'I marvel at you,' the Sultan cried. 'You seem to think nothing but ill of Aladdin. Surely you are jealous of him. You were present yourself when I gave him this land to erect a palace for my daughter. The man who could present a dowry of such jewels can surely build a palace in one night.'

Realizing that the King loved Aladdin too well to be aroused against him, the Vizier prudently held his peace and said no more.

As for Aladdin, when he felt that the time was ripe to present himself at the royal palace, he rubbed the lamp and said to the jinnee: 'I must now go to the Sultan's court; today is the wedding feast. I want you to bring me ten thousand dinars.'

The jinnee vanished, and in a twinkling returned with ten thousand dinars. Aladdin got up and mounted, and his slaves rode before and behind him. All along the way he scattered gold among the people, who now made him their idol on account of his munificence. As soon as he approached the palace the courtiers and officers of the guard hurried to inform the King of his arrival. The Sultan went out to receive him; he embraced and kissed him, and taking him by the hand led him into the hall and seated him on his right. The entire city was decorated; and in the palace performers sang and made music.

The Sultan now gave orders for the banquet to begin. He sat at table with Aladdin and all the courtiers, and they ate and drank until they were satisfied. Nor was the merriment confined to the royal palace; all the people of the kingdom, great and small alike, rejoiced on this auspicious occasion. Viceroys

and governors had come from the remotest provinces to see
Aladdin's wedding and the bridal celebrations. Deep in his
heart the Sultan marvelled at Aladdin's mother, how she had
come to him in tattered garments while her son was master of
such extraordinary riches. And when the guests saw Aladdin's
palace, they were amazed that such a dwelling could have been
built in one night. They called down blessings upon him,
crying: 'May Allah give him joy and long life!'

When the banquet drew to an end, Aladdin rose and took
leave of the Sultan. He mounted his horse and, escorted by his
servants, rode over to his own palace to prepare himself for
meeting his bride. As he rode along he threw handfuls of gold
to right and left amidst the benedictions of the people and,
on reaching his house, alighted and took his seat in the
audience-hall. Sherbets were brought to him, and when he had
drunk he bade the servants and slave-girls, and everyone else
in the palace, make ready to receive his bride. In the cool of the
afternoon, when the heat of the sun had abated, the Sultan
ordered his captains, amirs, and viziers to go down and take
their places in the parading ground opposite his court. They
all went down, including the Sultan; and Aladdin presently
joined them, mounted upon a horse unequalled among all the
Arabian steeds for beauty. He galloped and sported round the
square, excelling all the others in his display of horsemanship.
Badr-al-Budur watched him from one of the windows; she
was captivated by his good looks and equestrian skill, and fell
in love with him outright. When all the cavaliers had played
their rounds the Sultan returned to his palace and Aladdin to
his.

In the evening the viziers and high dignitaries called on
Aladdin and took him in a great procession to the Royal Baths.
There he bathed and perfumed himself, and, changing into a
more magnificent suit, rode home escorted by amirs and
soldiers. Four viziers walked about him with unsheathed
swords, while all the townsfolk, natives and foreigners alike,
marched ahead with candles and drums, pipes, and all manner
of musical instruments. Reaching the palace, he dismounted
and sat down with the amirs and viziers. The slaves brought

sherbets and sweetmeats, and served with drinks the innumerable men and women who had accompanied him in the procession. Then, at Aladdin's bidding, the slaves went out to the palace gate and scattered gold among the people.

Meanwhile, on returning from the square, the Sultan had ordered his household to take Badr-al-Budur in procession to Aladdin's palace. The troops and courtiers immediately mounted; the servants and slave-girls went out with lighted candles, and Badr-al-Budur was brought in splendid procession to her husband's palace. Aladdin's mother walked by her side; in front marched the wives of the viziers, amirs, noblemen, and courtiers; while in her train followed the eight-and-forty slave-girls whom Aladdin had given her, each carrying a torch of camphor and amber set into a gold candlestick encrusted with gems. They took her up to her chamber, and, after displaying her in her bridal garments, ushered her into her husband's room, accompanied by Aladdin's mother. Presently Aladdin came in; he lifted her veil, and his mother gazed in wonderment upon Badr-al-Budur's loveliness and beauty. She also marvelled at the bridal chamber, which was all wrought with gold and jewels, and at its golden chandelier, studded with emeralds and rubies. Nor was Badr-al-Budur less astonished than Aladdin's mother at the magnificence of the palace. By and by the table was brought in, and they ate and drank and made merry, while eighty slave-girls, each holding a musical instrument, plucked the strings and played enchanting tunes. Badr-al-Budur was so entranced with the music that she stopped eating, and listened with rapt attention. Aladdin plied her with wine; the two rejoiced in each other's love. It was a glorious night, such as not even Alexander spent in all his life. When the feast was finished and the table was removed, Aladdin rose and took possession of his bride.

In the morning Aladdin got up and dressed himself in a magnificent suit which his chief eunuch had prepared for him. He was served with coffee flavoured with amber; then, bidding the slaves saddle his horses, he rode with a numerous escort to the Sultan's palace. The Sultan at once rose to receive him, and, after embracing and kissing him as though he were his own son, seated him on his right. The King, together with the viziers, amirs, and courtiers, congratulated him and wished him joy. Breakfast was then served, and when they had finished eating, Aladdin turned to the Sultan and said: 'Sir, would your majesty honour me with your presence at lunch today with the Princess Badr-al-Budur, your dear daughter? Let your majesty be accompanied by all your viziers and the nobles of your kingdom.'

The Sultan gladly accepted and, at once ordering his courtiers to follow him, rode over with Aladdin to his palace. When he entered, he marvelled at that edifice, whose stones were all of jasper and agate; his reason was confounded at the sight of such luxury, wealth, and splendour.

'What do you say now?' he exclaimed, turning to the Vizier. 'Have you ever seen anything like this in all your life? Has the greatest monarch in the world such wealth and gold and jewels as can be seen in this palace?'

'Your majesty,' replied the Vizier, 'this prodigy is beyond the power of mortal kings. Not all the people of the world could build a palace like this; no masons are to be found who can produce such work. As I told your majesty before, only magic could have brought it into being.'

But the King realized it was envy that prompted his minister to speak in this way. 'Enough, Vizier,' he cried. 'I know why you are telling me this.'

The Sultan now came under the lofty dome of the palace, and his amazement knew no bounds when he saw that all the windows and lattices were made of emeralds, rubies, and other precious stones. He walked round and round, bewildered at those extravagent marvels, and presently caught sight of the window which Aladdin had deliberately left unfinished.

'Alas, poor window, you are unfinished!' observed the Sultan. And, turning to the Vizier, he asked: 'Do you know why that window and its lattice have not been properly completed?'

'Perhaps because your majesty hurried Aladdin over the wedding,' replied the Vizier. 'He may not have had time enough to complete it.'

Aladdin, who had meanwhile gone to inform his bride of her father's arrival, now returned, and the Sultan addressed to him the same question.

'Your majesty,' he replied, 'the wedding took place at so short a notice that the masons had no time to complete it.'

'Then I would like to finish it myself,' said the Sultan.

'Allah grant your majesty everlasting glory!' Aladdin cried. 'May it stand a memorial to you in your daughter's palace!'

The Sultan at once sent for the jewellers and the goldsmiths, and ordered his lieutenants to give them all the gold and jewels they required out of his treasury. The jewellers and goldsmiths presented themselves before the Sultan, and he bade them complete the ornamentation.

While this was going forward, Badr-al-Budur came out to meet her father. Noticing her happy smile, he took her into his arms and kissed her; then he went with her to her apartment, followed by all his courtiers. It was now lunch-time; one table had been prepared for the Sultan, Badr-al-Budur, and Aladdin, and another for the Vizier, the officers of state, the high dignitaries, the chamberlains, the nabobs, and the captains of the army. The King sat between his daughter and his son-in-law, and as he ate he marvelled at the delicacy of the meats and the excellence of the dishes. Before them stood a troupe of eighty slave-girls, so fair and radiant that each of them might have said to the moon: 'Begone, that I may take your place!' They tuned their instruments, plucked the strings, and made such sweet music as cannot be heard in the courts of kings and emperors. Wine flowed freely; and when all had eaten and drunk, they repaired to an adjoining chamber, where they were served with fruits and sweetmeats.

Then the Sultan rose to inspect the jewellers' work, and to see how it compared with the workmanship of the palace. He went up to the unfinished window, but was disappointed to find that the difference was too marked, and that they lacked the art to match the perfection of the whole. The jewellers informed him that they had brought all the gems that they could find in his treasury, and that they needed more. He ordered that the great imperial treasury should be opened and that they should be given all they required; if that was not enough, they were to use the jewels which Aladdin had sent him. The jewellers did as the Sultan had directed, but found that all those gems were not sufficient to ornament one-half of the lattice. The Sultan next commanded that all the precious stones that could be found in the houses of the viziers and rich notables should be taken. The jewellers took all these and worked with them, but still they needed more.

Next morning Aladdin went up to the jewellers and, finding that they had not finished even half of the lattice, bade them undo their work and restore the gems to their owners. The jewellers did so, and went to inform the Sultan of Aladdin's instructions.

'What did he say to you?' inquired the Sultan. 'Why did he not allow the window to be completed? Why did he destroy what you had done?'

'We do not know, your majesty,' was their reply.

The Sultan called for his horse, and rode at once to his son-in-law's palace. Now when Aladdin dismissed the jewellers, he had entered his chamber and rubbed the lamp. The jinnee appeared before him, saying: 'Ask what you will. Your slave is at your service.'

'I want you to complete the unfinished window,' Aladdin commanded.

'It shall be as you wish,' the jinnee replied.

He vanished, and in a short while returned, saying: 'Master, the task is accomplished.'

Aladdin climbed up to the dome of the palace and saw that all its windows were now complete. Whilst he was examining them, his eunuch came in to inform him that the Sultan had come. Aladdin went down at once to receive him.

'Why did you do that, my son?' cried the Sultan as soon as he saw him. 'Why did you not let the jewellers complete the lattice, so that there should remain nothing amiss in your palace?'

'Great King,' Aladdin replied, 'it was left unfinished at my own request. I was not incapable of completing it myself; nor would I wish to receive your majesty in a palace where there was something missing. May it please your highness to come up and see if there is anything imperfect now.'

The Sultan mounted the stairs and went into the dome of the palace. He looked right and left, and was astonished to see that all the lattice-work was now complete. He took Aladdin into his arms and kissed him.

'What an extraordinary feat, my son!' he exclaimed. 'In a single night you have accomplished a task that would have occupied the jewellers for months. By Allah, there cannot be anyone like you in the whole world!'

'Allah keep your majesty and prolong your life!' replied Aladdin. 'Your servant is unworthy of such praise.'

'By Allah, my son,' the Sultan cried, 'you are worthy of all praise, because you have done that which no jeweller on earth could ever do.'

The Sultan went down to visit Badr-al-Budur, and rejoiced to see her so happy in her magnificent new home. After resting a while in her apartment, he took his leave and rode back to his own palace.

Thenceforth Aladdin went out in the city every day, his slaves scattering gold before him as he rode along. The hearts of all the people, natives and foreigners alike, were drawn to him on account of his munificence and charitable deeds. He increased the alms for the needy and the poor, and himself distributed it to them with his own hand. His fame spread far and wide throughout the realm; amirs and notables ate at his table and there was none, high or low, who did not swear by his precious life. Badr-al-Budur loved him more ardently than ever, and bethought herself of Allah's goodness in preserving her, after all that had passed between her and the Vizier's son, for her true husband Aladdin.

Thus every day Aladdin's good name and reputation were enhanced in the people's eyes, and their love for him increased. It also happened at that time that certain enemies marched against the Sultan, who mustered his armies and appointed Aladdin chief commander. Aladdin led the troops to the battlefield, unsheathed his sword, and with reckless valour charged the opposing forces. A bloody battle ensued, in which the foe was routed and put to flight. Aladdin plundered their goods and belongings and returned in a glorious triumph to the capital, which had been gaily decked to receive him. The Sultan came out to meet him; he congratulated him on his victory, took him into his arms and kissed him amidst the rejoicings of the people. Then he and his son-in-law went into Aladdin's palace. Badr-al-Budur received her husband in an ecstasy of joy and, kissing him between the eyes, took him into her own apartment. After a little while the Sultan joined them, and they all sat down, drinking sherbets. The Sultan ordered the entire kingdom to be decorated in honour of Aladdin's victory. The soldiers and all the people now looked only to Allah in heaven and to Aladdin on earth. They loved him more than ever on account of his generosity and patriotism, his horsemanship and heroic courage. So much for Aladdin.

Now to return to the Moorish sorcerer. When he had left Aladdin to perish in the cave, he journeyed back to his own land and passed his days bewailing the vain hardships and fruitless toil he had endured to secure the lamp. It galled him to reflect how the long-sought morsel flew out of his hand just when it had reached his lips, and he cursed Aladdin in the extremity of his rage.

'I am very glad,' he would sometimes say to himself, 'that the little wretch has perished under the ground. The lamp is still safe in the treasure, and I may get it yet.'

One day he cast his divinatory sand, marked the resultant forms, and set them out with care to ascertain Aladdin's death and the exact position of the lamp. He scanned the figures attentively, both the origins and derivations; but he saw no lamp. Angrily he cast the sand a second time to verify that the boy was dead, but he did not see him in the treasure-house. His fury mounted when he learnt that Aladdin was alive; he realized that he must have come up from the cave and gained possession of the lamp, for which he himself had undergone such perils and ordeals.

'I have suffered many hardships, and endured pains such as no other man could bear, on account of the lamp,' he thought to himself. 'Now this damned wretch has taken it pat. It is all too clear that, if he has discovered its magic power, he must now be the wealthiest man on earth. I must seek to destroy him.'

He cast the sand once more and scrutinized the figures. He found that Aladdin was master of incalculable riches, and that he was married to the Sultan's daughter. Demented with envious rage, he rose and set out immediately for China. After a long and arduous journey he reached the capital where Aladdin lived and secured a lodging at a traveller's inn. There he heard the people talk of nothing but the magnificence of Aladdin's palace. When he had rested a little, he changed his clothes and went out for a walk in the streets of the city. Wherever he passed he heard tell of nothing but Aladdin's palace and its regal splendour, the beauty of Aladdin and his manly grace, his generosity and sublime virtues. The Moor went up to someone who was praising Aladdin in these terms and said: 'Tell me, my good friend, who is this man of whom you speak so highly?'

'Why, sir, you must be a stranger in these parts,' the man replied. 'But even if you are, have you never heard of Prince Aladdin? Surely he is renowned among all men. His palace is one of the wonders of the world. How is it that you have never heard of it, nor even the name of Aladdin, Allah increase his glory and give him joy?'

'I would very much like to see the palace,' said the Moor. 'Would you be so kind as to direct me to it? I am a stranger in the city.'

'Why, gladly,' the man replied, and walking before the Moor, brought him to Aladdin's palace.

The magician looked at the building and realized at once it was the work of the enchanted lamp.

'Ah,' he thought to himself, 'I must dig a pit for this cursed tailor's son who could never earn an evening's meal before. If fate allows it, I will destroy him utterly, and send his mother back to her spinning-wheel.'

Oppressed with sorrow and envy, he returned to his lodging and took out his divining board. He cast the sand to find out where the lamp was hidden, and saw that it was in the palace and not on Aladdin's person. At this he rejoiced exceedingly, and cried: 'My task is easier now. I know a way of obtaining the lamp.'

He went off to a coppersmith and said to him: 'Make me a few copper lamps. I will pay you handsomely if you finish them fast enough.'

'I hear and obey,' replied the coppersmith, and set to work at once.

When they were finished, the Moor paid him without haggling, took the lamps, and returned to his lodging. There he placed them in a basket, and went about the streets and markets, crying: 'Who will exchange an old lamp for a new one?'

When the people heard his cry, they laughed at him. 'No doubt the man is mad,' they said to each other. 'Who would go round offering to change old lamps for new?'

A great crowd followed at his heels, and the street boys ran after him from place to place with shouting and laughter. But the Moor took no notice of them and proceeded on his way until he came in front of Aladdin's palace. Here he began to shout louder and louder, while the children chanted back: 'Madman, madman!' At length Badr-al-Budur, who chanced to be in the hall of the latticed dome, heard the clamour in the street and ordered one of the maids to go and find out what was happening. The girl went out to look, and saw a man crying: 'Who will exchange an old lamp for a new one?' Children were hooting at him.

The maid returned to Badr-al-Budur and said: 'Mistress, outside the gate there is an old man crying: "Who will exchange an old lamp for a new one?" Little boys are laughing at him.'

Badr-al-Budur laughed too at this strange offer. Now Aladdin had left the lamp in his apartment and forgotten to lock it up. One of the girls, who had chanced to see it there, said: 'Mistress, there is an old copper lamp in my master Aladdin's apartment. Let us take it down to the old man and see if he will in truth exchange it for a new one.'

'Fetch it to me, then,' said the Princess.

Badr-al-Budur knew nothing of the lamp or its magic powers, nor was she aware that it was this that had brought Aladdin such vast riches. She merely wished to see what manner of whim it was that drove the Moor to change old things for new.

The maid went up to Aladdin's chamber and returned with the lamp to her mistress, who then ordered the chief eunuch to go and exchange it for a new one. The eunuch gave the lamp to the Moor, took a new one in return, and carried it to the Princess. Badr-al-Budur examined it and, finding that it was really new, burst out laughing at the old man's folly.

When the Moor recognized the lamp he quickly hid it in the breast of his robe and flung his basket with all its contents to the jeering mob. He ran on and on until he came outside the city and reached the empty plains. Then he waited for the night and, when all was darkness, took out the lamp and rubbed it. At once the jinnee appeared before him, saying: 'I am here, master. Ask what you will.'

'Slave of the lamp,' said the Moor, 'I order you to lift up Aladdin's palace with all that it contains and to transport it, and me as well, to my own country in Africa. You know my native city; there you shall set it down, among the gardens.'

'I hear and obey,' replied the jinnee. 'Shut your eyes and open them, and you shall find yourself in your own land with the palace.'

At once the thing was done. In a flash the Moor and Aladdin's palace, together with all that it contained, were carried off to Africa. So much for the Moorish sorcerer.

Now to return to the Sultan and Aladdin. When the King rose next day he opened the window and looked out, as was his custom every day, in the direction of his daughter's palace. But he saw nothing there, only a vast bare space, as in the former days. He was greatly astonished and perplexed; he rubbed his eyes, in case they were clouded or bedimmed, and looked again. But he saw not a trace or vestige of the palace, and could not understand how or why it had vanished. He wrung his hands in despair and the tears began to roll over his beard, for he did not know what had become of his daughter. At once he summoned the Vizier; and when the Vizier came in and saw the Sultan prostrated with grief, he cried: 'Allah preserve your majesty from all evil! Why do I see you so distressed?'

'Is it possible that you do not know the reason?' the Sultan asked.

'By Allah, I know nothing,' returned the Vizier. 'Nothing at all.'

'Then you have not looked towards Aladdin's palace?' the Sultan cried.

'No,' answered the Vizier. 'It is still shut.'

'Since you know nothing about the matter,' groaned the Sultan, 'pray have a good look from the window and see where Aladdin's palace is, which you say is still shut.'

The Vizier crossed over to the window and looked out towards Aladdin's palace. He saw nothing there, neither palace nor anything else. Confounded at the mystery, he returned to the Sultan.

'Well,' said the King, 'do you know now the reason of my grief? Could you see Aladdin's palace, which you said was still shut?'

'Great King,' answered the Vizier, 'I have told your majesty time and time again that the palace and the whole affair was magic from beginning to end.'

'Where is Aladdin?' exclaimed the Sultan, blazing with rage.

'Gone to the hunt,' replied the Vizier.

The Sultan instantly ordered a troop of officers and guards to go and bring Aladdin before him manacled and bound with chains. The officers and guards rode off on their mission, and when they met Aladdin they said: 'Pardon us, our master. We are commanded by the Sultan to take you to him manacled and in chains. We beg you to excuse us; we are acting under royal orders, which we cannot disregard.'

Aladdin was dumbfounded at these words, for he did not know the reason. Then, turning to the officers he said: 'Good friends, do you know why the Sultan gave these orders? I know I am innocent; I have committed no crime against the Sultan or his realm.'

'Master,' they replied, 'we know nothing at all.'

'Then you must carry out your orders,' said Aladdin, dismounting. 'Obedience to the King is binding on all his loyal subjects.'

The officers chained their captive and dragged him in fetters to the capital. When the citizens saw Aladdin treated in this way they realized that he was to be beheaded by the Sultan. But, since they all loved him, they crowded in the street and, arming themselves with clubs and weapons, pressed at his heels to see what would happen.

The troops brought Aladdin to the palace and informed the Sultan, who thereupon commanded the executioner to behead him. When the citizens learnt of this order they locked up the gates of the palace and sent a warning to the Sultan, saying: 'This very hour we will pull down your dwelling over your head and all who are in it, if Aladdin comes to the slightest harm.'

The Vizier went in and delivered the warning to the Sultan. 'Your majesty,' he said, 'this order will be the end of us all. It would be far better to pardon Aladdin, or the consequences will be terrible indeed. Your subjects love Aladdin more than us.'

Meanwhile the executioner had spread his mat and made Aladdin kneel upon it. He had just bandaged his eyes and walked round him three times, waiting the King's final command, when the Sultan saw his subjects storming at the palace and scaling its walls to destroy it. At once he ordered the executioner to stay his hand and bade the crier go out among the people and proclaim that the King had spared Aladdin's life.

Freed from his fetters, Aladdin walked up to the Sultan and said: 'Your majesty, since you have been graciously pleased to spare my life, I beg you to tell me what I have done to earn your displeasure.'

'Traitor,' exclaimed the Sultan, 'dare you pretend not to know your crime?' Then turning to the Vizier he said: 'Take him, and let him see from the window where his palace is now!'

The Vizier led Aladdin to a window, and he looked out in the direction of his palace. He found the site desolate and empty, with not a trace of any building there. He returned, utterly bewildered, to the Sultan.

'What did you see?' the Sultan asked. 'Where is your palace? And where is my daughter, the flower of my heart, my only child?'

'Great King,' Aladdin answered, 'I know nothing of all this, nor do I know what has happened.'

'Listen, Aladdin,' cried the Sultan. 'I have reprieved you only that you may go and investigate this mystery and seek out my daughter for me. Do not return without her. If you fail to bring her back, I swear by my life that I will cut off your head.'

'I hear and obey, your majesty,' Aladdin replied. 'Only grant me a delay of forty days. If I do not bring her to you by that time, cut off my head and do with me what you will.'

'Very well,' said the Sultan. 'I grant you the delay. But do not think you can escape my reach; for I will bring you back even if you are above the clouds.'

The people were overjoyed to see Aladdin at large. He came out of the palace delighted at his escape; but the disgrace of what had happened and the triumphant glee of his enemies caused him to hang his head. For two days he wandered disconsolately about the town, not knowing what he should do, while certain friends secretly brought him food and drink. Then he struck aimlessly into the desert and journeyed on until he came to a river. Careworn and sick at heart, he abandoned all hope and would have incontinently thrown himself into the water; but, being a true servant of the One God, he reminded himself of Allah's reckoning and, instead of taking his life, knelt down upon the bank to make his ablutions. He took up the water in the hollow of his hands and began to rub between his fingers; and in so doing he rubbed the ring which the Moor had given him. Thereupon a jinnee appeared, saying: 'I am here. Your slave stands before you. Ask what you will.'

Aladdin rejoiced at the sight of the jinnee, and cried: 'Slave of the ring, bring me back my wife and my palace with all that it contains.'

'Master,' the jinnee replied, 'that which you have asked is beyond my power, for it concerns only the slave of the lamp.'

'Very well,' said Aladdin. 'Since you cannot do this, take me away and set me down beside my palace, wherever it may be.'

'I hear and obey, my master.'

So saying, the jinnee carried him up, and in the twinkling of an eye set him down beside his palace in Africa in front of his wife's apartment. Night had fallen; and, as he looked at his palace, his cares and sorrows left him. He prayed hopefully to Allah, after he had given up all hope, to unite him with his wife again; and he began to ponder over the mysterious workings of the Almighty (glory to His omnipotence!) – how He had provided him with the ring, and how he would have yielded to despair had Allah not aided him with the slave of the ring. Therefore he rejoiced, and forgot all his troubles. As he had had no sleep for four days on account of his anxiety and excessive grief, he stretched himself out beside the palace and slept under a tree; for, as I have told you, the palace stood amongst the gardens of Africa, outside the town.

Thus, despite the anxious thoughts that haunted him, he slept soundly under the tree till daybreak, when he awoke to the singing of birds. He rose and, betaking himself to a nearby river which flowed into the town, washed his hands and face, made ablutions, and recited the morning prayer. Then he returned and sat down under the window of Badr-al-Budur's apartment.

The Princess was sorely grieved at being separated from her husband and her father and at all that had befallen her at the hands of the vile magician. She neither ate nor drank and passed her days and nights weeping. As luck would have it, however, on that morning one of the maids came in to dress Badr-al-Budur, and, opening the window to cheer her mistress with the delightful view, saw Aladdin her master sitting under the apartment.

'Mistress, mistress!' she exclaimed. 'There is my master Aladdin, sitting under the apartment!'

Badr-al-Budur rushed to the window, and the parted lovers recognized and greeted each other in a transport of joy.

'Come up, quickly!' the Princess shouted. 'Enter by the secret door. The magician is not here now.'

Her maid ran down and opened a secret door, by which Aladdin gained access to his wife's apartment. Laughing and crying, they fell into each other's embrace and kissed most joyfully.

'Before all else, Badr-al-Budur,' said Aladdin when they had both sat down, 'tell me what became of that copper lamp which I left in my room when I went out hunting.'

'Alas, my love!' sighed Badr-al-Budur. 'That lamp and nothing else was the cause of our ruin.'

'Tell me everything,' said Aladdin.

Badr-al-Budur recounted to him all that had happened from first to last; how they had exchanged the old lamp for a new one.

'Next morning,' she added, 'we suddenly found ourselves in this country. And the man who cheated us told me that it was all done by his witchcraft and the power of the lamp; that he was a Moor from Africa, and that we were now in his own city.'

'What does the fiend intend to do with you?' asked Aladdin, when Badr-al-Budur had finished speaking. 'What does he say to you? What does he want of you?'

'He comes to me once every day,' she replied, 'and seeks to win my heart. He wants me to forget you and to take *him* for my lover. He says that the Sultan has cut off your head, that you come of a poor family, and that you owe your wealth to him. He tries to endear himself to me, but gets nothing in return except silence and tears. He has never heard me speak a kind word to him.'

'Now tell me where he keeps the lamp,' said Aladdin.

'He always carries it with him,' replied Badr-al-Budur, 'and is never parted from it even for a moment. But he once drew it from his robe and showed it to me.'

Aladdin was very glad to hear this.

'Listen to me, Badr-al-Budur,' he said. 'I want to go out now, and will return after changing my clothes. Do not be taken aback to see me disguised. Post one of the maids at the secret door, so that she should let me in as soon as I get back. I have hit upon a plan to kill this foul magician.'

With this Aladdin went out of the palace. Setting off in the direction of the city, he presently met a peasant on the way.

'Good friend,' he said, 'take my clothes and give me yours.'

The peasant refused; so Aladdin laid hold of him, and, after forcing him to cast off his clothes, put them on himself and gave him his own costly robes in return. Then he walked on to the city and made his way to the perfume-sellers' market, where he bought a potent drug. Returning to the palace, he went in by the secret door to Badr-al-Budur's apartment.

'Listen, now,' he said to the Princess. 'I want you to array yourself in your finest robes and jewels and to dismiss your gloom. When the Moor comes, give him a joyful welcome and receive him with a smiling face. Invite him to dine with you; pretend that you have forgotten your husband and your father, and that you are deeply in love with him. Ask him for red wine, and drink his health with a great show of merriment. When you have given him two or three glasses, drop this powder into his cup and fill it to the brim with wine. As soon as he has drunk it off, he will fall over on his back like a dead man.'

'That would be difficult for me,' replied the Princess. 'Yet it must be done if we are to rid ourselves of that abominable fiend. To kill such a man is certainly lawful.'

Then Aladdin ate and drank with the Princess, and when he had satisfied his hunger he rose and left the palace with all speed.

Badr-al-Budur sent for her maid, who combed her hair, perfumed her, and dressed her in her fairest garments. By and by the Moor came in. He was delighted to see her so changed, and agreeably surprised when she received him with a welcoming smile. His passion for her increased and his longing grew more violent than ever. She took him by the hand and seated him by her side.

'If you wish, my love,' she said in a tender voice, 'come to my room tonight and we will dine together. I have had my fill of grief; and were I to sit mourning for a thousand years, Aladdin would never come back from the grave. I have reflected on what you told me yesterday, and do believe that my father the Sultan may well have killed him in his sorrow at being parted from me. Therefore you must not be astonished to see me so changed; I have resolved to take you as my lover and intimate friend instead of Aladdin, for now I have no other man but you. Pray let us meet tonight, that we may have dinner and drink a little wine together. I would particularly like to taste your African wine; perhaps it is better than ours. I have here some wine from our own country, but would much prefer to try some from yours.'

Perceiving the love which Badr-al-Budur displayed towards him, and the unwonted gaiety of her demeanour, the Moor concluded that she had given up all hope of Aladdin. Therefore he rejoiced, and said: 'My love, I hear and obey your every wish. I have in my house a cask of African wine, which I have stored deep under the earth these eight years. I will now go and fetch from it sufficient for our needs, and return to you without delay.'

But to coax him more and more, Badr-al-Budur replied: 'Do not leave me alone, dearest. Send one of your servants to bring us some, and sit here by my side, that I may cheer myself with your company.'

'Dear mistress,' answered the Moor, 'no one knows where the cask is but myself. I shall not be long.'

So saying he went out, and after a little while returned with a flaskful of the wine.

'Dearest,' said Badr-al-Budur when he entered, 'you have tired yourself on my account.'

'Not at all, my love,' replied the Moor. 'It is an honour for me to serve you.'

Badr-al-Budur sat beside him at the table, and the two ate

together. The Princess asked for a drink, and her maid filled her cup and then the Moor's. They drank hilariously to each other's health, Badr-al-Budur using her cunning to captivate him with her artful words. Elated with wine and oblivious of the whole world, the unsuspecting Moor supposed all this to be heartfelt and true; he did not know that this love of hers was but a snare to destroy him. When they had finished eating and the wine had mastered his brain, Badr-al-Budur said: 'We have a custom in our country: I do not know if you observe it here.'

'And what is this custom?' he asked.

'When dinner is over,' she replied, 'each lover takes his beloved's cup and drinks it.'

She thereupon took his cup and filled it with wine for herself; then she bade the maid give him her cup, in which the wine had already been mixed with the drug. The girl acted her part well, for all the maids and servants in the palace wished his death and were in league with their mistress against him. So the girl gave him the cup, while the infatuated Moor, overwhelmed by this show of love, imagined himself Alexander the Great in all his glory.

'Dearest,' said Badr-al-Budur, swaying from side to side and placing her hand in his, 'here I have your cup and you have mine. Thus do lovers drink from one another's cup.'

Badr-al-Budur kissed his glass and drank it; then she went over to him and kissed him on the cheek. The delighted Moor wanted to do the same; he raised the cup to his lips and gulped it down, without noticing if there was anything in it or not. At once he rolled over on his back like a dead man, and the cup fell from his hand. Badr-al-Budur rejoiced, and the maids rushed out to the door of the palace to admit their master Aladdin.

Aladdin hastened to his wife's apartment and found her sitting at the table, with the Moor lying motionless before her. He took her joyfully into his arms and thanked her for all that she had done.

'Now go with your maids into the inner chamber,' he said to her, 'and leave me to myself a while. I have some work to accomplish.'

When they had all retired, Aladdin locked up the door behind them and, going over to the Moor, thrust his hand into the breast of his robe and took out the lamp, then he drew his sword and cut off the Moor's head. Having dispatched his enemy, he rubbed the lamp, and at once the jinnee appeared before him, saying: 'I am here, master, I am here. What would you have?'

'I order you,' said Aladdin, 'to lift up this palace and set it down where it stood before, in front of the Sultan's dwelling in China.'

'I hear and obey, my master,' the jinnee replied.

Aladdin went in and sat down with his wife; he embraced and kissed her, and she kissed him back. Meanwhile the jinnee carried the palace and set it down on its former site, in front of the Sultan's dwelling. Aladdin ordered the maids to bring the table, and he and the Princess feasted and made merry to their hearts' content. Then they repaired to the drinking chamber, where they sat dallying together until the sun of the wine shone in their heads and sleep overcame them.

Next morning Aladdin got up and awakened his wife. The maids came in and dressed Badr-al-Budur, and Aladdin dressed himself also. The two looked eagerly forward to meeting the Sultan. So much for them.

Now to return to the Sultan. After releasing Aladdin he continued to grieve over the loss of his daughter; he passed his days wailing for her like a woman, for she was his one and only child. Every morning, as he left his bed, he would look out towards the spot where Aladdin's palace had been and weep until his eyes were dry and his eyelids sore. Rising that day as usual, he opened the window and looked out – and saw before him a building. He rubbed his eyes and stared intently at it, until he had no doubt that it was Aladdin's palace. He at once called for his horse and rode to his son-in-law's dwelling.

When Aladdin saw him approaching, he went down and met him in the middle of the square; he took him by the hand and led him up to the Princess's apartment. Badr-al-Budur was overjoyed at her father's arrival. The Sultan caught his daughter in his arms, and the two mingled their joyful tears together. Then he asked her how she was and what had happened to her.

'Father,' she replied, 'my spirits did not revive until yesterday, when I saw my husband. He rescued me from a foul Moorish magician, a filthier man than whom is not to be found in the whole world. Had it not been for Aladdin, I would have never escaped from him, nor would you have ever seen me again in all your life. I had been pining with grief, not only because I was taken away from you, but also because I was separated from my husband, to whom I shall ever be bound in gratitude for delivering me from that wicked enchanter.'

Badr-al-Budur recounted to the Sultan all that had befallen her. She told him how the Moor had disguised himself as a lamp-seller, and how she had exchanged her husband's lamp for a new one.

'Next morning, father,' she continued, 'we found ourselves in Africa, together with the palace and all its contents. I did not know the power of the lamp which I had changed, until my husband came to us and devised a trick against the Moor, by means of which we escaped from him. Had not my husband come to my rescue the villain would have taken me to his bed by force. Aladdin gave me a powder; I mixed it with his wine and offered it to him to drink. As soon as he had drunk it off he fell over on his back like a dead man. Thereupon my husband rushed in; I do not know what he did, but the next moment we were here in this country.'

'Your majesty,' said Aladdin, 'when I came up and found him lying drugged and senseless, I said to Princess Badr-al-Budur: "Go with the maids into your inner chamber." She got up and went with her maids. I then bent over the Moor, thrust my hand into the breast of his robe and pulled out the lamp, which Badr-al-Budur told me he always carried there. Then, summoning the slave of the lamp, I ordered him to carry the palace and set it down where it belonged. If you doubt my words, your majesty, pray come along and look at the damnable Moor.'

The King followed Aladdin into the apartment and saw the

Moor. He at once ordered them to take out the corpse and burn it, and to scatter its ashes to the winds. Then he embraced Aladdin and kissed him, saying: 'Forgive me, my son, for the wrong I have done you on account of that evil enchanter who cast you into this pit. I may well be excused for what I did, since I found myself bereft of my only daughter, who is dearer to me than all my kingdom. You know the great love parents bear their children; mine is greater still, for I have none besides Badr-al-Budur.'

And the Sultan went on excusing himself to Aladdin and kissing him.

'Great King,' replied Aladdin, 'you have done me no wrong, nor have I offended against your majesty. It was all the fault of that abominable Moor.'

The Sultan ordered the city to be decorated. The streets were gaily decked, and there was great rejoicing among the people. He also bade the crier proclaim that that day was a public festival, and that a month of celebrations was to be observed in all the kingdom, to mark the return of Princess Badr-al-Budur and her husband.

Nevertheless Aladdin was not yet entirely secure from the cursed magician, although his body had been burnt and its ashes scattered to the winds. The damnable wretch had a brother viler than himself and as skilled in magic and divination; as the proverb has it, they were as like as the two halves of a split bean. Each dwelt in a different corner of the earth and filled it with his witchcraft, guile, and malice. Now it chanced one day that this magician wished to know what had become of his long-since-parted brother. He therefore cast the sand, marked out the figures, and scrutinized them carefully. He learnt to his dismay that his brother was dead. He cast the sand a second time, to see how he had died and where. He discovered that he had died a hideous death in China at the hands of a youth called Aladdin. Thereupon he rose and, making ready for the journey, travelled over deserts and plains and mountains for many months until he arrived in China and entered the capital where Aladdin lived. There he put up at the foreigners' inn, and, after resting a little, went down to walk about the streets, seeking some means to avenge his brother's death. Presently he came to a coffee-shop in the market. It was a large place, and many people were gathered there, some playing at dice, others at backgammon, and others at chess. He sat at one of the tables, and heard those next to him talking of a saintly woman called Fatimah, who practised her devotions in a cell outside the town and came to the city only twice a month; she was renowned for her healing powers.

'Now I have found what I was seeking,' said the Moorish sorcerer to himself. 'Allah willing, by means of this woman I shall accomplish my design.'

Then, turning to the people who were extolling her virtues, he said to one of them: 'Good sir, who is this holy woman, pray, and where does she live?'

'Why, man,' his neighbour exclaimed. 'Who has not heard of Mistress Fatimah's miracles? It is evident you are a stranger here, never to have heard of her long fasts, devout exercises, and goodly piety.'

'You are right, sir, I am a stranger,' said the Moor. 'I arrived in your city only last night. Pray tell me about the miracles of this good woman and where she lives. I am beset with ill-fortune and wish to go to her and seek her prayers, so that Allah may deliver me from my troubles.'

The man informed him of the miracles of Holy Fatimah, her piety and saintliness. Then he took him by the hand, and leading him outside the city, showed him the way to her dwelling in a cave at the top of a little mountain. The Moor thanked the man for his kindness and the trouble he had taken and then returned to his lodgings.

As chance would have it, however, the following day Fatimah herself came down to the city. The Moor left his lodgings in the morning, and noticed the people crowding in the street. He went up to inquire the cause of the hubbub, and found the holy woman standing in their midst. All the sick and ailing thronged about her, seeking her benedictions and her prayers; as soon as she touched them they were cured. The Moor followed her about till she returned to her cave, and then waited for nightfall. When evening came he entered a wineshop, drank a glass of spirits, and made his way to Holy Fatimah's cell. Arriving there, he found her fast asleep, lying on her back upon a piece of matting. He stole towards her without a sound, sat on her stomach, and drew his dagger, shouting in a terrible voice. She opened her eyes, and was terrified to see a Moor crouching upon her breast with a dagger in his hand, about to kill her.

'Listen!' he cried. 'If you breathe one syllable or scream, I will kill you upon the instant. So get up and do everything I tell you.'

And he swore to her that if she did his bidding he would not harm her. Rising immediately, he helped her to her feet.

'First,' he said, 'take my clothes and give me yours.'

She gave him her clothes, together with her headdress, shawl, and veil.

'Now,' said the Moor, 'you must stain me with some ointment, to make my face the same colour as yours.'

The old woman went to a corner and fetched a jar of ointment; she took some in her palm and rubbed his face with it until its colour became like hers. She also gave him her staff and taught him how to walk with it, and what to do when he went down to the city. Finally she placed her rosary round his neck and handed him a mirror, saying: 'Look! There is not the slightest difference now between us.'

The Moor looked into the mirror and saw that he was indeed her very image. Having attained his purpose, he broke his oath. He asked her for a rope and, when she had brought him one, he grabbed her by the neck and hanged her with it in her cave. Then he dragged her body outside, cast it into a pit, and returned to her cell, where he slept the night.

In the morning he rose, and, making his way to the city, stood in front of Aladdin's palace. The people gathered round him, taking him for Holy Fatimah. He did exactly as she used to do, laying his hand on the sick and ailing and reciting for them prayers and verses from the Koran. Badr-al-Budur heard the tumult in the street and bade her servants go and see what it was about. The chief eunuch went out to look, and soon returned saying: 'Mistress, it is Holy Fatimah, curing people by her touch. If it be your wish, I will call her in, so that you may receive her blessing.'

'Go and bring her to me,' said Badr-al-Budur. 'I have long heard of her miracles and virtues, and would much like to see her.'

The chief eunuch brought in the Moorish sorcerer, disguised in Fatimah's clothes. On coming to the Princess he offered up a long prayer for her continued health, and no one doubted that he was the saint herself. Badr-al-Budur rose to receive him; she greeted him and made him sit down by her side.

'Mistress Fatimah,' she said, 'I wish you to stay with me always, so that I may obtain your blessing and follow your example in the ways of piety and goodness.'

This invitation was the very thing which the magician wanted. But to complete his deception, he said: 'I am a poor woman, my lady. I pass my days in the wilderness. Hermits like myself are not fit to dwell in the palaces of kings.'

'Do not be troubled over that,' replied the Princess. 'I will give you a room of your own in my house, where you can worship undisturbed. You will serve Allah here better than in your cave.'

'I hear and obey, my lady,' said the Moor. 'The words of princes cannot be contradicted or opposed. Only I beg of you that I may be allowed to eat and drink and sit in my chamber all alone, with no one to intrude upon my privacy. I need no dainty food. Be so generous as to send me every day a crust of bread and a drink of water; when hunger presses, I shall eat in my own room by myself.'

The cunning Moor requested this for fear lest he should lift his veil while eating and thus expose his plot on account of his beard and his moustache.

'Fear nothing, Mistress Fatimah,' said Badr-al-Budur. 'It shall be as you wish. Rise up now, and I will show you your room.'

The Princess got up and led the disguised magician to the place she had assigned for the holy woman's use.

'Mistress Fatimah,' she said, 'this apartment is yours alone. Here you shall live in peace and quiet.'

The Moor thanked her for her kindness and called down

blessings upon her. Badr-al-Budur then showed him the jewelled dome with its four-and-twenty windows, and asked him what he thought of it.

'By Allah, my daughter, it is truly beautiful,' the Moor replied. 'There cannot be another place like it in the whole world. Yet I can see that it lacks one thing.'

'And what may that be, Mistress Fatimah?' she inquired.

'The egg of a bird called the roc,' the magician answered. 'If that were hung up from the middle of the dome, this hall would be the wonder of the world.'

'What is this bird,' asked the Princess, 'and where can its egg be found?'

'It is a huge bird, my lady,' the Moor replied. 'Its strength and size are such that it can carry camels and elephants in its claws and fly with them. This bird is mostly found in the Mountain of Kaf. The builder who constructed this palace can bring you one of its eggs.'

It was now lunch-time. The slave-girls laid the table, and Badr-al-Budur invited her guest to eat with her. The magician, however, declined. He retired to his own room, where he ate by himself.

In the evening Aladdin returned from the hunt. Badr-al-Budur greeted him, and he embraced and kissed her. Finding her preoccupied and anxious, he asked her the cause in some alarm.

'It is nothing at all, dearest,' she answered. 'I always thought there was nothing missing or deficient in our palace. Yet . . . if only a roc's egg was hung up from the dome of the jewelled apartment, our palace would be unrivalled in the world.'

'If that is all,' Aladdin replied, 'there is nothing simpler. Cheer up, my sweet. Just name the thing you fancy and I will bring it to you upon the instant, even if it be hidden in the darkest caverns of the earth.'

Leaving his wife, Aladdin went into his room, took out the lamp, and rubbed it; and at once the jinnee appeared before him, saying: 'Ask what you will!'

'I wish you to bring me a roc's egg,' said Aladdin, 'and to hang it up in the dome of the palace.'

But the jinnee scowled on hearing these words.

'Ungrateful human!' he roared. 'Are you not content to have me and all the other slaves of the lamp at your beck and call? Must you also command me to bring you our mistress and hang her up in the dome of the palace for your amusement? By Allah, you and your wife deserve to be burnt to ashes this very instant and scattered to the winds. But as you are both ignorant of this offence and have no knowledge of its consequences, I forgive you. You are not to blame. The culprit is that cursed magician, the Moor's brother, who is now staying in your palace disguised as Holy Fatimah. He put on her clothes and killed her in her cave; then he came here to avenge his brother's death on you. It was he that incited your wife to make this request.'

And so saying the jinnee vanished.

Aladdin was thunderstruck at these words, and all his limbs trembled with fear. He soon recovered himself, however, and went back to his wife, saying that his head ached; for he knew that the holy woman was renowned for her healing powers. The Princess sent at once for Fatimah, so that she might lay her hand on his head.

'Fatimah will soon cure you of your pain,' she said.

'And who is Fatimah?' asked Aladdin.

Badr-al-Budur told him that she had invited Holy Fatimah to stay with her in the palace. Presently the Moor entered; Aladdin rose to receive him, and pretending to know nothing of his intent, welcomed him as he might have welcomed Fatimah herself. He kissed the hem of his sleeve, saying: 'Mistress Fatimah, I beg you to do me a kindness. I have long heard of your consummate skill in curing ailments. Now I have a violent pain in my head.'

The damnable Moor could scarcely believe this invitation, for he wished for nothing better. He came near and, laying one hand on Aladdin's head, stretched the other under his robe and drew out his dagger to kill him. But Aladdin was on his guard; he caught him by the hand, wrenched the weapon from him, and thrust it into his heart.

'O what a woeful crime!' exclaimed the terrified Princess.

'Have you no fear of Allah to kill Fatimah, this virtuous and saintly woman, whose miracles are the wonder of our time?'

'Learn,' Aladdin replied, 'that the wretch whom I have killed was not Fatimah, but the man who murdered her. This is the brother of the Moorish magician who carried you off by his magic to Africa. He came to this country and devised these tricks. He murdered Fatimah, and, disguising himself in her habit, came here to avenge his brother's blood on me. It was he who exhorted you to ask for a roc's egg, seeking thereby to bring about my ruin. If you doubt my words, come and see who it is that I have slain.'

Aladdin lifted off the Moor's veil, and Badr-al-Budur saw a man with a beard all over his face. At once the truth dawned upon her.

'My love,' she said, 'this is the second time I have thrown you into a deadly peril.'

'Never mind, Badr-al-Budur,' replied Aladdin. 'For your eyes' sake I gladly accept whatever befalls me through you.'

Badr-al-Budur threw her arms round his neck and kissed him.

'Does my love mean so much to you?' she murmured. 'I confess I have never done justice to your love.'

Then Aladdin took her into his arms and kissed her, and they loved each other more than ever.

At that moment the Sultan arrived. They related to him all that had happened, and showed him the sorcerer's body. The Sultan ordered that he should be burnt and his ashes scattered to the winds, like his brother's.

Aladdin dwelt with the Princess in serenity and joy, and thenceforth escaped all dangers. When the Sultan died he inherited his throne and reigned justly over the kingdom. All his subjects loved him, and he lived happily with Badr-al-Budur until they were visited by the Destroyer of all earthly pleasures, the Annihilator of men.

THE TALE OF
KAFUR THE BLACK EUNUCH

KNOW, my friends, that when no more than eight years of age I had already cultivated a remarkable habit of telling one big lie a year.

Unable to bear with me any longer, my old master, who was a slave merchant, decided to sell me. He took me to his broker and ordered him to cry through the market-place: 'Who will buy a little slave with one fault?'

While the broker was thus declaiming the terms of the bargain, a certain merchant came forward and inquired what my fault might be. He was told that I lied once a year, and he finally agreed to buy me, fault and all, for the moderate sum of six hundred dirhams. Thereupon the broker took me to the merchant's house, and departed after receiving his commission.

My new master clad me in a fine suit of clothes, and I remained in his service for the rest of that year. With the new year the merchants hailed a season of fruitfulness and abundance, regaling each other at convivial feasts. When his turn came, my master made elaborate preparations for a pleasure-trip to a garden not far from the city. On the appointed day he and his guests went there and sat eating and carousing till noon, when my master, having forgotten something at his house, ordered me to ride back and return with it posthaste.

At once I mounted my mule and set out on my errand. But as soon as I drew near the house, I began to cry out and to shed a flood of tears. The neighbours, old and young, flocked around me; and, hearing my cries, my master's wife and daughters rushed to the door and asked me what had happened. With tears running down my face, I sobbed: 'My master and his guests were sitting in the garden beneath an old wall, and the wall fell down on them and crushed them to death. I mounted my mule and came with all speed to tell you.'

When they heard this, my master's wife and daughters shrieked and rent their clothes and beat their faces, while the neighbours thronged around to comfort them. My mistress proceeded to mourn her husband's death in a noble fashion. She set the entire house in chaos, smashing up the furniture, tearing down the doors and the windows, and smearing the walls with mud and soot. When half the business of destruction had been accomplished, she cried out to me to help her in the mourning rites. I gladly offered my services, setting myself the task of making havoc of all that remained. I knocked out the cupboards, pulled down the shelves with all that stood upon them, shattered to fragments the vessels and the china, and went around battering at the walls and the ceilings until the whole house lay in ruin. And all the while I cried: 'My master, oh, my master!'

Then my mistress rushed out into the street, with face unveiled and tresses flowing, followed by all her sons and daughters. 'Come, Kafur,' they cried, 'lead us to the place where your master lies buried, so that we may take him from beneath the ruins, and lay him in a coffin, and give him a fitting funeral!'

So I marched ahead of them, crying out: 'My master, oh, my master!'

A great multitude of men, women, and children followed at our heels, all beating their faces and joining in a chorus of shrill lament. I led them at an easy pace from one end of the city to the other; and, as we advanced from street to street, more and more people joined the procession, crying, when they learnt of the tragedy: 'There is no strength or help save in Allah!'

Just before we reached the gates of the city, some neighbours counselled my mistress to report the disaster to the Governor. When he heard the news, the Governor rose at once and, ordering some labourers to follow him with spades and baskets, joined the vast crowd; and they all resumed the march towards the garden.

Wailing aloud, beating my face, and scattering dust upon my head, I ran on as fast as I could go until I left the mourners far behind me. As soon as I approached the gates of the garden, I began to howl: 'My mistress, oh, my mistress! Who will ever be as kind to me as my poor, dead mistress!'

Alarmed at my lament, my master rushed out to meet me. He cried: 'In Allah's name, Kafur, what has happened?'

'Sir,' I replied, 'when I reached home, I found that the walls of the house had fallen down upon my mistress and her children.'

My master stood aghast.

'But my wife!' he exclaimed. 'Was she not saved?'

'Alas, she was not,' I answered. 'They were all crushed beneath the ruins; your eldest daughter was the first to die.'

'But my youngest girl!' he cried 'Did she not escape?'

'Alas, she did not,' I replied.

'And what became of my mule?' he then cried. 'Is she safe?'

'No, by Allah,' I answered. 'The walls of both the house and the stable collapsed and buried beneath them every living thing, even the sheep, the geese, and the hens. Nothing is now left but a heap of decaying flesh.'

'But my eldest son?' he exclaimed.

'Dead, dead!' I moaned. 'Not a trace is left of house or family. As for the sheep, the geese, and the hens, the cats and dogs of the entire neighbourhood are even now devouring their dead flesh.'

The world darkened before my master's eyes. Stunned by the terrible news and trembling all over, he could scarcely stand upright and was like one suddenly stricken with the palsy. He rent his clothes, tore his beard, hurled his turban to the ground, and beat his face until his cheeks were covered with blood 'My wife!' he cried out. 'My children! Oh, my great sorrow!'

His friends the merchants gathered around him, wailing and tearing their clothes.

Still beating himself about the head with great violence, my master staggered forward towards the road, followed by his guests. Scarcely had he reached the gates of the garden, when he saw in the distance a great cloud of dust, from which proceeded cries of wild lamentation. And soon the Governor appeared with my master's family, together with the rest of the mourners.

My master was confounded at the sight of his own wife and children hurrying towards him. For a moment he stood speechless, and then broke out into a fit of laughter.

'Thank Allah you are alive!' shouted his wife and children, throwing themselves upon him.

'Thank Allah you are safe!' exclaimed my master.

'But how were you rescued from beneath the ruins of the wall, you and your friends the merchants?' cried his wife.

'What happened to you in the house?' asked my master.

'We are all safe and well,' answered his wife. 'Nothing has happened save that your servant Kafur came to us unturbaned and with his clothes all torn, telling us that the garden wall had fallen upon you and killed you.'

'But, by Allah,' burst out my master, 'Kafur came to me just now and told me that you were all crushed beneath the ruins of the house!'

Here my master turned round and saw me still wailing and throwing dust upon my bare head. He beckoned me to draw near, crying: 'Ill-omened slave, son of a pitch-faced whore, damned offspring of a monstrous race, what is the reason of this fiendish act? By Allah, I will flay your skin from your flesh and tear your flesh from your bones!'

'Upon my life,' I retorted, 'you can do no such thing. You have bought me with my fault; and there are honest men who will bear witness that you did so knowing that my fault was the telling of one lie a year. Now this, let me hasten to add, is only half a lie. The other half shall be told before the year is out.'

'Dog, and son of a dog!' exclaimed my master. 'Do you call that half a lie? Why, it is an entire calamity! By Allah, let the world note, I free you here and now: you are no more slave of mine!'

'By Allah,' I rejoined, 'if you are willing to free me, I will not free you until my year is ended and I have treated you to the other half of my lie. Then, and only then, you can take me to the market-place and sell me. But you must sell me with my fault. Free me you cannot, for I know no trade with which to earn a living. Such is the law of the land.'

While we were thus arguing, the great crowd, headed by the Governor and his men, gathered around us. My master and the other merchants explained what had happened, adding: 'This, mark you, is only half a lie.'

The crowd marvelled greatly, but everyone said that it was a whole lie, and a big one. So they reviled me and showered curses on my head, while I stood grinning at them.

'How can my master punish me,' I laughed triumphantly, 'when he bought me with my fault?'

When at last we returned to the town and entered the quarter where my master lived, he found a heap of ruins where his house once stood. But my mistress chose to forget her own exploits and told him that I had done all the damage.

'Son of a whore!' he cried, foaming with rage. 'If this was only half a lie, what would have happened if you had told a whole one? A couple of cities, I suppose, would have been levelled to the ground!'

With that he dragged me to the Governor's house, where I was treated to such a trouncing that I at length dropped down unconscious. Whilst I was lying senseless they called in a barber, who cut off my testicles and cauterized the wound: so that when I recovered my senses I found myself a eunuch with nothing left. My master wagged his finger at me with evident satisfaction, saying: 'You have taken away from me things that I valued dearly: I have taken away from you things which you held most precious.'

Soon afterwards, he took me to the market-place and sold me at an enormous profit, for I was now a eunuch.

Thus I continued to bring trouble and misfortune to every household that employed me until at length I entered the service of the Prince of the Faithful. But now, alas, my old spirit is broken; for I have lost much of my youthful vigour since I became a eunuch.

That, my friends, is the story of my castration; and peace be with you.

THE PORTER AND THE
THREE GIRLS OF BAGHDAD

ONCE upon a time there lived in the city of Baghdad a young
bachelor who was by trade a porter.

One day, as he sat in the market-place leaning idly against
his basket, a young woman, dressed in rare silks and cloaked
in a gold-embroidered mantle of Mosul brocade, stopped
before him and gently raised her veil. Beneath it there showed
dark eyes with long lashes and lineaments of perfect beauty.

'Lift up your basket, porter,' she said in a sweet voice, 'and
follow me.'

At once the porter took up his basket and followed her,
thinking to himself: 'This is indeed a blessed day!' until she
stopped at the door of a house and knocked. The door was
opened by a Christian, who gave her, in return for a piece of
gold, a measure of olives and two casks of wine. These she put
into the basket and said to the porter: 'Follow me.'

'By Allah,' thought the porter, 'this is surely my lucky day!'

He took up his basket and followed her until she stopped at
a fruiterer's, where she bought Syrian apples and Othmani
quinces, Omani peaches, cucumbers from the Nile, Egyptian
lemons and Sultani citrons, sweet-scented myrtle and henna
flowers, camomile, anemones, violets, sweet-briar, and pome-
granate-blossom. All these she put into the basket and again
said to the porter: 'Follow me.'

She stopped at a butcher's stall and said to him: 'Cut me
ten pounds of meat.' She wrapped the meat in a large banana-
leaf and, putting it into the basket, ordered the porter to
follow her. She next made her way to a grocer's shop, where
she bought pistachios, nuts and raisins, and thence to a confectioner's, where she chose a platter of dainty sweetmeats
stuffed with almonds and flavoured with musk, lemon cakes,

pastry crescents, Zainab's combs, and honey tarts. And all these she placed into the porter's basket.

'Had you told me,' observed the porter, 'I would have brought a mule to carry all these things!'

The young woman smiled at the porter's remark and, bidding him hold his tongue, stopped at a perfume-seller's and bought ten different essences, rose-water, willow-water and musk-rose dew, two loaves of sugar, a sprinkling-bottle, frankincense, aloe-wood, ambergris, and candles of Alexandrine wax. Again the porter took up his basket and followed her until she came to a magnificent, lofty house facing a great courtyard. Its doors were of ebony plated with red gold.

Here the young woman unveiled her face and knocked, and the door was opened by a girl of surpassing beauty. Her forehead was white as a lily and her eyes were more lustrous than a gazelle's. Her brows were crescent moons, her cheeks anemones, and her mouth like the crimson ruby on King Solomon's ring. Her teeth were whiter than a string of pearls, and like twin pomegranates were her breasts.

At the sight of this girl the porter was so overwhelmed with wonder that the basket nearly fell off his head.

'Surely this is the most auspicious day of my life!' he thought.

'Pray come in, sister,' said the girl who had opened the door, 'and let this weary porter put down his burden.'

The porter followed the two girls into a spacious and nobly vaulted hall. The ceiling was wondrously carved in patterns of elaborate design, and the walls were hung with tapestry of silk and rich brocade. In the centre of the hall a fountain played in a pool of crystal water, and near the far side stood a couch of alabaster inlaid with diamonds and covered with a red silken quilt embroidered with pearls. A third girl, slim and exquisitely beautiful, was reclining on the couch. Her face was radiant as the full moon and all the witchcraft of Babylon was in her eyes. A paragon of Arabian grace, she was like a star twinkling in a cloudless sky or a golden dome shimmering in the night.

The girl, who was the oldest of the three, rose from her couch and, walking slowly to the middle of the hall, said to

her sisters: 'Why are you standing idly by? Come, let us take
down this heavy basket from the porter's head.'

The three girls helped the porter put down his basket, and
when they had taken out the contents and arranged them in
their proper places, they handed him two pieces of gold,
saying: 'Take this, and go your way.'

The porter looked at the young girls and marvelled at the
perfection of their beauty; never in all his days had he seen the

like. He noticed that there was no man in the house, and stood hesitant before them, gazing in wonderment at the plentiful drinks, fruits, and flowers.

'Why do you not go?' asked the eldest of the girls, the mistress of the house. 'Do you find your payment too little?' Then, turning to her sisters, she said: 'Give him another dinar.'

'By Allah, sweet ladies,' replied the porter, 'you have paid me well enough; my ordinary pay is but a few coppers. It is about you that my heart is troubled. How is it that you live alone in this house with no man to attend you? Do you not know that a feast cannot be merry with fewer than four companions, and that women cannot be truly happy without men? Now you are only three, my ladies. You need a fourth, a man of discretion who can be trusted with secrets.'

'But, porter,' replied the eldest, laughing, 'do you not see that we are young girls and should therefore be wary of confiding in strangers? "A secret shared," says the proverb, "is a secret lost."'

'I swear by your dear life,' he replied, 'that I am a discreet and honest man, lacking neither in wisdom nor in learning. Your secrets, ladies, shall be safe with me.'

'You must know,' said the second with a mischievous smile, 'that we have spent a large fortune on this house. Have you anything with which to pay us? We shall not allow you to sit in our midst and be our drinking-companion unless you contribute a sum of money. Does not the proverb say: "Friendship without gold is worth no more than a pip"?'

'Have you a well-lined purse, young man?' put in the youngest. 'If you have nothing, be off with nothing!'

But the mistress of the house cut short her sisters' pleasantry.

'By Allah,' she said, 'this man has not failed us today: another might have lost his patience. I myself will undertake to pay for him.'

'Stay with us, then, good porter,' cried her sisters, 'and be welcome in this house.'

At this the porter rejoiced. He thanked them and kissed the ground before them. Presently the eldest rose and, tying a girdle round her waist, began to make ready for the evening. She strained and poured out the wine, arranged the fruit and flowers, and set places for the feast beside the fountain. The three girls sat down with their delighted guest. The mistress of the house poured wine for herself and for her sisters, and then handed a cup to the porter.

'Drink this,' she said, 'and may it bring you joy!'

The porter quickly drained his cup. He kissed his hostesses' hands and recited verses in their praise, his head swaying from side to side. The three girls again filled their cups, and so did the porter.

'My lady,' he said, bowing low before the eldest, 'I am your servant, your bondsman.'

'Drink,' she cried, 'and may your wine be sweet and wholesome!'

When they had drained their cups a second time, they rose and danced round the fountain, singing and clapping their hands in unison. They went on drinking until the wine took possession of their senses and overcame their reason, and, when its sovereignty was fully established, the first girl got up and cast off all her clothes, letting down her long hair to cover her nakedness. She jumped into the fountain, frolicking and washing her body, filling her mouth with water and squirting it at the porter. At length she came out of the pool and threw herself into the porter's lap. Then she pointed down to that which was between her thighs and said: 'Darling master, what do you call that?'

'The gateway to heaven,' the porter answered.

'Are you not ashamed?' cried the girl, and, taking him by the neck, began to beat him.

'Then it is your crack.'

'Villain!' cried the girl, and slapped him on his thigh.

'It is your thing!'

'No, no,' she cried, shaking her head.

'Then it is your hornets' nest,' said the porter.

All three slapped him, laughing, until his flesh was red.

'Then tell me what *you* call it!' he shouted.

'The Buttercup,' the girl replied.

247

'At last,' cried the porter. 'Allah keep you safe and sound O Buttercup.'

They passed the wine round and round again. Presently the second girl took off her clothes and threw herself onto the porter's lap. Pointing to that which was between her thighs, she said: 'Light of my eyes, what is the name of this?'

'The thing!' he answered.

'A naughty word,' she cried. 'Have you no shame?' And she slapped him so hard that the hall echoed to the sound.

'Then it must be the Buttercup.'

'No, no,' she cried, and slapped him on the neck.

'Well, what do you call it, my sister?'

'Sesame,' the second girl replied.

After the wine had gone round once more, and the porter had somewhat recovered from his beatings, the last girl, the fairest of the three, got up and threw off her clothes. The porter began to stroke his neck, saying, 'Allah save me from yet another beating!' as he watched her descend, utterly naked, into the fountain. She washed her limbs, and sported in the water. He marvelled at the beauty of her face, which resembled the full moon rising in the night sky, at the roundness of her breasts, and her graceful, quivering thighs. Then she came out of the water and laid herself across his lap.

'Tell me the name of this,' she said, pointing to her delicate parts.

The porter tried this name and that, and finally begged her to tell him and stop beating him.

'The Inn of Abu Mansoor,' the girl replied.

'Allah preserve you,' cried the porter, 'O Inn of Abu Mansoor.'

The girls dressed themselves and resumed their seats. Now the porter got up, undressed, and went down into the fountain. The girls watched him as he sported in the water and washed as they had done. Eventually he came out of the fountain, threw himself into the lap of the first girl, and rested his feet on the knees of the second. Pointing to his rising organ, he demanded of the first girl, 'And what do you call this, my queen?'

The girls laughed till they fell over on their backs. To every guess they hazarded he answered 'No', biting each one in turn, and kissing, pinching, and hugging them, which made them laugh all the more. Finally they cried, 'Brother, what is its name, then?'

'Know that this,' the porter replied, 'is my sturdy mule which feeds on buttercups, delights in sesame, and spends the night in the Inn of Abu Mansoor.'

At these words the girls collapsed with laughter.

The four amused themselves till nightfall, when the girls said to the porter: 'In the name of Allah, our friend, rise, put on your clothes, and get out of this house.'

'By Allah,' replied the porter, 'my soul would more willingly leave my body than I your company. Pray let us join the night with the day, and when tomorrow comes we will bid each other farewell.'

Finding him a pleasant, witty rogue, the eldest of the girls said to her sisters: 'By my life, let him stay with us, so that we may beguile the night with his drollery.'

The others agreed, and said to the porter: 'You may pass the night here on one condition: that you obey us strictly and ask no questions about anything you see.'

'I agree to that, my mistresses,' he answered.

'Rise, then,' they said, 'and read the writing on the door.'

The porter went to the door, on which he found these words inscribed in letters of gold: 'He who speaks of that which does not concern him shall hear what will displease him.'

'Bear witness, my mistresses,' he said, 'that I will never speak of that which does not concern me.'

Presently the eldest of the girls set before them meat and drink, and when they had finished eating they lit lamps and candles and burned incense in the braziers. Then they moved to the other side of the hall and sat down to another bout, telling stories and reciting verses. Suddenly they heard a knocking at the door. One of the girls went to open it and soon came back, saying: 'Our company is now complete. There are three wandering dervishes at the door; their heads are clean-shaven, and so are their beards and eyebrows: and what is stranger still, each of them is blind in the left eye. They appear as though they have just arrived from a distant land. "Perhaps the master of this house," they said, "would give us leave to spend the

night in the stables. We are strangers in this city and do not know anyone who would give us shelter." Oh my sisters,' added the girl, laughing, 'the three have such an odd appearance!'

She spoke thus of the dervishes until she prevailed upon her sisters to admit them.

'Let them come in,' said the two girls. 'But you must first

warn them not to speak of that which does not concern them.'

The girl hastened eagerly to the door, and in a few moments came back leading the three strangers. They were each blind in the left eye and their beards and eyebrows were shaven. They bowed low before the girls, who received them courteously and invited them to be seated.

The dervishes marvelled at the beauty of the young girls, at the fragrance of the incense, and at the rich splendour of the house. They saw the drunken porter lying on the floor and, taking him for one of their order, whispered to each other: 'He must be a dervish like ourselves and a stranger here.'

Upon this the porter sprang to his feet, and staggered towards the three men.

'Hold your tongues!' he muttered, glaring fiercely in their faces. 'Have you not read the warning on the door?'

'We pray for Allah's pardon!' cried the dervishes. 'Our lives are at your mercy.'

The girls laughed, and rose to make peace between the porter and their one-eyed guests. They invited the dervishes to eat and drink; and again the cups went round.

'Brothers,' said the porter to the dervishes, 'have you not some tale of marvel to entertain us with?'

Encouraged by the porter's remark, the dervishes called for musical instruments. A tambourine, a lute, and a Persian harp were at once brought in. They each took up an instrument and together made music, the girls singing to their accompaniment. Soon, however, their merriment was interrupted by a second knocking on the door, and one of the girls rose to see who was there.

Now this was the reason of the second knocking on the door.

That night the Caliph Haroun al-Rashid went out into the streets and alley-ways of Baghdad in quest of new adventures. Disguised in merchant's attire, he was accompanied by Ja'afar, his vizier, and Masrur, his executioner. It so chanced that as they were roaming about the city they passed by the house of the three girls, and, hearing the sounds of music and voices singing, Al-Rashid said to Ja'afar: 'Would that we could enter this house, so that we may listen to the singers and find out who they are.'

'Prince of the Faithful,' replied the Vizier, 'they are doubtless a company of drunkards. If we go in, I fear that some harm may befall you.'

'We must go in,' insisted the Caliph. 'You shall invent some pretext for our entrance.'

'I hear and obey,' said Ja'afar.

He went up to the door and knocked. When the girl opened, the Vizier kissed the ground before her and said: 'Mistress, we are merchants from Tiberias. Ten days ago we arrived in Baghdad with our goods and took lodging at the Inn of the Merchants. A gentleman entertained us at his house tonight, but, as we left him at a late hour, we lost our way to the inn. Perhaps you would be so hospitable as to give us leave to pass the night under your roof; and may Allah reward your kindness.'

The girl looked closely at them, and, noticing their merchants' garb and distinguished appearance, went in to inform her sisters. They gave her leave to admit them, and when the Caliph and his companions were ushered into the hall the girls rose to greet them.

'As our guests you are welcome,' they said. 'But you must accept this one condition: that you shall not speak of that which does not concern you.'

'So be it,' they replied. And they all sat down together.

The Caliph marvelled at the grace and radiance of the young girls, and was astonished to see that each of the dervishes was blind in the left eye. The girls offered him a cup of wine, but he excused himself, saying: 'I am setting forth on a pilgrimage to Mecca shortly.' Thereupon one of the girls put down before him a small table, on which she placed a cup of Chinese porcelain. Into the cup she poured some rose essence and water; then she added to it a lump of ice and sweetened it with sugar. The Caliph thanked her and thought to himself: 'By Allah, I will reward her tomorrow for this good deed.'

When the wine had gone the rounds the mistress of the

house rose and, taking the youngest girl by the hand, said to her: 'Sister, we must now fulfil our duty.'

Upon this the second girl also rose; she cleared and tidied the hall and added more incense to the braziers. Then she invited the dervishes to sit in one corner, and the Caliph, Ja'afar, and Masrur in another, and, turning to the fuddled porter, ordered him to get up.

'What is your wish, mistress?' he muttered, staggering to his feet.

'You are no stranger in this house,' she replied. 'Come and help me.'

The porter followed her out of the hall and saw two black bitches with chains round their necks, which the girl ordered him to lead in. When he had done so, the mistress of the house pulled up her long sleeves and, taking up a whip, said to the porter: 'Bring one of the bitches near.'

As the porter dragged the bitch forward, she whined piteously and lifted up her eyes to the girl in sorrowful entreaty. But the young woman fell upon the bitch, whipping her mercilessly on the head, until the animal wept and howled and she herself could strike no more. Then she flung down the whip and, taking the bitch in her arms, pressed her tenderly to her breast, wiped away her tears and kissed her head.

'Take this one back,' she said to the porter, 'and bring me the other.'

He dragged the second bitch forward and the girl did with her as she had done with the first.

The Caliph was profoundly distressed at this sight and, anxious to learn the reason of the girl's conduct, looked questioningly at Ja'afar. But the Vizier motioned him to keep silent. Presently the mistress of the house turned to her youngest sister and said: 'Rise, and perform your task.'

She sat down with the other girl on the gold-encrusted couch, while the youngest went into a chamber and brought out a satin bag tasselled with green ribbons and fastened with buckles of gold, from which she took a lute. Then she tuned the instrument and, playing upon it, sang a mournful song.

When she heard the song the second girl wailed aloud and

beat her breast; then, rending her garments, she fell down in a swoon. Her body being uncovered as she lay on the floor, the Caliph was astonished to see on it the marks of lashing. But the youngest at once came to her sister's aid; she sprinkled her face with water, and helped her into a new robe.

The company watched the proceedings with pity and horror.

'Do you not see the sorrowful state of this young woman and the weals of whipping on her body?' whispered the Caliph to Ja'afar. 'I cannot keep silent any longer, and must find out the answer to the mystery of these girls and the bitches.'

'Prince of the Faithful,' replied Ja'afar, 'remember the condition: "Do not speak of that which does not concern you or you shall hear what will displease you."'

Whilst they were thus whispering, the youngest again took up the lute and, pressing it against her bosom, touched the chords and sang another song. Again the second girl wailed and tore her clothes and fell into swoon; and again her sister sprinkled her face with water and helped her into a new robe. This was followed by yet another song, and for the third time the girl wept and fell down fainting.

'Would that we had never set foot in this house,' said the dervishes to each other, 'but had rather passed the night outside the city among the garbage heaps! What we have just witnessed has wrung our hearts with horror.'

Overhearing their whispers, the Caliph said to the dervishes: 'Are you not of this house, then?'

'No,' they replied. 'We have never been in this place before.'

'Perhaps that man there knows the answer,' said the Caliph pointing to the porter.

They all turned to the porter and inquired of him the reason of the girls' behaviour.

'I have never set foot in this house before,' the porter replied. 'By Allah, I have seen some strange things here this evening.'

The company conferred together and at length the Caliph said, 'We are seven men to three girls. Let us question them about their mystery; if they do not answer willingly, they shall do so by force.'

They all agreed to this except Ja'afar, who said: 'This is not a wise counsel. Remember that we are their guests and that they have laid down a condition which we promised to observe. It is now almost morning, and soon each of us will go his way.'

He winked at the Caliph and, drawing him aside, continued: 'Prince of the Faithful, we have but one hour more in this house. As soon as we return to the palace I will have them brought before you, and then you can command them to tell their story.'

'I have not the patience to wait till morning,' said the Caliph angrily. 'Let these dervishes question them.'

Ja'afar wavered, whilst the company sought each other's counsel; but opinion differed widely amongst them as to who should speak first. At length they decided that the porter should be their spokesman.

'What are you whispering about?' inquired the eldest of the sisters.

'Mistress,' said the porter, rising to his feet, 'my friends desire to know the history of the two black bitches and why you whipped them and then fondled them and kissed them. They are also anxious to learn the cause of the weals upon your sister's body.'

'Is it true that this is your wish?' asked the young woman.

'Yes,' replied the Caliph and the dervishes.

'By Allah,' exclaimed the girl, 'you have done us a most grievous wrong! You swore that you would abide by our condition. Was it not enough for you to come into our house and eat and drink with us? But perhaps you are less to blame than our sister who persuaded us to let you in.'

With this she pulled up her long sleeves above her writsts and stamped her foot against the floor three times, crying: 'Make haste, make haste!'

Suddenly a door in the hall was flung open and through it entered seven black slaves with unsheathed swords in their hands.

'Lay hold of these babbling fools,' she cried, 'and chain them one to the other.'

The slaves did so. 'One sign from you, gracious lady,' they said, 'and their heads shall be struck off.'

'First,' said the young woman, 'I wish to question them and find out what sort of men they are.'

'For the sake of Allah,' whimpered the porter, 'do not kill me for an offence of which I am innocent. These men have wronged you, but I have not. By Allah, how joyous would our night have been had we not set eyes on these dervishes! Why, their ill-omened presence would make a flourishing city fall in ruin. Fair mistress, does not the poet say: "Forgiveness is never so noble as when extended by the mighty to the weak"?'

The young woman laughed at the porter's words and said sternly: 'Each of you will now tell us the true story of his life. You have but one hour to live.'

'Woe to you, Ja'afar!' whispered the Caliph. 'Speak to her nobly: tell her who we are, or she will have us put to a miserable death.'

'Is that not what we deserve?' rejoined the Vizier. But the Caliph grew very angry and said: 'There is a time for pleasantry and a time for earnestness.'

'Are you brothers?' asked the mistress of the house, turning to the dervishes.

'No, by Allah,' they replied. 'We are poor wanderers who met by mere chance.'

Then, addressing one of the three, she said: 'Were you born blind in one eye?'

'No,' he replied. 'My story is very strange; if it were written with a needle on the corner of an eye, it would yet serve as a lesson to those who seek wisdom.'

She put the same question to the second and the third, and they both replied: 'Fair mistress, we are the sons of illustrious kings. Each of us was born in a different land.'

'Well, then,' said the girl, addressing the company, 'each of you shall tell us his story and the reason of his coming to this house. He whose tale is truly strange shall gain his liberty and go his way.'

The first to speak was the porter. 'Mistress,' he said, 'I am a humble porter; one whom this fair sister of yours hired and led from a wine merchant's house to a butcher's stall, from a fruiterer's to a grocer's, from a confectioner's to a perfume-seller's, and thence to this house, where that has happened which was destined to happen. That is the long and the short of my story; and peace be with you.'

'Porter, you may go,' said the mistress of the house, laughing. 'You have gained your freedom.'

'By Allah,' he replied, 'I will not leave this house until I have heard the stories of my companions.'

Then the first of the dervishes came forward and said:

The Tale of the First Dervish

KNOW, mistress, that my father and my father's brother were both kings and that they ruled over two neighbouring cities. It chanced that on the day of my birth a son was also born to my uncle, so that as the years passed away my cousin and I reached manhood together.

It was my custom every year to spend several months in my uncle's city, and on the last occasion I visited him my cousin received me sumptuously, slaughtering fatted sheep in my honour and regaling me with the rarest wines. When we were both overtaken in drink, he said to me: 'Son of my uncle, I beg you to grant me an urgent favour.'

'With all my heart,' I replied, and at his request solemnly swore that I would do whatever he desired.

Immediately rising, he went away, and after a short while came back with a veiled woman, richly perfumed and decked with precious ornaments. Pointing to his companion, my cousin begged me to take her to a certain graveyard and to await him there. As I had pledged him my assistance, I accompanied the woman to the burial ground, where my cousin presently joined us, bringing with him a basin filled with water, a bag containing plaster, and a little axe.

He carried these to a tomb in the middle of the graveyard, and with the axe removed its stones one by one. Then he dug in the ground beneath until he uncovered an iron slab the size of a small door. This he lifted, revealing a vaulted staircase. My cousin turned to his companion and motioned her to draw near, saying: 'Now make your choice.'

The woman went down the stairs and disappeared below. Then he said to me: 'Son of my uncle, I must now ask you to fulfil your promise. When I have descended, put back the iron cover and the earth, mix the plaster, and rebuild this tomb as it was before, so that none should suspect that it was lately opened. I have been working on this tomb for a whole year:

and no one knew except Allah. Farewell, cousin, and may the Merciful keep you!'

With that he went down the stairs and vanished from my sight. I replaced the trap-door, covered it with earth, and laboured at the tomb until it appeared exactly as before. Then I returned to my uncle's palace, and, finding that he was away hunting, lay down and slept the night through.

When morning came I thought over all that had happened the previous day and bitterly repented what I had done; but, alas, repentance was too late. I hastened back to the burial ground and searched all day for the tomb which my cousin had entered, but could nowhere find it. With a heavy heart I returned at nightfall to the palace, and could neither eat nor drink for thinking of my cousin. Tormented by the thought of my own guilt, I passed the night on a sleepless bed and at daybreak made my way again to the burial ground, where I searched in vain among the tombs till evening. I thus continued my quest for seven days and, at length, half-demented with grief and fear, set out for my father's kingdom.

Scarcely had I reached the gates of the city when I was set upon by an armed band who bound me with strong chains. I was utterly confounded at this encounter, seeing that I was the King's own son and that among my captors were servants of my father and myself. Suspecting that some evil chance had befallen my father, I questioned my assailants about him but received no answer. At length, one of my slaves who was among them said to me: 'Fortune has betrayed the King. The troops have mutinied and the Vizier has killed him . We were sent here to lie in ambush for you.'

Prostrate with grief at the death of my father, I was carried by my captors to the Vizier's presence. Now the Vizier had long borne me a grudge which resulted from my passion for the crossbow. For it chanced one day that, as I was standing on the roof of our palace, a bird alighted on the Vizier's terrace, where he happened to be walking. I shot my bolt, but, as ill luck would have it, missed the bird and hit the Vizier in the eye, knocking it out. The angry Vizier could not demand justice because my father was the King of the city; but now, when I stood before him manacled and bound with chains, he gave orders that my head be struck off.

'What is my crime?' I asked.

'What crime is greater than this?' he cried, pointing to his missing eye.

'That was done by accident,' I protested.

'If you did it by accident,' he replied, 'I will do it by design.'

He ordered his men to bring me near, and, thrusting his finger in my left eye, plucked it out.

That was how I became one-eyed.

Then the Vizier had me locked into a chest, which he delivered to his executioner. 'Carry this chest out of the city,' he said to him. 'Put the prisoner to death and leave his body to the vultures and the wild beasts.'

The executioner brought me outside the gates of the city, took me out of the chest, and was about to bandage my eyes when I began to weep and bewail my evil fortune in sorrowful verses. Hearing my lament, the executioner, who had until so recently served my father and received many favours at my hands, exclaimed: 'How can I, your own slave, put you to death?' Then he added: 'Fly for your life! But never return to this city, or you shall die and be the cause of my death also.'

I kissed his hand and left him, scarcely believing in my freedom. I hastened to my uncle's city, and, as I journeyed on, I consoled myself for the loss of my eye by reflecting on my escape from death. When I at length saw my uncle and told him of the murder of my father and the injury that had been done me, he wept bitterly, crying: 'You have added a heavy sorrow to my sorrows. My own son has been missing for many days and no one knows what has become of him.'

Here my uncle wept again and fell back fainting; then, recovering himself, he added: 'Remember, my child, it is better to have lost an eye than to have lost your life.'

At this I could keep silent no longer about my cousin's disappearance. I told my uncle the whole truth, and he was much relieved to learn what had happened.

'Take me to the tomb at once,' he cried.

I told him of my vain endeavours to find it, but he insisted on another search. We set out together for the burial ground, and this time, after a thorough scrutiny of all the tombs, I recognized the one we sought. My uncle and I rejoiced; we removed the stones, displaced the earth, and, lifting the iron slab, went down the stairway. After descending some fifty steps a dense cloud of smoke blinded our eyes, but my uncle pronounced those comforting words which banish all fear: 'There is no strength or help save in Allah the Most High!'

We made our way through the smoke and at length came to a spacious hall well-stored with sacks of flour and grain and many kinds of provisions. In the centre of the hall we saw a curtained bed, and on this bed my cousin was lying in the arms of the woman who had gone down with him. But they were both black as charcoal, as though they had been thrown into a pit of fire.

My uncle spat in the face of his dead son, crying: 'Wretch, this is your reward in this world, but your punishment in the world to come will be more terrible!'

So saying, he took off his sandal and struck the corpse of his son with it. Astonished at this callous act, and grieved to see my cousin and the girl reduced to cinders, I cried: 'Uncle, restrain yourself, I pray you! I am horrified at the fate of your son and his companion, but even more at seeing you, his father, treat his remains with such irreverence.'

'Son of my brother,' he replied, 'you must know that this youth was in love with his half-sister from his earliest days. When they were children I forbade him to see her and consoled myself that they were young and foolish; but when they grew older they committed evil together and I was informed of the outrage. I was scarcely able to believe my ears and rebuked my son sharply, saying: "Beware of these infamous deeds which Allah has forbidden and man condemned; or we shall be dishonoured and held to shame till the end of time. Caravans will carry our tale from land to land. Take heed, or I shall surely kill you in my rage!" Thenceforth I kept the two apart, but the wicked girl's passion for her brother was as great as his, and their souls willingly yielded to Satan's promptings.

'When my son saw that his sister was kept away from him, he made this secret hiding-place, stored it with these provisions, and, taking advantage of my absence at the hunt, came here with her.

'Then the scourge of Allah smote them, and his fire consumed them both together. But their punishment in the world to come will be more terrible.'

We both wept, and my uncle said to me: 'Henceforth you shall be my son.'

I sat there for some time pondering over the sorrowful ways of the world. And when I thought of my father's death and his Vizier's treachery, the loss of my eye and the strange end which had overtaken my cousin, I wept again from a full heart.

At length we came out of the tomb and, after we had replaced the earth and restored the stones, we returned to the palace. Scarcely had we seated ourselves, however, when we heard a fierce and warlike din in the streets. The air was filled with the sounds of drums and trumpets, the neighing of horses, and the clang of armour; and the town was enveloped in a cloud of dust raised by galloping hoofs. We were greatly alarmed at the tumult, and upon inquiry the King was told: 'The Vizier who usurped your brother's throne has mustered an innumerable force of mercenaries and bedouins and stormed his way into your kingdom; and the people, unprepared and powerless to resist him, have opened the gates and surrendered the city.'

I was overcome with despair at this crowning stroke of ill fortune, and thought to myself: 'If I am found by the people of the city or the Vizier's soldiers, they will surely kill me.' So I shaved my beard, put on these garments, and fled my uncle's kingdom. I journeyed to this city, hoping to find someone who would take me to the Caliph of Allah, the Prince of the Faithful, that I might tell him my woeful story.

It was only this evening that I arrived in Baghdad, and, as I stood uncertain whither to bend my steps, I met by chance this other dervish and we were soon joined by our third companion. Recognizing each other as strangers, we walked on in the darkness together till Destiny led us to this house, my mistress.

This is the story of my lost eye and shaved beard.

*

When she had heard the tale of the first dervish, the mistress of the house said to him: 'You may go.'

But he replied: 'By Allah, I will not leave this house until I have heard the tales of my companions.'

They all marvelled at the story, and the Caliph whispered to Ja'afar: 'Never in all my life have I heard a more extra-ordinary adventure.'

Then the second dervish came forward and, kissing the ground before the mistress of the house, began:

The Tale of the Second Dervish

KNOW, mistress, that this eye of mine was not sightless from my birth. My story is of such marvel that if it were written with a needle on the corner of an eye, it would yet serve as a lesson to those who seek wisdom.

Though you see me in these rags, I am a king and the son of a king. I have read the Koran in each of the seven traditions, studied ancient books under the most eminent tutors, and per-used the writings of all the poets. I mastered the lore of the stars and excelled in the other sciences, so that I surpassed in learning all the men of my time. My fame spread far and wide as a calligrapher; and I became renowned in all countries and among all kings.

When the King of India heard tell of me, he requested my father to let me visit him, accompanying his invitation with regal and priceless presents. My father equipped for me six ships and I set sail, together with my retinue.

After a month's voyage we sighted land and, casting anchor, disembarked our horses, loaded ten camels with presents for the King of India, and set out on the inland journey. We had not gone far, however, when there appeared a great cloud of dust in the distance which drew closer and closer, filling the earth and sky with sand, and presently revealed a mounted band of Arab highwaymen, armed to the teeth and as fierce as lions. When they saw our treasure-laden caravan they galloped towards us, charging with their spears. We made signs to them that we were envoys to the illustrious King and begged them not to molest us. But they replied: 'This is not his land, nor are we his subjects.' At once they slew some of my slaves and fell to plundering the caravan, while the rest of us took to flight, myself receiving a serious wound.

I ran on and on, grieving at this sudden stroke of ill-fortune, and at nightfall came to the top of a mountain, where I took shelter in a cave. Next morning I made my way down the mountain and journeyed painfully on until at length I reached a flourishing city surrounded by high walls. Winter with its icy breath had passed away, and spring had decked its gardens with fresh flowers, so that the air was filled with the singing of birds and the murmur of gushing brooks.

I rejoiced to find myself in this city, worn out as I was by the journey, sick and pale from my wound, and utterly fallen from my former state. I wandered along the streets and, uncertain whither to turn my steps, entered the shop of a tailor and exchanged greetings with him. He received me courteously, invited me to sit down, and asked me whence I had come. I recounted to him all that had befallen me from first to last, and he was both grieved and alarmed at my story.

'My son,' he said, 'you must on no account repeat this tale to any other man in this city, for our King is a sworn enemy of your father. Indeed, I greatly fear for your safety.'

He placed some food and drink before me, and we ate and drank, conversing together till the fall of evening. Then he gave me a mattress and a quilt, and I slept that night in a corner of his shop. I lodged with him for three days, and at the end of that time he inquired if I knew any trade with which I could make a living.

'I am deeply versed in the Law,' I replied, 'and well-schooled in the arts and sciences. Also I am a mathematician and a scribe of high repute.'

'None of this, my friend,' he said, 'will earn you a living in this city. No one here knows anything of the arts or sciences; their sole concern is to make money.'

THOS. WILLIAMS. 82

When I answered that I was skilled in nothing else, he said: 'Courage, my son. Take an axe and a rope, and go out and cut wood in the forest, till Allah relieves your distress. But tell no one who you are or they will kill you.'

The tailor bought me an axe and a rope, and introduced me to a band of woodcutters, to whose special care he commended me. I went out with them to the forest, and, when I had chopped a load of faggots, carried them back on my head and sold them in the city for half a piece of gold. I bought some food with a few coppers, laying the rest aside. And in this fashion I continued to labour for a whole year.

One day, however, I entered a densely wooded glade and began to dig round the stump of a fallen tree. As I was loosening the soil about its roots my axe struck against a ring of brass set into a wooden slab. I cleared away the earth, lifted the slab aside and saw below it a flight of stairs. I went down the stairs and, opening a door at the bottom, found myself in the spacious courtyard of a magnificent palace. In this courtyard I saw a young woman more beautiful than a priceless pearl and as radiant as the sun; her lips were scarlet, her cheeks fresh and smooth, and her breasts round and shapely. At the sight of her all my sorrows were forgotten, and I knelt down in adoration before the Creator who had fashioned so fair a form.

She gazed at me and said: 'Are you a man or a jinnee?'

'A man, my mistress,' I replied.

'Who then has brought you down to this palace,' she asked, 'where for five-and-twenty years I have not beheld a human face?'

Enthralled by her sweet voice, I answered: 'Mistress, it was Allah who led me to your dwelling so that all my troubles and misfortunes might be forgotten.'

I told her my story from first to last and her eyes filled with tears as she listened to my adventure. Then she herself told me her story.

'Know,' she began, 'that I am the daughter of King Iphitamus, lord of the Ebony Island. My father had wedded me to my cousin, but on my bridal night I was carried away by Jerjees the Jinnee, son of Iblees himself, and imprisoned in this palace, to which he had conveyed all that I could need of jewels and ornaments, of robes and silks, of furniture and food and wine. He visits me every ten days and spends one night with me, hurrying away at the first light of dawn; for he had ravished me without the consent of his tribe. He has told me that should I have need of anything, be it by day or night, I have but to touch the two lines inscribed upon that dome and he would at once appear before me. He was here four days ago, and it will be six more before he comes again. Therefore you may stay with me for five days and go on the day before he arrives.'

'With all my heart,' I answered, transported with joy.

Thereupon she rose and, taking me by the hand, conducted me through a vaulted doorway to a warm and splendid bath, where we both undressed and bathed together. Then she seated me by her side upon a couch and offered me delicate meats and a cooling drink scented with musk. After we had eaten and talked for a long time, she said: 'Sleep and rest a while, for you must be weary.'

I lay down and slept, forgetting all my worldly cares. When I awoke she was still at my side, gently caressing my feet. I called down blessings on her and we again sat talking together.

'By Allah,' she sighed at last, 'how great has been my sorrow all these years, living alone in this palace with no human being to speak to. Praise be to Him who has sent you to me!'

Love and joy reigned in my heart. Folded in each other's arms, we drank deep till the fall of evening, and all night I lay with her in an ecstasy of bliss. Memorable indeed was that night. When morning came I staggered to my feet elated with wine and passion, and cried: 'Rise, my love! I will take you from this underground prison and deliver you from the jinnee!'

'Be content and say no more,' she replied, laughing. 'The jinnee has but one night in ten; the other nine are yours.'

But in my drunkenness I cried: 'I will now destroy this dome with its magic words and kill the jinnee when he appears. I am accustomed to the slaying of jinn!'

She turned pale at my words and begged me to restrain myself. But, paying no heed to her entreaties, I gave a violent kick at the side of the enchanted dome. Scarcely had my foot touched the wall, however, when the palace was suddenly overcast with darkness, the earth shook, and peals of thunder rattled in the distance.

'The jinnee has come!' exclaimed the woman. 'Did I not warn you? By Allah, you have wronged me! Fly by the way you came and save yourself!'

Seized with fear, I rushed to the stairway, leaving behind my sandals and my axe. When I had mounted a few steps, I hastened back to look for them; but the earth suddenly opened and there appeared a hideous jinnee, crying to the woman: 'What can you mean by this fearful summons? What calamity has befallen you?'

'No calamity,' she replied. 'I was oppressed with gloom, and, rising to fetch some drink to cheer my solitude, my head struck against the dome.'

The jinnee looked right and left and, noticing my sandals and my axe, cried: 'You lie, vilest of whores! What are these things, and what man has been here?'

'I never saw them before this instant,' she replied. 'They might have been hanging from the back of your clothes.'

'Absurd and shameless lies!' exclaimed the angry jinnee. 'None of your tricks, harlot!'

So saying, he stripped her naked, tied her to four stakes planted in the middle of the courtyard, and, beating her cruelly, charged her to confess the truth.

Unable to endure her cries, I ran in terror up the stairs and, gaining the entrance, put back the wooden slab and covered it over with earth. I was stricken with remorse at what I had done, and, as I hurried back to the city, I wept as I thought of the young woman's beauty and of the torture to which she was being put on my account, of my father and his kingdom, and of the abject state to which I had fallen.

When I returned to the tailor's shop I found my friend waiting for me anxiously. 'I could not sleep last night,' he said, ' fearing that you had been killed by a wild beast or had met with some luckless accident in the forest. Praise be to Allah for your safe return!'

I thanked the good man and sat down in my accustomed corner, my mind troubled with disquieting thoughts. Presently the tailor came to me, saying: 'At the door there is an old man, a foreigner, who is asking for you. He has your axe and sandals and has been calling on all the woodcutters saying that he found them on his way to the morning prayers at the first call of the muezzin. The woodcutters recognized them and directed him to this shop. Go and thank him, and take your sandals and your axe.'

I was greatly dismayed at these words, and before I could stir from my corner the ground opened and the supposed old man, who was none other than the jinnee, appeared before me.

Now the jinnee had put the young woman to the cruellest of tortures, but when she had refused to confess he took up my axe and sandals and said: 'You shall see how Jerjees, the true grandchild of Iblees, can find the owner of these things!' Thereupon he changed himself into the guise of a foreigner and traced me among the woodcutters by the trick you have just heard of.

In a twinkling the jinnee sprang upon me, lifted me over his shoulder, and, after flying with me high into the air, dived through the earth and set me down in the courtyard of his palace. When I beheld the woman naked and with blood flowing from her sides, I wept bitterly. But the jinnee laid hold of her, crying: 'Harlot, here is your lover!'

The young woman looked at me and said: 'I do not know him. I have never seen him before.'

'What!' exclaimed the jinnee. 'Will you not confess?'

But she replied: 'I do not know him. I have never seen him in my life, nor is it lawful in the sight of Allah that I should say what is untrue about him.'

'If you do not know him,' said the jinnee, 'take this sword and strike off his head.'

She took the sword and stood before me. With tears running down my cheeks, I silently entreated her to spare me. She gazed long into my face and murmured: 'You are the cause of all this!' But she understood my sorrowful look and threw the sword at the feet of her tormentor, saying: 'How can I kill an innocent man whom I have never seen before?'

Then the jinnee turned to me and said: 'Son of Adam, do you know this woman?'

'I have never set eyes on her in all my life,' I replied.

He handed me the sword, saying: 'Cut off her head, and you shall go unharmed.'

I grasped the sword, quickly stepped forward, and raised my arm; but she looked at me as though she would say: 'Did I betray you?' So I threw away the sword and cried: 'Mighty and valiant jinnee, if she, a woman lacking in faith and reason, deemed it unlawful to harm me, how can I, who am a man, bear to cut off her head, especially when I do not know her? I will not charge myself with so great a sin though I should drink the cup of death.'

'Now I know there is love between you!' exclaimed the jinnee, and with four strokes of his sword he cut off the hands and the feet of the unfortunate woman, while I looked on in an agony of grief. She made a last sign to me with her eyes as though she would bid me farewell; but, alas, the jinnee perceived the wink.

'Wretch, would you commit adultery with your eyes?' he shrieked, and struck off her head with another blow of his sword. Then, turning to me, he said: 'Know, son of Adam, that among us jinn the penalty of adultery is death. I carried away this girl on her wedding night, when she was twelve years of age and still untouched by man. I brought her to this palace and visited her every tenth night in the semblance of a foreigner. But I have now killed her because I found her unfaithful: even if it was only with her eyes. As for you, since I am not sure that you have sinned with her, I shall be content to inflict some kind of scourge upon you. Therefore choose your punishment.'

I rejoiced to hear that I was to escape with my life, and answered: 'What punishment can I choose, mighty jinnee?'

'Choose,' he roared, 'into what shape I shall change you! A dog, an ass, or an ape?'

Hoping for pardon, I replied: 'Spare me, valiant jinnee,

and so will Allah spare you. He will surely reward you if you show mercy to an honest Moslem who has done no harm.'

In vain I thus continued to beseech him, until he cut me short, saying: 'Enough, or you shall die. Bewitch you I must!'

With this he snatched me up, leapt through the earth, and soared with me so high into the air that the world beneath appeared like a little bowl of water. At length he set me down upon a mountain and, taking a handful of dust, muttered some mysterious charm and scattered it over me, crying: 'Cast off your human form and turn into an ape!'

At that moment I became an ape, ugly, and a hundred years of age. Prostrate with grief at my transformation, I lay on the earth bewailing the tyranny of Fortune. But soon fortifying myself with courage and patience, I made my way down the mountain and, after journeying for a whole month, came to the beach of the salt sea. When I had rested there for a while I saw a sail heading with a favourable breeze towards the shore. I hid behind a rock and waited; and, as soon as the crew cast anchor, I leapt into the ship.

'Throw out the ill-omened beast!' cried one of the passengers.

'Kill it!' exclaimed another.

'Yes, kill it with a sword!' shouted a third.

Upon this I threw myself at the captain's feet and, clinging to the skirt of his robe, burst into bitter tears. The captain took pity on me and said to the passengers: 'This ape has sought my protection and he shall have it. Let no one molest him or interfere with him.'

He spoke kind words to me, all of which I understood, and made me his personal servant on the ship. Aided by favourable winds, we sailed for fifty days and nights and at length cast anchor in the harbour of a city so vast that Allah alone could tell the number of its people. As soon as the ship was moored, some slaves from the King's palace came on board and, after welcoming the passengers, gave them, with the greetings of their master, a scroll of parchment on which each man was asked to write a line in his best hand. For the King's vizier, an eminent calligrapher, had died and the King had sworn never to appoint any man in his place who could not write as well as he.

At once I sprang upon the men and snatched the scroll from their hands. Afraid lest I should tear it to bits or throw it into the sea, they pursued me round the deck with threats and curses; but, ape though I was, I made a sign to them that I wished to write.

'Let him try,' said the captain. 'If he scribbles we will chase him away, but if he writes with a fair hand I shall adopt him as my son. For never in all my life have I seen a more intelligent ape.'

I took the pen, dipped it into the inkpot, and began to write. I wrote out six couplets, each in a different script: the first in *ruk'i*, the second in *rihani*, the third in *thulthi*, the fourth in *naskhi*, the fifth in *tumar*, and the sixth in *muhaqqiq*. When I finished I handed the scroll to the passengers, and each in turn inscribed a line in his best hand.

The slaves carried back the parchment to the King, and of all the writing none pleased him more than mine. He said to his attendants: 'Go to the writer of these lines, invest him with this robe of honour, mount him on the finest of my mules, and bring him to me in a triumphal march.'

They all smiled at his words, so that the King grew angry and cried: 'Do you dare laugh at my orders?'

'Great King,' they replied, 'the writer of these lines is no human but an ape, the property of a ship's captain.'

At this the King marvelled greatly and then burst out laughing.

'I must buy this ape!' he cried, and ordered his courtiers to go down to the ship with the mule and the robe of honour and bring the ape to his presence. 'You must dress him in this robe,' he added, 'and escort him to the palace mounted on the mule.'

At once they came down to the harbour and bought me from the ship's captain. They clad me in the robe of honour, set me upon the mule, and led me through the city at the head of a long procession. Great crowds lined the streets and all were filled with wonder at the prodigious sight.

When I was brought before the King I thrice kissed the ground before him, and he invited me to be seated. I sat down upon my knees, with such accomplished grace that all who were present, and especially the King, marvelled at the courteousness of my behaviour. Presently he dismissed his attendants, except for a eunuch and a little slave, and called for food. A table richly spread with all manner of delicate meats was at once brought in, and the King invited me by signs to eat. I rose and, after kissing the ground before him seven times, sat down and ate with him. Finally, when the table was removed, I washed my hands, took up an inkpot, pen and paper, and, improvising half a dozen verses in praise of his hospitality, handed the poem to the King.

He read the lines with great astonishment and exclaimed: 'Can an ape possess such eloquence? By Allah, this is a rare marvel!'

The slaves brought the King his chessboard and he asked me if I could play. I nodded, and, arranging the pieces, began to play with him. Twice I beat him, so that his amazement knew no bounds.

'Were this beast human,' cried the King, 'he would be the wisest man of all our time!' Then he said to the eunuch: 'Go to my daughter and ask her to come quickly. I wish her to see this wondrous ape.'

The eunuch went out and soon returned with the Princess, who no sooner saw me than she covered her face with her veil.

'Father,' she said, 'how is it that you are pleased to summon me into the presence of a stranger?'

'Daughter,' replied the King, 'here are only my little slave, the eunuch who brought you up, this ape, and your father. Who is the stranger of whom you speak?'

'Know, then,' she said, 'that this ape is an illustrious prince, the son of King Iftiyamarus. He was bewitched by Jerjees the Jinnee, a grandchild of Iblees, who has also killed his own wife, daughter of King Iphitamus, lord of the Ebony Island. Indeed, that which you suppose an ape is a wise and learned man.'

Amazed at her words, the King looked at me closely and asked: 'Is it true what the Princess has said of you?'

I nodded and wept.

'How do you know that he is bewitched?' asked the King, turning to his daughter.

'Father,' she replied, 'when I was a child I had an old nurse, a skilled enchantress deeply versed in sorcery, who taught me witchcraft. I have committed all its rules to memory and know a hundred and seventy codes of magic, by the least of which I could raze your city to the ground and scatter its stones as far as the Mountain of Kaf, turn your kingdom into a bottomless sea, and change its people into wriggling fishes.'

'Then in Allah's name,' cried the King, 'restore this man so that I may make him my vizier.'

'Gladly,' the Princess replied.

She took a knife engraved with Hebrew words and with it marked a circle in the middle of the palace. This she filled with talismanic names and magic inscriptions and, standing in the centre, pronounced an incantation. Suddenly the palace was overcast with darkness and the jinnee appeared before us in his most hideous shape, with hands like pitchforks, legs like the masts of a ship, and eyes that resembled flaming torches. We were all overcome with terror at the sight, except the Princess, who exclaimed: 'Ill-met and unwelcome!'

'Traitress, you have broken your oath!' roared the jinnee. 'Did we not swear that neither of us would molest the other? You well deserve the end which now awaits you!'

So saying, he suddenly changed himself into a lion, which opened wide its jaws and sprang upon the girl. But in a twinkle she plucked a hair from her head and waved it with her fingers, mumbling a magic charm, so that it turned into a sharp sword with which she cut the lion in two. Presently the lion's head became a scorpion which scurried towards the Princess, but the girl instantly changed to an enormous serpent which hurled itself upon the scorpion and grappled with it in a most deadly fashion. Then the scorpion became an eagle and the serpent a vulture, which swooped upon its foe and pursued it for a long while. Escaping, the eagle changed into a black

cat, whilst the Princess transformed herself into a wolf. Long
and fiercely the cat and the wolf battled with each other, until
the cat, seeing itself overcome, turned into a large red pomegranate, which bounced into the fountain of the palace. The wolf
dived in after it, but the pomegranate bounded into the air and
fell on the ground, breaking into pieces and scattering its grains
all about the marble courtyard. Thereupon the wolf changed
into a cock, which pecked at the grains one by one and swallowed them except for a single grain which, as Fate would
have it, lay hidden in a crack beside the fountain. The cock
crowed, flapped its wings, and made signs to us with its beak,
but we did not understand what it was trying to say. At length
it uttered so fearful a cry that we thought the palace was falling down upon us. Feverishly the cock hopped round and
round the courtyard until it found the grain which was hidden
in the crack beside the fountain. But, when the cock had
pounced upon it and picked it up, the grain fell into the water
and was transformed into a fish which sank to the bottom of
the basin. Whereupon the cock changed to an enormous
whale which plunged into the fountain and, diving after the
fish, disappeared for an hour. At length we heard a loud din
which set us all in a tremble of fear, and out of the fountain
rose the jinnee, a mighty flame of fire, with smoke pouring
from his eyes, his mouth, and his nostrils. Behind him came
the Princess, and she too was all on fire, as though she were a
burning coal. Headlong she rushed at the jinnee and battled
with him until they were locked together in a mass of flame
and all the palace was filled with smoke. Terrified of being
burnt alive, we were about to throw ourselves into the water
when the jinnee broke loose from his adversary with a deafening cry and, throwing himself upon us in the middle of the
courtyard, blew fire in our faces. But the girl swiftly overtook
him and blew fire in his face, so that flames fell upon us from
them both. Those coming from her did us no harm, but a
spark, darting from the jinnee, blinded my left eye, another
burned the lower part of the King's face and knocked out all
his nether teeth, while a third, striking the eunuch in the chest,
burned him to death upon the instant.

Whilst we were thus resigned to certain death, we suddenly heard a voice crying: 'Allah alone is great! Allah alone is mighty! His is the victory, His is the triumph! He has destroyed the infidel who denied the Faith of Mohammed, the Prince of mankind!'

It was the girl who spoke: the jinnee had become a pile of ashes.

'Make haste!' cried the Princess, hurrying towards us. 'Fetch me a bowl of water!'

When this was brought, she murmured some mysterious words over it and sprinkled me with the water, saying: 'In the name of the only Truth, in the name of Allah the Most High, return to your natural state!'

The spell was broken. A quiver passed through my body and I became a man as I had been before, except that I was now blind in one eye.

'Flames!' cried the Princess. 'Oh, these tormenting flames! Father, my hour is come, and I must die. Had my enemy been a man I could have destroyed him at the first encounter. It was the breaking of the pomegranate that led to my ruin, for the grain which I did not swallow was the one that held the soul of the jinnee. Had I found it he would have perished upon the instant; but Destiny ordained otherwise. So I was forced to battle with him under the earth and in the air and beneath the water, and each time he tried a weapon against me I used another more powerful, until at length he employed the weapon of fire. When that weapon is used none can survive its peril. Before I killed him I adjured him to embrace Islam, but he refused, and Fate enabled me to burn him before I was burnt myself. Now I die. May Allah grant you another in my place.'

She contended with the flames until black sparks enveloped her breast and mounted to her head. When they reached her face, she exclaimed through her tears: 'I bear witness that there is no god but Allah! I bear witness that Mohammed is His prophet!' Then she fell, a pile of ashes, beside the jinnee.

We were stricken with grief at the sight, and I wished that I could have died in her place rather than see her delicate body reduced to cinders, this innocent princess who had saved me; but, alas, none can revoke the decrees of Allah.

When the King saw his daughter fall down in ashes, he plucked at the remnant of his beard, beat his face, and tore his robes. I, too, rent my clothes, and we both mourned over her, until the chamberlains and officers of the court came and found their King unconscious beside two heaps of cinders. They stood around him in bewilderment until at length he recovered his senses and told them all that had happened to the Princess. They fell to weeping and wailing, and so did all the women and the slave-girls of the palace.

When the seven days of mourning were over, a monument was erected at the King's orders over the ashes of his daughter, and in it were hung lighted lamps and candles, while the ashes of the jinnee were flung to the wind, under the curse of Allah.

Worn out with sorrow, the King fell into a grave illness which lasted for a whole month. When he had recovered his strength a little he called me to his side and said: 'Young man, before you came we lived in serenity and joy, secure from the vicissitudes of time. With you came trouble and misfortune. Would that we had never set eyes on your ill-omened face, which has brought down on us desolation and ruin. First, you have caused the death of my daughter, whose life was worth a hundred men; second, you were the cause of my disfigurement; and third, through you my faithful eunuch also perished. And yet it was not your fault. It was the will of Allah. Praise be to Him, then, who has ordained that my child should restore you at the cost of her own destruction. Leave our kingdom, my son, for we have suffered enough on your account. Yes, it was all decreed by Fate. Go hence in peace.'

I went out of the King's presence, scarcely believing in my salvation and not knowing whither to turn my steps. I pondered over all that had befallen me from beginning to end: how I had escaped from the highwaymen of the desert and how I had met the tailor; my amorous sojourn with the young woman in the secret palace and my deliverance from the jinnee; my life as an ape and my purchase by the King; the loss of my eye and the breaking of the spell. Nevertheless I thanked Allah, saying: 'Better a lost eye than death.'

Before leaving the city I went down to the public baths, where I shaved my beard and put on these rags. I journeyed through many countries and only tonight reached Baghdad, the City of Peace, where I hoped to tell my story to the Prince of the Faithful. By chance I met this other dervish and while we were exchanging greetings, we were joined by our third companion. Recognizing each other as strangers, we walked on together till Destiny brought us to your house, my mistress.

That is the story of my lost eye and shaved beard.

*

When the second dervish ended, the mistress of the house said to him: 'Your story is strange indeed. You may now go.'

But he replied: 'I shall not leave this house until I have heard the tales of my other companions.'

Then the third dervish came forward and said:

The Tale of the Third Dervish

NOBLE lady, my story is even more extraordinary than the tales of my two companions. The misfortunes which befell these two were ordained by Destiny and Fate, but the sorrowful events which led to the loss of my eye and the shaving of my beard were brought about through my own fault.

I am a king and the son of a king. When my father died I succeeded to his throne and reigned in justice and wisdom over my people.

I had a great passion for seafaring, for my capital lay by the sea and many of the neighbouring islands were subject to my rule. Wishing one day to visit my dominions, I set sail with a fleet of ten ships, provisioned for a whole month. We voyaged for twenty days, and at the end of that time contrary winds sprang up in mid ocean, raging throughout the night till morning. At sunrise, when the tempest subsided and the sea was calm again, we sighted a little island, and there we went ashore, prepared a meal, and rested for two days. Then we resumed our voyage and sailed for another twenty days until we found ourselves in a strange ocean, unknown even to the captain. We sent a watch to look out from the masthead, and when he came down he said to the captain: 'On my right I saw fishes floating on the water, and far off, in the middle of the sea, beheld an object looming black and white by turns.'

At these words the captain was much dismayed; he hurled his turban on the deck and tore at his beard.

'Alas, we are lost!' he cried. 'Not one of us will escape alive!'

Alarmed at his lament, we gathered round him, inquiring what the watch had seen.

'My lord,' he replied, 'we have been drifting off our course these twenty days and there is no favouring wind to carry us back. Tomorrow we shall come to a cliff of black rock called the Magnetic Mountain, against which the headlong current will hurl our ship and shatter it to pieces. All her nails will dart from her and cling to the Magnetic Mountain, for Allah has endowed its stone with such power that it draws all things of iron to itself. He alone knows what mass of wreckage lies scattered among its rocks. On its summit there is a dome of brass held up by ten pillars, and upon this dome stands a horseman on a brazen steed, with a spear of brass in his hand and a leaden tablet on his breast, inscribed with talismanic names. Know, great King, that so long as this rider stays upon his horse, all ships that pass below shall be destroyed and all their sailors drowned. Until he has fallen from his horse no mariner can be safe.'

The captain wept, and we, resigning ourselves to certain death, began to bid each other farewell.

Early next morning we came in sight of the Magnetic Mountain. The current drove us swiftly along, and as soon as we approached its base the nails flew from the ship and shot off towards the mountain. The vessel fell to pieces and we were all flung into the raging sea. Most of us were drowned outright, and the few who saved themselves never met again, such was the fury of the wind and tide. As for myself, the Almighty spared my life, in order to afflict me with great trials. I clung to a floating piece of wreckage and in the evening was cast on land at the foot of the mountain.

Not far from the shore I found a pathway hewn in the rock and winding upwards. I called on Allah and prayed to Him with all fervour, so that through His grace the wind was stilled and I was able to climb by the jutting crags to the summit. I rejoiced at my escape and, entering the dome, knelt down in prayer and thanked the Almighty for my deliverance.

Worn out with toil, I stretched myself under the dome and slept. In my sleep I heard a voice saying to me: 'Son of Khaseeb, when you wake, dig the earth beneath your feet and you shall find a bow of brass and three leaden arrows engraved with talismans. With these shoot the horseman above the dome, and thus you shall rid mankind of a grievous scourge. When you have shot the horseman he will fall into the sea and the bow will drop upon the ground. Bury it where it has fallen and the sea will forthwith surge and rise up to the summit of the mountain. Then you shall see a boat approaching with another man on board, also of brass, carrying an oar in his hand. Get into this boat, but, while you are there, you must on no account utter the name of Allah. The man of brass will row you for ten days and then you will come to safe waters, where you shall find one who will convey you to your country. All this shall come to pass provided you do not pronounce the name of Allah.'

I woke and, quickly rising, did as the voice had bidden me. With the bow and arrows I shot the horseman and he fell into the sea. I buried the bow where it had fallen, and at once the sea surged and rose up to the summit of the mountain. Presently I saw a boat approaching from the middle of the ocean, at the sight of which I rendered thanks to Allah. In it was a man of brass bearing upon his chest a leaden tablet carved with talismanic names. Without a word I climbed into the boat, and the man of brass rowed me for ten successive days until at length I came in sight of an island. Transported with joy, I glorified my Creator, crying: 'There is no god but Allah! Praise to the Most High!'

Scarcely had I uttered these words when I was thrown into the sea, while the boat and its oarsman vanished beneath the waves. Being a good swimmer, I managed to keep afloat till nightfall, and then, utterly exhausted, commended myself to Allah and prepared to meet my end. But a mighty billow as high as a castle swept me forward and flung me onto the shore of the island, so that Allah's will might be fully accomplished.

I made my way up the beach and, after I had wrung out my clothes and spread them on the sand to dry, lay down and slept all night. At daybreak I put on my garments and, striking inland, came to a little valley covered with trees. I walked round and round it, and soon found that I was on a solitary island set in the middle of the sea.

'No sooner do I escape from one evil,' I thought to myself, 'than I fall into another far worse.'

As I was thus reflecting on my plight and wishing earnestly for death, I descried a vessel heading towards the island. I climbed into a near-by tree and, concealing myself among its branches, saw the ship anchor and ten slaves come ashore, each carrying a spade. They made their way to a certain spot in the middle of the island, where they dug in the earth until they uncovered a trap-door, which they lifted. Then they returned to the vessel and unloaded from it a great store of provisions: bread and flour, butter and honey, sheep, and all manner of household goods; and all these they carried down the trap-door. After that the slaves brought out from the ship magnificent garments and, as they came nearer, I saw in their midst a decrepit old man leading by the hand a boy of such beauty that he might have been cast in the very mould of perfection. They all went down by the entrance, but after an hour reappeared without the boy and, returning to the ship, hoisted sail and vanished from sight.

I climbed down the tree and, hastening to the spot, removed the earth again and came to a great wooden cover the size of a millstone. This I lifted with Allah's help and saw beneath a vaulted stairway. Going down to the bottom, I found a spacious hall spread with rare carpets and hung with silken tapestries, and there, among flowers and bowls of fruit, I saw the boy reclining on a couch with a fan in his hand. When he saw me he started back, but I wished him peace.

'Fear nothing, my master,' I said. 'I am no evil spirit, but a king and the son of a king. Destiny has guided me here to comfort you in your solitude. But what is your story, pray, and what is the reason of your sojourn in this cell?'

Reassured by these words, the boy welcomed me courteously and invited me to be seated.

'Know, my brother,' he began, 'that I am the only son of a wealthy jeweller, renowned throughout the world for his argosies and caravans. My father was not blessed with a child till he was past the prime of life. One night he dreamt that he was soon to have a son but that the child would die before his parents. He awoke with a heavy heart; and at the end of nine months my mother brought me into the world. Despite the ominous portent of his dream my father rejoiced at my birth, holding sumptuous feasts and lavishing alms on the poor and needy. But the astrologers and the sages of the land warned him that at the end of my fifteenth year I would be killed by a king named Ajeeb son of Khaseeb, fifty days after he had thrown the Knight of the Magnetic Mountain into the sea. My father was sorely troubled at these forebodings. When I had nearly attained my fifteenth year, the astrologers came again and told him that the brass rider had been cast into the sea, and that the man who threw him was King Ajeeb, son of Khaseeb. Broken by grief, my father brought me here that I might hide in safety in this unknown island.'

I marvelled greatly at these words, knowing that it was I, Ajeeb, the son of King Khaseeb, who had shot down the horseman into the sea. 'By Allah,' I thought, 'never shall this youth come to grief at my hands!'

'May Allah preserve you, my child, from all misfortunes and all sorrows!' I said. 'Have no fears; I will stay with you and protect you from all harm. The day will surely come when both of us will return home in safety.'

The youth rejoiced and thanked me. We talked all day, and

when night came I lit more candles and burned incense in the braziers, and we ate and drank together in amity and peace. When he woke next morning I took a basin filled with warm water to him, and he washed his face.

'My friend,' he said, 'if ever I escape from this King Ajeeb and outlive my predicted term, you shall not lose your reward.'

For nine-and-thirty days we stayed together on the island, whiling away the hours with sport and merriment. On the evening of the fortieth day my young companion bathed himself and, after resting on his couch for a while, told me that he wished to eat. I brought him a melon upon a plate and climbed on his couch to reach a knife which lay on a shelf above him. But, as Fate would have it, my foot slipped and I fell down over the youth, the knife being planted through his heart.

Overwhelmed with horror, I wailed and beat my face and rent my clothes. But the boy was dead. The will of Allah was done and the prophecy of the sages was fulfilled.

In despair I rushed up the stairway, shut the trap-door, and covered it over with earth. Scarcely had I done this when, looking towards the sea, I saw the ship approaching.

'When these men find the youth slain,' I said to myself, 'they will know that I killed him and will put me to a cruel death.'

So I climbed into a tall tree overlooking the hiding place and concealed myself among the leaves. Presently the old sheikh with his slaves came ashore, and, hurrying to the spot, cleared away the soil and went down. When he found his son pierced to the heart with a knife, the old man fell down fainting, and the slaves, raising a loud lament, carried their master up the stairs and laid him down near the entrance. They wrapped the youth's body in a large silken shawl and placed it beside their master, who, recovering himself a while, uttered an agonizing cry and dropped down lifeless. Wailing aloud and scattering dust upon their heads, the slaves carried the two corpses to the ship and sailed away.

Alone and sick at heart, I wandered for many days about the island. One day, however, I noticed that the sea was receding hour by hour, leaving to the west a vast expanse of dry sand, so that after a few days there was no more water on that side of the isle. I rejoiced at the prospect of a speedy rescue, and, crossing over the sand, came at length to the coast of the opposite mainland, where I beheld a blaze of light in the distance. When I drew nearer I found that this was a lofty palace built of brass glowing in the rays of the declining sun. I sat down on the ground admiring its splendour, and presently saw, coming out of the gates, an old sheikh accompanied by ten richly dressed youths who, to my astonishment, were each blind in the left eye. When they saw me they came round and bade me a çourteous welcome, inquiring who I was and where I had come from. I related to them all that had befallen me and they were much amazed at my adventures.

The one-eyed men led me to their palace, where, in the central courtyard, I saw ten couches spread with blue quilts, and a smaller couch in their midst. On this the sheikh sat down, and the young men stretched themselves on their couches.

'Be seated, sir,' they said to me, 'but, pray, ask no question about our lost eyes or anything you may see us do.'

After we had rested a while, the sheikh rose and placed before us meat and wine. When we had finished eating and drinking, the youths said to the old man: 'We must now fulfil our task.'

The old man left the court and, entering an adjoining chamber, brought back ten basins covered with blue lids, which he set down before the youths together with ten lighted candles. When each had removed the lid from his basin I saw that they contained soot and ashes and powdered charcoal. Pulling up their sleeves, the young men blackened their faces, smeared their robes, and beat their breasts and cheeks, lamenting: 'Alas, we were the authors of our own ruin!' This they continued to do all night, and at daybreak they washed in warm water which the old man brought them and changed into fresh garments.

I was profoundly distressed at these proceedings and begged them to tell me the reason of their strange behaviour. But they replied: 'We have warned you. Beware of temptation.'

I stayed with them for a whole month, and night after

night this performance was repeated. At length I could hold my peace no longer and cried: 'In Allah's name, my friends, explain to me your mystery or I shall surely die of grief.'

'Unhappy man,' they replied, 'would you bring ruin on yourself? That which has happened to us will happen to you, and it will be your own fault.'

I gave no heed to their exhortations, and at length they brought in a ram which they killed and flayed, saying to me: 'You will be sewn in the skin of this animal and be left in the courtyard of the palace. By and by a giant bird called the roc will swoop on the skin and, carrying it up in its talons, will fly with you and set you down on the top of a mountain. You must cut the skin with a knife and get out at once, so that the roc will take fright and fly away. Walk half a day's journey and then you will come to a palace sheeted with red gold and decked with emeralds and rubies. Enter through the doorway, as we have entered, and you shall see what we have seen. On leaving it each of us lost his left eye and thereafter passed every night in mourning.'

When the youths saw that I was fixed in my resolve, they handed me a knife, sewed me up in the skin of the ram and left me in the courtyard. Suddenly I felt myself lifted from the ground by the talons of a huge bird, which flew with me through the void and at length set me down on the summit of a mountain. I slit the skin with the knife and leapt out, whereupon the frightened bird flew off. After journeying a few hours I came to the palace of which the one-eyed men had told me. I made my way through the door and, entering a great hall saw forty young girls, each as beautiful as the rising moon. They got up when they saw me and received me joyfully.

'Welcome to this house, dear master,' they said. 'We have been waiting for you these thirty days. Praise be to Allah who has brought you to us!' Then, seating me upon a dais, they added: 'You shall henceforth be our lord and master, and we your obedient slaves.'

Five of the girls spread a rich carpet at my feet, which they covered with flowers and fruit. They served me with the choicest meats and wines, and as I ate they sang and made music. We sat drinking for many hours, and I was so flushed with joy that every worldly care was banished from my heart. At midnight they said to me: 'It is now bedtime. Choose one of us, dear master.'

I chose the fairest of them, a girl of surpassing beauty, with black eyes, black tresses, and lips like rubies. She led me to her chamber and I passed with her a night of such bliss as I had never before experienced. Next morning they took me to the bath of the palace, washed me, and robed me in splendid garments. In this fashion I lived with them for a whole year, revelling away the nights with each of the forty girls in turn. On the last day of the year they all came to me with tears running down their cheeks.

'The day has come,' they said, 'when we must part; and if you fail to do our bidding we shall never meet again.'

'But why must you leave me?' I asked in astonishment.

'Know,' they replied, 'that we are princesses of royal blood. We have lived here for many years, but at the end of every year we go away for forty days. Here are the keys of all the forty doors of the palace. You may delight your eyes with all the treasure behind these doors; but beware of opening the fortieth door or you shall lose us for ever.'

I swore never to open it and promised to wait for them till they returned. One by one they threw their arms round my neck and, bidding me farewell, departed.

Left alone with the keys in my hands, I loitered about the palace all day. When evening came I opened the first door and saw a garden covered with fruit trees and watered by crystal brooks. Apples, plums, and quinces hung in clusters from the boughs and the air was filled with the twitter of birds and the fragrance of multi-coloured flowers. I wandered among the trees, marvelling at all that I beheld, and at nightfall returned to my chamber and lay down to sleep.

Next morning I rose betimes, and, opening the second door, found myself in another garden shaded by palm-trees and refreshed by a gently flowing stream. On its banks bloomed the rose and the violet, jasmine and narcissus and eglantine, their rich perfume scenting the air and dazzling the senses.

Next I opened the third door and saw a spacious hall, paved with coloured marble inlaid with gold and silver, and decked with precious stones. From the ceiling hung cages made of sandal and aloe-wood, in which merles and pigeons, bulbuls and turtle-doves, sang in praise of the Most High. Entranced by their melodies, I stayed in that hall all night and next morning opened the fourth door. There I saw a great pavilion with forty doors, each opening on a vault stacked with pearls and rubies, chrysolites and emeralds and other priceless gems. I was dumbfounded at these marvels and thought to myself: 'Such treasures cannot be found in the courts of mighty kings. Surely I am the richest man of all my time. Praise be to Allah who led me to this palace and made me sole master over the forty girls who dwell in it!'

Thus every day I opened one of the doors, being more and more amazed at each new wonder, until the fortieth day arrived. But the thought of the forbidden door weighed heavy on my heart and I was tempted to open it. At length, yielding to Satan's promptings, I unlocked the door and made my way into another spacious hall. I had not gone far, however, when I was suddenly overcome by a scent so strong that I fell down fainting. When I recovered my senses I found that the floor was strewn with saffron; in the centre there were candles and golden lamps perfumed with musk and ambergris, and on either side two great braziers in which incense and honeyed aloe-wood were burning. Among the lamps, before a manger of clearest crystal filled with sifted sesame, and a trough holding musk-rose dew, stood a magnificent horse, black as midnight. He was richly bridled and his saddle was of red gold. I marvelled at the sight of this prodigy and, seduced by the Evil One, led the horse into the courtyard and mounted him. I spurred him on with my heels, but he did not move; so I struck him with a whip and at once he spread a pair of mighty wings, gave an ear-splitting neigh, and soared with me high up into the air.

After flying through the void for some time the horse came to earth on the terrace of that brass palace from which I had set out. Here he hurled me from his back and, as I lay on the ground, knocked out my left eye with a violent blow of his tail. Then he spread his wings and vanished into the air. I made my way down the terrace and found the one-eyed youths in the courtyard.

'Fool!' they exclaimed. 'We have no welcome for you. Begone this instant!'

'I am now one of you,' I replied. 'Let me stay here, that I may cast ashes upon my head each night.'

But they cried: 'Begone this instant. We cannot receive you back amongst us.'

Thus I left them, with tears in my eye and anguish in my heart. I journeyed many days with a shaved beard and in the rags of a wandering dervish, and only tonight arrived in Baghdad, the City of Peace. I soon fell in with these other two and greeted them, saying: 'I am a stranger.' They replied that they too were strangers, and the three of us walked on together till Destiny brought us to your house, my mistress.

That is the story of my lost eye and shaved beard.

*

When she heard the tale of the third dervish, the mistress of the house said to him: 'You may go. You have gained your liberty.'

But he replied: 'By Allah, I shall not go till I have heard the stories of my other companions.'

The young woman turned to the Caliph, Ja'afar, and Masrur, and bade them relate their stories. The Vizier told her the invented tale which he had told her sister at the door. When he ended, the mistress of the house said: 'I pardon you all. Go your ways in peace.'

Out in the street the Caliph asked the dervishes whither they were going and, when they answered that they did not know, he ordered his vizier to take them to his house and bring them before him in the morning.

Ja'afar did as he was bidden, and the Caliph returned to his palace, where he lay sleepless for the rest of the night. Next morning he rose and, sitting upon his throne, received the officers of his court. When these had departed he said to the

Vizier: 'Bring before me the three young girls with the two bitches and the three one-eyed men.'

Ja'afar ushered them in and, after seating the three girls behind a curtain, said to them: 'We were unknown to you and yet you treated us with kindness. Therefore you are pardoned. Now learn that you are in the presence of the fifth of the royal line of Al-Abbas, Haroun al-Rashid, Prince of the Faithful. Tell him nothing but the truth.'

When the Vizier had thus spoken for his master, the eldest of the girls came forward and said:

The Tale of the First Girl

KNOW, Prince of the Faithful, that we three were born of one father but not of the same mother; these black bitches, on the other hand, were, before they were bewitched, full sisters to me, myself being the youngest of the three though older than the other two.

On his death our father left us five thousand pieces of gold, and when we had each taken our share of the inheritance my stepsisters went to live with their mother, while I and my two sisters continued to live together. Soon afterwards my elder sisters married and their husbands bought with their dowries a quantity of merchandise and went away to trade in foreign lands, taking their wives with them and leaving me alone.

My sisters were away for four years, and during that time their husbands gambled away their fortunes and abandoned them in a strange land. After much hardship they returned to me, destitute and in beggars' rags. At first I did not recognize them, and when they told me who they were I questioned them anxiously about their troubles.

'Sister,' they replied, 'words cannot help us now. All that happened to us was decreed by Allah.'

I sent them to the bath and gave them new garments to put on, saying: 'Sisters, I am younger than you; to me you stand as father and mother. My inheritance has prospered by Allah's grace. You shall share in its benefits and live with me in comfort and honour.'

I treated them with kindness and they stayed with me for a year, enriching themselves with the gold that I gave them. One day, however they said: 'It would be better for us to marry again; we cannot live alone any longer.'

'Marriage will not make you happy,' I said, 'for honest men are hard to find these days. You tried marriage once and nothing came of it but ruin.'

They paid no heed to my counsel and married without my consent. I gave them clothes and money, and they went away with their husbands as before.

It was not long, however, before their new husbands deceived them and made off with their dowries. Penniless and broken, they returned to me, saying: 'Pray do not be angry with us. We are older than you but you are wiser than we. We promise never again to speak of marriage.'

'Welcome to this house, my sisters,' I replied, 'there are none dearer to me than you.' I kissed them and comforted them and invited them to stay with me as before.

After we had lived together for another year, I felt a great longing to travel abroad in quest of profit and amusement. I made preparations for a long voyage and fitted out a large vessel with provisions and merchandise. I asked my sisters whether they preferred to come with me or stay at home. They decided to accompany me, and we all set sail from Basrah. But first I divided my gold into two equal parts, one of which I took with me and the other I stored away in case some evil chance befell the ship and we returned home empty-handed.

We voyaged for many days and nights, but by ill fortune the captain lost his course and we were driven into an unknown ocean. Carried by a steady wind for ten days, we at length descried a city in the distance and asked the captain what its name might be.

'By Allah, I do not know,' he answered. 'I have never seen it in my life, nor have I ever sailed this sea before. We are now out of danger. There you can land your goods and offer them for sale; if you cannot sell them we will rest for two days, take in fresh provisions, and resume the voyage.'

We disembarked and brought our merchandise ashore. In a few minutes the captain, breathless with excitement, returned to us, saying: 'Come into the city and behold the wonder which Allah has wrought upon its people. Pray to Him, that He may preserve you from His scourge!'

We entered the city and were amazed to see that all the inhabitants had been turned into black stone, while everything else in the shops and markets, from rich fabrics to ornaments of gold and silver remained as it had been. We were puzzled at what we saw and said to each other: 'Surely there must be some strange reason for all this.' Then, separating in the streets, we each went in a different direction to gaze upon the treasures of the city.

I made my way to the citadel and, entering the King's palace, found it richly decked with plate of gold and silver. In the hall, among the stone figures of his viziers, chamberlains, and courtiers, I saw the King sitting on his throne arrayed in gold-embroidered robes of astonishing splendour. His throne was encrusted with pearls and jewels twinkling like brilliant stars, and about him stood fifty silk-clad slaves with unsheathed swords in their hands.

I marvelled greatly at the sight, and walked on until I entered the hall of the harem. On the walls were hangings and silken curtains wrought with thread-of-gold, and in the middle I saw the queen, a figure of black stone, reclining on a couch. She was dressed in a robe sewn with pearls and crowned with a diadem of the rarest gems, with diamond collars and necklaces about her neck. Through an open door I came to a staircase of seven steps and, climbing this, entered a marble hall spread with carpets of tissued gold. Here I saw a couch of alabaster studded with pearls and jewels and upholstered with precious silk, with a great light shining by its side. Drawing near, I found that the light came from a diamond, as large as an ostrich's egg, which, as it lay on a stool beside the couch, shed such brilliance around it that the entire hall was flooded with its lustre.

Near the couch I also saw lighted candles and, inferring that some human hand must have lit them, went on searching through the other halls. I was so enraptured with the splendour of all I beheld that I forgot my sisters, the ship, and the voyage which brought me to that city. When night came I tried to leave the palace, but, unable to find my way, retraced my steps to the hall with the lighted candles. There I lay down on the couch and, covering myself with a silken quilt, recited some verses from the Koran and endeavoured to compose my mind for sleep.

But I could not sleep, and at midnight I suddenly heard a low, melodious voice intoning the Koran. I rose at once and, hastening in the direction from which the sound proceeded, came to a chamber with an open door. I entered softly, and found that the room was a shrine of worship. It was lighted by lamps and candles and on the floor lay a prayer-rug upon which a handsome young man was reading the Koran aloud. Marvelling how he alone could have escaped the fate of all the city, I walked towards him and wished him peace. He turned his eyes upon me and answered my greeting.

'I adjure you by the words which you are reading from the Book of Allah,' I said, 'to tell me the history of this city and how you alone survived the fate which overtook its people.'

The young man smiled at me.

'First, gracious lady,' he said, 'tell me how it is that you have found your way to this chamber, and then I will answer any question you may wish to ask.'

When he had listened to my story, the youth put away his Koran in a satin bag and invited me to sit by his side. I did so and, as I gazed intently at him, I was captivated by his beauty and his manly grace.

'Know, gracious lady,' he began, 'that my father was the King of this city; he it was whom you found petrified upon his throne; the Queen you saw was my mother. The people all were pagans, worshippers of fire who swore by fire and light, by heat and shade, and by the turning sun.

'For many years my father had no children. I was the child of his old age and he nursed me carefully until I grew to boyhood. By good fortune there was an old woman in the palace who secretly believed in Allah and His prophet, though in public she conformed with the observances of my people. My father had great confidence in her as a chaste and honest woman; he lavished on her bounteous favours and firmly believed that she held the same faith as himself. When I grew up he committed me to her care, charging her to give me a sound education and to train me in the practices of his religion.

'The old woman received me and from the outset instructed me in the Moslem faith, teaching me its rites of purification and absolution and the forms of all its prayers. She expounded to me the whole of the Koran, and, when she had schooled me in all she knew, charged me to keep my faith from my father lest he should kill me. Shortly afterwards the old woman died, and one day, while the inhabitants of the city persisted in their ignorance and idolatrous unbelief, a voice like thunder was heard far and near, saying: "People of the city, renounce the worship of fire and serve the one Almighty King!"

'Seized with terror, the people flocked to my father's palace, asking what the fearful voice might portend. But the King told them not to be frightened or perturbed and urged them to stand firm in their ancient faith. Their hearts inclined to my father's words, and for another year they continued to worship fire. Then the voice thundered once again, and this it did on the same day for the next three years. But the people still persisted in their evil ways, until one morning, in the faint light of dawn, wrath and vengeance fell upon them from the sky and they were turned to black stone, together with their cattle and all their beasts. I alone was saved.

'Since then I have spent my days in fasting and prayer, with no human being to cheer my solitude.'

'Noble youth,' I said, 'will you not come with me to the city of Baghdad? There you will meet divines and sages deeply versed in Islam, and through them you will increase in faith and knowledge. I myself am mistress among my household, with a following of slaves and servants; also I have a ship here laden with merchandise. Fate cast me upon this shore and

Destiny has brought us together.' In this manner I spoke to him until he consented to go with me.

That night I slept in joy at the feet of the young man. When morning came we chose from the treasures of the palace all that was light and valuable and, leaving the citadel, went down to the city where we met the captain and my slaves who had long been searching for me. They rejoiced to see me again and marvelled greatly at the young man's story. But when my sisters saw me with the youth they were filled with envy and, in the malice of their hearts, began to scheme against me.

Blissfully happy with the young man at my side I embarked with the others, and after waiting for a favouring wind we weighed anchor and sailed away. My sisters never left us alone, and one day, as we sat talking together, they asked me what I proposed to do with my young companion. I told them that I intended to marry him and, turning towards him, I said: 'Sir, I wish to become your slave. Do not refuse me this, I pray you.'

'With all my heart,' he answered.

'This youth is all that I desire,' I said to my sisters. 'The riches I have on board I give to you.'

'May your marriage prosper,' they replied. But in their hearts they plotted evil.

We voyaged through the Unknown Ocean until we came to the Sea of Safety and saw, after a few days, the walls of Basrah looming far off on the water. That night we dropped anchor and lay down to sleep.

Whilst we were fast asleep my sisters rose and, carrying up the young man and myself, cast us, beds and all, into the sea. The youth, who could not swim, was drowned; for it was Allah's will that he should die a martyr. As for myself (would that I had perished with him!) Allah threw into my way a piece of timber, and to this I clung until I was cast by the waves on the shore of an island. I wandered about all night, and next morning, when the sun rose, I dried my garments and made my way inland. Reaching the other side, I found a footpath joining the island with the mainland, and along this I walked until I came within two hours' journey from Basrah. Suddenly

I saw a little snake hurrying towards me, pursued by a great serpent which was striving to devour it. I was moved with pity for the little snake, which was so tired out that its tongue trailed on the ground. So I took up a great boulder and threw it at the head of the serpent, killing it upon the instant. To my great astonishment, the little snake spread a pair of wings and, climbing high into the air, vanished from sight.

Worn out by the long journey, I lay down on the sand and slept for an hour. When I awoke I found a young girl caressing my feet, with two black bitches by her side. I sat up in great alarm and asked her who she was and what she wanted.

'Have you already forgotten me?' she cried. 'You have just now done me a great service in killing my enemy. I am a jinniyah and was in the semblance of that little snake whom you saved from the great serpent, himself a jinnee and a sworn enemy of mine. As soon as you rescued me I flew to the ship from which your two sisters threw you. I changed them into these black bitches, transported all the treasure to your house in Baghdad, and then sank the ship to the bottom of the ocean.'

She carried me in her arms, together with the two bitches, and, flying with us through the void, set us down on the terrace of my house, where I found all the treasure and the goods ranged in the courtyard. Before she vanished the jinniyah said: 'I swear by the sacred words engraved on Solomon's seal that, if you do not give each of these bitches three hundred strokes every day, I shall come back and change you into the same shape.'

'I hear and obey,' I replied.

And ever since, Prince of the Faithful, I have whipped them every day and shed compassionate tears over them.

That is my story.

*

The Caliph marvelled at this tale, and, turning to the second girl, said: 'Now tell me, young woman, what caused the weals on your body.'

The second girl came forward and began:

The Tale of the Second Girl

SOON after my father's death, Prince of the Faithful, I married one of the richest men of Baghdad. But a year later my husband passed into eternal rest, leaving me a fortune of eighty thousand dinars in gold. From that time I took to sumptuous living, dressing myself in such splendour that the least of my robes cost a thousand dinars.

One day, as I was sitting in my house, a hideous old woman was admitted to my presence. Her face was deeply wrinkled, her hair wild and shaggy, and her teeth were broken.

'Gracious lady,' she said, kissing the ground before me, 'I have an orphan daughter who is to be wedded tonight. I beg you to honour with your presence the marriage feast of this humble girl, and Allah will reward you. Alas, she is broken-hearted, for we are strangers in this city and there is none to befriend her except Allah.'

She wept and kissed my feet, so that I took pity on her and consented.

'I will now leave you, gracious lady,' she said, 'and if you will prepare yourself I will come back for you at nightfall.' Then, calling down blessings upon me, she kissed my hand and departed.

I rose and dressed myself. In the evening the old woman came and said: 'Honoured lady, the house is already full of the bridegroom's kinsfolk. I told them you were coming and they are joyfully waiting to receive you.'

I called some of my slave-girls to accompany us and, putting on my veil, walked with the old woman until we came to a pleasant, well-watered street in which a cool breeze was blowing. Presently we stopped at an arched gateway surmounted by a great marble dome, through which we saw a palace towering so high that it almost touched the clouds. The old woman knocked and we were admitted into a carpeted vestibule lighted by lamps and candles and decked with jewels and rich ornaments. Through this vestibule we passed into a hall of unparalleled splendour. The floor was spread with silken rugs and in the midst stood a couch of alabaster, inlaid with pearls and jewels and canopied with satin curtains. Upon our entrance a young girl, as fair as the full moon, rose from the couch and received me courteously, saying: 'A sweet welcome to you, my sister.' Then, seating me by her side, she continued: 'I must tell you that I have a brother, young and handsome, who saw you once at a wedding feast and has pined for you ever since. It was he who brought you here by this harmless trick; he desires to marry you in full observance of the Law of Allah and His prophet, and he therefore has no shame in seeking to do what is lawful.'

When I realized that there was no escape, I said to the girl: 'I hear and obey.' She rejoiced, and clapped her hands. At this signal a door was opened and through it came in a young man of such beauty that I felt my heart leap on seeing him. He was followed by a cadi and four witnesses, who greeted me and sat down. The cadi drew up my contract with the young man and, when the ceremony was over, all went away, leaving us alone.

The young man turned to me, saying: 'May our night be blessed!' He then told me that he wished to bind me with a vow and, bringing a Koran, said: 'Swear on this sacred book never to cherish or at all incline to any man but myself.'

I gladly took this oath and he threw his arms about my neck in passionate joy. Slaves served us with meat and wine, and when the feast was finished he took me to his bed and all night long we lay in each other's arms.

I loved the youth with all my heart, and for a full month we lived happily together. One day I asked my husband's leave to go to the market-place to buy some fabrics for a dress. I veiled myself and went there in company with the old woman, who took me to the shop of a young merchant whom she knew and recommended for the quality of his goods. My companion asked him to show us the finest of his silks and, while he did so, she went on praising him to me in the most endearing terms.

'Pray cease your chatter,' I said at last. 'I have come here only to buy what I need and then we will go home.'

I chose a length of stuff, but when I offered him the money, the merchant refused to touch it. 'Pray accept this silk,' he said, 'in return for the honour you have done my shop.'

'If he will not take the money,' I said to the old woman, 'give him back the silk.'

'By Allah, I will take nothing,' he replied. 'This is a present from me for a single kiss, which I shall value more highly than all the goods in my shop.'

'But what will a kiss profit you?' laughed the old woman. Then to me she added: 'Do you hear what the young man says, my daughter? There is no harm in a little kiss. Think, you shall get all you want for nothing.'

'Woman,' I rejoined, 'do you not know that I am bound by oath to my husband?'

'Let him have one little kiss,' she answered. 'If you do not speak of it you will lose nothing.'

The old woman went on persuading me until I put my head, as it were, into the bag and consented. I covered my eyes and stretched my cloak behind me so that no passer-by should see us, and the young man passed his head under my veil and, bringing his lips to my cheek, kissed me. But, in the excess of his passion, he bit my cheek so violently that the flesh was torn.

I fell down fainting and, when I came to, found myself laid on the knees of the old woman, who was making a great show of grief. The shop was closed and the young man nowhere to be found. At length the old woman said: 'Thank Allah it is nothing worse! Come, let us go home. When we are there pretend to be ill and take to your bed. I shall bring you an ointment to heal the wound.'

I rose and walked back in great fear to my husband's house. On reaching home I went forthwith to my chamber, telling the servants that I was ill. At nightfall my husband came in to see me. 'My love,' he said, 'what accident befell you while you were out?'

'Nothing,' I replied, 'I am a little unwell.'

He brought the candle close to my face and said: 'But what is the wound on your cheek, in its softest part?'

'When, with your leave, I went to the market-place today,' I replied, 'a camel loaded with firewood drove against me in the crowd, so that a faggot tore my veil and grazed me as you see. You know how narrow are the lanes of Baghdad.'

'Tomorrow,' he cried, 'I will complain to the Governor and he will hang every woodcutter in the city.'

'In Allah's name,' I pleaded, 'spare your soul the burden of so great a sin! It was all my fault; I was riding on a donkey which reared and threw me, so that my cheek was torn by a piece of wood on the ground.'

'Tomorrow,' he exclaimed, 'I will report this outrage to Ja'afar the Vizier, and he will put to death every donkey-boy in the city.'

'Would you kill all these men on my account?' I replied. 'It was only an accident, ordained by Allah.'

The more I pleaded with him the angrier he became, and at length he cried: 'Traitress, you have broken your oath!'

He called out in a terrible voice and at once seven black slaves burst into the room. They dragged me from my bed, threw me down on the floor, and then, at my husband's bidding, one held me by the shoulders, another seized my feet, and a third stood over me with an unsheathed sword in his hand.

'Cut her in two, good Sa'ad,' cried my husband to the slave, 'and throw her into the Tigris to be eaten by fishes. Thus shall perjurers be punished!'

'Recite your prayers and make your will,' said the Negro, lifting his sword. 'Your hour is come.'

In vain I besought my husband to spare me, but, as I was bewailing my fate and commending myself to Allah, the old woman rushed into the room and threw herself at the feet of her master.

'By the love with which I nursed you,' she pleaded, 'I implore you to pardon this girl, for she has done nothing worthy of such a punishment. You are still young, my son, and her life will be on your head.'

She wept and entreated, until, relenting, my husband said: 'For your sake I will pardon her. But she must bear upon her body the marks of shame until her dying day.'

He ordered the slaves to strip me naked and, taking up a
quince branch, beat me about the back and sides till I fell down
unconscious. Then he charged them to carry me away in the
night and to throw me into my own house.

The slaves did as their master bade them. Next morning,
when I recovered myself, I treated my wounds with various
ointments, but though they healed after a time, the weals can
still be seen upon my body.

After four months, when I was quite restored, I went to see
the house where I had suffered such agony. But I found the
palace a pile of rubble, and the once-flourishing street in which
it stood a desolate waste strewn with garbage heaps. And for
all my inquiries I could not learn the cause.

I betook myself to my half-sister and with her I found these
two bitches. We each recounted our story, and at last she said:
'Dear sister, no one in the world is secure from the assaults of
Fortune. Praise be to Allah we are all alive.'

Thenceforth we lived together, never allowing the thought of marriage to cross our minds again. Soon afterwards we were joined by our youngest sister, who went down every day to the market-place to buy what we needed. Yesterday she went out as was her custom and brought back the porter with her shopping. In the evening the dervishes came and then you others in the guise of merchants. What happened afterwards is not unknown to you, Prince of the Faithful.

Such is my story.

*

The Caliph marvelled at the tales of the two girls. He gave orders that they be recorded on parchment and that the manuscript be kept in the royal library. Then he said to the first girl: 'Now, honoured lady, have you no news of the jinniyah who bewitched your sisters?'

'Prince of the Faithful,' replied the girl, 'before she left me she gave me a lock of her hair and told me that if ever I needed her I had but to burn one of the hairs and she would promptly appear before me, were she at the other side of the Mountain of Kaf.'

'Give me the lock,' said the Caliph.

She handed it to him, and he burned one of the hairs. No sooner had they smelt the fume than they heard a noise like thunder which shook the entire palace, and the jinniyah appeared before them. Being a Believer, she greeted Al-Rashid, saying: 'Peace be with you, Caliph of Allah!'

'And on you be peace,' he answered, 'with Allah's blessing and mercy.'

'Know, my master,' said the jinniyah, 'that this girl has done me so great a kindness that I can never reward her sufficiently for it. She killed my enemy and delivered me from death; and I, having witnessed what her sisters had done to her, avenged her by turning them both into bitches. I spared their lives only because their death might have deeply grieved her. But if you wish it, Prince of the Faithful, I will restore them to their human shape, for your sake and for the sake of their sister.'

'Do so,' said the Caliph, 'and after that we will see what can be done for the girl with the scars. If what she says be true I shall justly avenge her on the man who treated her so villainously.'

'Prince of the Faithful,' she replied, 'you shall presently know the name of the man who flogged this girl and deprived her of her possessions. He is your nearest kinsman.'

She took a bowl of water and, muttering a mysterious charm over it, sprinkled the bitches, saying: 'Return to your natural state!'

Thereupon the bitches changed to beautiful girls, and the jinniyah turned to the Caliph, saying: 'Prince of the Faithful, the husband of the young woman is your own son, Al-Amin!'

When the Caliph had heard the story of the second girl from the jinniyah's own lips, he cried: 'By Allah, I will do a deed that shall be long remembered after me!'

At once he called his son to his presence and, when Al-Amin had truthfully told him all that had passed between him and his wife, the Caliph sent for cadis and witnesses and had him reunited to the girl. Then the eldest of the girls was married to the first dervish, her once-bewitched sisters to the other two dervishes, and the Caliph himself wedded the youngest of the five.

Al-Rashid appointed the dervishes chamberlains to his court, giving each a splendid palace to live in and endowing them with large annuities. He passed that night with his bride, and on the following day he set apart a magnificent mansion for her and assigned numerous slaves to her service.

THE TALE OF
KHALIFAH THE FISHERMAN

ONCE upon a time, in the reign of the Caliph Haroun al-Rashid, there lived in the city of Baghdad a fisherman who was so poor that he could not afford to take even one woman in marriage. He was called Khalifah.

It so happened one morning that he took his net upon his back and went down to the river, before the other fishermen arrived. When he reached the bank, he rolled up his sleeves and tucked his skirt into his belt; then he spread his net and cast it into the water. He cast his net ten times, but did not catch a single fish. In despair he threw himself upon the river bank, crying: 'There is no strength or help save in Allah! He gives bread to whom He will, and denies it to whom He pleases.' Then thought Khalifah: 'Trusting in Allah, I will cast my net once more.'

So saying, he rose and, wading knee-deep into the water, threw his net as far as his arms could send it. He waited a long time, and then pulled hard on the cords. But when at last he managed, with much skill and effort, to haul the heavy net ashore, he was astonished to find in it a lame, one-eyed ape. His astonishment, however, soon gave way to anger. He tied the ape to a tree upon the river bank, and would have fallen upon the beast with his whip had not Allah made the ape speak with an eloquent tongue.

'Stay your hand, Khalifah,' said the ape, 'and do not whip me. Leave me tied here to this tree and cast your net again. Allah will give you all that you desire.'

On hearing the ape's words, the fisherman once more spread his net and cast it into the water. Shortly afterwards he felt the net grow heavy; but when he had succeeded in bringing it to land, he found in it another ape of even more

303

grotesque appearance. His eyelids were darkened with kohl, his hands dyed with henna, and he wore a tattered vest about his middle. His front teeth, set wide apart, gleamed as he stared at the fisherman with an awkward grin.

'Praise be to Allah who has changed the fishes of the river into apes!' exclaimed the amazed Khalifah. Then, running towards the first beast, he cried: 'Look upon the fruit of your counsel, monster of ill omen! I began the day with the sight of your deformity and I shall doubtless end it in starvation and ruin.'

He lifted his whip high above his head and was again about to fall upon the one-eyed ape, when the beast begged him for mercy, crying: 'Spare me, Khalifah, in the name of Allah! Go to my brother: he will give you good advice.'

The bewildered fisherman flung away his whip and turned to the second ape, who said: 'If you mark my counsel and do my bidding, Khalifah, you shall prosper.'

'What would you have me do?' asked the fisherman.

'Leave me on this bank,' said the second ape, 'and once more cast your net.'

Khalifah spread his net again and cast it into the water. He waited patiently and, when he felt the net grow heavy, he gently hauled it in, only to find in it yet another ape. His hair was red, his eyelids lengthened with kohl, his hands and feet dyed with henna, and he wore a blue vest about his middle.

'Glory to Allah, King of the Universe!' exclaimed Khalifah when he saw the third ape. 'Surely this is a blessed day from first to last! It began with a sinister-looking monkey; and if the contents of a scroll can be divined from its title, this must indeed be a day of monkeys! There is not a single fish left in the river and we shall catch nothing today but apes!' Then, turning to the red-haired beast, he cried: 'In heaven's name what are you?'

'Do you not know me, Khalifah?' replied the ape.

'I do not, indeed,' protested the fisherman.

'Know, then,' said the beast, 'that I am the ape of Abu Sa'adah the Jew, chief of the money-changers. To me he owes his good fortune and all his riches. On greeting me in the morning he gains five pieces of gold, and on bidding me good night he gains five more.'

'Mark that,' said Khalifah, turning to the first ape. '*You* cannot boast of such liberality: seeing your face this morning has brought me nothing but ill luck!'

'Leave my brother in peace, Khalifah,' said the red-haired ape, 'and cast your net once more into the river. Then come back and show me your catch. I shall instruct you how to use it to your best advantage.'

'I hear and obey, king of all monkeys!' answered the fisherman.

Khalifah did as the ape told him, and when he drew in his net he rejoiced to find a splendid fish with a large head, broad fins, and eyes that glittered like gold coins. Marvelling at the quaintness of his prize, he carried it to the red-haired ape and showed it to him.

'Now gather some fresh grass,' said the beast, 'and spread it at the bottom of your basket: lay the fish upon it and cover it with more grass. Then carry the basket to the city of Baghdad. Should anyone speak to you on your way, you must make no answer, but proceed directly to the market of the money-changers. In the midst of it stands the shop of Abu Sa'adah the Jew, chief of the money-changers. You will find him seated on a mattress with an embroidered cushion at his back, surrounded by his slaves and servants. In front of him you will see two coffers, one for gold and one for silver. Go up to him, and set your basket before him, and say: "Sir, I went down to the Tigris this morning and in your name cast my net. Allah sent me this fish." He will ask: "Have you shown it to any other man?" "No, by Allah," you must answer. Then he will take the fish and offer you one dinar. You must refuse to sell it for that price. He will offer you two dinars, but you must still refuse. Whatever he offers, you must not accept, though it be the fish's weight in gold. He will ask: "What, then, would you have?" And you will reply: "I will sell this fish only for a few plain words." "What are they?" he will ask, and you will answer: "Stand up and say: 'Bear witness, all who are present in this market, that I give Khalifah the fisherman my ape in exchange for his ape, and that I barter my fortune for his fortune.' That is the price of my fish: I demand no gold." If the Jew consents to this,' continued the red-haired ape, 'you will become my master; I will bless you every morning and every evening, and you will every day gain ten pieces of gold. As for Abu Sa'adah, he will be cursed with the sight of my lame, one-eyed brother, and daily afflicted with extortionate tolls and taxes until he is reduced to beggary. Bear in mind what I have told you, Khalifah, and you shall prosper.'

'I will obey you in every particular, royal ape!' said the fisherman. He unbound the three beasts, who leapt into the water and disappeared.

Khalifah washed the fish, placed it in his basket upon some fresh grass, and covered it over. Then he set out for the city, singing merrily.

As he made his way through the streets of Baghdad, many people greeted him and asked him if he had any fish to sell. But he walked on, heeding no one, until he entered the market of the money-changers and stopped before the shop of Abu Sa'adah the Jew. The fisherman found him surrounded by numerous servants, who were attending him with such ceremony as can be found only in the royal courts of Khorasan. He went up to him and stood before him.

'What can we do for you, Khalifah?' asked Abu Sa'adah. 'If any man has wronged or slandered you, we will gladly take up your cause with the Governor, and you shall have justice.'

'Chief of the Jews,' replied Khalifah, 'I come to you with no such grievance. This morning I went down to the Tigris, and in your name cast my net. I caught this fish.'

Khalifah opened the basket and proudly held out the fish to the money-changer.

'By the Five Books of Moses, the Psalms, and the Ten Commandments,' cried the delighted Jew, 'a holy man appeared to me in a dream last night, saying: "You shall receive a present from me tomorrow." This must be the present; only tell me, on your life, have you shown this fish to any other man?'

W. HARVEY.   THOS. WILLIAMS.

'I swear by Allah, chief of the Jews,' replied the fisherman, 'and by the honoured memory of Abu Bakr, that no one else has seen it.'

When he heard this the Jew turned to one of his slaves and said: 'Take this fish to my house and ask my daughter to have it dressed for dinner: tell her to fry one half and to grill the other.'

'Do you hear, my lad?' echoed Khalifah. 'Tell your mistress to fry one half and to grill the other. Tell her it is a most excellent fish.'

'I hear and obey,' answered the slave, and departed with it to his master's house.

The Jew took a dinar from one of his coffers and offered it to Khalifah, saying: 'Spend this on your family.' Now Khalifah, who had never before earned such a sum for a single day's labour, impulsively held out his hand and took the coin. But as he was about to leave the money-changer, he remembered the ape's instructions.

'Take your dinar and give me back my fish,' he cried, throwing down the coin before the Jew. 'Would you make a laughing-stock of me?'

Thinking that the fisherman was jesting with him, the Jew smiled and handed him three dinars; but Khalifah refused the gold, saying: 'Since when have you known me to sell any fish for such a trifle?'

The Jew then gave him five dinars and said: 'Take these and do not be greedy.'

The fisherman took the five dinars and left the shop, scarcely believing his eyes. 'Glory be to Allah!' he thought. 'The Caliph himself has not as much gold in his coffers as I have in my purse today!' It was not until he had reached the end of the market-place, however, that he remembered the ape's advice. He hurried back to the Jew and again threw down the coins before him.

'What has come over you, Khalifah?' asked Abu Sa'adah. 'Would you rather have the money in silver?'

'I want neither your gold nor your silver,' returned the fisherman. 'Give me back my fish.'

'I have given you five dinars for a fish that is not worth one dirham,' cried the money-changer impatiently, 'and yet you are not satisfied. In heaven's name what is your price?'

'A few plain words,' replied Khalifah.

When he heard this the Jew grew so angry that his eyes sank into their sockets. 'You nail-paring of the Moslems!' he exclaimed, grinding his teeth with rage. 'Would you have me give up my faith, renounce my religion, and disavow the laws of my holy ancestors for a mere fish?' Then, turning to his slaves, he cried: 'Take hold of this rascal and beat him soundly!'

The slaves immediately set upon the fisherman and beat him until their master cried: 'Enough!' But as soon as they let go of him, Khalifah rose to his feet as though he felt no pain at all.

'Sir,' said the fisherman, 'you should have known that Khalifah can take more blows than ten donkeys put together.'

At this the Jew laughed heartily, and said: 'Enough of this fooling. How much do you wish me to pay you?'

'I ask only for a few brief words,' repeated Khalifah, 'and these have nothing to do with your religion; for if you were to become a Moslem, your conversion would neither benefit the Moslems nor harm the Jews; and if you persist in your error, your heresy will neither benefit the Jews nor harm the Moslems. I wish you only to rise up and say: "Bear witness, all who are present in this market, that I give Khalifah the fisherman my ape in exchange for his ape, and that I barter my fortune for his fortune."'

'Nothing can be easier than that,' said the Jew. And he instantly rose to his feet and proclaimed the words in the market-place. Then, turning to Khalifah, he asked: 'Is there any other thing that I am required to do?'

'No,' answered the fisherman.

'Then peace be with you,' said the money-changer.

Khalifah placed the empty basket upon his shoulder and hurried back to the river. As soon as he reached the bank he spread his net and cast it into the water. When he drew it in he found it filled with fish of every kind. Presently a woman came up to him with a basket on her shoulder, and bought a dinar's worth of fish. Then there passed by a slave who also bought a dinar's worth. When the day was done Khalifah had earned ten dinars. And he continued to earn ten dinars a day until he piled up a hundred pieces of gold.

Now Khalifah the fisherman dwelt in a hovel of a house at the end of the Lane of the Merchants. One night, as he lay in his lodging befuddled with hashish, he thought to himself: 'All your neighbours, Khalifah, think that you are a penniless, unfortunate fisherman. They have not seen your hundred pieces of gold. But they will soon hear of your wealth; and before long the Caliph himself will get to know of it. One day, when his treasury is empty, he will send for you and say: "I need some money. I hear that you have a hundred dinars. You must lend them to me." "Prince of the Faithful," I will answer, "your slave is a poor, humble fisherman. The man who told you that is a wicked liar." The Caliph, of course, will not believe me. He will hand me over to the Governor, who will strip me naked and whip me mercilessly. The best course for me now is to inure my body to whipping. I will rise and prepare myself.'

Khalifah rose and put off all his clothes. He placed beside him an old leather cushion and, taking up his whip, began lashing himself, aiming every other stroke at the cushion and yelling out: 'A wicked lie! Oh! Oh! I have no money!'

His cries, and the sound of the whipping, echoed in the stillness of the night and startled the neighbours out of their slumbers. They all rushed out into the street inquiring the cause of the disturbance. Thinking that thieves had broken in upon the fisherman, the neighbours hurried to his rescue; but they were surprised to find the door of his lodging locked and bolted.

'The thieves must have got in from the neighbouring terrace,' they said to each other. So they climbed up to the adjoining terrace and from there descended into the fisherman's house, only to find him thrashing his naked body.

'What demon has possessed you tonight, Khalifah?' they cried in amazement. And when he had told the neighbours the very secret he had been so anxious to keep from them, they laughed at him and said: 'Enough of this jest! May Allah give you no joy in your treasure!'

When the fisherman woke up next morning his mind was still obsessed with the fear of losing his gold. 'If I leave my hundred dinars at home,' he thought, 'it is certain they will be stolen; if I carry them in my belt, thieves will lie in wait for me in some deserted place, and cut my throat, and rob me of them. I must think of a better device.' At length Khalifah decided to sew a pocket in the breast of his robe, and to carry in it the hundred dinars tied in a bundle. This done, he took up his net, his basket, and his staff, and went down to the Tigris.

When he reached the river he stepped down the bank and cast his net into the water. But the net brought up nothing at all. Farther and farther away he moved along the bank, until he had travelled half a day's journey from the city; but all to no purpose. At last he summoned up all his strength and hurled the net with such desperate force that the bundle of coins flew from his pocket and plunged into the river.

At once Khalifah threw off his clothes and dived after his gold; but it was swept away by the swift current, and he soon had to abandon the search. Bedraggled and utterly exhausted, he walked back to the spot where he had left his clothes. But his clothes, too, had disappeared and were nowhere to be found. In despair he wrapped himself in his net and, like a raging camel or a rebel jinnee just let loose from King Solomon's prison-house, he began jumping blindly in all directions. So much for Khalifah the fisherman.

Now it so chanced that the Caliph Haroun al-Rashid (who is the other hero of our tale) had at that time a friend among the jewellers of Baghdad called Ibn-al-Kirnas. He was known to all the merchants of the city as the Caliph's own broker; and his influence was such that nothing choice or rare, from jewels to eunuchs and slave-girls, was put up for sale that was not first shown to him.

One day, as Ibn-al-Kirnas was attending to his customers, the chief of the brokers ushered into his shop a slave-girl of incomparable beauty. Not only was she peerless in her physical perfection, but she was also graced with rare accomplishments; she could recite pretty verses, sing, and make music upon all manner of instruments. Her name was Kut-al-Kulub. Ibn-al-Kirnas bought her upon the instant for five thousand dinars; and after he had arrayed her in rich robes and adorned her with jewels worth a thousand more, he took her to the Prince of the Faithful.

Al-Rashid spent that night with Kut-al-Kulub, and was so delighted with her talents that next morning he sent for Ibn-al-Kirnas and gave him ten thousand dinars in payment for the girl. The Caliph loved his new favourite with such violent passion that he forsook for her his wife, the Lady Zubaidah, and all his concubines. He stayed a whole month by her side, leaving her chamber only for the Friday prayers.

It was not long, however, before resentment grew among the Caliph's lieutenants and the officers of his court. They could keep silent no longer, and voiced their complaints before Ja'afar the Vizier.

The following Friday, whilst he was attending upon the Caliph at the mosque, Ja'afar discreetly broached the subject of his infatuation with Kut-al-Kulub.

'By Allah, Ja'afar,' replied the Caliph, 'my will is powerless in this matter; for my heart is caught in the snares of love and, try as I may, I cannot release it.'

'Prince of the Faithful,' said Ja'afar, 'this girl Kut-al-Kulub is now a member of your household, a servant among your servants; and it is a common saying that what the hand possesses the soul never pines for. Think of the pleasures of riding and hunting and other sports; for these may help you to forget her.'

'You have spoken wisely, Ja'afar,' replied the Caliph. 'Come, we will go hunting this very day.'

As soon as the service was over they mounted their steeds and rode out into the open country, followed by the troops.

It was a hot day. When they had travelled a long way from the city, Al-Rashid felt very thirsty, and, looking round to see if there was any sign of an encampment near by, he faintly descried an object far off upon a mound.

'Can you see what that is?' he asked Ja'afar.

'It seems to be the figure of a man,' replied the Vizier. 'He is perhaps the keeper of an orchard or a cucumber garden. He can no doubt give us some water. I will ride and fetch some.'

But Al-Rashid ordered Ja'afar to stay and wait for the troops, who had lingered behind, and he himself galloped off, more swiftly than the wind that blows in the wilderness or the cataract that thunders down the rocks. On reaching the mound he saw a man swathed in a fishing-net, with hair dishevelled and dusty, and bloodshot eyes blazing like lurid torches.

Al-Rashid greeted the strange-looking figure, and Khalifah muttered a few angry words in reply.

'Have you a drink of water to give me?' asked the Caliph.

'Are you blind or mad?' broke out the fisherman. 'Can you not see that the Tigris flows behind this mound?'

Al-Rashid walked round the hillock and, finding that the river did indeed run behind it, drank and watered his horse. Returning to Khalifah, he said: 'What are you doing here, and what is your trade?'

'That question is even sillier than the last!' cried Khalifah. 'Do you not see the implement of my trade about my shoulders?'

'So you are a fisherman,' said the Caliph. 'But where have you left your cloak, your gown, and your belt?'

It so chanced that those were the very things of which the fisherman had been robbed. Therefore, when he heard the Caliph name them, he did not doubt that the thief stood before him. At once he darted, like a flash of lightning, from the top of the mound and caught the Caliph's horse by the bridle, crying: 'Give me back my clothes and stop this foolish joke!'

'By Allah, my friend,' replied the Caliph, 'I have never seen your clothes; nor do I understand what you are shouting about.'

Now Al-Rashid had a small mouth and round, plump cheeks; so that Khalifah took him for a professional piper. 'Give me back my clothes, you scraper of beggarly tunes,' threatened the fisherman, 'or I will cudgel your bones with this staff till you wet your drawers!'

When he saw the fisherman brandishing his heavy staff, the Caliph thought to himself: 'By Allah, even a light stroke from this cudgel would be too much for me.' He at once took off his splendid satin cloak and handed it to Khalifah, saying: 'Take this in place of the things you lost.'

'My clothes were worth ten times as much as this frivolous garment,' muttered Khalifah, as he turned the cloak about with evident contempt. At length, however, he was prevailed upon by Al-Rashid to try it on. But finding it too long, he took the knife which was tied to the handle of his basket and cut off the lower third of its skirt, so that it hung just above his knees.

'Tell me, good piper,' said the fisherman, 'how much a month does your playing bring you?'

'Ten dinars,' replied the Caliph.

'By Allah,' said Khalifah, 'you make me feel sorry for you. Why, I make ten dinars every day. If you are willing to enter my service, I will teach you my trade and share with you my gain. You will thus become my partner and earn a good round sum every day. And should your old master have any objections, this staff of mine will protect you.'

'I accept your offer,' replied the Caliph.

'Then get off your ass,' said the fisherman, 'and follow me. We will begin work at once.'

Al-Rashid dismounted, and having fastened his horse to a near-by tree he rolled up his sleeves and tucked his robe into his belt.

'Hold the net thus,' said the fisherman, 'spread it over your arm thus, and cast it into the water – thus . . .'

Al-Rashid summoned up all his strength and did as the fisherman told him. When, after a few moments, he tried to draw in the net, it was so heavy that the fisherman had to come to his aid.

'Piper of ill omen!' burst out Khalifah, as the two tugged together at the cords. 'A moment ago I was willing to accept your cloak in compensation for my clothes: but now, if you cause my net to be torn or damaged, I will take from you your ass and beat you black and blue. Do you hear?'

When they at length succeeded in hauling the net ashore, they rejoiced to find it filled with fish of every kind and colour.

'Although you are but an ill-favoured piper,' said Khalifah, 'you may yet become an excellent fisherman. Ride now to the market-place and fetch me two large baskets. I will stay here and watch over the fish till you return. We will then load the catch on your ass's back and take it to the fish market. All that you have to do there is to hold the scales and receive the money. Be off, and waste no time!'

'I hear and obey,' replied the Caliph and, mounting his horse galloped away, scarcely able to repress his laughter.

When Al-Rashid had rejoined Ja'afar and the troops, the Vizier, who had become anxious about his master's delay, said: 'You no doubt came upon some pleasant garden on the way and rested there all this while.'

At this the Caliph burst out laughing and proceeded to tell the company of his adventure with the fisherman. 'My master is now waiting for me,' he continued gleefully. 'He and I are to go to the market-place and sell the fish and share the profit.'

'Then let me provide you with some customers,' laughed the Vizier.

But a mischievous fancy suddenly took possession of the Caliph's mind. 'By the honour of my holy ancestors,' he cried, 'whoever brings me a fish from my master Khalifah shall receive one gold dinar.'

Thereupon the crier proclaimed the Caliph's wish among the guards and they all made at once for the river, in the direction of the mound.

While the fisherman was waiting for Al-Rashid, the guards swooped down upon him like vultures, each grabbing as many fish as his hands could hold.

'There must surely be something miraculous about these fishes!' cried Khalifah in terror and amazement. Then, holding one fish in each hand, he jumped into the water, crying: 'O Allah, send your servant the piper quickly to my aid!'

The guards wrapped up the spoil in their large, gold-embroidered handkerchiefs and rode back to their master at full gallop. As soon as they were gone, however, the chief of the Caliph's eunuchs (who had been delayed through his horse stopping on the road to make water) appeared on the bank of the river.

'Come here, fisherman,' said the Negro, when he saw Khalifah holding up the fish.

'Be off, impudent scoundrel,' answered Khalifah.

But the eunuch drew nearer. 'Give me your fish,' he said persuasively. 'I will pay you well.'

The fisherman still refused, and the slave lifted his lance and aimed it at him.

'Dog, do not throw!' cried Khalifah. 'I would rather give you all than lose my life.'

So saying, he contemptuously flung the fish at the Negro, who picked them up and wrapped them in his handkerchief. Then the chief of the eunuchs put his hand in his pocket in order to pay the fisherman. But, as chance would have it, he found not a single coin.

'I fear you have no luck today,' he said, 'for, by Allah, I have not one piece of silver about me. But if you will come to the Caliph's palace tomorrow and ask for Sandal the black eunuch, you shall receive a hearty welcome and a generous reward.' With this the slave leapt upon his horse and galloped away.

'This is indeed a blessed day!' groaned Khalifah. In despair, he threw his net upon his shoulder and set out for the city.

As he walked through the streets of Baghdad, the passers-by were puzzled to see the fisherman wrapped in a cloak worth a thousand dinars. Presently he entered the market-place and passed by the shop of the Caliph's tailor, who recognized the garment which he himself had made for the Prince of the Faithful.

The tailor stopped Khalifah, saying: 'How did you come by that cloak?'

'What is that to you?' returned the fisherman angrily. 'Yet, if you must know, it was given me by an apprentice of mine. The rascal had stolen all my clothes; but I took pity on him and, rather than have his hand cut off for theft, I contented myself with this cloak, which he offered me in their place.'

The tailor was greatly amused to hear this, and understood at once that the fisherman was the victim of one of the Caliph's latest pranks.

Meanwhile, a plot against Kut-al-Kulub was being hatched at the Caliph's palace. For when the Lady Zubaidah, the Caliph's queen and cousin, learnt of her husband's new attachment, she was stung with such consuming jealousy that she thenceforth refused meat and drink and eagerly awaited an opportunity to avenge herself on Kut-al-Kulub. Now, when she heard that Al-Rashid had gone out hunting, she held a sumptuous feast and sent for her husband's favourite to entertain the guests with her music.

Not knowing what Destiny held in store for her, the girl took up her instruments and allowed herself to be conducted to the Queen's chambers.

When her eyes fell upon Kut-al-Kulub, the Lady Zubaidah marvelled in her heart at the girl's exquisite beauty and, concealing her bitter thoughts with a welcoming smile, requested her to be seated. Kut-al-Kulub sang to the accompaniment of the lute and the tambourine. So sweetly did she sing that her audience were charmed into a magic trance, the birds paused in their flight, and the whole palace echoed with a thousand mellifluous voices.

'Al-Rashid is hardly to blame for loving her,' thought the Lady Zubaidah, as the girl ended her performance and gracefully bowed to the ground before her.

Presently the servants set before Kut-al-Kulub a dish of sweetmeats in which the Queen had cunningly mixed a potent drug. Scarcely had the girl swallowed one morsel when her head fell backward and she sank to the ground unconscious. The Lady Zubaidah ordered her women to carry the girl to her private chambers. She then had it announced that Kut-al-Kulub had choked while eating and died, threatening her attendants with a cruel death if they betrayed her secret. Lastly she ordered a mock burial to take place and a marble tomb to be erected in the grounds of the palace.

When the Caliph returned from the hunt and the news of the supposed death of his favourite was broken to him, the world darkened before his eyes and he was overwhelmed with grief. He bitterly wept for Kut-al-Kulub and stayed by the tomb a full hour.

Her plot having succeeded, the Lady Zubaidah gave orders that the senseless Kut-al-Kulub be locked into a chest and carried to the market-place. She instructed one of her trusted slaves to sell the chest without delay, making it a condition that the contents should not be declared beforehand. And she ordered the slave to give away the money in alms.

Now to return to the fisherman. Early next morning, Khalifah thought to himself: 'I can do nothing better today than go to the Caliph's palace and demand of the black slave the debt he owes me.'

So he rose and betook himself to Al-Rashid's court. As soon as he entered the great portals of the palace, he saw Sandal, the chief eunuch, in the doorway, with a crowd of slaves waiting upon him. As the fisherman drew closer, one of the slaves rose to bar his way and would have turned him back had not Khalifah called out to the black eunuch: 'I have not failed you, my golden tulip!'

Recognizing the fisherman, Sandal greeted him with a laugh and put his hand into his pocket to produce his purse. It so chanced, however, that at that moment a great shout announced the approach of Ja'afar. At once Sandal sprang to his feet and, heedless of his creditor, hurried off to the Vizier and fell into a long conversation with him.

Khalifah repeatedly tried to draw the slave's attention to his presence, but all to no purpose. At length, observing the fisherman's impatient gesticulations, Ja'afar asked: 'Who is that stranger?'

'That,' replied Sandal, 'is the self-same fisherman whose fish we seized yesterday at the Caliph's orders.' And he proceeded to explain to Ja'afar the occasion of Khalifah's visit.

When he had heard Sandal's account, the Vizier smiled and said: 'This fisherman is the Caliph's instructor and business partner. He has come at a time when we need him most. Today our master's heart is heavy with grief for the death of his beloved, and perhaps nothing can cheer him better than this fisherman's antics. Let him stay here while I ask the Prince of the Faithful if he wishes to see him.'

Ja'afar left the eunuch and hurried back to the Caliph's chamber. He found him bowed down with sorrow, still brooding over the loss of Kut-al-Kulub. The Vizier wished him peace, and bowing low before him, said: 'On my way to you just now, Prince of the Faithful, I met at the door your teacher and partner, Khalifah the fisherman. He is loud in his complaint against you. "Glory to Allah!" I heard him say. "Is this how masters should be treated? I sent him to fetch me a couple of baskets and he never came back. What kind of partnership is this, I ask?" Now, I pray you, Prince of the Faithful,' went on Ja'afar, 'if you still have a mind to be his partner, let him know of it; but if you wish to end your joint labours, tell him that he must seek another man.'

The Caliph smiled at Ja'afar's words, and his sorrow seemed to be lightened. 'Is this true, Ja'afar?' he asked. 'Upon my life, this fisherman shall have his reward!' Then added Al-Rashid with a mischievous twinkle in his eye: 'If it is Allah's wish that he should prosper through me, it shall be done; and if it is His wish to scourge him through me, it shall be done also.'

So saying, Al-Rashid took a large sheet of paper and, cutting it into numerous pieces, said to the Vizier: 'Write down on twenty of these papers sums of money from one dinar to a thousand, and all the dignities of the State from the smallest office to the Caliphate itself; also twenty kinds of punishment from the lightest beating to a hideous death.'

'I hear and obey,' replied Ja'afar, and did as the Prince of the Faithful bade him.

Then said the Caliph: 'I swear by my holy ancestors and by my kinship with Hamzah and Akil that Khalifah the fisherman shall have the choice of one of these papers, and that I will reward him accordingly. Go and bring him before me!'

'There is no strength or help save in Allah,' thought Ja'afar, as he left the Caliph's chamber. 'Who knows what lies in store for this poor wretch! But the Caliph has sworn; and that which Allah has ordained must surely come to pass.'

When he found Khalifah, Ja'afar took him by the hand and, followed by a crowd of slaves, proceeded with him through seven vast vestibules until they stood at the door of the Caliph's chamber.

'Be careful,' said the Vizier to the terrified fisherman. 'You are about to be admitted to the presence of the Prince of the Faithful, Defender of the Faith.' With this, he led him in;

and Khalifah, who was so perplexed at the commotion that he could not understand the Vizier's words, suddenly saw the Caliph seated on a couch with all the officers of his court standing around him. The fisherman recognized his former apprentice with a shout of surprise.

'It is good to see you again, my piper!' he cried. 'But was it right to go away and leave me by the river all alone with the fish, and never to return? Know, then, that thanks to your truancy I was attacked by a band of mounted slaves, who carried off the entire catch. Had you returned promptly with the baskets, we would have made a hundred dinars. And what is worse, the treacherous rogues have now arrested me. But, tell me, who has imprisoned *you* in this place?'

Al-Rashid smiled and held out the cuttings to the fisherman, saying: 'Come closer, Khalifah, and draw one of these papers.'

'Only yesterday you were a fisherman,' replied Khalifah. 'Now I see that you have turned astrologer. But you have doubtless heard the common adage: "A rolling stone gathers no moss."'

'Enough of this chatter,' interrupted Ja'afar. 'Draw one of these papers at once, and do as the Prince of the Faithful bids you.'

The fisherman took one paper and handed it to the Caliph, saying: 'Read me my fortune, good piper, and keep nothing back.'

Al-Rashid passed the paper to Ja'afar and asked him to read out the contents. Such was Khalifa's luck, however, that his choice decreed a hundred blows of the stick. Accordingly, he was at once thrown down and given a hundred strokes.

'This unfortunate man has come to the river of your bounty, Prince of the Faithful,' said Ja'afar. 'Pray do not turn him back with his thirst unquenched.' And the Vizier persuaded the Caliph to let the fisherman draw again.

The second paper decreed that Khalifah be given nothing at all. Ja'afar, however, prevailed upon the Caliph to let the fisherman draw a third. Khalifah drew again, and the Vizier unfolded the paper and announced: 'One dinar.'

'What!' cried the angry fisherman. 'One dinar for a hundred strokes? Then may Allah justly requite you.'

The Caliph laughed, and Ja'afar took the fisherman by the hand and led him from his master's presence.

As Khalifah was about to leave the palace, Sandal called out to him, saying: 'Come, my friend, give me my share of the Caliph's reward.'

'You want your share, do you, sunshine?' broke out Khalifah. 'All I have earned was a hundred strokes and one dinar. You would indeed be welcome to half of my beating; as for the miserable coin, why, you can have that too!' So saying, he flung the dinar at him and rushed out, bursting with indignation.

Moved with pity, the eunuch ordered some slaves to run after him and bring him back. They did so, and Sandal took out a red purse and emptied from it a hundred dinars into the fisherman's hands, saying: 'Take this in payment of my debt, and go in peace.'

Khalifah rejoiced. He put the gold into his pocket, together with the dinar which Al-Rashid had given him, and went out of the palace, his troubles all forgotten.

Now it so chanced that as the fisherman was walking along the streets, lost in happy fancies, Destiny conducted his steps to the market-place, where he saw a great concourse of people. Pushing his way among the wealthy merchants, he found the centre of attention to be a large chest with a young slave seated upon it. Beside the chest stood an old man calling out: 'Gentlemen, merchants, worthy citizens! Who will be the first bidder for this chest of unknown treasure from the harem of the Lady Zubaidah, daughter of Al-Kasim, wife of the Prince of the Faithful?'

'By Allah,' said one of the merchants, 'there is much risk in this; but I will say twenty dinars.'

'Fifty!' cried another.

'A hundred!' shouted a third.

'Who will give more?' cried the auctioneer.

Breathless with excitement, Khalifah the fisherman lifted his voice, crying: 'Be it mine for a hundred and one dinars!'

At this the merchants laughed incredulously; but the auctioneer, who was impressed by the fisherman's earnestness, replied: 'The chest is yours: hand in your gold, and may Allah bless the bargain!'

Having paid the slave, Khalifah placed the chest upon his shoulder, and carried it to his house. As he staggered along under its weight, he wondered what the precious contents might be. Presently he reached his dwelling and, after he had managed to get the chest through the door, he applied himself to opening it. But the chest was securely locked.

'What devil possessed me to buy a box that cannot even be opened!' he cried. Then he decided to break the chest to pieces: but it stoutly defied all his kicks and blows. Utterly exhausted, he at length stretched himself out on the lid and sank into a heavy sleep.

Scarcely an hour had passed, however, when the fisherman was awakened by a sound of movement beneath him. Half-demented with terror, he leapt to his feet, crying: 'This chest must be haunted by jinn! Praise be to Allah who prevented me from opening it! For had I freed them in the dark they would have put me to a miserable death!'

His terror increased as the noise gradually became more distinct. He searched in vain for a lamp and finally rushed out into the street yelling at the top of his voice: 'Help! Help, good neighbours!'

Roused from their sleep, the neighbours appeared at every door and window. 'What has happened?' they shouted.

'Jinn! Jinn!' cried the fisherman. 'My house is haunted! Give me a lamp and a hammer, in the name of Allah!'

The neighbours laughed. One gave him a lamp and another lent him a hammer. His confidence restored, the fisherman went to his house determined to break open the chest. He battered its locks with the hammer and pulled back the lid.

Inside, he was astonished to see a girl as beautiful as a houri. Her eyes were half-open, as if she had just waked from a heavy sleep. Khalifah marvelled at her loveliness. 'In Allah's name, who are you?' he whispered, kneeling down before her.

Kut-al-Kulub opened her eyes and murmured: 'Bring me Jasmine and Narcissus.'*

'Alas, my mistress,' he replied, 'I have nothing here but a few henna flowers.'

On hearing the stranger's words the girl completely regained her senses. 'Who are you? Where am I?' she asked, gazing intently into his face.

'I am Khalifah the fisherman, and you are in my house,' he answered.

'Am I not in the palace of the Caliph Haroun al-Rashid?' asked the girl.

'Are you mad?' exclaimed the fisherman. 'Let me tell you at once that you belong to no one but me; it was only this morning that I bought you for a hundred and one dinars. Allah be praised; my luckless star has turned auspicious!'

Khalifah would have long continued in this strain had not Kut-al-Kulub, who was beginning to feel the pangs of hunger, interrupted him, saying: 'Give me something to eat.'

'By Allah,' replied the fisherman, 'there is nothing to eat or drink in this house. I myself have scarcely tasted anything for two days past.'

'Have you any money, then?' she asked.

'Allah preserve this chest!' he answered bitterly. 'This bargain has swallowed up every dirham that I had.'

'Then go to your neighbours,' she said, 'and bring me something to eat, for I am very hungry.'

The fisherman rushed out into the street, crying: 'Good neighbours, who will give a hungry man something to eat?' This he repeated several times at the top of his voice, until the unfortunate neighbours, once more awakened by his cries, opened their windows and threw down some food to him: one gave him half a loaf of bread, another a piece of cheese, a third a cucumber.

Returning home, he set the food before Kut-al-Kulub and invited her to eat. But the girl said: 'Bring me a drink of water; I am very thirsty.'

So Khalifah took up his empty pitcher and again ran out

* The names of two slave-girls.

into the street, begging the neighbours for some water. The neighbours replied with angry curses; but, unable to stand his persistent cries any longer, they carried water to him in jugs, pails, and ewers. Khalifah filled his pitcher and took it to the slave-girl.

When she had eaten and drunk her fill, the fisherman asked her how she had come to be locked into the chest. She recounted to him all that had happened at the Caliph's palace, adding: 'All this is no doubt destined to make your fortune. For when Al-Rashid hears the news of my rescue you shall not lose your reward.'

'But is not this Al-Rashid the dull-witted piper whom I but recently taught fishing?' cried Khalifah. 'Never in all my life have I met such a niggardly rascal.'

'My friend,' said the girl, 'you must cease this churlish talk and make yourself worthy of the new station that awaits you. Above all, you must bear yourself respectfully and courteously in the presence of the Prince of the Faithful.'

Such was the influence of Kut-al-Kulub's words on Khalifah that a new world seemed to unfold before him. The dark veil of ignorance was lifted from his eyes and he became a wiser man.

The fisherman and the girl slept (the two lying far apart) till morning, when Kut-al-Kulub asked Khalifah to bring her pen, ink, and paper. She wrote to Ibn-al-Kirnas, the Caliph's jeweller, informing him of her whereabouts and of the events of the previous day. Then she directed Khalifah to the shop of Ibn-al-Kirnas and asked him to deliver the letter without delay.

When he entered the jeweller's shop the fisherman bowed to the ground before him and wished him peace. But, taking Khalifah for a common beggar, the merchant ordered one of his slaves to give him half a dirham and show him out. Khalifah refused the coin, saying: 'I beg no alms. Read this, I pray you.'

As soon as he finished reading the girl's letter, the jeweller lifted it to his lips and, rising, bade the fisherman a courteous welcome. 'Where is your house, my friend?' he asked.

Khalifah directed him to his dwelling. The merchant then called two of his servants and said to them: 'Take my friend to the shop of Muhsin the money-changer and ask him to pay him a thousand dinars in gold. Then return with him forthwith.'

The servants took the fisherman to the money-changer, and he was paid a thousand dinars. When they returned with him to their master's shop, Khalifah found the jeweller mounted on a magnificent dappled mule with all his servants gathered around him. Near by stood another splendid mule, richly saddled and bridled, which Ibn-al-Kirnas invited Khalifah to mount. The fisherman, who had never been on a mule's back in all his life, at first refused, but, having been finally prevailed upon by the merchant, he decided to risk a trial and resolutely leapt upon the animal's back – facing the wrong way and grasping its tail instead of the bridle. The mule reared at once, and Khalifah was violently thrown to the ground to the cheers and shouts of the onlookers.

Ibn-al-Kirnas left the fisherman behind and rode off to the Caliph's palace. Al-Rashid was overjoyed to hear the news of his favourite's deliverance, and he ordered the merchant to bring her immediately to his court.

When the girl was admitted to the Caliph's presence, she kissed the ground before him, and he rose and welcomed her rapturously. Kut-al-Kulub related to him the story of her adventure and told him that her rescuer was a fisherman called Khalifah. 'He is now waiting at the door of the palace,' she added.

Al-Rashid sent at once for the fisherman, and when he entered upon him he kissed the ground before him and humbly wished him joy and everlasting glory.

The Caliph marvelled at the fisherman's transformation, his humility and politeness. He bestowed upon him a generous reward, giving him fifty thousand dinars, a magnificent robe of honour, a noble mare, and slaves from the Sudan.

When his audience with the Caliph ended, the fisherman again kissed the ground before him and left his chamber a proud, rich man. As he passed through the gates of the palace,

Sandal approached him and wished him joy of his new fortune. Khalifah produced from his pocket a purse containing a thousand dinars and offered it to him. But the slave refused the gold and marvelled at his liberality and the goodness of his heart.

Then Khalifah mounted the mare which Al-Rashid had given him and, with the help of two slaves who held her by the bridle, rode majestically through the streets of the city until he reached his house. As he dismounted, his neighbours flocked around him inquiring about his sudden prosperity. The fisherman related to them all that had happened and they marvelled at his story.

Khalifah became a constant visitor at the court of Al-Rashid, who continued to lavish on him high dignities and favours. He bought a magnificent house and had it furnished with rare and costly objects. Then he married a well-born, beautiful maiden, and lived happily with her until he was visited by the Spoiler of worldly mansions, the Dark Minister of the graveyard.

THE DREAM

THERE lived once in Baghdad a merchant who, having squandered all his wealth, became so destitute that he could make his living only by the hardest labour.

One night he lay down to sleep with a heavy heart, and in a dream a man appeared to him, saying: 'Your fortune lies in Cairo. Go and seek it there.'

The very next morning he set out for Cairo and, after many weeks and much hardship on the way, arrived in that city. Night had fallen, and as he could not afford to stay at an inn he lay down to sleep in the courtyard of a mosque.

Now as the Almighty's will would have it, a band of robbers entered the mosque and from there broke into an adjoining house. Awakened by the noise, the owners raised the alarm and shouted for help; then the thieves made off. Presently the Chief of Police and his men arrived on the scene. They entered the mosque and, finding the man from Baghdad lying in the courtyard, seized him and beat him with their clubs until he was nearly dead. Then they threw him into prison.

Three days later the Chief of Police ordered his men to bring the stranger before him.

'Where do you come from?' asked the chief.

'From Baghdad.'

'And what has brought you to Cairo?'

'A man appeared to me in a dream, saying: "Your fortune lies in Cairo. Go and seek it there." But when I came to Cairo, the fortune I was promised proved to be the blows your men so generously gave me.'

When he heard this, the Chief of Police burst out laughing. 'Know then, you fool,' he cried, 'that I too have heard a voice in my sleep, not just once but on three occasions. It said: "Go to Baghdad, and in a cobbled street lined with palmtrees you will find such-and-such a house, with a courtyard of grey marble; at the far end of the garden there is a fountain of white marble. Under the fountain a great sum of money lies buried. Go there and dig it up." But would I go? Of course not. Yet, fool that you are, you have come all the way to Cairo on the strength of one idle dream.'

Then the Chief of Police gave the merchant some money. 'Here,' he said, 'take this. It will help you on the way back to your own country.'

The merchant recognized at once that the house and garden just described were his own. He took the money and set out promptly on his homeward journey.

As soon as he reached his house he went into the garden, dug beneath the fountain, and uncovered a great treasure.

Thus the words of the dream were wondrously fulfilled, and Allah made the ruined merchant rich again.

THE TALE OF JUDAR AND
HIS BROTHERS

ONCE upon a time there was a merchant called Omar who had three sons: the eldest was named Salem, the second Seleem, and the youngest Judar. He reared them all to manhood, but the youngest he loved more than his brothers, so that they grew jealous of Judar and hated him. When Omar, who was by now well advanced in years, noticed that the two hated their brother, he feared that after his death Judar might come to mischief at their hands. He therefore summoned his kinsfolk together with some learned men and a number of property-dividers from the Cadi's court, and said to them: 'Bring me my money and all my goods.' They brought him his money and his goods, and Omar said: 'Friends, divide these things into four portions according to the law.'

They did so; and he gave each of his sons a portion and kept the last for himself, saying: 'This is the sum of my property and I have divided it among my children in my lifetime, so that all disputes should be avoided. They shall have nothing to claim from each other after my death. The portion which I have kept for myself shall belong to my wife, the mother of these children, that she may have the wherewithal to support herself when I am gone.'

Shortly afterwards old Omar died, and the two elder brothers, not content with their inheritance, claimed a part of Judar's share, saying: 'Our father's wealth has fallen into your hands.'

Judar referred the matter to the judges, and the Moslems who witnessed the division came and gave testimony. The judge dismissed their claim; but as a result of the dispute Judar lost a part of his property and so did his brothers. Yet it was not long before they plotted against him a second time, so that he was obliged to go to law again. The three lost more money at the hands of the judges. Bent on ruining Judar, his brothers pursued their claim from court to court; they lost, and he lost, until at length they were reduced to penury.

The two elder brothers then came to their mother; they cheated her of her money, beat her, and threw her out. In this state she came to Judar and told him what his brothers had done to her, cursing them bitterly.

'Mother, do not curse them,' Judar replied. 'Allah will requite them for their deeds. We are paupers now; we have lost all our inheritance in suing one another and incurred disgrace in the sight of men. Am I to sue them again on your account? No, we must resign ourselves. Stay with me, and the bread I eat I will share with you. Allah will sustain us both. As for my brothers, leave them to Allah's judgement.' And he went on comforting his mother until he persuaded her to stay with him.

He bought a net, and every day he went to the river and the neighbouring lakes. One day he would earn ten coppers, another day twenty, and another thirty, so that he and his mother ate and drank well.

Meanwhile the two brothers squandered away the money which they had taken from their mother. Misery and ruin soon overtook them, for they neither bought nor sold, nor had any trade with which to earn a living. Naked and destitute, they would come from time to time humbling themselves before their mother and complaining of hunger. Her heart being compassionate, the old woman would feed them on mouldy bread or any remnants from the previous night's supper.

'Eat this quickly,' she would say, 'and go before your brother returns; for if he sees you here he will harden his heart against me and I shall justly earn his displeasure.'

So they would eat in haste and leave her. One day, however, as they sat eating the bread and cooked meat she had placed before them, their brother Judar came in. Confused and ashamed, his mother hung her head and looked at the ground, fearing his anger. But Judar smiled at them.

'Welcome, my brothers,' he cried, 'and may this day bring you joy! How is it that you have honoured me today with this visit?'

Then he embraced them lovingly, saying: 'I never thought that you would keep away from me and your mother.'

'By Allah, we have longed to see you, brother,' they replied. 'But we were stricken with remorse over what had passed between us, and shame prevented us from coming. That was the work of Satan, Allah's curse be upon him! We have no blessing but you and our mother.'

'And I have no blessing but you two,' Judar answered.

'May Allah bless you, my son,' exclaimed the old woman, 'and shower His abundance upon you. You are the most generous of us all!'

'Stay and be welcome in this house,' said Judar to his brothers. 'Allah is bountiful; there is plenty here for all.'

He thus made peace with them, and they ate and stayed the night in his house.

Next morning, after they had breakfasted, Judar took up his net and went to work, trusting in Allah's bounty. His brothers also went out, and came back at noon to eat with their mother. In the evening Judar returned, bringing meat and vegetables. In this way they lived together for a whole month, Judar paying for their daily needs with his fishing and his brothers eating their fill and making merry.

Now it chanced that one day Judar went down to the river, cast his net, and brought it up empty. He cast it a second time, and again it came up empty.

'There are no fish in this place,' he muttered to himself, and moved to another spot. He cast his net there, but it still brought up nothing. In that way he moved farther and farther along the bank from morning till evening, but caught nothing at all.

'This is indeed a strange thing!' he exclaimed. 'Are there no fish left in the river? Or is there some other reason?'

Dejected and sick at heart, he took up his net and made for

home, troubled over his brothers and his mother; for he did not know what he could give them to eat. Presently he came to a baker's shop and saw the people crowding round the bread with money in their hands. He stopped and sighed.

'Welcome, Judar!' the baker cried. 'Do you want any bread?'

But Judar remained silent.

'If you have no money with you,' said the baker, 'take what you need. You can pay me some other time.'

'Give me ten halves' worth of bread,' said the fisherman.

The baker handed him the loaves together with ten halves, saying: 'You can bring me fish for the twenty tomorrow.'

Judar warmly thanked the good man. He took the loaves and the ten halves and bought meat and vegetables with the money. 'The Lord willing,' he said to himself, 'all will be well again tomorrow.'

His mother cooked the meal, and Judar had his supper and went to bed. Next morning he rose and took up his net.

'Sit down and eat your breakfast,' said his mother.

'You have breakfast,' he replied, 'and my brothers.'

He went down to the river and cast his net time after time, moving from place to place until the afternoon; but all to no purpose. In despair he carried up his net and walked away. The baker saw him as he passed by, and gave him bread and ten coppers, as on the day before.

'Here,' he cried, 'take this and go. If you had no luck today, you will have luck tomorrow.'

Judar wished to apologize, but the baker would not listen to him.

'There is no need for apologies,' he said. 'When I saw you empty-handed I knew you had caught nothing. If you have no luck tomorrow, come again and take your bread. Let shame not prevent you; I will give you time to pay.'

For the third day Judar went from lake to lake, but when evening came he had caught nothing, and was forced to accept the baker's loaves and coppers. Ill-luck pursued him for a whole week, and at the end of that time he said despondently: 'Today I will go to Lake Karoon.'

He journeyed to Lake Karoon, and was about to cast his net when there suddenly came up to him a Moor riding upon a mule and wearing a magnificent robe. The mule was richly saddled and bridled and bore upon its flank a saddle-bag embroidered with gold.

'Peace be to you, Judar son of Omar,' cried the Moor, dismounting.

'And to you peace, good pilgrim,' answered the fisherman.

'Judar,' said the Moor, 'I need your help. If you accept my offer you shall have much to gain and be my companion and trusted friend.'

'Good sir,' Judar replied, 'tell me what you have in mind and I will gladly do your bidding.'

'First,' said the Moor, 'recite the opening chapter of the Koran.'

Judar recited it with him, and then the stranger took out a silken cord and handed it to the fisherman, saying: 'Fasten my arms behind me as firmly as you can, then throw me into the lake and wait a little. If you see me lift up my hands out of the water, cast in your net and haul me quickly ashore. But if you see me put up my feet, you will know that I am dead. In that case leave me in the water and take the mule with the saddle-bag to the market-place. There you will find a Jew called Shamayah; give him the beast and he will pay you a hundred dinars. Take them and go your way. But you must on no account reveal the secret.'

Judar fastened the Moor tightly; then, at his request, he pushed him forward and threw him into the lake. After a little while he saw his feet come out of the water, and he knew that the Moor was dead. Leaving the body in the lake, Judar took the mule to the market-place, where he found the Jew sitting on a chair at the door of his shop.

'The man must have perished!' exclaimed the Jew when he saw the mule. 'It was greed that destroyed him.'

He took the beast and gave Judar a hundred pieces of gold, charging him to keep the matter secret.

Judar hastened to the baker's and, giving him a dinar, took as many loaves as he required. The baker made up his account and said: 'I now owe you enough for two days' bread.' He then bought meat and vegetables and returned home with the provisions, to find his brothers asking their mother for something to eat.

'I have nothing to give you,' she was saying. 'Have patience until your brother returns.'

'Take this,' Judar cried, throwing to them the bread. And the two fell upon the loaves like famished beasts.

Then Judar gave his mother the rest of the gold, saying: 'If my brothers come tomorrow, give them money to buy some food and eat while I am away.'

Next morning he went again to Lake Karoon, and was just about to cast his net when he was approached by another Moor, dressed more sumptuously than the first. He, too, was on a mule and had a saddle-bag which held a pair of little caskets.

'Peace be to you, Judar!' he cried.

'And to you peace, pilgrim,' replied the fisherman.

'Did you meet a Moor yesterday, mounted upon a mule like mine?' he asked.

Fearing lest he should be accused of having drowned the man, Judar denied all knowledge of him. But the Moor cried: 'Poor wretch! He was my brother. He came here before me. Was it not you that tied his hands behind him and threw him into the lake? And did he not say to you: "If you see my

335

hands come up through the water, haul me quickly ashore, but if my feet appear you will know that I am dead?" It was his feet that came up; you took the mule to Shamayah the Jew and he gave you a hundred pieces of gold.'

'If you know all that,' said Judar, 'why do you ask me?'

'Because I wish you to do with me as you did with my brother,' replied the Moor.

And he thereupon took out a silken cord and handed it to the fisherman, saying: 'Fasten my arms and throw me into the lake. If I meet the same end as my brother's, take my mule to the Jew and he will give you a hundred pieces of gold.'

'Very well,' Judar answered.

He tied his arms and threw him into the lake, and the Moor disappeared under the water. After a while his feet emerged.

'He is dead and finished,' said Judar to himself. 'May Allah send me a Moor each day to drown, that I may earn a hundred pieces of gold!'

Then he took the mule to the market-place.

'The second one is dead!' exclaimed the Jew when he saw him.

'May Allah give *you* long life!' cried the fisherman.

'That is the reward of avarice,' added the Jew. And he took the mule from him and gave him a hundred dinars.

Judar went home and gave the gold to his mother.

'My son,' she cried, 'where did you come by this?'

Judar recounted to her all that had happened.

'You should never go to Lake Karoon again,' said the old woman. 'I greatly fear that you may come to harm at the hands of these Moors.'

'But, mother,' replied Judar, 'it is at their request that I throw them into the lake. Am I to give up this trade which brings me every day a hundred dinars, and for such little labour? By Allah, I will go there day after day until I have drowned them all and not a single Moor has been left alive.'

The next day he went again to Lake Karoon; and presently a third Moor, even more richly attired than the other two, came riding on a mule with a saddle-bag.

'Peace be to you, Judar son of Omar!' he cried.

'How is that they all know my name?' thought Judar to
himself as he returned his greeting.

'Have any Moors passed by this lake?' inquired the stranger.

'Yes, two,' replied Judar.

'Where did they go?' he asked.

'I bound their arms and threw them into the lake,' replied
the fisherman. 'They were both drowned. I am ready to render
you the same service.'

'Miserable fool!' smiled the Moor. 'Do you not know that
every life has its predestined end?'

Then, dismounting, he gave the fisherman a silken cord and said: 'Judar, do with me as you did with them.'

'Turn round and let me bind your arms,' said the fisherman. 'Time is short and I am in a hurry.'

Judar threw the Moor into the lake and stood waiting for his feet to emerge from the water. But to his surprise a pair of hands came out instead, and he heard the Moor crying: 'Good fellow, cast out your net!'

He threw the net over him and, drawing him in, saw that in each hand he was holding a fish, red as coral.

'Open the two caskets,' cried the Moor, as he quickly rose to his feet.

Judar opened the caskets, and the Moor put a fish in each and securely shut them up. Then he threw his arms about the fisherman's neck and kissed him on both cheeks, saying: 'May the Most High preserve you from all hardships! By Allah, but for your help I would have surely perished.'

'Sir,' said Judar, 'I beg you in Allah's name to tell me the story of the drowned Moors, the red fish, and the Jew Shamayah.'

'The two who were drowned were my brothers,' the Moor replied. 'One was called Abdul Salam, and the other Abdul Ahad. My name is Abdul Samad, and the man whom you take to be a Jew is my fourth brother, a true Malikite Moslem whose real name is Abdul Rahim. Our father, Abdul Wadud, taught us the occult sciences, witchcraft, and the art of opening hidden treasures, to which we applied ourselves with such diligence that in the end we made the demons and the jinn our servants. When our father died we inherited all his wealth and divided his gold and his treasures, his talismans and his books; but a quarrel arose amongst us concerning a book called *The Lore of the Ancients*. It is unique among writings and cannot be valued in gold or jewels: for it holds the answer to all mysteries and the clue to every hidden treasure. Our father made it the study of his life, and we four conned a little of its contents. Each of us strove to gain possession of it, so as to be acquainted with its secrets. When our feud had reached its height, we were visited by the old sheikh who had reared our father and taught him magic and divination; his name was Al-Kahin al-Abtan. He ordered us to bring him the book, and he took it in his hand and said: "You are the sons of my son, and I cannot wrong any one of you. I therefore pronounce that none shall have this book but he that opens the Treasure of Al-Shamardal and brings me the Celestial Orb, the Vial of Kohl, the Ring, and the Sword. The Ring is served by a jinnee called Rattling Thunder, and he that wears it can vanquish kings and sultans and make himself master of the vast earth. The man who holds the sword and shakes it can rout whole armies, for flames as bright as lightning shoot forth from it at his bidding. By means of the Celestial Orb a man can view the world from east to west while sitting in his chamber: he has but to turn the orb towards the land he desires to see and, looking upon it, he shall behold that land with all its people. If he is incensed against a city and has a mind to burn it down, let him turn the orb towards the sun's disc, and all its dwellings shall be consumed with fire. As for the Vial, he that applies its kohl to his eyes shall see the buried treasures of the earth.

' "This then is the condition which I impose upon you. Whoever fails to open that treasure shall forfeit his claim to this book; but he that opens it and brings me the four precious things it holds shall become sole master of it."

'We all agreed to his condition, and the old sage went on: "Know, my children, that the Treasure of Al-Shamardal is under the power of the sons of the Red King. Your father told me that he himself had vainly tried to open it, for the sons of the Red King had fled away from him to Egypt. He pursued them to that land, but could not capture them because they had thrown themselves into an enchanted lake called Lake Karoon. When he returned and told me of his failure I made for him a computation and discovered that the treasure could be opened only under the auspices of an Egyptian youth called Judar son of Omar, who would be the means of capturing the Red King's sons. This youth was a fisherman and could be met with on the shores of Lake Karoon. He alone could break the spell that bound it, and it was for him to cast into the lake those who would tackle the sons of the Red King. The man whose destiny it was to vanquish them, his hands would come out of the water and Judar would bring him safe to land with his net. But those who were destined to drown, their feet would come out first and they would be abandoned to their fate."

'Two of my brothers said: "We will go, even though we perish," and I resolved to do the same. But my third brother, Abdul Rahim, said: "I will not risk my life." We thereupon arranged with him that he should go to Egypt in the guise of a Jewish merchant, so that if any of us perished in the attempt he should take the mule and the saddle-bag from Judar and pay him a hundred pieces of gold.

'My first brother was slain by the sons of the Red King, and so was my second brother. But against me they could not prevail and I took them prisoner.'

'Where did you imprison them?' Judar asked.

'Did you not see them?' answered the Moor. 'I shut them up in the two caskets.'

'But those were fish,' said Judar in amazement.

'No, they are not fish,' replied the Moor. 'They are jinn in the shape of fish. Now you must know that the treasure can be opened only in your presence. Will you agree to come with me to the city of Fez-and-Meknes and open the treasure? I will give you everything that you demand and you shall be my brother in the sight of Allah. When our quest has been accomplished, you shall return to your people with a joyful heart.'

'Sir,' Judar replied, 'I have a mother and two brothers to support. If I go with you, who will provide for them?'

'A poor excuse,' rejoined the Moor. 'If it is money that prevents you, I will give you a thousand dinars for your mother to spend and my promise that you shall return within four months.'

On hearing mention of this sum, the fisherman cried: 'Give me the thousand dinars, my master. I will at once carry them to my mother and set out with you.'

He handed him the gold, and Judar hastened to his mother

and recounted to her all that had passed between him and the Moor.

'Take these thousand dinars,' he said, 'and spend them on yourself and my brothers. I am going away to Maghreb with the Moor, and shall be back within four months. I may return with a vast fortune.'

'My son, I shall be desolate without you,' said the old woman. 'I greatly fear for your safety.'

'No harm can befall the man who is in Allah's protection,' he replied. 'Besides, the Moor is a good and honest fellow.'

And he went on praising him to her until his mother said: 'May Allah incline his heart towards you! Go with him, my son; perhaps he will reward your labours.'

He took leave of his mother and returned to the Moor.

'Have you consulted your mother?' Abdul Samad asked.

'Yes,' he replied, 'and she has given me her blessing.'

The Moor bade Judar mount behind him on the mule, and they rode from midday till late in the afternoon. By that time the fisherman felt very hungry, and, noticing that his companion had nothing with him to eat, he remarked: 'Sir, you have forgotten to bring any provisions for the journey.'

'Are you hungry?' asked the Moor.

'I am indeed,' Judar replied.

They both dismounted from the mule.

'Bring down the saddle-bag,' said the Moor.

Judar brought it down.

'Now, my brother, what would you like?' his companion asked.

'Anything will do,' Judar answered.

'In Allah's name, tell me what you would rather have,' said the Moor.

'Some bread and cheese,' replied the fisherman.

'Poor Judar,' said the Moor, 'you surely deserve better than that. Ask for some excellent dish.'

'Anything would be excellent to me just now,' Judar replied.

'Would you like some roast chicken?' asked the Moor.

'I would,' answered the fisherman.

'And some honeyed rice?' asked the Moor.

'Yes, by Allah,' replied Judar.

'And such-and-such a dish,' went on the Moor, until he had named four-and-twenty dishes.

'The man is mad,' thought Judar to himself. 'Where will he bring me all these dishes from when he has no cook and no kitchen?' Then, aloud, he said: 'That is enough. But why do you make my mouth water when I cannot see a thing?'

'You are welcome, Judar,' said the Moor with a smile. And, putting his hand into the bag, he took out a gold plate with two roast chickens upon it steaming hot. He thrust his hand in a second time and there appeared a plate filled with kebab. And he went on bringing dishes out of the bag until he had produced the two dozen courses he had named.

'Now eat, my friend,' said the Moor.

'Sir,' exclaimed the confounded Judar, 'you must surely have a kitchen and numerous cooks in that saddle-bag of yours!'

'It is enchanted,' replied the Moor, laughing. 'It is served by a jinnee. If we were to ask for a thousand dishes every hour, the jinnee would come and prepare them for us immediately.'

'Upon my life,' Judar exclaimed, 'that is an excellent bag!'

The two ate together, and when they were satisfied the Moor threw away what remained of the meal and replaced the empty dishes into the bag. He put his hand in again and brought out a ewer filled with water. They drank, made their ablutions, and recited the afternoon prayers; then, returning the ewer to the bag, they mounted on the mule and resumed their journey.

Presently the Moor said to Judar: 'Do you know how far we have travelled from Egypt?'

'No, by Allah,' Judar replied.

'We have travelled a whole year's journey,' said the Moor. 'You must know that this mule of mine is a jinnee and can make a year's journey in a single day. But for your sake it has been going at an easy pace.'

For four days they travelled westwards, riding every day till midnight and having all their food provided by the enchanted bag. Judar demanded of the Moor whatever he fancied, and the Moor supplied it promptly upon a gold dish. On the fifth day they reached Maghreb and entered the city of Fez-and-Meknes. As they made their way into the town, everyone who met the Moor greeted him and kissed his hand. At length they halted before a certain house; the Moor knocked, and the door was opened by a girl as radiant as the moon.

'Rahmah, my daughter,' said the Moor, 'open for us the great hall.'

'Welcome, father,' the girl replied, and went in, swinging her hips.

'She must be a princess,' said Judar to himself, marvelling at her beauty.

The girl opened the great hall, and the Moor took the saddle-bag off the mule.

'Go,' he said to the beast, 'and may Allah's blessing be upon you!'

At once the earth opened, swallowed up the mule, and closed again.

'Praise be to Allah,' Judar exclaimed, 'who kept us safe on the creature's back!'

'Do not be amazed, Judar,' said the Moor. 'Did I not tell you that the mule was a jinnee? Come now, let us go into the hall.'

Judar followed him into the hall and was astounded at the abundance of fine carpets, the rare ornaments, and the hangings of gold and jewels which decked its walls. As soon as the two were seated the Moor bade his daughter bring him a certain bundle. She fetched it to him and he took out from it a robe worth a thousand dinars.

'Put this on, Judar,' he said, 'and be welcome in this house.'

Judar put it on and was so transformed that he looked like some Moroccan king. Then the Moor plunged his hand into the bag and drew from it dish after dish until he had spread out before his guest a banquet of forty courses.

'Eat, sir,' he said, 'and pardon us our shortcomings. We

do not know what kind of food you fancy. Tell us what you relish and we will set it before you without delay.'

'By Allah,' Judar replied, 'I like every kind of food and hate nothing. Do not ask me what I fancy; give me whatever comes into your mind and I will do nothing but eat.'

He stayed with the Moor twenty days, receiving from his host a new robe every day and feasting with him on the provisions of the enchanted bag. On the morning of the twenty-first day the Moor came to him and said: 'Rise, my friend. This is the day appointed for opening the Treasure of Al-Shamardal.'

Judar walked with the Moor to the outskirts of the city, where he found two mules with two slaves in attendance. The Moor mounted one beast and Judar the other, and they rode on and on, followed by the slaves. At midday they came to a running river and dismounted. The Moor made a sign to the slaves, who took the mules and went off with them. Presently they returned, one carrying a tent, which he pitched, and the other a mattress and cushions, which he spread inside. Then one of them went and brought the two caskets containing the two fish, and the other brought the enchanted bag.

The Moor drew several dishes out of the bag and, seating Judar by his side, invited him to eat. As soon as the meal was over he took the caskets in his hands and mumbled a magic charm over them.

'At your service, dread enchanter!' cried the two fish from within. 'Have mercy upon us!'

He repeated his incantation, and they pleaded louder and louder, until the caskets burst in fragments and there appeared two creatures with their arms chained behind them.

'Pardon us, great enchanter!' they cried. 'What would you do with us?'

'Swear to open the Treasure of Al-Shamardal,' roared the Moor, 'or I will burn you both!'

'We will open it on one condition,' they answered. 'You must bring the son of Omar, Judar the fisherman. The treasure cannot be opened except in his presence. None but he may enter it.'

'Here stands the very man of whom you speak,' replied the sorcerer. 'He beholds and hears you.'

Thereupon they swore to open the treasure and the Moor broke the spell that bound them. He placed two tablets of red carnelian upon a hollow reed; then he took a brazier filled with charcoal and set it alight with one breath. After that he brought some incense and said to Judar: 'I am about to throw the incense and recite my conjuration. Once I begin the charm I cannot speak again, or the spell will be broken. Therefore I will now tell you what you are to do so as to achieve your end.'

'Speak,' Judar replied.

'Know,' said the Moor, 'that as soon as I have cast the incense and begun my charm, the water of the river will dry up and on the sloping bank there will appear a door of gold, as high as the city gate, with a pair of metal rings. Go down to that door, knock lightly on it, and wait a little. Then knock louder and wait again. After that knock three times in succession, and you will hear a voice say from within: "Who knocks at the door of the treasure-house and yet cannot solve the Riddle?" You will reply: "I am the son of Omar, Judar the fisherman." The door will open and reveal a man bearing a sword in his hand, who will say: "If you are that man stretch out your neck, that I may strike off your head." Stretch out your neck to him and have no fear; for no sooner will he raise his sword and smite you than he will fall on the ground, a body without a soul. You will feel no pain from the blow, nor will any harm befall you. But if you defy him he will kill you.

'When you have thus broken the first charm, go in and you will find another door. Knock on it, and the door will be opened by a horseman bearing a lance upon his shoulder, who will say: "What brings you to this place, forbidden alike to man and jinnee?" He will brandish his lance at you. Bare your breast to him and he will strike you and fall on the ground, a body without a soul. But if you defy him he will kill you.

'You will make your way to a third door, which will be opened by a man armed with a bow and arrow. He will shoot

345

at you with his weapon. Bare your breast to him and he will at once fall on the ground, a body without a soul. But if you defy him he will kill you.

'After that go in to the fourth door and knock. An enormous lion will rush out and leap upon you, opening its jaws apart to eat you. Do not flinch or run away; give it your hand and it will fall down lifeless upon the instant.

'Then knock at the fifth door. A black slave will open it to you, saying: "Who are you?" Say: "I am Judar," and he will reply: "If you are that man, go and open the sixth door."

'At the sixth door you must cry: "Jesus, bid Moses open the door." The door will swing ajar. Go in, and two huge serpents, one on the right and the other on the left, will hurl themselves at you with open mouths. If you stretch out a hand to each they will do you no harm. But if you resist them they will kill you.

'The seventh door will be opened by your mother. "Welcome, my son," she will say. "Come near that I may greet you." You must answer: "Stay where you are and put off your clothes!" "My child," she will say, "I am your mother, who suckled you and brought you up. How would you see me naked?" You must reply: "Put off your clothes, or I will kill you." Look on your right, and you will find a sword hanging from the wall: take it down and threaten her with it. She will plead with you and humble herself before you; have no pity on her, and each time she takes anything off, cry: "The rest!" Go on threatening her until she has put off all her clothes. Then she will fall at your feet.

'At that moment all the charms will be annulled and all the spells broken. Safe and sound, you will enter the hall of the treasure and see the gold lying in heaps. But pay no heed to that. At the opposite end you will find a small pavilion with a curtain over it. Draw aside the curtain and you will see the Magician Al-Shamardal sleeping on a couch of gold, with a round object above his head shining like the moon. That is the Celestial Orb. You will find the Sword on his side, the Ring on his finger, and the Vial of Kohl hung from a chain about his neck. Bring back these four talismans. Be on your guard lest you forget any of my instructions; if you go against them you shall rue it.'

The Moor repeated his directions until Judar assured him that he had them all by heart.

'But who can face the charms you speak of?' the fisherman then cried. 'Who can brave such mighty perils?'

'Have no fear, Judar,' the Moor replied. 'They are but phantoms without souls.'

Judar commended himself to Allah, and the Moor threw the incense on the fire and began his incantation. Presently the water of the river vanished and the door of the treasure-house appeared below. Judar went down to the door and knocked.

'Who knocks at the door of the treasure-house and yet cannot solve the Riddle?' cried a voice from within.

'Judar, son of Omar,' he answered.

The door was opened and a man with an unsheathed sword appeared, crying: 'Stretch out your neck!' Judar stretched out his neck, but no sooner did he raise his sword and smite Judar than the man fell down on the ground. Then Judar passed on to the other doors, breaking their spells in turn. When he reached the seventh door, his mother came out and greeted him.

'What are you?' Judar asked.

'I am your mother,' she answered. 'I suckled you and brought you up. I carried you for nine months, my son.'

'Put off your clothes!' cried Judar.

'But you are my son!' the old woman exclaimed. 'How can you strip me naked?'

She pleaded long with him, but Judar repeated his demand, threatening her with the sword which he had taken from the wall, until she had put off all but one of her garments.

'Is your heart of stone, my son?' she cried. 'Would you see your mother utterly naked? Do you not know that this is unlawful?'

'You are right, mother,' answered Judar. 'That is enough.'

Scarcely had he uttered these words when the old woman exclaimed: 'Beat him! The man has failed!'

At this the guardians of the treasure fell upon him with mighty blows and gave him a thrashing which he never forgot for the rest of his life. Then they flung him out of the treasure-house and slammed the golden gate behind him.

When the Moor saw the fisherman thrown outside the door he hurriedly dragged him from the water, which was already tumbling back into the river-bed, and recited charms over him until he recovered his senses.

'What have you done, you fool?' he cried.

Judar recounted to him all that happened after he had met his mother.

'Did I not charge you to observe all my instructions?' shouted the Moor. 'By Allah, you have wronged me, and yourself too. Had the woman unrobed herself entirely we would have gained our end. Now a whole year will have to pass before we can renew our attempt.'

He at once called the slaves, who struck the tent and brought back the mules. And the two rode back to the city of Fez.

Judar stayed with the Moor another year, feasting to his heart's content and dressing in a splendid new robe each morning. When the appointed day arrived, the Moor took him outside the city, and there they saw the black slaves with the mules. On reaching the river bank they pitched the tent and ate the midday meal. Then the Moor arranged the reed and the tablets as before, lit the charcoal, and said to Judar: 'Listen again to these instructions.'

'You need not repeat them, sir,' Judar cried. 'I shall forget them only when I forget my thrashing.'

'Do you remember every detail?' asked the Moor, and, when the fisherman assured him that he did, went on: 'Keep your wits about you. Do not think that the woman is really your mother; she is no more than a phantom which has taken on your mother's semblance to mislead you. You came out alive the first time; but, if you slip this time, you shall assuredly perish.'

'If I slip this time,' Judar replied, 'I shall deserve burning.'

The Moor cast the incense on the fire and as soon as he began his conjuration the river dried up and Judar went down to the golden door. Spell after spell was broken until he came to his mother.

'Welcome, my son!' she cried.

'Wretched woman!' Judar shouted. 'Since when have I been your son? Put off your clothes!'

The old woman undressed herself, pleading with him the while, until only her drawers remained.

'Off with them, wretch!' he cried.

And as she removed her drawers she dropped at his feet, a phantom without a soul.

Judar entered the seventh door and, paying no heed to the piles of gold that lay within, went up straight to the pavilion. There he saw the Wizard Al-Shamardal lying, with the Sword at his side, the Ring on his finger, the Vial of Kohl upon his chest, and the Celestial Orb above his head. He ungirt the Sword, pulled off the Ring, unclasped the Vial, took down the Orb, and made for the door again. Suddenly a burst of music sounded in his praise, and the guardians of the treasure cried: 'Rejoice, Judar, in that which you have gained!' The music went on playing until he was outside the gate of the treasure-house.

As soon as he saw him, the Moor ceased his fumigation

and his charms, and, quickly rising, threw his arms about the fisherman's neck. Judar gave him the four talismans and the Moor called the slaves, who carried away the tent and returned with the mules.

When they were back in the city the Moor brought out a variety of meats, and the two feasted and ate their fill. Then the magician said: ' Judar, you left your native land on my account and have fulfilled my dearest wish. Therefore name your reward; ask whatever you desire and Allah will grant it through me. Do not be shy; you have earned it well.'

'Sir,' replied the fisherman, 'I can ask for nothing better than this saddle-bag.'

The Moor bade his slave fetch the bag, and then handed it to Judar, saying: 'It is yours. You have earned it. Had you asked me for anything else I would have as willingly given it to you. But, my friend, this saddle-bag will provide you only with your food. You have exposed yourself to great perils for my sake, and I promised to send you home with a contented heart. I will give you another bag filled with gold and jewels and bring you safe to your own land. There you can set up as a merchant, and satisfy your needs and your family's. As for the first bag, I will now tell you how to use it. Stretch your hand into it and say: "Servant of the Bag, by the mighty names that have power over you, bring me such-and-such a dish." He will at once provide you with whatever you demand, even if you call for a thousand different dishes every day.'

The Moor sent for a slave and a mule and, filling a second bag with gold and jewels, said to Judar: 'Mount this mule. The slave will walk before you and be your guide until he brings you to the door of your own house. On your arrival take the two bags and return the mule to the slave, so that he may bring it back. Admit none to your secret. And now go with Allah's blessing.'

Judar thanked the Moor with all his heart, and, loading the two bags on the beast, rode off. The mule followed the slave all day and all night, and early next morning Judar entered the Victory Gate. There he was astounded to see his mother sitting by the roadside.

'Alms, in the name of Allah,' she was crying.

Judar quickly dismounted and threw himself with open arms upon the old woman, who burst into tears on seeing him. He mounted her on the mule and walked by her side until they reached their dwelling. There he took down the saddle-bags and left the mule to the slave, who returned with it to his master; for they were both devils.

Judar was profoundly distressed at his mother's plight.

'Are my brothers well?' he asked as soon as they went in.

'Yes, they are well,' she answered.

'Then why are you begging on the streets?' he inquired. 'I gave you a hundred pieces of gold the first day, a hundred more the next day, and a thousand the day I left home.'

'My son,' she replied, 'your brothers took all the money, saying they wished to buy some merchandise. But they deceived me and threw me out, so that I was forced to beg or starve.'

'Never mind, mother,' said Judar. 'All will be well with you now that I am home again. Here is a bag full of gold and jewels. Henceforth we shall lack nothing.'

'Fortune has smiled upon you, my son,' cried the old woman. 'May Allah bless you and ever give you of His bounty! Rise now and get us some bread. I have had nothing to eat since yesterday.'

'You are welcome, mother,' Judar replied, laughing. 'Tell me what you would like to eat and it shall be set before you this very instant. There is nothing I need to buy or cook.'

'But I can see nothing with you, my son,' said his mother.

'It is in the bag,' he answered. 'Every kind of food.'

'Anything will serve, if it can fill a hungry woman,' she replied.

'That is true, mother,' said Judar. 'When there is no choice one has to be content with the meanest thing: but when there is plenty one must choose the best. I have plenty: so name your choice.'

'Very well, then,' she replied. 'Some fresh bread and a slice of cheese.'

'That scarcely befits your station, mother,' Judar protested.

'If you know what is fitting,' she answered, 'then give me what I ought to eat.'

'What would you say,' he smiled, 'to roast meat and roast chicken, peppered rice, sausage and stuffed marrow, stuffed lamb and stuffed ribs, kunafah swimming in bees' honey, fritters and almond cakes?'

'What has come over you, Judar?' exclaimed the old woman, thinking her son was making fun of her. 'Are you dreaming or have you taken leave of your senses? Who can afford these wondrous dishes, and who can cook them?'

'Upon my life,' Judar replied, 'you shall have them all this very moment. Bring me the bag.'

His mother brought the bag; she felt it and saw that it was empty. Then she handed it to Judar, who proceeded to take out from it dish after dish until he had ranged before her all the dishes he had described.

'My child,' cried the astonished woman, 'the bag is very small, and it was empty; I felt it with my own hands. How do you account for these numerous dishes?'

'Know, mother, that the bag is enchanted,' he replied. 'It was given me by the Moor. It is served by a jinnee who, if invoked by the Mighty Names, provides any dish that a man can desire.'

Thereupon his mother asked if she herself might call the jinnee. Judar gave her the bag, and she thrust in her hand, saying: 'Servant of the Bag, by the mighty names that have power over you, bring me a stuffed rib of lamb!'

She at once felt the dish under her hand. She drew it out, and then called for bread and other meats.

'Mother,' said Judar, 'when you have finished eating, empty the rest of the meal into other plates and restore the dishes to the bag. That is one part of the secret. And keep the bag safely hidden.'

The old woman got up and stowed away the bag in a safe place.

'Above all, mother,' he resumed, 'you must on no account disclose the secret. Whenever you need any food bring it out

of the bag. Give alms and feed my brothers, alike when I am
here and when I am away.'

The two had scarcely begun eating when Judar's brothers
entered the house.

They had heard the news of his arrival from a neighbour,
who had said to them: 'Your brother has come home, riding
on a mule and with a slave marching before him. No one ever
wore the like of his rich garments.'

'Would that we had never wronged our mother,' they said
to each other. 'She is bound to tell him what we did to her.
Think of the disgrace!'

'But mother is soft-hearted,' one of them remarked. 'And
supposing she does tell him, our brother is kindlier still. If
we apologise to him he will excuse us.'

Judar jumped to his feet as they entered, and greeted them
in the friendliest fashion. 'Sit down,' he said, 'and eat with us.'

They sat down and ate ravenously, for they were quite faint
with hunger.

'Brothers,' said Judar when they could eat no more, 'take
the rest of the food and distribute it among the beggars.'

'But why, brother?' they replied. 'We can have it for
supper.'

'At supper-time,' said he, 'you shall have a greater feast
than this.'

So they went out with the food, and to every beggar that
passed by they said: 'Take and eat.' Then they brought the
empty dishes back to Judar, who bade his mother return them
to the bag.

In the evening Judar went into the room where the bag
was hidden and drew from it forty different dishes, which his
mother carried up to the eating-chamber. He invited his
brothers to eat, and, when the meal was over, told them to
take the remainder of the food and distribute it among the
beggars. After supper he produced sweets and pastries for
them; they ate their fill, and what was left over he told them
to carry to the neighbours.

In this fashion he regaled his brothers for ten days, and at
the end of that time Salem said to Seleem: 'What is the

meaning of all this? How can our brother provide us every day with such lavish feasts morning, noon, and evening, and then with sweetmeats late at night? And whatever remains he distributes among the poor and needy. Only sultans do such things. Where could he have got this fortune from? Will you not inquire about these various dishes and how they are prepared? We have never seen him buy anything at all or even light a fire; he has no cook and no kitchen.'

'By Allah, I do not know,' replied Seleem. 'Only our mother can tell us the truth about it all.'

Thereupon they contrived a plan and, going to their mother in Judar's absence, told her that they were hungry. She at once entered the room where the bag was hidden, invoked the jinnee, and returned with a hot meal.

'Mother, this food is hot,' they said. 'And yet you did not cook it, nor did you even blow a fire.'

'It is from the bag,' she answered.

'What bag is that?' they asked.

'A magic bag,' she replied.

And she told them the whole story, adding: 'You must keep the matter secret.'

'No one shall know of it,' they said. 'But show us how it works.'

Their mother showed them and they proceeded to put in their hands, each asking for a dish of his own choice.

When the two were alone, Salem said to Seleem: 'How long are we to stay like servants in our brother's house, living abjectly on his charity? Can we not trick him and take the bag from him, and keep it for our own use?'

'And how shall we do that?' asked Seleem.

'We will sell our brother to the chief captain of Suez,' Salem replied. 'We will go to the captain, and invite him to the house with two of his men. You have only to confirm whatever I say to Judar and by the end of the night you will see what I shall do.'

When they had thus agreed to sell their brother, they went to the chief captain of Suez and said to him: 'Sir, we have come upon some business that will please you.'

'Good,' said the captain.

'We are brothers,' they went on. 'We have a third brother, a worthless ne'er-do-well. Our father died and left us a small fortune. We divided the inheritance and our brother took his share and squandered it on lechery and all manner of vices. When he had lost all his money, he began complaining of us to the judges, saying that we had defrauded him of his inheritance. He took us from one court-of-law to another and in the end we forfeited all our fortune. Now he is at us again. We cannot bear with him any longer and want you to buy him from us.'

'Can you bring him here upon some pretext?' the captain asked. 'Then I can send him off to sea forthwith.'

'No, we cannot bring him here,' they answered. 'But you come to our house and be our guest this evening. Bring two of your sailors with you – no more. When he is sound asleep the five of us can set upon and gag him. Then you can carry him out of the house under cover of darkness and do whatever you please with him.'

'Very well,' said the captain. 'Will you sell him for forty dinars?'

'We agree to that,' they replied. 'Go after dark to such-and-such a street and there you will find one of us waiting for you.'

They returned home and sat talking together for a while. Then Salem went up to Judar and kissed his hand.

'What can I do for you, brother?' Judar asked.

'I have a friend,' he said, 'who has invited me many times to his house and done me a thousand kindnesses, as Seleem here knows. Today I called on him and he invited me again. I excused myself, saying: "I cannot leave my brother." "Let him come too," he said. I told him you would never consent to that and asked him and his brothers to dine with us tonight. His brothers were sitting there with him and I invited them, thinking they would refuse. However, they all accepted, and asked me to meet them at the gate of the little mosque. I now regret my indiscretion and feel ashamed for asking them without your leave. But will you be so kind as to give them hospitality tonight? If you would rather not, allow me to take them to the neighbours' house.'

'But why to the neighbours'?' Judar protested. 'Is our house too small or have we no food to give them? Shame on you that you should even ask me. They shall have nothing but the choicest dishes. If you bring home any guests and I happen to be out, you have only to ask our mother and she will provide you with all the food you need and more. Go and bring them. They shall be most welcome.'

Salem kissed Judar's hand and went off to the gate of the little mosque. The captain and his men came at the appointed hour and he took them home with him. As soon as they entered, Judar rose to receive them. He gave them a kindly welcome and seated them by his side, for he knew nothing of their intent. Then he bade his mother serve a meal of forty courses and the sailors ate their fill, thinking that it was all at Salem's expense. After that he produced for them sweets and pastries; Salem served the guests with these, while his two brothers remained seated. At midnight the captain and his men begged leave to retire, and Judar got up with them and went to bed. As soon as he fell asleep the five men set upon him and, thrusting a gag into his mouth, bound his arms and carried him out of the house under cover of darkness. The sailors took their victim to Suez, and there, with irons on his feet, he toiled for a whole year as a galley-slave in one of the captain's ships. So much for Judar.

Next morning the two brothers went in to their mother and asked her whether Judar had woken up.

'He is still asleep,' she said. 'Go and wake him.'

'Where is he sleeping?' they asked.

'With the guests,' she answered.

'There is no one there,' they said. 'Perhaps he went off with them whilst we were still asleep. It seems our brother has acquired a taste for visiting foreign lands and opening hidden treasures. Last night we overheard him talking to the Moors. "We will take you with us, and open the treasure for you," they were saying.'

'But when did he meet the Moors?' she asked.

'Did they not dine with us last night?' they answered.

'It is probable, then, that he has gone with them,' said the old woman. 'But Allah will guide him wherever he goes, for he was born under a lucky star. He is bound to come back laden with riches.'

Upon this she broke down and wept, for she could not bear to be parted from him.

'Vile woman!' they exclaimed. 'Do you love our brother so much? Yet if *we* went away or returned home, you would neither shed tears nor rejoice. Are we not your sons as much as he?'

'Yes, you are my sons,' she answered. 'But how wicked and ungrateful! Ever since your father died I have not had a moment's joy with you. But Judar has always been good and kind and generous to me. He is worthy of my tears, for we are all indebted to him.'

Stung by her words, the two abused their mother and beat her. Then they went in and searched the house until they found the two bags. They took the gold and jewels from the second bag, saying: 'This is our father's property.'

'No, by Allah,' their mother replied. 'It is your brother's. Judar brought it with him from the Moors' country.'

'You lie!' they shouted. 'It is our father's property. We will dispose of it as we choose.'

They divided the gold and jewels between them. But over the magic bag they fell into a hot dispute.

'I take this,' said Salem.

'No, I take it,' said Seleem.

'My children,' pleaded the old woman, 'you have divided the first bag, but the second bag is beyond price and cannot be divided. If it is split into two parts, its charm will be annulled. Leave it with me and I will bring out for you whatever food you need, contenting myself with a mouthful. Buy some merchandise and trade with it like honest men. You are my sons, and I am your mother. Let us live in amity and peace, so that you may incur no shame when your brother comes back.'

However, they paid no heed to her and spent the night quarrelling over the magic bag. Now it chanced that an officer of the King's guards was being entertained in the house next door, of which one of the windows was open. Leaning out of the window, he listened to the angry words that passed between the two brothers and understood the cause of the dispute. Next morning he presented himself before Shams-al-Dowlah, King of Egypt, and informed him of all he had overheard. The King sent at once for Judar's brothers and tortured them until they confessed all. He took the two bags, threw the brothers into prison, and appointed their mother a daily allowance sufficient for her needs. So much for them.

Now to return to Judar. After toiling for a whole year in Suez, he set sail one day with several of his mates; a violent tempest struck their ship and, hurling it against a rocky cliff, shattered it to pieces. Judar alone escaped alive. Swimming ashore, he journeyed inland until he reached an encampment of bedouin Arabs. They asked him who he was, and he recounted to them his whole story. In the camp there was a merchant from Jedda, who at once took pity upon him.

'Would you like to enter our service, Egyptian?' he said. 'I will furnish you with clothes and take you with me to Jedda.'

Judar accepted the merchant's offer and accompanied him to Jedda, where he was generously treated. Soon afterwards his master set out on a pilgrimage to Mecca, and took Judar with him. On their arrival Judar hastened to join the pilgrims' procession round the Ca'aba. Whilst he was thus engaged in his devotions, he met his friend Abdul Samad the Moor, who greeted him warmly and inquired his news. Judar wept as he recounted to him the tale of his misfortunes, and the Moor took him to his own house and dressed him in a magnificent robe.

'Your troubles are now ended, Judar,' he said.

Then he cast a handful of sand on the ground and, divining all that had befallen Salem and Seleem, declared: 'Your brothers have been thrown into prison by the King of Egypt. But you are welcome here until you have performed the season's rites. All shall be well with you.'

'Sir,' said Judar, 'I must first go and take my leave of the merchant who brought me here. Then I will come to you straightway.'

'Do you owe him any money?' asked the Moor.

'No,' Judar replied.

'Go, then,' said the Moor, 'and take leave of him. Honest men must not forget past favours.'

Judar sought out the good merchant and told him that he had met a long-lost brother.

'Go and bring him here, that he may eat with us,' said the merchant.

'There is no need for that,' Judar answered. 'He is a man of wealth and has a host of servants.'

'Then take these,' said the merchant, handing him twenty dinars, 'and free me of all obligations towards you.'

Judar took leave of him and went out. On his way he met a beggar and gave him the twenty dinars. Then he rejoined the Moor, and stayed with him until the pilgrimage rites had been completed. When it was time to part, the magician gave him the ring which he had taken from the treasure of Al-Shamardal.

'This ring,' he said, 'will grant you all that you desire. It is served by a jinnee called Rattling Thunder. If you need anything, you have but to rub the seal and he will be at hand to do your bidding.'

The Moor rubbed the seal in front of him, and at once the jinnee appeared, saying: 'I am here, my master! Ask what you will and it shall be done. Would you restore a ruined city, or lay a populous town in ruin? Would you slay a king, or rout a whole army?'

'Thunder,' cried the Moor, 'this man will henceforth be your master. Serve him well.'

Then he dismissed the jinnee and said to Judar: 'Go back to your country and take good care of the ring. Do not make light of it, for its magic will give you power over all your enemies.'

'By your leave, sir,' Judar replied, 'I will now set forth for my native land.'

'Rub the seal,' said the Moor, 'and the jinnee will take you there upon his back.'

Judar said farewell to the Moor and rubbed the seal. At once the jinnee appeared before him.

'Take me to Egypt this very day,' he commanded.

'I hear and obey,' Thunder replied. And carrying Judar upon his back flew with him high up into the air. At midnight he set him down in the courtyard of his mother's house and vanished.

Judar went in to his mother. She greeted him with many tears and told him how the King had tortured his brothers, thrown them into prison, and taken from them the two bags.

'Do not grieve any more over that,' Judar replied. 'You shall see what I can do. I will bring my brothers back this very instant.'

He rubbed the ring, and the jinnee appeared, saying: 'I am here, my master! Ask, and you shall be given.'

'I order you,' Judar said, 'to free my brothers from the King's prison and bring them back forthwith.'

The jinnee vanished into the earth and in the twinkling of an eye emerged from the floor of the prison-house, where the two men lay lamenting their plight and praying for death. When they saw the earth open and the jinnee appear, the brothers fainted away with fright; nor did they recover their senses until they found themselves at home, with Judar and their mother seated by their side.

'Thank Allah you are safe, brothers!' said Judar when they came round. 'I am heartily pleased to see you.'

They hung their heads and burst out crying.

'Do not weep,' said Judar. 'It was Satan, and greed, that prompted you to act as you did. How could you sell me? But I will think of Joseph and console myself; his brothers behaved to him worse than you did to me, for they threw him into a pit. Still, never mind. Turn to Allah and ask His pardon: He will forgive you as I forgive you. And now you are welcome; no harm shall befall you here.'

He thus comforted them until their hearts were set at ease.

Then he related to them all he had suffered until he met the Moor and told them of the magic ring.

'Pardon us this time, brother,' they said. 'If we return to our evil practices, then punish us as you deem fit.'

'Think no more of that,' he answered. 'Tell me what the King did to you.'

'He beat us and threatened us,' they replied. 'And he took away the two bags.'

'By Allah, he shall answer for that!' Judar exclaimed. And so saying he rubbed the ring.

At the sight of the jinnee the brothers were seized with terror, thinking that he would order him to kill them. They threw themselves at their mother's feet, crying: 'Protect us, mother! Intercede for us, we beg you!'

'Do not be alarmed, my children,' she answered.

'I order you,' said Judar to the jinnee, 'to bring me all the gold and jewels in the King's treasury. Also fetch me the two bags which the King took from my brothers. Leave nothing there.'

'I hear and obey,' replied the jinnee.

He thereupon vanished and instantly returned with the King's treasures and the two bags.

'My master,' he said, 'I have left nothing in all the treasury.'

Judar put the bag of jewels into his mother's charge and kept the magic bag by his side. Then he said to the jinnee: 'I order you to build me a lofty palace this very night and to adorn it with liquid gold and furnish it magnificently. The whole must be ready by tomorrow's dawn.'

'You shall have your wish,' replied the jinnee, and disappeared into the earth.

Judar sat feasting with his family and, when they had taken their fill, they got up and went to sleep. Meanwhile Thunder summoned his minions from among the jinn and ordered them to build the palace. Some hewed the stones, some built the walls, some engraved and painted them, some spread the rooms with rugs and tapestries; so that before day dawned the palace stood complete in all its splendour. Then the servant of the ring presented himself before Judar, saying: 'The task is accomplished, my master. Will you come and inspect your palace?'

Judar went forth with his mother and brothers to see the building and they were amazed at its magnificence and the peerless beauty of its structure. Judar rejoiced as he looked at the edifice towering high on the main road and marvelled that it had cost him nothing.

'Would you like to live in this palace?' he asked his mother.

'I would indeed,' she answered, calling down blessings upon him.

He rubbed the ring again, and at once the jinnee appeared saying: 'I am here, my master.'

'I order you,' said Judar, 'to bring me forty beautiful white slave-girls and forty black slave-girls, forty white slave-boys and forty black eunuchs.'

'I hear and obey,' the jinnee replied.

The slave of the ring at once departed with forty of his attendants to India, Sind, and Persia, and in a trice returned with a multitude of handsome slaves to Judar's palace. There he made them stand in full array before their master, who was greatly pleased to see them.

'Now bring each a splendid robe to put on,' said Judar, 'and rich garments for my mother, my brothers, and myself.'

The jinnee brought the robes and dressed the slave-girls.

'This is your mistress,' he said to them. 'Kiss her hand and obey her orders; serve her well, you blacks and whites.'

He also clothed the slave-boys, and one by one they went up to Judar and kissed his hand. Finally the three brothers put on their fine robes, so that Judar looked like a king and Salem and Seleem like viziers. His house being spacious, Judar assigned a whole wing to each of his brothers with a full retinue of slaves and servants, while he and his mother dwelt in the main suite of the palace. Thus each one of them lived like a sultan in his own apartment. So much for them.

Next morning the King's treasurer went to take some valuables from the royal coffers. He entered the treasury, but found nothing there. He gave a loud cry and fell down fainting; when he recovered himself, he rushed to King Shams-al-Dowlah, crying: 'Prince of the Faithful, the treasury has been emptied during the night.'

'Dog,' cried the King, 'what have you done with all my wealth?'

'By Allah, I have done nothing, nor do I know how it was ransacked,' he replied. 'When I was there last night the treasury was full, but this morning all the coffers are clean empty; yet the walls have not been pierced and the locks are unbroken. No thief could have possibly entered there.'

'And the two bags,' the King shouted, 'have they also gone?'

'They have,' replied the treasurer.

Aghast at these words, the King jumped to his feet and, ordering the old man to follow him, ran to the treasury, which he found quite empty.

'Who dared to rob me?' exclaimed the infuriated King. 'Did he not fear my punishment?'

Blazing with rage, he rushed out of the room and assembled his court. The captains of his army hastened to the King's presence, each thinking himself the object of his wrath.

'Know,' exclaimed the King, 'that my treasury has been plundered in the night. I have yet to catch the thief who has dared to commit so great an outrage.'

'How did it all happen?' the officers inquired.

'Ask the treasurer,' shouted the King.

'Yesterday the coffers were full,' said the treasurer. 'Today I found them empty. Yet the walls of the treasury have not been pierced, nor the door broken.'

The courtiers were amazed at the treasurer's words and did not know what to answer. As they stood in silence before the King, there entered the hall that same officer who had denounced Salem and Seleem.

'Your majesty,' said he, 'all night long I have been watching a great multitude of masons at work. By daybreak they had erected an entire building, a palace of unparalleled splendour. Upon inquiry I was informed that it had been built by a man called Judar, who had but recently returned from abroad with vast riches and innumerable slaves and servants. I was also told that he had freed his brothers from prison and now sits like a sultan in his palace.'

'Go, search the prison!' cried the King to his attendants.

They went and looked, but saw no trace of the two brothers. Then they came back to inform the King.

'Now I know my enemy,' the King exclaimed. 'He that released Salem and Seleem from prison is the man who stole my treasure.'

'And who may that be, your majesty?' asked the Vizier.

'Their brother Judar,' replied the King. 'And he has taken away the two bags. Vizier, send at once an officer with fifty men to seal up all his property and bring the three of them before me, that I may hang them! Do you hear? And quickly, too!'

'Be indulgent,' said the Vizier. 'Allah himself is indulgent and never too quick to chastise His servants when they disobey Him. The man who could build a palace in a single night cannot be judged by ordinary standards. Indeed, I greatly fear for the officer whom you would send to him. Therefore have patience until I devise some way of discovering the truth. Then you can deal with these offenders as you think fit, your majesty.'

'Tell me what to do, then,' said the King.

'I advise your majesty,' replied the Vizier, 'to send an officer to him and invite him to the palace. When he is here I shall converse with him in friendly fashion and ask him his news. After that we shall see. If he is indeed a powerful man, we will contrive some plot against him; if he is just an ordinary rascal, you can arrest him and do what you please with him.'

'Then send one to invite him,' said the King.

The Vizier ordered an officer called Othman to go to Judar and invite him to the King's palace.

'And do not come back without him,' the King shouted.

Now this officer was a proud and foolish fellow. When he came to Judar's palace, he saw a eunuch sitting on a chair outside the gateway. Othman dismounted, but the eunuch remained seated on his chair and paid no heed to the distinguished courtier, despite the fifty soldiers who stood behind him.

'Slave, where is your master,' the officer cried.

'In the palace,' replied the eunuch, without stirring from his seat.

'Ill-omened slave,' exclaimed the angry Othman, 'are you not ashamed to lounge there like a fool while I am speaking to you?'

'Be off, and hold your tongue,' the eunuch replied.

At this the officer flew into a violent rage. He lifted up his mace and made to strike the eunuch, for he did not know that he was a devil. As soon as he saw this movement the door-keeper sprang upon him, threw him on the ground, and dealt him four blows with his own mace. Indignant at the treatment accorded to their master, the fifty soldiers drew their swords and rushed upon the eunuch.

'Would you draw your swords against me, you dogs?' he shouted and, falling upon them with the mace, maimed them in every limb. The soldiers took to their heels in panic-stricken flight, and did not stop running until they were far away from the palace. Then the eunuch returned to his chair and sat down at his ease, as though nothing had troubled him.

Back at the palace the battered Othman related to the King what had befallen him at the hands of Judar's slave.

'Let a hundred men be sent against him!' cried the King, bursting with rage.

A hundred men marched down to Judar's palace. When they came near, the eunuch leapt upon them with the mace and cudgelled them soundly, so that they turned their backs and fled. Returning to the King, they told him what had happened.

'Let two hundred go down!' the King exclaimed.

When these came back, broken and put to rout, the King cried to his vizier: 'Go down yourself with five hundred and bring me this eunuch at once, together with his master Judar and his brothers!'

'Great King,' replied the Vizier, 'I need no troops. I would rather go alone, unarmed.'

'Do what you think fit,' said the King.

The Vizier cast aside his weapons and, dressing himself in a white robe, took a rosary in his hand and walked unescorted to Judar's palace. There he saw the eunuch sitting at the gate; he went up to him and sat down courteously by his side, saying: 'Peace be to you.'

'And to you peace, human,' the eunuch replied. 'What is your wish?'

On hearing himself addressed as a human, the Vizier realized that the eunuch was a jinnee and trembled with fear.

'Sir, is your master here?' he asked.

'He is in the palace,' replied the jinnee.

'Sir,' said the Vizier, 'I beg you to go in and say to him: "King Shams-al-Dowlah invites you to a banquet at his palace. He sends you his greeting and requests you to honour him with your presence."'

'Wait here while I tell him,' the jinnee answered.

The Vizier waited humbly, while the eunuch went into the palace.

'Know, my master,' he said to Judar, 'that this morning the King sent to you an officer with fifty guards. I cudgelled him and put his men to flight. Next he sent a hundred, whom I beat, and then two hundred, whom I routed. Now he has sent you his vizier, unarmed and unattended, to invite you as his guest. What answer shall I give him?'

'Go and bring the Vizier in,' Judar replied.

The jinnee led the Vizier into the palace, where he saw Judar seated upon a couch such as no king ever possessed and arrayed in greater magnificence than any sultan. He was confounded at the splendour of the palace and the beauty of its ornaments and furniture, and, Vizier that he was, felt himself a beggar in those surroundings. He kissed the ground before Judar and called down blessings upon him.

'What is your errand, Vizier?' Judar demanded.

'Sir,' he answered, 'your friend King Shams-al-Dowlah sends you his greetings. He desires to delight himself with your company, and begs your attendance at a banquet in his palace. Will you do him the honour of accepting his invitation?'

'Since he is my friend,' returned Judar, 'give him my salutations and tell him to come and visit me himself.'

'It shall be as you wish,' the Vizier replied.

Upon this Judar rubbed the ring and ordered the jinnee to fetch him a splendid robe. The jinnee brought him a robe, and Judar handed it to the Vizier, saying: 'Put this on. Then go and inform the King what I have told you.'

The Vizier put on the robe, the like of which he had never worn in all his life and returned to his master. He gave him an account of all that he had seen, enlarging upon the splendour of the palace and its contents.

'Judar invites you,' he said.

'To your horses, captains!' the King exclaimed and, mounting his own steed, rode with his followers to Judar's house.

Meanwhile, Judar summoned the servant of the ring and said to him: 'I require you to bring me from among the jinn a troop of guards in human guise and station them in the courtyard of the palace, so that when the King passes through their ranks his heart may be filled with awe and he may realize that my might is greater than his.'

At once two hundred stalwart guards appeared in the courtyard, dressed in magnificent armour. When the King arrived and saw the formidable array, his heart trembled with fear. He went up into the palace and found Judar sitting in the spacious hall, surrounded with such grandeur as cannot be found in the courts of kings or sultans. He greeted him and bowed respectfully before him; but Judar neither rose in his honour nor invited him to be seated. The King grew fearful of his host's intent and, in his embarrassment, did not know whether to sit down or go out.

'Were he afraid of me,' he thought to himself, 'he would have shown me more respect. Is it to avenge his brothers' wrong that he has brought me here?'

'Your majesty,' Judar said at last, 'is it proper for a king to oppress his subjects and seize their goods?'

'Sir, do not be angry with me,' the King replied. 'It was avarice, and fate, that led me to wrong your brothers. If men could never do wrong, there would be no pardon.'

He went on begging forgiveness and humbling himself in this fashion until Judar said: 'Allah forgive you,' and bade him be seated. Then Judar dressed the King in the robe of safety and ordered his brothers to serve a sumptuous banquet. When they had finished eating, he invested all the courtiers with robes of honour and gave them costly presents. After that the King took leave of him and departed.

Thenceforth the King visited Judar every day and never held his court except in Judar's house. Friendship and amity flourished between them and they continued in this state for some time. One day, however, the King said to his vizier: 'I fear that Judar may kill me and usurp my kingdom.'

'Have no fear of that, your majesty,' the Vizier answered. 'Judar will never stoop so low as to rob you of your kingdom, for the wealth and power he enjoys are greater than any king's. And if you are afraid that he may kill you, give him your daughter in marriage and you and he will be for ever united.'

'Vizier, you shall act as our go-between,' the King said.

'Gladly, your majesty,' the Vizier replied. 'Invite him to your palace, and we will spend the evening together in one of the halls. Ask your daughter to put on her finest jewels and walk across the doorway. When Judar sees her he will fall in love with her outright. I will then lean towards him and tell him who she is. I will speak adroitly to him and encourage him by hint and suggestion, as though you know nothing about the matter, until he asks you for the girl. Once they are married, a lasting bond will be ensured between you and, when he dies, the greater part of his riches will be yours.'

'You have spoken wisely, my Vizier,' said the King.

He thereupon ordered a banquet to be given, and invited him. Judar came to the royal palace and they sat feasting in the great hall till evening.

The King had instructed his wife to array the Princess in her finest ornaments and walk with her past the doorway. She did as the King bade her and walked past the hall with her daughter. When Judar caught sight of the girl in her incomparable beauty, he uttered a deep sigh and felt his limbs grow numb and languid. Love took possession of his heart, and he turned pale with overpowering passion.

'I trust you are well, my master,' said the Vizier in a whisper. 'Why do I see you so distressed?'

'That girl,' Judar murmured, 'whose daughter is she?'

'She is the daughter of your friend the King,' replied the Vizier. 'If you like her, I will ask him if he will marry her to you.'

'Do that, Vizier,' Judar said, 'and you shall be handsomely rewarded. I will give the King whatever dowry he demands and the two of us will be friends and kinsmen.'

'Allah willing, you shall have her,' the Vizier replied.

Then, turning to the King, he whispered to him.

'Your majesty,' he said, 'your friend Judar desires to marry your daughter, the Princess Asiah. Pray accept my plea on his behalf. He offers you whatever dowry you wish to ask.'

'I have already received the dowry,' the King answered. 'My daughter is a slave in his service. I marry her to him. If he accepts her I shall be greatly honoured.'

Next morning the King assembled his court, and in the presence of Sheikh al-Islam Judar wedded the Princess. He presented the King with the bag of gold and jewels as a dowry for his daughter and the marriage-contract was drawn up amidst great rejoicings. Judar and the King lived together in harmony and mutual trust for many months; and when the King died the troops requested his son-in-law to be their sultan. At first Judar declined, but when they continued to press him he accepted and was proclaimed their king. He built a great mosque over the tomb of Shams-al-Dowlah and endowed it munificently. Judar's house was in the Yemenite Quarter, but since the beginning of his reign the entire district has been known as Judariyah.

Judar appointed Salem and Seleem his viziers, and the three of them lived in peace for one year, no more. At the end of that time Salem said to Seleem: 'How long are we to stay as we are? Are we to spend the whole of our lives as servants to Judar? We shall never taste the joy of sovereignty or power as long as Judar is alive. Can we not kill him and take the ring and the bag from him?'

'You are cleverer than I am,' Seleem replied. 'Think out some plot for us whereby we can destroy him.'

'If I contrive to bring about his death,' said Salem, 'will you agree that I shall become sultan and you chief vizier? Will you accept the magic bag and let me keep the ring?'

'I agree to that,' Seleem replied.

Thus for the sake of power and worldly gain, the two conspired to kill their brother. They betook themselves to Judar and said to him: 'Brother, will you do us the honour of dining with us this evening?'

'To whose house shall I come?' he asked.

'To mine,' Salem replied. 'Then you can go to my brother's.'

'Very well,' said Judar.

He went with Seleem to Salem's house, where a poisoned feast was spread before him. As soon as he had swallowed a mouthful his flesh fell about his bones in little pieces. Salem thereupon rose to pull the ring off his finger, and, seeing that it would not yield, cut off the finger with his knife. Then he rubbed the ring, and the jinnee appeared before him, saying: 'I am here! Demand what you will.'

'Take hold of my brother and put him to instant death,' Salem said. 'Then carry the two bodies and throw them down before the troops.'

The jinnee put Seleem to death, then carried out the two corpses and cast them down in the midst of the palace hall, where the army chiefs were eating. Alarmed at the sight, the captains lifted their hands from the food and cried to the jinnee: 'Who has killed the King and his vizier?'

'Their brother Salem,' he replied.

At that moment Salem himself entered the hall.

'Captains,' he said, 'eat, and set your minds at rest. I have become master of this ring, which I have taken from my brother Judar. The jinnee who stands before you is its faithful servant. I ordered him to kill my brother Seleem so that he should not scheme against my throne. He was a traitor and I feared he would betray me. Judar being dead, I am your only

King. Will you accept my rule, or shall I order this jinnee to slay you all, great and small alike?'

The captains answered: 'We accept you as our King.'

Salem gave orders for the burial of his brothers, and assembled his court. Some of the people walked in the funeral and some in Salem's procession. When he reached the audience-hall, Salem sat upon the throne and received the allegiance of his subjects. Then said he: 'I wish to take in marriage my brother's wife.'

'That may not be done,' they answered, 'until the period of her widowhood* has expired.'

But Salem cried: 'I will not hear of such trifles. Upon my life, I will go in to her this very night.'

Thus they wrote the marriage-contract and sent to inform Judar's widow.

'Let him come,' she said.

When he entered, she welcomed him with a great show of joy. But she mixed poison in his drink and so destroyed him.

Shams-al-Dowlah's daughter took the ring and broke it to pieces, so that none should ever use it. She also tore the magic bag. Then she sent to inform Sheikh-al-Islam of what had happened and to bid the people choose a new king.

*Four months and ten days, according to Islamic law.

THE TALE OF
MA'ARUF THE COBBLER

ONCE upon a time there lived in the city of Cairo a poor and honest cobbler who earned his living by patching old shoes. His name was Ma'aruf.

He was married to a spiteful termagant called Fatimah, nicknamed by her neighbours 'The Shrew' on account of her sour disposition and scolding tongue. She used her husband with heartless cruelty, cursing him a thousand times a day and making his life a burden and a torment. Ma'aruf was a sensitive man, jealous of his good name, and in time he grew to fear her malice and dread her fiery temper. All his daily earnings he gladly spent on her, but if, by ill fortune, he returned home with an empty purse, she abused and scolded him, giving him no rest and making his night hideous as her scowl.

It happened one day that his wife came to Ma'aruf and said: 'See that you bring me a kunafah cake tonight, and let it be dripping with sweet honey.'

'May Allah send me good custom today,' replied the cobbler, 'and you shall gladly have one. At present I have not a single copper, but the bounty of Allah is great.'

'A fig for the bounty of Allah!' rejoined the shrew. 'If you do not bring me back a kunafah, dripping with sweet honey, I will make the night blacker for you than the fate which cast you into my hands!'

'Allah is merciful,' sighed Ma'aruf. Perplexed and downcast, he left his house and went to open his shop, saying: 'O Allah, grant me this day the means to buy a honey-cake for my wife, that I may save myself from the spleen of that wicked woman!'

But, as ill luck would have it, no customer entered his shop that day and he did not earn enough even to buy a loaf of bread. Weary and sick at heart, he locked his shop and walked along the street. Presently he came to a pastry-cook's, and as he gazed upon the delicacies displayed in the window, his eyes filled with tears. Noticing his dejected countenance, the pastry-cook called out to him, saying: 'Why so sad, Ma'aruf? Come in, and tell me your trouble.'

When the cook had heard the cause of the cobbler's unhappiness, he laughed and said: 'No harm shall come to you, my friend. What quantity of kunafah do you require?'

'Five ounces,' muttered Ma'aruf.

'I will gladly let you have it,' said the cook, 'and you can pay me some other time.'

He cut a large slice of kunafah and added: 'I fear that I have no honey, but only sugar-cane syrup. I assure you it is just as good.'

The cook put the kunafah in a dish and poured syrup and melted butter over it until it was worthy of a king's table. Then he handed the dish to the cobbler, together with a cheese and a loaf of bread for his supper. Ma'aruf could scarcely find words to express his gratitude and, calling down fervent blessings on the good man, went off to his house.

As soon as his wife saw him she cried: 'Have you brought me the kunafah?'

Ma'aruf placed the dish before her, but no sooner had the vixen set eyes on the cake than she burst out in a menacing voice: 'Did I not tell you it must be made with honey? You have brought me a syrup cake to spite me! Did you think I would not know the difference?'

Abjectly Ma'aruf stammered out his explanation, saying: 'Good wife, I did not buy this cake; it was given me on credit by the kind-hearted pastry-cook.'

'This babble will not help you!' shrieked the furious woman. 'There, take your miserable syrup dish!' And she flung the cake in her husband's face and ordered him to go and fetch her another made with honey. Then she dealt him a savage blow on the jaw, knocking out one of his teeth, so that the blood trickled down his beard and chest.

Losing all patience, the long-suffering Ma'aruf impulsively lifted his hand and gave the woman a mild slap on the head. At this the termagant flew into a desperate rage; she gripped his beard with both her hands, and, raising her voice to its loudest pitch, shrieked out: 'Help, good Moslems! Help, my husband is murdering me!'

Hearing her cries, the neighbours came rushing into the house. After a long struggle they succeeded in freeing the

cobbler's beard from his wife's clutches, but when they saw the injury she had inflicted on him and heard the cause of the dispute, they rebuked her and said: 'We are all content to eat syrup kunafah, and find it as good as the other kind. What has your poor husband done that you should torment him so?'

At length, thinking that peace had been restored between husband and wife, the neighbours went their way. Left alone with Fatimah, Ma'aruf attempted to pacify her. He gathered up the scattered remnants of the kunafah and offered it to her with a trembling hand, saying: 'Eat a little of this, my love, and tomorrow, if Allah wills, I shall bring you a kunafah dripping with honey.'

But the shrew gave no heed to his entreaties and swore that nothing would persuade her to touch it. At last, beginning to feel the pangs of hunger, Ma'aruf sat down to eat the kunafah himself. This he did to the accompaniment of an uninterrupted flow of abuse from his wife; and she continued to call down curses on him throughout the night.

Early next morning Ma'aruf went to the mosque and prayed to Allah to grant him the means wherewith to gratify his wife's demand. Then he opened his shop, but had scarcely sat down to his work when two guards burst in upon him, saying: 'We hold a warrant from the Cadi So-and-so for your arrest.' With this they manacled the cobbler and dragged him to their master's court.

When he was led into the Cadi's presence, Ma'aruf saw his wife standing all in tears, with a bandaged arm and her head wrapped in a blood-stained veil.

'Wretch!' cried the Cadi, as soon as he set eyes on Ma'aruf. 'Have you no fear of Allah that you beat this poor woman and break her arm and knock out her tooth?'

The cobbler was utterly confounded, and proceeded to tell the Cadi what had passed between him and his wife. Convinced that the unhappy man was telling the truth, the Cadi took pity on Ma'aruf and gave him a quarter of a dinar, saying: 'Take this and buy her a honey kunafah.' Then he exhorted the pair to use each other kindly and, having made peace between them, dismissed them from his presence.

Ma'aruf gave his wife the quarter of a dinar and returned to his shop. Presently, however, the guards who had marched him to the court came back to demand payment. When Ma'aruf told them that he had not a copper in his purse, they dragged him out into the market-place and would have given him a sound beating had he not instantly sold his cobbler's tools and paid them half a dinar.

As he sat in his empty shop brooding over his ill fortune, two ruffianly guards from the court of another cadi burst in, saying: 'We have a warrant for your arrest.' Without more ado they led him to the court, where Ma'aruf was astounded to see his wife standing as before, with bandaged arm and a blood-stained veil about her head, heaping up monstrous charges against him.

Again the cobbler related his story to the judge, adding: 'The Cadi So-and-so had but an hour ago made peace between us.'

'Woman,' cried the Cadi, addressing the shrew, 'if you are already reconciled, why have you come to me?'

'He has beaten me again!' protested Fatimah.

The Cadi rebuked them both and, after ordering Ma'aruf to pay the guards, dismissed them from his presence.

The harassed cobbler parted with his last copper and trudged dolefully back to his shop. Scarcely an hour had passed, when one of his friends came running to the door and cried: 'Rise, Ma'aruf, and fly for your life, for the shrew has brought an action against you at the Governor's court! His guards are even now on their way to arrest you!'

The terrified cobbler closed his shop and made off towards the Victory Gate. It was a grey winter afternoon, and as soon as he came to the outskirts of the city and found himself amongst the garbage heaps the rain began to fall in torrents, drenching him to the skin. On and on he ran, and at nightfall came to a ruined hovel where he took shelter from the storm. He sat down on the ground and wept bitterly, crying: 'Oh, how shall I save myself from this fiend? O Allah, help me fly to some far-off land, where I shall never see her more!'

Whilst he was thus lamenting, the wall of the hovel suddenly opened and there appeared before him a colossal jinnee whose fearsome aspect struck terror in his soul.

'Son of Adam,' roared the jinnee, 'what calamity can have befallen you that you disturb my midnight slumbers with your wailing? I am the jinnee of this ruin and have dwelt here these hundred years; yet have I never seen the like of this behaviour.' Then, moved with pity, the jinnee added: 'Tell me what you desire, and I will do your bidding.'

Ma'aruf told him the story of his misfortunes, and the jinnee said: 'Mount on my back, and I will take you to a land where your wife shall never find you.'

The cobbler climbed onto the back of the jinnee, who

flew with him between earth and sky all night and at day-break set him down on the top of a mountain.

'Son of Adam,' said the jinnee, 'go down this mountain and you will come to the gates of Ikhtiyan-al-Khatan. In that city you will find refuge from your wife.' And, so saying, the jinnee vanished.

Amazed and bewildered, Ma'aruf remained where the jinnee had left him until the sun rose. Then he climbed down the mountain and at length came to a well-built city surrounded by high walls. He entered the gates, and, as he walked through the streets, the townsfolk stared at him with wondering eyes and gathered about him, marvelling at his strange costume. Presently a man stepped forward and asked him whence he had come.

'From Cairo,' replied Ma'aruf.

'When did you leave Cairo?' inquired the man.

'Last night,' he answered, 'just after the hour of evening prayers.'

At these words his questioner laughed incredulously, and, turning to the bystanders, cried: 'Listen to this madman! He tells us that he left Cairo only last night!'

The crowd greeted this remark with loud laughter, and, pressing round Ma'aruf, shouted: 'Have you taken leave of your senses? How was it that you left Cairo only last night? Do you not know that Cairo is a year's journey from this city?'

Ma'aruf swore that he was speaking the truth, and to prove his story took from his pocket a loaf of Cairo bread and showed it to them. They were all astonished to see the loaf, which was of a kind unknown in their country, and still soft and fresh. A few believed him, whilst others ridiculed him. As this was going forward, a wealthy merchant, followed by two slaves, came riding by and, stopping near the crowd, admonished them sternly, saying: 'Are you not ashamed to make game of this stranger?'

Then, turning to Ma'aruf, the merchant spoke to him kindly and invited him to his house.

There his host clad Ma'aruf in a merchant's robe worth a thousand dinars, seated him in a splendid hall, and entertained him at a sumptuous meal. When they had finished eating, the merchant said to the cobbler: 'Pray tell me, my brother, what land you have come from, for by your dress you would seem to be an Egyptian.'

'You are right, my master,' replied Ma'aruf. 'I am an Egyptian, and Cairo is the city of my birth.'

'What is your trade?' inquired the merchant.

'I am a cobbler; I patch old shoes.'

'In what part of Cairo did you live?'

'In Red Lane,' replied Ma'aruf.

'What folk do you know there?'

Ma'aruf named several of his neighbours in that street.

'Do you know Sheikh Ahmed the perfume-seller?' asked the merchant eagerly.

'Do I know him?' laughed Ma'aruf. 'Why, he is my next-door neighbour!'

'How is he faring?'

'Thanks be to Allah, he is in the best of health,' replied the cobbler.

'How many sons has he now?'

'He has three sons: Mustapha, Mohammed, and Ali.'

'What do they do for their living?' inquired the host.

'The eldest, Mustapha,' replied Ma'aruf, 'is a schoolmaster. Mohammed, the second, is a perfume-seller and has set up a shop of his own next to his father's. His wife has but recently borne him a son, whom they called Hassan. As for Ali, he was the playmate of my childhood. Together we would enter the churches of the Christians and steal their prayer-books; then we would sell them in the market-place and buy sweet-meats with the money. One day the Christians caught us red-handed and complained to our parents. They threatened Ali's father, saying: "If you do not restrain your son, we will inform the King of this sacrilege." Sheikh Ahmed gave his son a thrashing and poor little Ali ran away from home. No news has been heard of him these twenty years.'

Here the merchant threw his arms round the cobbler's neck and wept for joy, crying: 'Praise be to Allah! O Ma'aruf, I am that very Ali, the son of Sheikh Ahmed the perfume-seller!'

Then Ali asked his friend what had brought him to Ikhtiyan-al-Khatan, and the cobbler recounted to him the tale of his misfortunes and all that had befallen him since his disastrous marriage. He explained how he had chosen to fly the city rather than remain at the mercy of his heartless wife, how he met the jinnee in the ruined hovel, and how he was carried overnight to Ikhtiyan-al-Khatan. Then Ma'aruf asked his friend to tell him how he rose to such prosperity.

'After I left Cairo,' said Ali, 'I wandered for many years from place to place and at length arrived, forlorn and penniless, in this city. I found its people honest and kind-hearted, hospitable to strangers and always ready to help the poor. I told them that I was a rich merchant, the owner of a great caravan which would shortly arrive in their city. They believed my story and gave me a splendid mansion for my use. Then I borrowed a thousand dinars, telling my creditor that I needed a few necessities before my merchandise arrived. With this money I bought a quantity of goods and sold them the following day at a profit of fifty pieces of gold. I bought more goods, and, to enhance my reputation, I sought the acquaintance of the richest merchants in the town and entertained them liberally in my house. I continued to buy and sell until I had amassed a large fortune.

'The old proverb says: "Where candour fails, cunning thrives." Now, my friend, if you tell the people of this city that you are a poor cobbler, that you have run away from a nagging wife and left Cairo only yesterday, no one will believe you and you will become the laughing-stock of the whole town. If you tell them that you were carried here by a jinnee, you will frighten everyone away and they will think: "This man is possessed with an evil spirit." No, my friend, this will not do.'

'Then what am I to do?' asked the perplexed Ma'aruf.

'Tomorrow morning,' said Ali, 'you shall mount my finest mule and ride to the market-place, with one of my slaves walking behind you all the way. There you will find me sitting among the richest merchants of the city. When I see you I will rise and greet you, I will kiss your hand and receive you with the utmost deference. When you have taken your seat among the other merchants, I shall question you about many kinds of merchandise, saying: "Have you such-and-such a cloth?" And you must answer: "Plenty! Plenty!" When they ask me who you are, I shall say you are a merchant of great wealth, and praise your munificence. If a beggar holds out his hand to you, give him gold. These proceedings will earn you great consideration in the merchants' eyes. They will seek your acquaintance and wish to trade with you, and before long you will become indeed a merchant of great wealth.'

Next morning Ali dressed Ma'aruf in a magnificent robe, gave him a thousand dinars, and mounted him upon his best mule. At the appointed time the cobbler rode to the market-place, where he found his friend sitting among the merchants. As soon as Ali saw him approaching he rose, threw himself at his feet, kissed his hand, and helped him from his mule, saying: 'May your day be blessed, great Ma'aruf!'

When the newcomer had gravely taken his seat, the wondering merchants came to Ali one after another and asked him in a low voice: 'Who may this sheikh be?' Ali replied: 'He is one of the chief merchants of Egypt. His wealth and the wealth of his father and forefathers is of proverbial fame, and his munificence is boundless as the sea. He possesses shops and storehouses in all the corners of the earth, and his agents and partners are the pillars of commerce in every city from Egypt and Yemen to India and the far-flung hills of Sind. Indeed the wealthiest merchant in this city is but a poor pedlar when compared with him.'

Hearing this encomium, the merchants thronged around Ma'aruf, vying with each other to welcome him and offering him sherbets. The chief of the merchants himself came to greet him, and questioned him eagerly about the goods he had brought.

'Doubtless, my master,' he said, 'you have many bales of yellow silk?'

'Plenty! Plenty!' answered Ma'aruf, without a moment's hesitation.

'And gazelle blood-red?' asked another.

'Plenty! Plenty!' replied the cobbler gravely.

To all their questions he made the same answer, and when one of the merchants begged him to show them a few samples, Ma'aruf replied: 'Certainly, as soon as my caravan arrives.' Then he explained to the company that he was expecting a caravan of a thousand mules within the next few days.

Now whilst the merchants were chatting together and marvelling at the extraordinary richness of the caravan, a beggar came round and held out his hand to each in turn. A few gave him half a dirham, some a copper, but most of them gave him nothing. Ma'aruf, however, calmly drew out a handful of gold and gave it to the beggar.

The merchants marvelled at this, and thought to themselves: 'By Allah, this man must be richer than a king!'

Then a poor woman approached him, and to her also he gave a handful of gold. Scarcely believing her eyes, the woman hurried away to tell the other beggars and they all came flocking round Ma'aruf with outstretched hands. The cobbler gave each a handful of gold, until the thousand dinars were finished. Then he clapped his hands together, saying: 'By Allah, to think there are so many beggars in this city! Had I known of this I would have come prepared, for it is not my way to refuse alms. What shall I do now if a beggar solicits me before my caravan arrives? If only I had, say, a thousand dinars!'

'Do not let that trouble you,' said the chief of the merchants. And he at once sent for a thousand dinars and handed the money to Ma'aruf.

The cobbler continued to give gold to every beggar who passed by. When the muezzin's call summoned the Faithful to afternoon prayers, he went with the merchants to the mosque, and what remained of the thousand dinars he scattered over the heads of the worshippers.

As soon as the prayers were over he borrowed another thousand, and these also he gave away. By nightfall Ma'aruf had obtained five thousand dinars from the merchants and given them all away, while the dismayed Ali watched the proceedings helplessly. And to all his creditors he said: 'When my caravan arrives, if you want gold, you shall have gold; and if you want goods, you shall have goods: for I have vast quantities of them.'

That night Ali entertained the merchants at his house. Ma'aruf was given the seat of honour, and all night spoke of nothing but jewels and rich silks. And whenever they asked him if he had this or that merchandise in his caravan, the cobbler replied: 'Plenty! Plenty!'

Next morning he again went to the market-place, where he talked to the merchants about his caravan and borrowed more money and gave it to the beggars. This he repeated each day for twenty days, and by the end of this time he had taken sixty thousand pieces of gold on credit. And still no caravan arrived; no, not as much as a half-cooked pie.

At length the merchants, who were becoming impatient at the caravan's delay, began to clamour for their money. They voiced their anxiety to their friend Ali, who, himself alarmed at the cobbler's munificence, took him aside and remonstrated with him, saying: 'Have you taken leave of your senses? I told you to toast the bread, not to burn it! The merchants are demanding their money and say that you owe them sixty thousand dinars. You have squandered all this gold among the beggars; how will you ever pay it back, idle as you are, with no work to do or goods to trade with?'

'No matter,' replied Ma'aruf. 'What is sixty thousand dinars? When my caravan arrives, if they want gold, they shall have gold; and if they want goods, they shall have goods: for I have vast quantities of them.'

'Now glory be to Allah!' exclaimed Ali. 'What goods are you talking about?'

'Why, the goods in my caravan,' replied Ma'aruf. 'I have countless bales of merchandise.'

'Impudent dog!' cried Ali. 'Are you telling me that story? Why, I will denounce you to the whole world!'

'Be off!' said Ma'aruf. 'Did you suppose I was a poor man? Know, then, I have priceless riches on the way. As soon as my caravan arrives, the merchants shall be repaid two-fold!'

At this Ali grew very angry and cried: 'Scoundrel! I will teach you to lie to me!'

'Do your worst!' replied the cobbler. 'They must wait until my caravan arrives, and then they shall have their money back and more.'

In despair Ali left Ma'aruf and went away thinking: 'If I now abuse him after so highly commending him, I shall, as the saying goes, be a twofold liar.'

When the merchants returned, inquiring the outcome of his audience with Ma'aruf, the harassed Ali replied: 'My friends, I had not the heart to speak to him about his debts, for I myself have lent him a thousand dinars. When you advanced him so much money, you did not seek my advice; therefore you cannot hold me responsible. Speak to him yourselves. If he fails to pay his debts, denounce him to the King as an impostor and a thief.'

The merchants went in a body to the King and told him all that had passed between them and Ma'aruf. 'Your majesty,' they said, 'we are in great perplexity about this merchant, whose generosity knows no bounds. He has borrowed sixty thousand dinars from us and scattered them in handfuls among the poor. Were he a poor man, he would never be so foolish as to squander such a fortune; and if he is indeed a man of wealth, why has his vaunted caravan not yet arrived?'

Now the King was an avaricious old miser. When he heard the merchants' account of Ma'aruf's prodigality, greed took possession of his soul and he said to his Vizier: 'This merchant must surely be a man of extraordinary wealth, or he would never have been capable of such munificence. His caravan is certain to arrive. Now I will not suffer these wolves of the market-place to grab all the treasures for themselves, for they are already too rich. I must seek his friendship, so that when his caravan arrives I, too, will have a share. Why, I might even give him my daughter in marriage and join his wealth to mine.'

But the Vizier replied: 'This man is an impostor, your majesty. Beware of avarice, for avarice brings ruin and repentance.'

'I will put him to the test,' said the King, 'and we will soon discover if he is a trickster. I will show him a costly pearl and ask him his opinion. If he can tell its worth, we shall know that he is a man of affluence accustomed to such rarities. If he cannot, then we shall know that he is a liar and a fraud, and I will put him to a cruel death.'

The Vizier sent at once for Ma'aruf, and when he had been admitted to the King's presence and exchanged greetings with him, the King asked: 'Is it true that you owe the merchants sixty thousand pieces of gold?'

When Ma'aruf replied that it was true, he asked: 'Why do you not pay them their money?'

'The day my caravan arrives,' replied Ma'aruf, 'they shall be paid twofold. If they want gold, they shall have gold; if they want silver, they shall have silver; and if they prefer goods, they shall have goods: for I have vast quantities of them.'

Then, to test Ma'aruf, the King handed him a rare pearl worth a thousand dinars. 'Have you such pearls in your caravan?' he asked.

Ma'aruf examined the pearl for a moment, and, throwing it disdainfully to the ground, crushed it beneath his heel.

'What is the meaning of this?' cried the King indignantly.

'This pearl,' replied the cobbler with a laugh, 'is scarcely worth a thousand dinars. I have vast quantities of infinitely larger pearls in my caravan.'

At this the King's avarice knew no bounds. He at once sent for the merchants, told them that their fears were groundless, and assured them that the caravan would soon arrive. Then he summoned the Vizier and said: 'See that the merchant Ma'aruf is received with all magnificence at the palace. Speak to him about my daughter the Princess. Perhaps he will consent to marry her and so we shall gain possession of all his wealth.'

'Your majesty,' replied the Vizier, 'I do not like the manner of this foreigner. His presence bodes evil to the court. I pray you to wait until we have visible proof of his caravan.'

Now the Vizier himself had once sought the Princess's

hand in marriage and his suit had been rejected. So when the
King heard this warning, he flew into a passion and cried:
'Treacherous dog, you slander this merchant only because
you wish to marry the Princess yourself. You would have her
left on my hands until she is old and unacceptable. Could
she ever find a more suitable husband than this accomplished,
generous, and opulent young man? Not only will he make her
a perfect husband, but he will make us all rich into the bargain!'

Afraid of the King's anger, the Vizier kept his own counsel
and said no more. He betook himself to Ma'aruf and said to
him: 'His majesty the King desires you to marry his daughter
the Princess. What answer shall I give him?'

'I am honoured by the King's proposal,' replied Ma'aruf with an air of dignified reserve. 'But do you not think it would be better to wait until my caravan arrives? The dowry of such a bride as the Princess would be a greater expense than I can at present afford. I must give my wife a marriage-portion of at least five thousand purses of gold. Among the poor of the city I shall have to distribute a thousand purses on the bridal night; to those who walk in the wedding procession I must give a thousand more; and I shall need another thousand to entertain the troops. On the next morning I must present a hundred rich diamonds to the Princess, and as many jewels to the slave-girls and the eunuchs of the palace. All this is an expense which cannot be met before my caravan arrives.'

When the Vizier went back to the King and repeated to him Ma'aruf's reply, the King was overwhelmed at the prodigious recital and sent the Vizier to bring him to his presence. As soon as the cobbler entered the King said: 'Honoured and most distinguished merchant, let us celebrate this happy union forthwith! I myself will meet the expenses of the marriage. My treasury is full; I give you leave to take from it all that you require. You can settle the Princess's dowry when your caravan comes in. By Allah, I will take no refusal!'

Without a moment's delay the King sent for the Imam of the royal mosque, who drew up a marriage contract for Ma'aruf and the Princess.

The city was gaily decorated at the King's orders, drums and trumpets sounded in the streets, and Ma'aruf the cobbler sat enthroned in the great parlour of the palace. A troop of singers, dancers, wrestlers, clowns, and acrobats capered round the court to entertain the guests, whilst the royal treasurer brought Ma'aruf bag after bag of gold to scatter among the merry throng. He had no rest that day, for no sooner had he come to Ma'aruf staggering under the weight of a hundred thousand dinars, than he was sent back for another load. The Vizier watched the spectacle with rage in his heart, whilst Ali the merchant, aghast at the proceedings, approached Ma'aruf and whispered in his ear: 'May Allah have no mercy upon you! Is it not enough that you have frittered away the wealth of all the merchants? Must you also drain the royal treasury?'

'What is that to you?' replied Ma'aruf. 'Be sure that when my great caravan arrives, I will repay the King a thousand-fold.'

The extravagant rejoicings lasted forty days, and then came the wedding-day. The King, accompanied by his viziers and the officers of his troops, walked in the bridal procession, and as he passed by, Ma'aruf threw handfuls of gold to the crowds that lined the way.

When the couple were at length left alone in the bridal chamber, and the Princess lay down beneath the velvet curtains of the bed, Ma'aruf sat on the floor and wrung his hands in despair. Perceiving his grief, the Princess tenderly asked him: 'Why so sad, my lord?'

'There is no strength or help save in Allah!' replied Ma'aruf with a sigh. 'It is all your father's fault!'

'How so?' she asked.

'He has exposed me to ridicule in the eyes of the whole world!' sighed Ma'aruf. 'Surely everyone must have noticed my meanness, my miserly treatment of you and the royal guests! If only he had waited till my great caravan arrived! At least I should have been able to give you a few rich presents befitting your degree, and bestow upon your women jewels and ornaments in honour of this happy occasion. But your father would hurry on the wedding and put me to this shame! It was like burning green grass!'

'Instead of worrying about such trifles,' replied the Princess, 'undress and come to bed. Put away all thoughts of presents and caravans, my dear, and gird your loins for the merry sport!'

Ma'aruf cast off his clothes and, climbing into bed, threw himself upon the Princess as she lay on her back. He clasped her tight, and she pressed close to him, so that tongue met tongue in that hour when men forget their mothers. He slipped his hands under her armpits and strained her to his breast, squeezing all the honey and setting the dainties face to face. Then, threading the needle, he kindled the match, put it to

387

the priming, and fired the shot. Thus the citadel was breached and the victory won.

After a night of such dalliance, Ma'aruf rose and went to the bath. Then he dressed himself in a princely robe and entered the King's council-chamber, where he sat down by the side of his father-in-law to receive the felicitations of the viziers and the chief officers of the kingdom. He sent for the treasurer and ordered him to give robes of honour to all who were present; then he called for sacks of gold and gave handfuls to every member of the royal palace from the highest courtier to the humblest kitchen boy. And for twenty days he thus continued to dissipate the King's treasure.

At the end of this time there was still no news of Ma'aruf's caravan, and at length the day came when the treasurer found his coffers empty. He went to the King with a heavy heart and said: 'Your majesty, the treasure chests are empty and the great caravan of your son-in-law has not yet come to fill them.'

Alarmed at these words, the King turned to his Vizier and said: 'By Allah, it is true there is still no sign of the caravan. What shall we do?'

'Allah prolong your days, my master,' replied the Vizier with an evil smile. 'Did I not warn you against the wiles of this impostor? I swear he has no caravan: no, not as much as a half-cooked pie! He has married your daughter without a dowry and defrauded you of all your treasure. How long will your majesty tolerate this vagabond?'

'If only we could find the truth about him!' sighed the King in great perplexity.

'Your majesty,' said the Vizier, 'no one is better able to find out a man's secrets than his wife. I beg you to call your daughter here and permit me to question her from behind the curtain.'

'It shall be done!' replied the King. 'On my life, if it be proved that he has deceived us, he shall die the cruellest of deaths!'

At once the King had a curtain drawn across the hall, and, summoning the Princess, bade her sit behind it and speak with the Vizier.

'What do you wish to know?' she asked.

'Honoured lady,' began the Vizier, 'the chests of the treasury are empty, thanks to the extravagance of Prince Ma'aruf, and the wondrous caravan, about which we have heard so much, has not yet come. Therefore the King has given me leave to ask what you know of this stranger and whether you have reason to suspect him.'

'Night after night,' replied the Princess, 'he has promised me pearls and jewels, and treasures without number. But of these I have yet seen nothing.'

'Your highness,' said the Vizier, 'I counsel you to question him tonight, that we may know the answer to this riddle. Beg him to tell you the truth, and promise to keep his secret.'

'I hear and obey,' replied the Princess. 'I will speak to Ma'aruf tonight and tell you what he says.'

In the evening, when the pair lay side by side, the Princess threw her arms around Ma'aruf and, assuming that sweet and endearing air with which subtle women coax their husbands, said to him: 'Light of my eyes and flower of my heart, may Time and Destiny never part us! Your love has kindled in my breast such fires that I will gladly die for you. Tell me the truth about your caravan and conceal nothing from me. How long will you delude my father with such lies? For I fear that he will find you out at last and make you pay dearly for this deception. Tell me everything, my love, and I will contrive a means to help you.'

'Sweet Princess,' replied Ma'aruf, 'I will tell you all. I am no wealthy merchant, no master of caravans. In my own land I was a poor cobbler, cursed with a vixen of a wife called . . .' And he recounted to the Princess the tale of his connubial misfortunes from the adventure of the honey-cake to his flight to Ikhtiyan-al-Khatan.

When she heard the cobbler's story, the Princess burst into a fit of laughter and said: 'Truly, Ma'aruf, you are a subtle rogue! But what are we to do? What will my father say when he learns the truth? The Vizier has already sown suspicions in his mind. He will surely kill you, and I shall die of grief. Take this fifty thousand dinars and leave the palace this very hour. Ride away to some far country, and then send a courier to acquaint me with your news.'

'I am at your mercy, mistress,' replied the cobbler.

After he had dallied with the Princess for a while, he rose, disguised himself in the livery of a slave and, mounting the fastest horse in the King's stables, rode out into the night.

Next morning, the King sat in the council-chamber with the Vizier by his side and summoned the Princess to his presence. When she had taken her seat behind the curtain as before, the King asked: 'Tell us, my daughter, what you have learned about Prince Ma'aruf.'

'May Allah confound all slanderous tongues,' exclaimed the Princess, 'and blacken the face of your Vizier, as he would have blackened mine in my husband's eyes!'

'How so?' asked the King.

'Last night,' continued the Princess, 'soon after my husband came to my chamber, the chief of the eunuchs brought in a letter from ten richly dressed slaves who begged an audience with their master Ma'aruf. I took the letter and read aloud: "From the five hundred slaves of the caravan to their master the merchant Ma'aruf. We would have you know that soon after you left us we were attacked by a host of two thousand mounted bedouin. A bloody battle ensued, and lasted thirty days and thirty nights. The caravan lost fifty of its slaves, a hundred mules, and two hundred loads of merchandise. This is the cause of our delay."

'Yet at this bad news the Prince was undismayed; he did not even ask further details from the waiting messengers. "What are two hundred bales and a hundred wretched mules?" he said. "At worst the loss cannot be more than seventy thousand pieces of gold. Think no more about it, my dear. One thing alone distresses me, that I shall have to leave you for a few days in order to go myself and hasten the arrival of the caravan." He rose with a carefree laugh, embraced me tenderly, and bade me farewell. When he had gone I looked through the window of my chamber and saw him chatting with ten handsome slaves dressed in uniforms of rare magnificence. Presently he mounted his horse and rode away with them to bring the caravan home. Allah be praised that I did not question my husband in the manner you requested,' added the Princess bitterly. 'I would have lost his love and he would have ceased to trust me. It was all the fault of your hateful Vizier, whose only thought is to revile my husband and discredit him in your eyes.'

The King rejoiced at these words and exclaimed: 'May Allah increase your husband's wealth and prolong his years, my daughter!' Then, turning to the Vizier, he rebuked him angrily and bade him henceforth hold his tongue. So much for the King, the Vizier, and the Princess.

As for Ma'aruf, he journeyed disconsolately far into the desert, his heart yearning for his beloved princess, until he came at midday to the outskirts of a little village. By this time he was tired and very hungry. Seeing a ploughman driving two oxen in a field, he went up to him and greeted him, saying: 'Peace be with you!'

The peasant returned his greeting and, noticing the stranger's garb, inquired: 'Doubtless, my master, you are one of the King's servants?'

When Ma'aruf replied that he was, the ploughman welcomed him, saying: 'Pray dismount and be my guest this day!'

The cobbler thanked the poor peasant for his generosity and politely declined. But the kind old man would take no refusal. 'Pray dismount,' he insisted, 'and grant me the honour

of entertaining you. I will go instantly to the village, which is close at hand, and bring you food and hay for your horse.'

'Since the village is so near, my friend,' protested Ma'aruf, 'I can easily ride there myself and buy food in the market-place.'

But the peasant smiled and shook his head. 'I fear you will find no market-place in a poor hamlet such as ours,' he replied. 'I beg you, in Allah's name, to rest here with your horse while I quickly run to the village.'

Not wishing to offend the old man, Ma'aruf dismounted and sat down on the grass, while his host hurried away.

As he waited for the peasant's return, Ma'aruf thought: 'I am keeping this poor man from his work. I will make up for his lost time by working at the plough myself.'

He rose and, going up to the oxen, drove the plough along

the furrow. The beasts had not gone far, however, when the share struck against an object in the ground and came to a sudden halt. Ma'aruf goaded the oxen on but, though they strained powerfully against the yoke, the plough remained rooted in the ground. Clearing away the soil about the share, Ma'aruf found that it had caught in a great ring of gold set in a marble slab the size of a large millstone. He exerted all his strength, and when he had moved the slab aside, he saw below it a flight of stairs. Going down the stairs he found himself in a square vault as large as the city baths containing four separate halls. The first was filled with gold from floor to ceiling; the second with pearls, emeralds, and coral; the third with jacinths, rubies, and turquoises; and the fourth with diamonds and other precious stones. At the far side of the vault stood a coffer of clearest crystal and upon it a golden casket no larger than a lemon.

The cobbler marvelled and rejoiced at this discovery. He went up to the little casket and, lifting its lid, found in it a gold signet-ring finely engraved with strange talismanic inscriptions that resembled the legs of creeping insects. He slipped the ring upon his finger and, as he did so, rubbed the seal.

At once a mighty jinnee appeared before him, saying: 'I am here, master, I am here! Speak and I will obey! What is your wish? Would you have me build a capital, or lay a town in ruin? Would you have me slay a king, or dig a river-bed? I am your slave, by order of the Sovereign of the Jinn, Creator of the day and night! What is your wish?'

Amazed at the apparition, Ma'aruf cried: 'Creature of Allah, who are you?'

'I am Abul-Sa'adah, the slave of the ring,' replied the jinnee. 'Faithfully I serve my master, and my master is he who rubs the ring. Nothing is beyond my power; for I am lord over seventy-two tribes of jinn, each two-and-seventy thousand strong: each jinnee rules over a thousand giants, each giant over a thousand goblins, each goblin over a thousand demons, and each demon over a thousand imps. All these owe me absolute allegiance; and yet for all my power, I cannot choose but to obey my master. Ask what you will, and it shall be done. Be it on land or sea, by day or night: should you need me you have but to rub the ring, and I will be at hand to do your bidding. Of one thing only I must warn you; if you twice rub the ring I shall be consumed in the fire of the powerful words engraved on the seal, and you will lose me for ever.'

'Abul-Sa'adah,' said Ma'aruf, 'can you tell me what this place is, and who imprisoned you in this ring?'

'This vault in which you stand, my master,' replied the jinnee, 'is the ancient treasure-house of Shaddad Ibn Aad, King of the many-columned city of Iram. While he lived I was his servant and dwelt in this ring. Just before his death he locked it away in this treasure-house, and it was your good fortune to find it.'

'Slave of the ring,' said the cobbler, 'can you carry all this treasure to the open?'

'That is very easy,' replied the jinnee.

'Then do so without delay,' said Ma'aruf, 'and leave nothing in this vault.'

Scarcely had he uttered these words when the earth opened and there appeared before him several handsome youths with baskets upon their heads. These they quickly filled with gold and jewels and carried them above ground; and in a few moments the four halls were emptied of their treasure.

'Who are these boys?' asked Ma'aruf.

'They are my own sons,' replied the jinnee. 'A light task such as this does not require the mustering of a mighty band of jinn. What else do you wish, my master?'

'I require a train of mules loaded with chests,' replied Ma'aruf, 'to carry these marvels to Ikhtiyan-al-Khatan.'

The jinnee uttered a great cry, and there appeared seven hundred richly saddled mules laden with chests and baskets, and a hundred slaves magnificently clad. In a twinkling the chests and baskets were filled with treasure and placed upon the mules, and the caravan stood in splendid array, guarded by mounted slaves.

'And now, slave of the ring,' said Ma'aruf, 'I require a few hundred loads of precious stuffs.'

'Would you have Syrian damask or Persian velvet, Indian brocade or Roman silk or Egyptian gaberdine?'

'A hundred loads of each!' cried Ma'aruf.

'I hear and obey,' replied the slave. 'I will at once dispatch my jinn to those distant lands, and they shall return tomorrow morning with all that you require.'

Then Ma'aruf ordered the slave of the ring to set up a pavilion and serve him food and wine. The jinnee promptly provided his master with a silk pavilion and a sumptuous meal, and departed on his mission.

As Ma'aruf was about to sit down to his feast, the old peasant returned from the village, carrying a large bowl of lentils for his guest and a sack of hay for the horse. When he saw the great caravan drawn up in the field, and Ma'aruf reclining in the tent, attended by innumerable slaves, he thought that his guest must be no other than the King. 'I will hurry back,' he reflected, 'and kill my two fowls and roast them in butter for him.'

The peasant was on the point of turning back when Ma'aruf saw him and ordered his slaves to bring him into the pavilion.

The slaves led the peasant to the tent, with his bowl of lentils and his sack of hay. Ma'aruf rose to receive him and welcomed him, saying: 'What is it you are carrying, my brother?'

'My master,' replied the peasant, all abashed, 'I was bringing you your dinner and some hay for your horse. Forgive my scant courtesy, I pray you. Had I known you were the King, I would have killed my two fowls and roasted them in butter for you.'

'Do not be dismayed, my friend,' replied Ma'aruf, 'I am not the King, but only his son-in-law. A certain misunderstanding arose between us and I left the palace. He has sent these messengers to fetch me and these presents as a token of his forgiveness. Tomorrow morning I shall return to the city.' Then Ma'aruf thanked the peasant for his generosity and seated him by his side, saying: 'By Allah, I will eat nothing but the food of your hospitality.'

He ordered the slaves to serve the peasant with the choice meats and ate the lentils himself. When the meal was finished he filled the empty bowl with gold and gave it to the peasant. 'Take this to your family,' he said, 'and if you come to see me at the palace, you shall receive a hearty welcome and a generous reward.'

The peasant took the gold and returned to the village, scarcely believing his good fortune.

When darkness fell, the slaves of the caravan brought into the tent beautiful young girls, who danced and made music. At daybreak Ma'aruf perceived a great cloud of dust in the distance and presently saw a long procession of mules approaching. They were laden with innumerable bales of merchandise, and at their head rode the jinnee in the semblance of a caravan-leader, alongside a four-pillared litter of pure gold inlaid with diamonds. When the caravan came to the tent, the jinnee dismounted and, kissing the ground before Ma'aruf, said: 'The task is accomplished, my master. Pray mount into this litter and put on the garment which I have brought especially for you. You will find it worthy of a king.'

'One thing more remains to be done,' said Ma'aruf. 'Before I set forth with the caravan, I wish you to hasten to Ikhtiyan-al-Khatan and announce my coming to the King.'

'I hear and obey,' replied the jinnee, and instantly transforming himself into the semblance of a courier made off towards the city.

He arrived at the palace just as the Vizier was saying to the King: 'Be no longer deceived, your majesty, by the lies of this impostor. Give no credence to your daughter's story; for I swear by your precious life that it was not to hurry on the arrival of his caravan that Prince Ma'aruf fled the city, but to save his skin.'

The Vizier had not finished speaking, when the courier entered the royal presence and kissed the ground before the King, saying: 'Your majesty, I bring you greetings from the illustrious Prince your son-in-law, who is now approaching the city with his noble caravan.'

With this the courier again kissed the ground before the King and hurried out of the palace. The King rejoiced, and, turning to the Vizier, exclaimed: 'May Allah blacken your face, traitor of ill omen! How long will you revile my son-in-law to my face and call him thief and liar?'

The dumbfounded Vizier hung his head, whilst the King hastened to give orders for the decoration of the city and to send out a procession to meet the caravan. Then he went to his daughter's chamber and told her the joyful news. The Princess was astounded to hear her father speak of the caravan, and thought: 'Can this be another of Ma'aruf's tricks? Or was he testing my love with an invented tale of poverty?'

But even more astonished than the Princess was her husband's friend, Ali the merchant. When he beheld the great commotion in the city and learnt the news of Ma'aruf's imminent arrival at the head of a splendid caravan, he thought: 'What new roguery is this? Can it be possible that this patcher of old slippers is really coming with a caravan? Or is it some fresh trick which he has contrived with the aid of the Princess? May Allah preserve my old friend from dishonour!'

Before long the procession, which had gone out to meet the caravan, returned to the city. Arrayed in a magnificent robe, Ma'aruf rode triumphantly by the King's side in the golden litter and, as the interminable caravan wound its way through the streets, the merchants flocked around their prodigal debtor and kissed the ground before him as he passed. Ali the merchant pushed his way through the throng, and whispered to Ma'aruf: 'How has this come about, sheikh of mad swindlers? And yet, by Allah, you deserve your good fortune!'

The procession halted at the royal palace, and Ma'aruf sat with the King in the great council-chamber. He ordered his slaves to fill the royal coffers with gold and jewels, and to unpack the bales of precious merchandise. He chose out the finest stuffs and said to the attendants: 'Carry these silks to the Princess that she may distribute them among her women; and take to her this chest of jewels that she may share its contents among the slaves and eunuchs.'

Then he proceeded to deal out the treasures to the officers of the King's troops, to the courtiers and their wives, to his creditors the merchants, and to the poor of the city, while the King writhed upon his throne in an agony of greed. As Ma'aruf threw handfuls of pearls and emeralds to right and left, the King would whisper to him: 'Enough, my son! There will be nothing left for us!' But Ma'aruf would answer: 'My caravan is inexhaustible.'

Soon the Vizier came and told the King that the treasury was full and could hold no more. And the King cried: 'Fill another hall!'

Then Ma'aruf hastened to his wife, who received him in a transport of joy and kissed his hand, saying: 'Was it to mock me or to test my love that you pretended to be a poor cobbler fleeing from a nagging wife? Whichever it was, I thank Allah I did not fail you.'

Ma'aruf embraced her and gave her a gown splendidly embroidered in gold, a necklace threaded with forty orphan pearls, and a pair of anklets fashioned by the art of mighty sorcerers. His wife cried out for joy as she saw these marvels, and said: 'I will keep them for festivals and state occasions only.'

'Not so, my love,' replied Ma'aruf, 'I will give you ornaments like these each day.'

Then he summoned the slave-girls of the harem and bestowed upon each of them an embroidered robe, adorned with ornaments of gold. Arrayed in this splendour, they were like the black-eyed houris of Paradise, whilst the Princess shone in their midst like the moon amongst the stars.

At nightfall the King said to the Vizier: 'What have you to say now? Does not the wealth of my son-in-law surpass all wonders?'

'Indeed, your majesty,' replied the Vizier, 'the Prince's prodigality is that of no ordinary merchant; for where can a merchant find such pearls and jewels as your son-in-law has thrown away? Kings and princes have not treasures like these. There must surely be some strange reason for his conduct. I suggest, my master, that you make Prince Ma'aruf drunk if you wish to discover the source of his riches. When he is overcome with wine, we will ply him with questions until he tells us all. Indeed, I already fear the consequences of this extraordinary munificence, for it is more than likely that he will in time win the troops with his favours and drive you from your kingdom.'

'You have spoken wisely, my Vizier,' said the King. 'To-morrow we must find out the whole truth.'

Next morning, whilst the King was sitting in his council-chamber, the grooms of the royal stables rushed in, begging leave to speak with him. 'Your majesty,' they cried, 'the entire caravan of Prince Ma'aruf is gone! All the slaves, the horses, and the mules disappeared during the night, and nowhere can we find a trace of them.'

Greatly troubled at this news, the King hastened to Ma'aruf's chamber and told him what had happened. But Ma'aruf laughed aloud.

'Pray calm yourself, your majesty,' he said. 'The loss of these trifles is nothing to me. For what is a caravan of mules?'

'By Allah,' thought the King in amazement, 'what manner of man is this, to whom wealth counts for nothing? There must surely be a reason for all this!'

When evening came, the King sat with Ma'aruf and the Vizier in a pavilion in the garden of the palace. Wine flowed freely; and, when Ma'aruf was flushed with drink so that he could not tell his left hand from his right, the Vizier said to him: 'Your highness, you have never told us the adventures of your life. Pray let us hear how you achieved your prodigious wealth, and the marvellous vicissitudes of fortune which have befallen you.'

Thereupon the drunken cobbler related the story of his life, from his marriage in Cairo to the finding of the magic ring in the peasant's field.

Then said the Vizier: 'Will you not permit us to see the ring, your highness?'

Without a moment's thought the foolish cobbler slipped the ring from his finger and handed it to the Vizier, saying: 'Look at the seal! My servant the jinnee dwells within it!'

The Vizier instantly passed the ring upon his own finger and rubbed the seal; and the jinnee appeared before him, saying: 'I am here! Ask and receive! Would you have me build a capital, or lay a town in ruin? Would you have me slay a king, or dig a river-bed?'

'Slave of the ring,' replied the Vizier, pointing to Ma'aruf, 'take up this rascal and cast him down upon some barren desert where he shall perish from hunger and thirst!'

At once the jinnee snatched up Ma'aruf and flew with him between earth and sky until he set him down in the middle of a waterless desert.

Then said the Vizier to the King: 'Did I not tell you that this dog was a liar and a cheat? But you gave no heed to my counsel.'

'You were right, my Vizier,' replied the King. 'Give me the ring that I may examine it.'

But the Vizier spat in his face and cried: 'Miserable old

fool, do you expect me to remain your servant when I can be your master?'

So saying, the Vizier rubbed the ring and said to the jinnee: 'Take up this wretch and cast him down by the side of his cobbler son-in-law!'

The jinnee at once carried the old man upon his shoulder and, flying with him through the void, set him down in the middle of the desert, where King and son-in-law sat wailing together. So much for them.

The Vizier summoned the nobles and the captains of the troops and proclaimed himself Sultan of the city. He explained that he had banished the King and Ma'aruf by the power of a magic ring, and threatened the assembly, saying: 'If anyone dares resist my rule, he shall join them in the desert of hunger and thirst!'

Perforce the courtiers swore fealty, and the Vizier, after exalting some and dismissing others, sent to the Princess, saying: 'Prepare to receive me this night, for my heart yearns for you!'

The Princess, who was stricken with grief at the downfall of her father and Ma'aruf, sent back to say: 'I cannot receive you until you have drawn up a marriage-contract and become my lawful husband.' But the Vizier replied: 'I know nothing of marriage-contracts, and accept no such excuses. I desire to visit you at once.'

'Come, then, you will be welcome,' answered the Princess through her eunuch.

When evening came she arrayed herself in silks and jewels, perfumed herself, and received the Vizier with a seductive smile. 'What an honour, my master,' she said. 'What a night we shall pass together!'

She seated him on her couch and dallied with him until he was roused to a frenzy of desire. But as he was about to throw himself upon her, she uttered a cry of terror and started back, covering her face.

'What is the matter, my mistress?' asked the Vizier.

'Would you show me naked to that stranger?' she cried.

'Where? Where?' exclaimed the Vizier angrily.

'There, in your ring!' she answered.

The Vizier laughed and said: 'Dear lady, that is no man, but only my faithful jinnee.'

But the Princess screamed still louder and cried: 'I am terrified of jinn! Put him away, for my sake!'

Impatient to do that for which he had come, the Vizier took off the ring from his finger and hid it under the cushions. The Princess let him approach and, when he had come near, kicked him so violently in the belly that he rolled over senseless on the floor. Thereupon she gave a loud cry, and at once forty slave-girls burst into the room and laid hold of the Vizier, whilst she hastily snatched up the ring and rubbed the seal, saying to the jinnee: 'Cast this traitor into a dark dungeon and bring me back my father and my husband!'

'I hear and obey!' replied the jinnee, and, carrying the Vizier on his shoulder, threw him in the darkest dungeon of the palace. Then he flew towards the desert and presently returned with the King and Ma'aruf, both half-dead with fright and hunger.

The Princess rejoiced to see them. She offered them food and wine and told them how she had outwitted the Vizier.

'We will tie him to the stake and burn him alive!' cried the King. 'But first give me back the ring, my daughter.'

But the Princess replied: 'The ring shall stay on my finger. I myself will look after it in future.'

Early next morning the King and Ma'aruf entered the council-chamber, and the courtiers, who were astonished to see them, kissed the ground before them and gave them a jubilant welcome. The stake was set up in the grounds of the palace and the Vizier was burnt alive in sight of all the people.

Ma'aruf was appointed Vizier and heir to the throne. He governed jointly with the King and lived happily with his wife, who after a few months gave birth to a son.

Five years later the King died, and soon the Princess followed him to eternal rest. Before she died she commended the young Prince to the care of Ma'aruf, and gave him the ring and counselled him to guard it well.

King Ma'aruf reigned wisely and justly for many years, so that all his subjects loved him. One night, however, when he had retired to his sleeping chamber, a hideous old woman jumped out of his bed and flung her arms around him.

'Allah preserve us from the wiles of the Evil One!' exclaimed Ma'aruf in terror. 'Who are you?'

'Have no fear!' replied the hag. 'I am your wife, Fatimah!'

Ma'aruf recognized her by her long teeth and her black ugliness. 'But how came you here?' he asked in amazement. 'Who brought you to this city?'

'Last night,' answered Fatimah, 'as I sat in a street by the wall of a ruined house, begging alms from the passers-by and bewailing my woeful plight, a jinnee appeared, saying: "Why are you weeping, old woman?" When I recounted to him my misfortunes since you left me and told him that my name was Fatimah, wife of Ma'aruf, one time cobbler in Red Lane, the jinnee said: "I know your husband. He is now King of Ikhtiyan-al-Khatan, and if you wish I will take you to him." The jinnee carried me upon his back and flew with me between earth and sky until he alighted on the roof of this palace and set me down upon your bed.'

The old shrew wept and, kneeling down before her husband, begged forgiveness of him. Ma'aruf took pity on his wife. He bade her rise and, seating her by his side, related to her all that had befallen him since his flight from Cairo. He set apart a magnificent palace for her use and assigned twenty slave-girls to her service.

When Fatimah saw, however, that her husband held aloof from her bed and sought his pleasure with other women, she became jealous and her evil soul prompted her to seek his ruin. One night, whilst Ma'aruf was fast asleep with the magic ring under his pillow, she entered the palace and stealthily made her way to his room. She softly approached her husband's bed and took the ring from under the pillow.

Now it so chanced that as she was stealing out, with the ring in her hand, Ma'aruf's son, the young Prince, was passing by the door of his father's room. He followed her unnoticed until she came to the vestibule of the palace. Here she slipped the ring on her finger and was about to rub the seal, when he drew his sword and struck her through the neck. With a piercing scream she dropped dead to the ground.

The young Prince hurried to his father's chamber and roused him from his sleep. Ma'aruf praised his son for his bravery and recovered the ring from his wife's finger. Then he called out to his attendants and ordered them to take the body and bury it in the grounds of the palace. Such was the end of Fatimah.

King Ma'aruf reigned through many joyful years, until he was visited by the Destroyer of all earthly pleasures, the Leveller of mighty kings and humble peasants.

EPILOGUE

Now during this time Shahrazad had borne King Shahriyar three sons. On the thousand and first night, when she had ended the tale of Ma'aruf, she rose and kissed the ground before him, saying: 'Great King, for a thousand and one nights I have been recounting to you the fables of past ages and the legends of ancient kings. May I make so bold as to crave a favour of your majesty?'

The King replied: 'Ask, and it shall be granted.'

Shahrazad called out to the nurses, saying: 'Bring me my children.'

Three little boys were instantly brought in; one walking, one crawling on all fours, and the third sucking at the breast of his nurse. Shahrazad ranged the little ones before the King and, again kissing the ground before him, said: 'Behold these three whom Allah has granted to us. For their sake I implore you to spare my life. For if you destroy the mother of these infants, they will find none among women to love them as I would.'

The King embraced his three sons, and his eyes filled with tears as he answered: 'I swear by Allah, Shahrazad, that you were already pardoned before the coming of these children. I loved you because I found you chaste and tender, wise and eloquent. May Allah bless you, and bless your father and mother, your ancestors, and all your descendants. O, Shahrazad, this thousand and first night is brighter for us than the day!'

Shahrazad rejoiced; she kissed the King's hand and called down blessings upon him.

The people were overjoyed at the news of Shahrazad's salvation. Next morning King Shahriyar summoned to his presence the great ones of the city, the chamberlains, the

nabobs, and the officers of his army. When they had all
assembled in the great hall of the palace, Shahriyar proclaimed
his decision to spare the life of his bride. Then he called his
Vizier, Shahrazad's father, and invested him with a magnificent robe of honour, saying: 'Allah has raised up your
daughter to be the salvation of my people. I have found her
chaste, wise, and eloquent, and repentance has come to me
through her.'

Then the King bestowed robes of honour upon the courtiers and the captains of his troops, and gave orders for the
decoration of his capital.

The city was decked and lighted; and in the streets and
market-squares drums rattled, trumpets blared, and clarions

sounded. The King lavished alms on the poor and the needy, and all the people feasted at the King's expense for thirty days and thirty nights.

Shahriyar reigned over his subjects in all justice, and lived happily with Shahrazad until they were visited by the Destroyer of all earthly pleasures, the Annihilator of men.

Now praise and glory be to Him who sits throned in eternity above the shifts of time; who, changing all things, remains Himself unchanged; who alone is the Paragon of all perfection. And blessing and peace be upon His chosen Messenger, the Prince of Apostles, our master Mohammed, to whom we pray for an auspicious

END

MORE ABOUT PENGUINS
AND PELICANS

Penguinews, which appears every month, contains details of all the new books issued by Penguins as they are published. From time to time it is supplemented by *Penguins in Print*, which is a complete list of all available books published by Penguins. (There are well over four thousand of these.)

A specimen copy of *Penguinews* will be sent to you free on request. For a year's issues (including the complete lists) please send 30p if you live in the United Kingdom, or 60p if you live elsewhere. Just write to Dept EP, Penguin Books Ltd, Harmondsworth, Middlesex, enclosing a cheque or postal order, and your name will be added to the mailing list.

Note: *Penguinews* and *Penguins in Print* are not available in the U.S.A. or Canada

CHAUCER

THE CANTERBURY TALES

Translated by Nevill Coghill

The Canterbury Tales stands conspicuous among the great literary achievements of the Middle Ages. Told by a jovial procession of pilgrims – knight, priest, yeoman, miller, or cook – as they ride towards the shrine of Thomas à Becket, they present a picture of a nation taking shape. The tone of this never-resting comedy is, by turns, learned, fantastic, lewd, pious, and ludicrous. 'Here,' as John Dryden said, 'is God's plenty!'

Geoffrey Chaucer began his great task in about 1386. This version in modern English, by Nevill Coghill, preserves the freshness and racy vitality of Chaucer's narrative.

POEMS OF HEAVEN AND HELL
FROM ANCIENT MESOPOTAMIA

Translated by N. K. Sandars

Babylon is a city whose name has become charged with symbolism for us; rich, luxurious, and decadent. Yet it was in fact the seat of one of the finest and most vigorous civilizations of the period 2000–500 B.C.

The five poems in this volume are products of this civilization; the translations are by N. K. Sandars, well known for her version of *The Epic of Gilgamesh*. They include *The Babylonian Creation*, a great liturgy which was recited each year at the New Year festival proclaiming the power of the god Marduk, and his conquest of Tiamat, goddess of water chaos; *Inanna's Journey to Hell*, which recounts the descent of the goddess of fertility into a gloomy underworld waste land of devils and darkness; and *Adapa: the Man*, a story of man's fall from grace, not through arrogant disobedience but through blind obedience. The two other poems are short and are called *The Sumerian Underworld* and *A Prayer to the God of Night*.

THE KORAN

Translated by N. J. Dawood

The Koran, as Mr Dawood claims, 'is not only one of the greatest books of prophetic literature but also a literary masterpiece of surpassing excellence'. Unquestioningly accepted by Muslims to be the infallible word of Allah as revealed to Mohammed by the Angel Gabriel over thirteen hundred years ago, the Koran still provides the basic rules of conduct fundamental to the Arab way of life. Mr Dawood has produced a translation which retains the beauty of the original, altering the traditional arrangement to increase the understanding and pleasure for the uninitiated.

BOCCACCIO

THE DECAMERON

Translated by G. H. McWilliam

The Decameron, here presented entire and unexpurgated in a new translation, remains one of the supreme monuments of world literature. The Black Death of 1348 lends a macabre setting to the hundred stories which are supposed to be recounted, during ten days, by a party of wealthy young patricians taking refuge in a villa outside Florence. With equal felicity they range over comedy and tragedy, morality and bawdy; and the skill with which Boccaccio matches the style and mood of his prose narrative to the tales and their tellers is as astonishing as the variety of a collection which has often been imitated but never bettered.

A PELICAN ORIGINAL

ANTHOLOGY OF ISLAMIC LITERATURE

Edited by James Kritzeck

The literature of Islam is among the richest and the greatest in the world. Whether it has found expression in Arabic, Persian, Turkish, or any other of a dozen languages, this is a body of writing which preserves a distinct character of its own, largely because of a common religious influence. In the West, however, Islamic literature is hardly known at all, except by the specialist.

In this new anthology, now published for the first time in Britain, Professor Kritzeck has assembled the best available translations in verse and prose to represent the various periods of Islamic writing. His collection opens with chapters from the Koran and a number of early Arabic poems, and then covers successively the age of the Caliphs, the surprisingly rich period (and not merely because of Umar Khayyam) of the Turkish and Mongol invasions (from 1050 to 1350), and finally the rise of the Ottoman Empire. The work he includes was all written before 1800.

These passages offer the general reader a unique introduction to a literature which, in the opinion of the experts, better exemplifies the Islamic genius than even the Alhambra or the Taj Mahal.

'A first-rate anthology of a rich and wonderful literature' – *New Yorker*

THE PENGUIN CLASSICS

Some Recent Volumes

THE SATIRES OF HORACE AND PERSIUS
Niall Rudd

CAO XUEQIN
The Story of the Stone Vol. 1: The Golden Days
David Hawkes

THE BOOK OF DEDE KORKUT
Geoffrey Lewis

DIDEROT
The Nun   *Leonard Tancock*

GREEK PASTORAL POETRY
Anthony Holden

THE LETTERS OF ABELARD AND HELOISE
Betty Radice

DEMOSTHENES AND AESCHINES
A. N. W. Saunders

BALZAC
The History of the Thirteen   *Herbert J. Hunt*

CICERO
Murder Trials   *Michael Grant*

GREGORY OF TOURS
The History of the Franks   *Lewis Thorpe*